KATIE GINGER lives by the sea in the south-east of England, and apart from holidays to very hot places where you can sit by a pool and drink cocktails as big as your head, she wouldn't really want to be anywhere else. *Spring Tides at Swallowtail Bay* is her fourth novel. She is also the author of *Snowflakes at Mistletoe Cottage* and the Seafront series – *The Little Theatre on the Seafront*, shortlisted for the Katie Fforde Debut Novel of the Year award, and *Summer Season on the Seafront*.

When she's not writing, Katie spends her time drinking gin, or with her husband, trying to keep alive her two children: Ellie, who believes everything in life should be performed like a musical number from a West End show; and Sam, who is basically a monkey with a boy's face. And there's also their adorable King Charles spaniel, Wotsit (yes, he is named after the crisps!)

For more about Katie, you can visit her website: www.keginger.com, find her on Facebook: www.facebook.com/KatieGAuthor, or follow her on Twitter: @KatieGAuthor.

Readers LOVE Katie Ginger

'This book is every sort of wonderful, with gorgeous characters, a stunning town and a friendship that turns into a romance you're not going to want to miss out on' *****

'Does jumping up and down, cuddling my Kindle and grinning from ear to ear count as a review?! … Katie writes with such warmth and humour and I could feel every word' *****

'Loved it!' *****

'A fantastic chick-lit page turner' *****

'Sweet, heart-warming, and very enjoyable. This book is like a warm chocolate chip cookie, you feel better for eating it, get a bite of exciting chocolate now and again all while just enjoying the experience. Love the book!' *****

'The perfect book to enjoy in a few days of quiet downtime' *****

'Absolutely loved this book. Couldn't put it down. Wonderful uplifting storyline. Can't wait to see what's next from this author!' *****

'*The Little Theatre On The Seafront* has to be one of my top ten books of 2018. I loved everything about the book … I can't wait to see what Katie Ginger comes up with next and I know that it will be another cracking read … a very well deserved 5* out of 5*' *****

'Faultlessly enjoyable' *****

Also by Katie Ginger

The Little Theatre on the Seafront
Summer Season on the Seafront
Snowflakes at Mistletoe Cottage
Summer Strawberries at Swallowtail Bay

Spring Tides at Swallowtail Bay

KATIE GINGER

This novel is entirely a work of fiction. The names, characters and incidents portrayed in it are the work of the author's imagination. Any resemblance to actual persons, living or dead, events or localities is entirely coincidental.

HQ
An imprint of HarperCollins*Publishers* Ltd
1 London Bridge Street
London SE1 9GF

First published in Great Britain by
HQ, an imprint of HarperCollins*Publishers* Ltd 2020

ISBN: 9780008380540

To my wonderful husband, Phil,
and our amazing children, Ellie and Sam.
I love you all millions.

Chapter 1

'Urgh! Arrgh!' Stella raised her hands in front of her face trying to deflect the water spraying out from under the sink. With a splutter she reached forward to grab the stopcock, her T-shirt bearing the brunt of the assault, and water pooled in her bra. 'Yuck. How do I turn the water off, Frank?' Frank, her King Charles spaniel cocked his head. Stella's lungs squeezed together in panic, forcing the air out, but she gulped some back in with a deep breath. Grabbing the stopcock with both hands she tugged hard but still it wouldn't budge. Frank lapped at the water flooding over the kitchen floor. 'Don't do that, you horrible dog. Go on, shoo.'

With a resigned harrumph, Stella sat back on her haunches. No amount of mental determination could turn the rusted thing and, as she moved away from the soggy cupboard, water splashed over her trainers. Stella stood and put her hands on her hips while she surveyed the huge wet patch on her top. 'Fabulous. I look like I've been in some sort of wet T-shirt competition at a 1950s holiday camp.' A soggy strand of hair fell onto her face. It was only then Stella realised how wet she truly was. It wasn't just her top that had been deluged; literally everything was damp, even down to her underwear. As well as being in her bra, where

1

the water had hit her jeans, she now looked like she'd wet herself. Things were not going well for the start of her new life.

The little town of Swallowtail Bay – her new home – was supposed to be a dream come true, but so far, on her very first day, she'd smashed a vase in her new shop, found that her new bedroom absolutely honked and came with a germ-infested bed, and now the kitchen had a leaky pipe.

When she'd said goodbye to her beloved city of Oxford early that morning, her eyes had filled with tears. Though leaving a tiny rented flat with black mould on the kitchen walls and a strange cheesy smell whenever she opened the airing cupboard door wasn't a hardship, she'd lived her whole life there and it was home. But the idea of a new start, leaving Isaac well and truly behind, had lifted her spirits. And if that hadn't done the trick, the view that met her when she drove towards the tiny seaside town had. The sea appeared on the horizon, its pale blue hue merging with the clear cloudless sky above and it was hard to tell where one ended and the other began.

Even though she was soaked through, a smile spread over her face as she remembered seeing it. She'd followed the long road dotted here and there with sweet little churches, to the shingled beach and a row of white beach huts interspersed with small fishing boats. On the green, purple crocuses burst into life and little clumps of daffodils raised their trumpety heads to the sky.

Spring was the perfect season to make a fresh start. It was so hopeful and bright and happy, but since stepping over the threshold of her new home, things hadn't gone exactly to plan. Standing in her hideous retro kitchen with cold wet toes was not how she'd imagined her new life would begin. But Stella Harris wasn't a sulker. She never had been and mustering some of her old self, the tiny bit that remained after her heart had been battered and bruised, she decided she had no intention of starting now.

When she summoned back the feeling of anticipation that had

brightened her journey early that morning, butterflies once again danced in her stomach. As soon as the offer had been accepted she'd started packing and yesterday contracts had been exchanged and the sale completed. She'd waited for this day for months and a few little problems were not going to spoil it now.

Gently pushing Frank back towards the doorway she searched the cupboards and found a plastic bowl to catch the water dripping down from the stopcock but the jet shooting out sideways was worrying. The bottom of the cupboard was soggy and springy and Stella pulled her phone from her pocket. A quick search of the internet listed a number of different plumbers but, unsure who to choose, she called the first one on the list. No answer. Stella quickly tried the second.

''Ello?' said a harsh male voice.

'Oh, hi. Is that Jim the plumber?'

'Who are you?'

Rude, thought Stella, but she carried on regardless. 'My name's Stella and I've just moved into Admiral's Corner. I've found a bit of a leak and I need some help to stop it.'

'Can't do anything until tomorrow at the earliest.'

Still rude, she thought again but maybe he was in the middle of something: fixing a pipe for a little old lady or stopping some kind of emergency. 'Oh. It's just that there's water spraying out everywhere and well, I—' The phone went dead. Stella took it away from her ear and stared at it. 'Well I hope the rest of Swallowtail Bay's residents aren't like that, Frank.' Frank simply stared at her with big soppy brown eyes. Muttering a few choice swear words, she dialled plumber number three.

'Sutton Plumbing.'

That sounded much more professional. Stella tried to keep her voice calm and steady, but knowing that water was still flooding out all over the kitchen floor, a note of panic began to creep in as she went through it all again.

'Admiral's Corner? You mean Herbert's old place?' plumber

number three asked and Stella scratched her temple. It seemed everyone knew everyone else in this tiny town. She hoped people hadn't been talking about her already.

'Yes, I tried turning the stopcock but it won't budge and I didn't want to force it. Can you come, or do you know if there's another way I can turn the water off?'

'Not without having a look. There might be a tap with your water tank. Do you know where that is?'

For some reason Stella looked around as if that might help her but of course, she had no idea where the water tank was. She'd only been in the flat once before, on her one and only visit. The shop and holiday lets had been somewhat of an impulse buy and she was really beginning to regret it. 'Sorry, I don't. I literally got the keys from the estate agent this morning.' She felt a stinging at the back of her eyes again but refused to let the tears get any further. She pinched the bridge of her nose and took a deep breath.

'I'm just finishing a job but I can be over in about twenty minutes. If you can't turn the water off, grab some towels and wrap them around the leak until I get there, okay?'

'Okay. Thank you so much.' At least something was beginning to go right. And it was a good idea; she didn't know why she hadn't thought of it before.

Stella rang off and found some towels. Telling herself to stop being a wimp because, let's face it, she was already about as wet as she could be, she wrapped the towels around the leak. Then finding a mop and bucket she began to clean up the floor, chasing Frank away whenever he came near. Once it was done, she left the kitchen of her new one-bedroom flat and walked back down the hall into the shop. At least with the shop and flat being together she didn't have a long commute to work. In Oxford she'd had to sit on the bus for nearly forty-five minutes because although she could drive, there was nowhere to park near her work. It hadn't been exactly fun. She always seemed to end up near the people who ate smelly food for breakfast or had halitosis.

4

One time, someone had actually eaten a tuna sandwich for breakfast and then proceeded to clean their teeth. Even flossing. No, commuting she definitely wouldn't miss.

In the shop, the air was musty and white sheets covered the fittings. Paintings were piled in the corner, and a large comfy-looking wingback chair was stacked high with cardboard boxes. The remnants of the vase she'd knocked over that morning sat in a pile in a black bin bag. It wasn't a great loss. The glaze had been somewhat vomit-coloured and she couldn't imagine it would sell. The place needed a good clean too and Stella would have to sort through and decide what stock to keep and what to bin. The weird stone statue of a woman kissing a fish would definitely have to go.

Rocking onto her soggy toes, Stella couldn't wait to get started. When her eyes rested on the till, she pictured herself sat behind it serving customers, helping them decide what they wanted and then wrapping it up in brown paper, fastened with twine. Possibly with cute little logo stickers if she ever got round to designing them. She could even keep the tatty upholstered wingback chair for Frank and he could sit beside her every day. The customers would love him. He was already making himself at home, sniffing his way around the room.

Stella's mind whirled with a mixture of joy, dread, fear and elation. It still didn't feel real. This was her shop. *Her shop!* And she could sell whatever she wanted. After a life in high-street retail she didn't have to try and sell store cards or ask customers if they'd like to save ten per cent by signing up to the catalogue. There'd be no more standing by the open door in the depths of winter, freezing her bits off, welcoming customers with fake cheer. She could sit behind the counter reading a book and greet them with a smile and a genuine, 'Hi, let me know if you need any help,' then let them browse unhindered. And as far as the holiday lets were concerned, how hard could that be?

Despite everything that had happened earlier, a little squeal of delight escaped from her mouth. Large old-fashioned dressers lined the back wall, sticky and damp with dust but piled high with hand-painted teapots, cups and small china saucers. Everywhere her eyes fell there were more delights, and a few horrors. Why Herbert, the previous owner, had decided to sell strange tiny sculptures of old men's scrunched-up faces she had no idea. And that assortment of rather buxom papier-mâché figurines had clearly been purchased in a moment of madness. Still, nothing could quell her excitement. She'd been waiting for this moment for so long. It had been the focus for all her hopes and dreams since her life had changed so suddenly the evening Isaac came home from work and announced he wanted a divorce.

It had been a bog-standard boring Tuesday. A Tuesday! Who asked for a divorce on a Tuesday? It had always seemed to Stella that divorces were a Monday or Friday thing. Tuesdays were for two-for-one pizza deals, not for life-changing decisions that she hadn't even been consulted about. After she'd thrown things at him and he'd hidden behind the sofa, apologetic but determined, she packed a bag and sought refuge at her sister Abby's house.

A searing pain shot into Stella's heart, thinking back on those first agonising hours, and when he'd gone and started a new relationship immediately after their split, she'd hated him more than she ever thought she could hate anyone. Until then, she'd used words like hate to describe how she felt about celery or reality TV, but never before had she been filled with such vitriol. It had soon faded to be replaced by hurt and a feeling of rejection, of not being good enough. Of being a failure.

'Well, Frank,' Stella said to the tubby dog who had found a quiet corner to settle in, 'I'm not wasting any more time, I've got too much to do.' She set about cleaning while she waited for the plumber to arrive. Having lived so much of her life with Isaac it still felt strange to be doing such big things on her own but there was also something wonderful, in that her new start was entirely her own. Her adventure. Pushing down the shadowy pain that lingered whenever she thought of him, she pressed on. About twenty minutes later, though with the water still hissing in the background it felt a lot longer, a car pulled up on the double yellow lines outside the shop. A very short, very, very round man climbed out of the car and grabbed a big bag of tools from the passenger seat. Stella went to meet him at the door.

''Ello love, I'm Derek.'

'Hello, Derek. I'm Stella.' She held out her hand for him to shake and he took it in his grimy, pudgy one. Derek's eyes flew down to her wet white T-shirt and back up again. Feeling a flush rise up her neck, Stella crossed her arms over her chest to hide her bra. She hadn't thought to change and wished now she hadn't got so het up. If she'd remained calm she'd have thought to nip out to the car and grab another top before he arrived. Diverting Derek's attention she said, 'It's this way.'

'I'm reckoning,' said Derek, wobbling along behind, 'it must have happened in the last week – we had snow last week. Loads of it. They said we'd only get a couple of centimetres and we got masses. You wouldn't think it now though, would you, with the lovely sun outside. I bet it's burst because of that. It must have frozen and then, bam.' He dropped his bag onto the kitchen counter as he said it for dramatic effect. Derek then edged past her and crouched down to look in the cupboard. Crouching seemed to be quite a difficult affair and Stella wondered, yet again, if she'd made the right choice. Maybe she should have had a proper look online and checked some ratings before phoning someone or she could have nipped next door to the lovely-looking café and asked in there, but it was too late now. Frustratingly, her nervousness was making her second-guess herself.

Derek removed the towels, pulled a small torch from his toolbox and had a look. 'Yep, that'll be the weather done that. Can you see this coupling 'ere's gone?' He pointed to a piece of pipe that, to Stella, looked exactly like the other bit of pipe above it.

'How much is it going to cost?' she asked, raising a hand and absent-mindedly biting her nails.

Sitting back, Derek scratched his head and sucked a breath in through his teeth. 'Well, I'll have to go and get a few bits and it'll take about an hour to do. I've got to cut this 'ere and then again 'ere.' He pointed to just above and just below the leak. 'Then put a new bit in.' He scratched some more. 'About hundred quid.'

'A hundred?' repeated Stella. She didn't have much spare money and what she did have she'd planned to spend on a new bed after discovering the disaster that was currently in her new bedroom. A hundred pounds was a lot, but however much it was, it had to be paid. She couldn't just ignore the problem or she'd have an internal swimming pool where her kitchen used to be.

'Yeah, well. I can probably do it for eighty if there ain't no complications.'

Please God don't let there be any complications, thought Stella. There was something decidedly cowboy about Derek. All he needed was chaps and a horse. Suddenly, Stella had an image of this short, rotund man trying to mount a horse and had to bite back a giggle. 'And can you do it now?'

'Yeah.' He stood up and pulled his T-shirt down but it failed to cover the bottom of his stomach and a small slit of podgy pink flesh poked out. 'I'll nip and get the bits now if you like?'

'That would be great, thank you, Derek.'

Once he'd shut the door behind him Stella sighed and looked at Frank. 'I don't know how I'm going to afford that and a new bed.' Running a hand through her hair again she decided the last couple of quid in her wallet was to be spent on necessities. 'Right, Frank. I'm going to nip next door and get a coffee, okay?' Frank wagged his tail in response. 'After spending money on this, I'm not going to be getting a new bed any time soon, so if I'm sleeping on the sofa for the foreseeable future, I think I deserve it, don't you?'

Thankfully, Frank replied with an assenting 'rup.'

Chapter 2

Lexi Durham was rudely awoken by two small pairs of icy cold hands and two pairs of freezing cold feet being pressed against her as the children jumped into bed.

'Mummy,' said Ralph, her six-year-old son. 'Taylor said I smell of poo and that I'm a baby.'

Rolling over with a groan, Lexi came face to face with her eight-year-old daughter, her blonde hair falling over her face so only her green eyes popped out. 'Yeah, well, Ralph said that I'm ugly and the worst singer in the whole wide world. Which I'm not!'

'Yeah, but you said I smelled like poo first—'

'I did not!' Her voice rose an octave, piercing Lexi's eardrums.

'Yes, you did.'

'No, I didn't.'

Lexi rubbed her eyes and pushed a mass of hair back from her face. As far as her sleep-deprived, addled brain could make out, there were two ways she could deal with this situation. The first option was to completely lose her shit and send them back to bed, shouting as loudly as possible. The second was just to ignore their silly bickering because they'd be bickering all day anyway, and give them both a kiss and a cuddle. Deciding on option two, Lexi wriggled her arms out from under her and squeezed them both in for a hug. She kissed the tops of their heads and smelled the baby shampoo she still used, remembering all those times they'd fallen asleep on her as newborns, their soft, chubby cheeks pressed against her skin. 'Good morning, you two little monsters. I love you.'

'Love you too, Mummy,' they said in unison. 'Can we go and play?' Ralph asked, the previous argument forgotten. He had a cute gap where he'd recently lost a tooth and Lexi smiled as he planted a kiss on her cheek.

'Yes, as long as you don't bicker.' *Fat chance* – but she had to say it anyway.

'We won't.'

And out of bed they scrambled to immediately begin arguing again. As their voices grew louder, Lexi groaned and rolled over for one more minute snuggled in her cosy duvet. Though being a single mum was the hardest job in the world, she did appreciate the perk of having the bed to herself so she could wrap the duvet around like a cocoon. Rudely, the alarm clock beeped, insisting that she get out of bed. Remembering that she was on an early shift in the café, and the kids had to be dropped at breakfast club at eight o'clock, she hastily climbed out and dressed in the outfit she'd picked the night before. The one good habit Lexi had was choosing her clothes each night rather than throwing something on in the morning. But then, a vintage look like hers required some planning. Once dressed, she brushed her hair, pulled it up into a chignon and pinned the sides into a 1940s style. After a quick flick of eyeliner, a coat of mascara and a swipe of red lipstick and she was good to go. Or at least, go and make packed lunches.

The kids, however, weren't quite working at the same speed. Ralph, his room trashed, was now sitting in his empty toy box wearing a fireman's helmet. Captain Cuddles, his favourite teddy bear, was squeezed in beside him as he ordered the anchor be heaved up and his loyal crew set sail. Taylor's room was equally messy but her teddies had been laid out in a more orderly fashion ready for teddy bear hospital. She was dressed as a ballerina and had on an old pair of Lexi's high heels, too busy dancing to actually tend to her patients.

Lexi decided to ignore the horrendous mess and pretend it wasn't there. In a minute she'd close their bedroom doors and forget about it until later. 'Time to get dressed, kids. Double quick, please.' But double quick didn't seem to mean anything to Ralph and Taylor, and despite her earlier attempts at calm she was soon shouting. By the time the kids were dressed and being dropped off at school, Ralph was almost in tears and Taylor was pouting more than Kim Kardashian. Lexi's heart melted under the tearful gaze of her gorgeous boy and his big blue eyes, and the usual guilt and self-loathing flooded back.

She'd tried so hard this morning not to be a crazy shouty mum but somehow it always ended up that way. Blame pulsed through her veins till every part of her body was saturated. What made it even worse was that the school was deserted as her kids had to go to breakfast club. *Again.* Ralph and Taylor pulled at her hands to go in but Lexi drew them back, wrapping them in one final hug. 'I love you two. Shall we have hotdogs for dinner tonight? And curly fries?' She couldn't really afford it, but she wanted them to know how much she loved them.

'Yeah!' they both shouted. 'And no vegetables?' asked Taylor.

Lexi smiled at their wide grins, all traces of the morning's upsets forgotten. 'Okay. No veg, but don't tell your teacher.'

They ran into school smiling and Lexi turned on her heel and hurried to work. Even though there wasn't much traffic at that time of the morning, it was still quarter past eight when she arrived. It was going to be another beautiful spring day, which meant lots of customers and, hopefully, lots of tips. Her mobile phone bill was coming up and she was running woefully short of funds. Another reason why she shouldn't be spending extra money on expensive branded food, but her kids deserved it.

'Morning,' came a small voice from the back of the shop. 'So you finally decided to turn up then?'

'Ha ha.' It was a good job Raina was so understanding, otherwise Lexi would always be in trouble. She tossed her bag down and began tying her apron, watching the early morning birds hop between the branches of a tree in the churchyard opposite. 'Sorry about that. After they'd trashed their bedroom, they wouldn't get dressed, then after I turned the telly off they got dressed even slower because they were constantly moaning at me to turn it back on. Ralph couldn't find his shoes, Taylor couldn't find her cardigan and neither of them could find their reading books. Sometimes I don't know why I bother. They can't be any more feral than they are already.'

'Nonsense. You're doing a grand job,' came her comforting Irish lilt. 'It's hard enough being a mammy without having to do it all on your own. I tell you what, you make me one of your amazing cappuccinos and I'll forget all about it.'

Lexi smiled to herself. They went through virtually the same routine whenever she was late, which was quite often. She didn't make a cappuccino better than anybody else, Raina just liked having someone else make it for her. And why not? She'd owned the café for almost forty years and magically, it was still going even with the fancy ones at the other end of the high street and the chain ones competing with them for business. But Raina was a sturdy old bird and had no plans of retiring any time soon. If she did, Lexi would miss her like crazy and be out of work, and that didn't bear thinking about. 'I think it's going to be another nice day today,' Lexi said to distract herself. 'The town's always busier when it's sunny.'

'Yes, I think so too.' Raina put another batch of freshly made baguettes into the oven. The smell of the first baked loaves filled the air and reminded Lexi she hadn't had any breakfast. The children would just be having theirs at school and another wave

12

of guilt hit her. How she wished she didn't have to put them into breakfast club, it meant such a long day for them, but at least she would be there to pick them up today. She much preferred that to them being the only ones left at the end of the day – the last ones collected from Sunset Club. But even that happened more times than she'd like. Being a divorced single parent was hard, hard work. Will was around at the weekends and loved his kids dearly, but the bulk of the responsibility still fell on Lexi's shoulders, and, she thought ruefully, it had ever since the kids were born.

Turning her back on the window, Lexi steamed some milk at the big posh machine and then gently poured it into the coffee. She handed the cup to Raina and they went and sat down. Lexi took a moment to appreciate the café she absolutely adored working in. There were only six tables, each one laid with a different linen tablecloth. None of this plastic rubbish. Raina hated the plastic ones even though using proper ones required more cleaning. On the centre of each table sat a small jam jar of flowers or herbs, depending on what Raina had picked on one of her walks. On a high shelf that ran all the way around the shop, were random pieces of china they'd both found at car boot sales, and in between them sat pretty shells the children had found while walking along the beach and presented to Raina as keepsakes. Lexi smiled. If her kids did things like that perhaps she wasn't doing such a bad job after all. 'Shall I do the till after this?'

Raina shook her head. 'No need. I've done it already.'

'I thought that was the purpose of the early shift? That, and sorting out the tables and chairs, and prepping the fillings.' Lexi looked over to the counter. 'Which I can see you've already done too.'

'I know, but I woke up at five and couldn't get back to sleep so I got up a bit earlier than usual. The older I get, the earlier I seem to wake up these days.' Raina took a sip of her coffee, closing her eyes and tipping her head back a little to savour the taste. 'I thought I might as well come and do the chopping. I left the chairs for you though. They're getting a bit heavy for me now.'

'I'll do those in a minute then.' Lexi cupped her cappuccino, feeling instantly more awake as the aroma of fresh coffee drifted up. 'The new woman's arriving next door today.'

Raina's wrinkled cheeks creased even more as she smiled. 'Oh, that's exciting. Do you think she'll keep the shop the same or start selling weird stuff like crystals and joss sticks?'

Lexi paused. 'Joss sticks?'

'Yeah, and healing crystals and all that hocus-pocus rubbish. You know those stinky shops that sell strange hippy clothing. All made of that horrid wool with swirly patterns. And dream catchers. I bloody hate dream catchers.'

'Would it matter if she did?'

'I suppose not,' Raina replied with a shrug. 'You get all sorts these days. But those sorts of shops do stink.'

'I don't think she will,' Lexi replied, sipping her coffee to hide her smile. 'The estate agent said she's going to sell arty stuff and homeware. Herbert left loads of stock so she'll probably sell that off first. I would. Maybe you should pop round later and introduce yourself?'

'Why don't you?' teased Raina. 'She'll be closer to your age than mine, I'm sure.'

'Because,' said Lexi, putting her cup down and adjusting a hairpin, 'I need to schmooze these customers so they leave me nice big tips. And you're the owner. It should definitely be you.'

As Raina was a widow with no children, comfortably off and incredibly kind, she allowed Lexi to keep all the tips. Since the divorce, the agreement had been that Lexi was to spend the money on herself, but so far that hadn't happened. Something or other always came up to stop her. Ralph's school shoes would come apart because the boy had toxic toes, or Taylor would need new leggings for PE because she'd had a growth spurt and was getting

14

cold ankles. Still, using the tip money was better than dipping even further into her overdraft.

Before long it was time to open up and no sooner had the sign on the door been flipped than the first of their usual customers poured in. The workmen were nice, pleasant boys – well, men really – and always told Lexi to keep the change. When they sat down with their bacon and sausage baguettes with lashings of ketchup they filled one whole side of the little café. Thankfully they ate quickly and were on their way by nine o'clock when the old ladies started arriving for their regular tea and toast after they'd been to the Post Office.

Lexi enjoyed preparing their favourite teapots and vintage cups and saucers, and each had their own one. These were her favourite customers even though they only left a small tip, but pensions weren't much these days. Lexi often chatted with them about her outfits and what they had worn back in the day. Some had even donated their old vintage clothes so that Lexi's closet at home was overflowing with items. Not all of them fitted, but she couldn't bear to throw such beautiful things away, or even give them to a charity shop. Most of all, she loved listening to their stories; Lexi usually had to pull herself away to clear the tables and keep the cakes and pastries stocked up as she heard about coming-out balls and dances during the war.

By ten o'clock that morning, the first rush of the day was over and as the older ladies settled with their second pot of tea and a selection of cakes, Lexi and Raina were enjoying a quick sit-down before lunch preparations began. The bell above the door tinkled and a pretty woman in a damp T-shirt with bobbed hair the colour of milky coffee walked in. The tip of her fringe was wet and had begun to curl, giving her a trendy look, but something about the baggy jeans and ill-fitting, damp T-shirt told Lexi this hadn't been done on purpose. 'Hi, what can I get you?' Lexi asked, as the woman's eyes scanned the chalkboard menu on the wall.

'Can I have a latte to take away, please? Better make it a big one.'

'That kind of a day is it?' Lexi turned and began to make the coffee.

'It definitely is.' An anxious note perforated her voice. 'I'm Stella by the way. Stella Harris. I just bought the shop next door.'

From the corner of her eye Lexi saw Raina peer around the doorway from where she was out the back, mixing cake batter in a large stand mixer. Lexi turned her attention back to her customer. She didn't look like she'd be selling crystals or stinking up the place with horrid joss sticks which should make Raina happy. 'It's lovely to meet you, Stella. I'm Lexi. I was hoping to pop by later and say hello. How's it going?'

'Not as well as I hoped. I've got a leak. But once that's sorted out I hope I can get cracking on clearing up. I wanted to open on Saturday.'

'Oh no. A leak?'

Stella nodded, concern clearly written on her face. 'Yeah, a pipe under the sink burst, or cracked or something. It's not too bad. I could just do without it on my first day.'

'I'm sure you could. Well, here you go. Hopefully this will help.' Lexi placed the takeaway cup on the counter. Just as she did, her mobile phone rang. It was the school. 'Oh, I'm sorry, Stella, I just need to take this.' She placed the phone to her ear while her stomach turned over. It always did whenever the school rang. There was no logic to it; she just feared something terrible had happened, like a fire or a terrorist attack, or something else completely horrific and really very unlikely. 'Hello?'

'Hello, Miss Durham, it's Mrs Brandon from the school.'

A senior teacher. This couldn't be good. 'Hello.'

'Nothing to worry about, I just wanted to let you know that during playtime this morning Ralph bashed heads with another child. We've applied some ice and he's perfectly fine but we like to let the parents know, as there's a little bit of a lump. We'll send

16

him home with an accident slip but I just wanted to reassure you everything was fine.'

'Oh, okay.' Lexi stiffened. 'Thanks for letting me know, Mrs Brandon. Goodnight – I mean, goodbye.' *Goodnight?* Why had she said goodnight? Now she looked like a complete idiot to the deputy headteacher. Though her exterior was calm, inside her heart was beating double time and her mind was screaming. Her baby boy had hurt himself. And a lump? How big was the lump? Where was the lump? How hard did they hit each other? Could he have concussion? Should she let him sleep tonight? Should she take him to A&E? She looked up to see Stella waiting patiently, smiling at her. As Lexi's mind returned to that of a normal, sane human being, her heartrate slowed as well. 'Nothing to worry about. Just my little boy had a bump with another kid. Both okay.'

'Oh, good,' Stella replied. 'It must be worrying when the school phones. My sister has kids and she told me she always thinks something really bad has happened. She's normally worried her son has burned down the building or something. He's a bit of a terror.'

Lexi laughed. 'That's normally my daughter. Thank you for waiting. Raina would have finished serving you, but she's up to her elbows in cream cheese frosting.'

Stella handed over her money and Lexi noticed how kind her eyes were. 'No problem at all. I saw the picture on your phone when it rang. Your kids are really cute.'

'When they've got their mouths shut they are,' Lexi replied. She was definitely going to enjoy having Stella as a neighbour.

'Here, you'd better have this too,' said Raina, emerging from the back with a large slice of chocolate cake in an open white box. She sealed the lid and gently stamped it with the shop's logo, then placed it on the counter.

'It looks delicious,' Stella replied eyeing the board for the price.

'On the house,' Raina said, as she went back out to her mixer. 'And the coffee too.'

'Oh no, I couldn't possibly.' Stella shook her head and her milky-brown hair jiggled too.

'Of course you can,' Lexi replied. 'There's no point trying to argue with Raina. Believe me, I've tried. Take it as a moving-in present. Welcome to Swallowtail Bay.' Stella balanced the coffee on top of the box and departed with the biggest smile Lexi had seen all morning. 'That was nice of you,' she said to Raina when Stella had left.

'Well, she seems nice enough.'

Coming from Raina that was a huge compliment. Lexi wiped the counter with a tea towel. 'Shall we finish our coffees then get going? Do you want me to prepare the regular orders or serve any walk-ins?'

'You can serve the walk-ins as you want the tips.' Raina squeezed her shoulder as she walked past. Though Raina wasn't one for large shows of affection these little gestures meant the world to Lexi. 'What do you think of Stella?'

'She seems nice,' said Lexi. 'Why?'

'No reason.' Raina cleaned the counter top next to Lexi.

'Come on, what is it?' She knew that sneaky tone of Raina's. She was up to something.

'Well, I just thought you could—'

'What?' asked Lexi.

Raina stroked her short-cropped grey hair. 'Oh, I don't know. Befriend her.'

Lexi pinned her with a stern glare. 'She not a lost puppy, Raina. She's a grown woman.'

'Yes, but she's just moved here and she doesn't know anyone. And you haven't got that many friends your own age either.'

'That's because I have horrible kids and no social life.'

Raina continued to clean the counter top, even though it was spotless. 'You have beautiful, lovely children. You've no social life because you never try and go out – that's all your own fault. You could help Stella settle in. Make friends with her.'

'We're not at school, Raina. She may not want people trying to be friends with her.'

'But she might.' She paused a moment. 'I heard her say she wants to reopen on Saturday.'

'So?'

'Aren't your kids at their dad's this Saturday?'

Reluctantly, Lexi said, 'Yes. So?'

'And haven't you got the day off? You could surprise her with coffee and cake at about eleven?' When Lexi didn't reply but looked at Raina from the corner of her eye, Raina said, 'Good. I'll have it ready. My treat. Besides, if she's going to try and sell the last of Herbert's stock I'm sure she won't be busy. That man had some of the worst taste I've ever seen. His wife should never have died and let him run the shop on his own.'

Repressing a grin, Lexi said, 'I'm sure she didn't mean to.'

'Now, what cake would you like to take?'

'This is happening, isn't it?' said Lexi. 'Whether I want it to or not. You've got your determined face on.'

Raina gave a triumphant smile. 'Yes it is.'

'Fine,' Lexi replied. It was true she did get quite lonely. She always missed the other mums because her kids were in breakfast or after-school club, or she was too stressed to make polite conversation. And she could never afford childcare for nights out with the few friends she used to have. Stella had seemed really nice. Plus Lexi would be in town to see Vivien anyway. 'You'd better make your special triple chocolate mousse cake then, or I'm heading straight back home.'

Raina simply winked, the battle well and truly won.

Chapter 3

Stella let Derek the plumber out the shop door and locked it behind him. With the leak now fixed, she could actually start cleaning and clearing out the rubbish. Her top was still a little damp and clinging to her cleavage but it couldn't be helped. There was no point changing if she was just going to get dirty again, and what's more, there was no one around to look at it.

Rearranging the shop would have to wait until tomorrow. There was no way she'd get all the stock cleared, the place cleaned up and then reorganised by the end of the afternoon, and tiredness was creeping into her bones, making her limbs feel heavy. She'd underestimated what an emotional day it would be. Not exactly underestimated – Stella had expected it to be full of happy emotions, just not the ups and downs she'd had so far. And she certainly hadn't envisaged thinking about Isaac as much as she had. She'd tried so hard to put him behind her but the anger and hurt at their relationship ending had felt fresh and new today.

Frank was asleep on the old sofa in the bright but dusty living room, so Stella nipped out and grabbed her portable radio from the car. It was a sunny, breezy day with off-white clouds scudding across the sky, and the wind carried a cold chill. Hearing the waves in the distance calmed her frenzied energy a little. Stella loved the sound of the sea and it had been one of the things that drew her to Swallowtail Bay. When she'd visited, she'd walked along the beach with Frank, dodging the white frothy edges of the waves as they petered out on the pebbles beneath her feet. The cold salt-sea air had filled her lungs and bitten her cheeks, and now, hearing it again was reassuring. Back in the shop she turned on the radio and began singing along while she cleaned out the stock, storing it in the living room. Frank would occasionally open an eye to watch for a moment, distinctly unimpressed, as Stella filled the room with box upon box of goods.

Before long piles of dust and debris were dotted around the shop floor ready to be swept up, and almost half the shop had been cleared. Checking her phone, she saw that it was almost four o'clock and her stomach gave a loud gurgle. She'd been so busy tackling her to-do list she hadn't realised how hungry she was. As she surveyed her new domain her heart soared; it seemed so much bigger with all the mess out.

The lovely paintings Herbert had left could be hung on the far side wall and the dressers, which were dark cherry wood and sucked in all the light, would look much better painted cream. They could hold all the painted china. Frank came to join her in the shop, nosing through the little piles of rubbish. 'Don't do that, Frank, I've just swept there.' Frank paid no attention and, realising she'd left the dustpan and brush in the car, Stella tried to squeeze through the door. She opened it just wide enough to get through but Frank, ready for a walk and eager to get outside for the first time that day, ran past her and into the street.

'Frank! Frank, you naughty boy, come back here.'

On the pavement, Frank turned and looked at her, wagging his tail. Stella's heart began to pound hard. As trained as he was, he did have a habit of not returning if something more interesting was happening. If she ran after him he'd think it was a game of chase and leg it. The road was so much busier now with cars going past all the time. She needed to tempt him back with a treat. Reaching into her pockets, she cursed. There was nothing there and her hands began to shake. If she lost Frank she didn't know what she'd do. Further up the road she could see a cyclist pedalling fast. Naughty old Frank loved chasing cyclists. She had to do something quick. 'Frank, come here, please.'

Stella glanced back to the shop to see if she'd put any treats on the counter as a male voice said, 'Hello, boy, what are you— Oww!'

Spinning back in panic, Stella turned around as she heard Frank give an angry snarl and a bark. The man was clutching his hand and Frank ran back to Stella, cowering behind her legs. She grabbed his collar and shoved him inside the shop before closing the door. 'Oh, Frank, what have you done now?'

'Excuse me,' demanded a deep angry voice. 'Your dog just bit me.'

'I'm so sorry,' said Stella, staring at the man's hand, trying to catch a glimpse of the wound. There was no blood pouring from between his fingers so it couldn't be that bad, but he could still report Frank as a violent dog and then Frank might get put down. The thought of it was terrifying and her throat closed over. Stella pulled her eyes away from the man's hand to see his face. His light brown curly hair was cut short and he had a confident stance, even though he was holding his hand like it was about to drop off. *Blimey*, thought Stella. He was incredibly handsome and a strange fluttering in her lower tummy made her squirm. His blue eyes darted down to her T-shirt, which though dry now, was grubby and dirty, then back to her face. 'I'm really, really sorry,' she began, her voice a little shaky. 'He's just a bit jumpy today. Everything's new. We just moved in.'

'What, here?' he asked in a dismissive tone. When she didn't answer instantly he said, 'Have you bought here?' speaking slowly as if she were stupid.

'Umm, yes. Yes, I have,' Stella replied. The hairs on the back of her neck stood up as her hackles rose. 'Look, is your hand okay? Can I see if it needs a plaster or anything?' She didn't have a plaster, but she needed to see if Frank had actually bitten him. The man ignored her and peered in through the windows. Though Stella was normally a calm, sensible sort of person, Mr Handsome had wound her up, speaking to her as if she were an idiot, and now nosing at her shop. 'Is your hand okay, or do you need some help?'

He didn't look at her. Instead, he walked to the window and stared into the shop. 'What are you going to do with the place? Old Herbert couldn't make it work. How are you planning to?'

Was it just her or was there a note of derision in his voice? Stella met his gaze. Mr Handsome might be gorgeous but he was also haughty and rude. She tried to keep her temper. 'I'm going to sell off the old stock then source some more from local artists and makers.'

'Makers?' he repeated with a scoff. 'Is that a newfangled word for craftsmen?'

Okay, enough was enough. 'Don't you mean craftspeople? It's a more modern and inclusive term – and gender-neutral – but yes, craftsmen. Anyway, do you need a plaster?' She said it in the same way old people ask foreign tourists if they speak English.

He shook out his hand as if to shake away the pain, then examined it. As far as Stella could make out there was nothing there. Frank hadn't even left a red mark let alone punctured the skin. He must have just growled. He'd never bitten anyone before and thank goodness he wasn't starting now. Mr Handsome was clearly just a wimp. He cleared his throat. 'You're lucky. He hasn't done much damage.'

'Much damage?' Stella replied, her voice growing higher as her temper flared. 'He hasn't done *any* damage.'

'He could have. What if I'd been a little kid? Then you'd have been in real trouble.'

'If it was a child Frank wouldn't have snapped. He loves kids. Did you grab his collar?'

Mr Handsome put his hands on his hips. 'I was trying to stop him running into the road.'

'Well, there you go,' Stella replied, triumphantly. It wasn't Frank's fault, it was his. 'If you grabbed his collar, he probably thought you were trying to steal him and he's all on edge today.'

'He's a menace.' The man's face was a stone wall and didn't seem anywhere near as attractive as he had at first glance.

'A menace?' Stella laughed. 'Look at him.' She pointed to the window where Frank was stood, his paws on the sill and his tail sweeping the ground as it wagged, a plump little body wiggling. 'Oh yes. He's a real menace.'

Mr Handsome stood taller and pulled his shoulders back. His blue shirt came slightly un-tucked from the top of his trousers to reveal a hint of skin. Stella tried to ignore how flat and sexy the muscled abs it revealed were. She couldn't deny that he was, annoyingly, very good-looking. 'I could report that dog.'

'You could, but then you'd have to show them your injuries, wouldn't you? And then they'd laugh at you.' Stella knew she shouldn't have said it the moment the words flew from her mouth but he was making her pulse race and not in a good way.

Mr Handsome's eyes flashed down to his hand then back to Frank whose wet nose had left a smear on the window. 'If he does anything like that again, I'll report him.'

Stella knew it was a small town – Derek the plumber had proved that – and she had to be friendly to everyone to get the customers in. The last thing she needed today, after everything, was this man going around telling the town she had a vicious dog. As the anger and fear over Frank's possible demise subsided, and knowing he was safely inside, she decided to be a little more conciliatory for the sake of her reputation. 'Look, I'm sorry, I didn't mean that. It was just an accident. And I didn't mean to be rude. It's just been a difficult day so far.'

He didn't speak but nodded as he considered his response. 'Fine,' he said eventually, though it clearly wasn't, which annoyed

Stella even more after trying to be nice. 'I suppose we should try and get along as we're neighbours.'

Stella knew her face registered the shock she felt inside. Typical. Of course they'd be neighbours. That would make her new life awkward as well as frightening. She watched a grin spread across his face. Was he enjoying seeing her so uncomfortable? 'Neighbours?'

'Yes. I live practically next door. My name's Miles. Miles Parker.' He spun on his heel and sauntered off down the street, heading into the café.

Stella's normally positive attitude was waning fast and her shoulders sagged from tiredness and stress. As she stepped back into the shop, just as she'd done only hours earlier, she realised she hadn't made herself a happy new life by the sea. She'd made the scariest and most reckless decision of her life and worst of all, there was no going back.

Chapter 4

The next few days passed in a blur of activity for Stella who worked from eight every morning until late into the evening, sorting the stock and repainting the shop. Her only breaks were to take Frank for walks along the seafront, breathing in the fresh air and watching the world go by as she strolled along, daydreaming of what the shop would look like once it was finished. She compared it to the fabulous boutique shops that lined the beach-front with their arty window displays, knowing one day hers would be just as good. When her spirits failed or thoughts of Isaac filled her head and flared the pain in her heart, the sound of the tide ebbing and flowing, keeping its own time, revived her. On the beach she could calm and refocus.

By Saturday morning she was ready to reopen with all the old stock Herbert had left. He'd been in such a hurry to jet off to Málaga and start his retirement, he'd agreed to sell the shop with any stock left in it at the end of his last day. For Stella, this was both good and bad news. It meant she didn't have to source anything immediately and could open as soon as she wanted, but it also meant some of the weird stuff he'd bought over the years was still sitting there staring at her. As well as the big stone statue of a woman kissing a fish, the papier-mâché buxom ladies and the stone tiles with grumpy men's faces on, she'd found a pile of very unattractive rugs and badly crocheted cushions. Frank had been quite taken with one that had an angry-looking tortoise on, so Stella had kept it and placed it on the wingback chair, ready for him to take his seat on Saturday morning. The others though, she wasn't sure what to do with. Big red 'SALE' signs had been stuck to the windows so with any luck by the end of her first day, she'd be rid of a lot of the rubbish and could start getting new things.

Opening her eyes on Saturday morning, the feeling of excitement Stella had imagined on all those lonely nights in her smelly one-bedroom flat in Oxford flooded through her. Her chest felt light and adrenalin swamped her body. She jumped out of bed with a huge smile on her face even though it was barely light outside. Seagulls cawed overhead and circled by the bins, hoping for food, but the trees in the churchyard opposite barely moved. When the sun began to rise it flooded the sky with colour. An incredible palette that ranged from warm burnt-orange to the palest creamy-yellow fell across the sky. It was going to be a beautiful windless day. Though Stella didn't need to be up that early there was no way she could go back to sleep, especially as she was still using the old sofa in the living room as a bed. She hadn't even started to clean out the bedroom yet. The shop had had to take priority.

Deciding the best way she could start the day was with a long walk on the beach, she pulled her feet out from under Frank who was still fast asleep and snoring loudly, and dressed in her old joggers and a huge paint-splattered sweatshirt. She pulled her hair back into a ponytail, brushed her teeth, and then found Frank's lead.

It was colder outside than she was expecting as Frank guided her to the beach and she shivered a little in the strong, fresh breeze. All was quiet as the sky turned from deep lilac to pale blue, and clouds drifted above. The salty tang hit her nose. She headed down to the shore and Frank bounded over the pebbles, running back from the waves that splashed at his feet. Stella kept him on his lead, mindful of her run-in with snooty Mr Handsome, or Miles Parker. She had to stop calling him Mr Handsome because every time she did her stomach gave a funny squiggle and she was afraid she might actually say it out loud. Strands of seaweed had washed ashore from the strong winds and waves they'd had the night before and Stella stepped over one, careful to lead Frank away before he could eat it, or worse, roll on it.

After a quick breakfast, Stella took the ugly angry tortoise cushion and placed it on the wingback chair she'd positioned in the corner, next to the till. Frank sniffed at it then pulled it off onto the floor and sat on it. 'You can't sit there, you silly dog. You'll get in the way of the masses of people queuing at the till.' Fetching his basket, Stella placed it at the end of the counter but with just enough room to move around. Mindful of his quick escape last time, she clipped on his lead and tied it to her stool. She'd tuned the portable radio to a jazz channel and at exactly nine o'clock opened the shop for her first day's trading. She took a moment to stare at the full-length shop windows. The old white paint was chipping a little on the door and window frames, but it was nothing a coat of paint couldn't fix. Before long, the tired and worn facade would be shiny, bright and new.

Even though she hadn't expected a queue waiting at the door, a little part of her had hoped all the same. 'I'm sure we'll get some customers soon, Frank,' she said as, unimpressed and still damp from the morning walk, he went to sleep. Gazing around at all she'd achieved over the last few days, Stella beamed proudly. She hadn't painted the walls yet, but one was hidden by paintings and the other was covered by the dressers she'd painted in cream chalk paint. The shop was now light and airy and while there was still work to do, it was slowly getting there.

About an hour later, a steady stream of customers began to

arrive and more came throughout the morning, happy to see the shop open once more or just so see if anything was different. A lot of the ugly rugs were sold now the price was knocked down, and by lunchtime, Stella was happy-dancing as she'd even sold some of the ugly crocheted cushions – the squinting giraffe had gone, as had a rather gormless-looking fish and a pouting Schnauzer. When things quietened down, Stella read her book, reminding herself that there were slow periods in every shop. It was nothing to worry about.

'Oh, wow.' It was Lexi, the waitress from next door, looking absolutely incredible. Her curvaceous, hourglass figure had been poured into a 1950s tea dress in emerald-green with a sweet little collar. Her black hair was piled up into a high bun and wispy strands fell from it, softening her face. Bright green eyes stood out thanks to a thick swipe of eyeliner that flicked up at the ends. Stella looked down at her baggy jeans decorated with paw prints left by Frank, and her thick cable-knit jumper flecked with dog hair, and made a mental note to sort herself out.

'I can't believe this is the same shop,' said Lexi. 'It looks amazing. So bright and sunny. Is this all Herbert's old stock?'

Glowing at the compliment, Stella replied, 'At the moment it is. I'm trying to sell off some of the old tat and then I'll get some new pieces in. I'm thinking nice ceramics and glass, maybe some jewellery too. I want to keep the paintings and find some different local artists as well. Maybe broaden the range.'

'You've done such a fantastic job.' Lexi placed a tray of takeaway coffee cups and a white cardboard box on the counter. 'I brought you coffee and cake to celebrate opening day.'

Stella paused. 'Really? Oh my gosh, thank you. That's so kind. If it's as good as the cake I had the other day I'm in for a treat.'

Lexi smiled back, evidently pleased that she'd made Stella's day. As Stella opened the box Lexi said, 'I wasn't sure what you liked so got a piece of Victoria sponge, and a bit of chocolate mousse cake.'

'I can't possibly eat all this on my own. Will you share some with me?'

'No, no, I can't do that. I brought it for you.'

'Please? I really can't eat all this on my own or I'll fall asleep at the till this afternoon.'

Lexi smiled again. 'Okay then. Shall we have one each or just dive in and share?'

'Let's share.'

'And I remembered how you liked your coffee so here's a latte for you and a cappuccino for me.'

Stella couldn't believe that a stranger could be so kind. Oxford was friendly enough but she'd never got to know her neighbours when she and Isaac were together, and when she'd moved into her little flat after the divorce, she hadn't felt able to. Mourning the end of her marriage, she couldn't bring herself to pretend she was fine and be cheerful and jolly. The warmth of Lexi's smile radiated through Stella. 'I'll grab some forks.' She ran out to the kitchen and checking they were actually clean – she hadn't sorted the kitchen out yet either – brought them through.

'It must be hard moving to a new place and not knowing anyone. I think you're incredibly brave.'

'Or stupid,' Stella replied. 'I'm leaning more towards stupid at the moment.'

'Nonsense. You've done amazingly well already. This place looks so different. Old Herbert was lovely but the shop was a mess. I remember it always felt so dark and crowded. There was just stuff everywhere.'

Stella forked some of the chocolate mousse cake into her mouth and gasped. 'This is amazing.'

'I know,' Lexi replied, having some herself. 'Raina's an incredible baker.'

'There's still quite a lot of stock in the living room,' said Stella. 'I couldn't get it all in here. But I'm hoping most of that will come in tonight when I restock ready for Monday. I noticed none of the other shops are open tomorrow?'

'No, Sundays are dead. I wouldn't bother if I were you.'

Frank woke up at the smell of food and stretched in his basket. Lexi bent down and gave him a fuss and he pushed his head into her hands. 'He's gorgeous,' she said. 'What's his name?'

'Frank,' Stella replied. 'And he's an absolute tart. He's on his lead at the moment because we had a bit of an incident the other day.'

'I heard,' said Lexi, taking a fork and cutting a piece of the Victoria sponge. Jam and cream oozed down the sides. 'Miles told me about it.'

Stella felt a chill as Lexi said his name. Was he telling everyone about her vicious dog and warning them to stay away from the shop? She tried to keep her voice casual. 'Did he?'

'Don't worry, he wasn't rude about you. Just said that your dog nipped him, but I can't imagine that,' Lexi said to Frank.

'He was just scared because what's his name grabbed his collar.' She'd been about to call Miles Mr Handsome but pulled it back just in time. Stella felt as protective towards Frank as other people did their children. 'Frank's a bit scared of men. He was a rescue puppy. I got him when he was six months old and he'd been treated quite badly, I think. He's really nervous around blokes but he loves children.'

'I think he's lovely,' said Lexi, forking off another bit of cake. 'Don't worry about Miles, his bark's worse than his bite. He was probably just jealous because he wanted this place.' She motioned around at the shop.

'Did he?' Stella was astounded. She couldn't imagine that man losing out on anything he wanted. Or being the type to want to run a shop for that matter. He'd have to be nice and talk to people, which didn't seem to come naturally to him at all.

'Yeah. He thought he could make a better go of the business than old Herbert had and he was close to getting it because there hadn't been much interest until you. Herbert said you swept him off his feet.'

'Me?' It had been a long time since Stella had swept anything except the floor and considering how rejected she'd felt by Isaac who'd gone headlong into a new relationship the moment their split was official, the compliment lifted her spirits.

Lexi chewed another piece of cake. 'He thought you were lovely and just the person to take over from him. But Miles is a nice bloke too. He just doesn't do well not getting his own way. I think Herbert enjoyed teasing him about it actually.'

'So they knew each other quite well?'

'Very well. I think Miles had tried a bit of a charm offensive but Herbert saw through it. Miles kept popping in as he lives just over the road there but charm isn't exactly his thing. Shame really, as you're neighbours.'

Miles had said they were neighbours and the idea of living near him after the start they'd had made Stella slightly panicky. She didn't like awkwardness or confrontation and tried to keep any hint of worry from her voice. 'Where exactly "over the road" does he live?'

After taking a swig of her coffee, Lexi walked to the side window and pointed down the road. 'He lives in that cottage there. The one with the white shutters and blue front door. It's called the Old Post House.'

Stella followed and looked to where Lexi was pointing. He lived in one of the larger cottages and the property was definitely worth a few quid. Mr Handsome must be loaded. 'What does he do?'

'He's a salesman for a big pharmaceutical company. He travels a lot. That's why he wanted to buy this place and really settle down.'

For a moment Stella felt a little guilty, but just as quickly the feeling disappeared. On balance, her need had probably been greater than his. Finding this place had saved her from feeling so utterly hopeless. Plus Miles was awful.

They headed back to the counter and tucked in to more cake. Stella's mind turned over everything Lexi had told her and even when she tried to pull her thoughts away from Miles they didn't seem to want to budge. It was a shame he was such a snob.

'I really can't believe how different this place looks,' said Lexi while Stella cleared away the box and forks. 'You've made it so bright and clean. Even the old rubbishy stuff looks good.'

Stella had artistically draped some horrid blankets and the ugly cushions over the wide windowsill in one corner of the room, and beside them stood a large wicker basket containing long rolls of fabric. Old Herbert really had offered an eclectic range of things. He must have purchased whatever he fancied selling at the time or what was at a knockdown price. Lexi wandered over and studied the bolts of cloth.

'How much are you selling the teapot print for?'

'I've knocked it down to six quid a metre but they've been here for ages according to Herbert's records. Why? Are you interested?'

'I make dresses,' said Lexi. She held out the skirt of her own dress. 'This is one of mine and I really like this mustard colour. It'll be lovely for autumn.'

Stella hadn't been sure about the mustard fabric with little black teapots on but she wasn't about to turn down a sale and to be fair, it was obvious Lexi knew much more about fashion than she did. 'It's a forty-metre roll but I'll let you have it for a hundred quid if you want the whole thing?'

'I can't really afford that. I can't even afford the few metres I'd need for a dress,' Lexi replied, sighing. 'I've got a phone bill to pay this month. Never mind though.'

Stella couldn't imagine anyone else buying it; so far that morning, no one had even looked at it. Lexi had been so incredibly kind, Stella found herself saying, 'I tell you what, if it's still here at the end of the day I'll let you have it for fifty and you can pay me later.'

'It might have to be in tips,' Lexi said. 'Or a little bit each week.'

'That's fine,' Stella replied. 'It's the least I can do as you've been so welcoming.'

'Cooee?' An elderly voice sounded from the doorway and in walked a very glamorous old lady. She wore a large woollen coat, a black pillbox hat with a small veil, and her aged but smiling face was made up with mascara and a dab of blusher.

'Vivien,' Lexi replied, giving her a hug. 'You look lovely today, as usual.' Stella couldn't tell how old Vivien was but her slim, frail frame and slight stoop was that of a woman pushing eighty. 'Come and meet Stella.' Lexi held her arm out for Vivien who took it and leaned on her walking stick with the other.

'I love what you've done with the place, young lady,' Vivien said as they approached the counter.

'Thank you. Would you like a chair?'

'Oh, that'd be lovely. Thank you.' Stella motioned to the wing-back chair and Vivien lowered herself into it. 'You've done wonders here already. Herbert was a lovely old man but a terrible shop-keeper. No head for business.' She shook her head, then peered around like an owl.

'Did you know him well?' asked Stella, moving back behind the counter and edging onto her stool while Lexi fussed Frank who was wagging his tail delightedly.

'Yes, dear. I've lived here for nearly sixty years and Herbert was born and bred here.'

'Vivien was an opera singer,' Lexi said. 'She's our local super-star.'

'Really?' asked Stella, as Vivien puffed with pride. 'How exciting.'

'Oh yes, dear. It was a long time ago now but I remember it so vividly. I sang all across the world, you know. London, New York, Vienna, Rome. And I used to record the screams for the *Hammer Horror* films back in the Sixties.'

'That's amazing,' Stella replied, genuinely impressed. She loved those films. There was nothing better than snuggling up on a Saturday night with a terrible movie and a bucket of popcorn. Isaac had hated cheesy movies though, so she'd often watch them on her own while he did something else.

Strangely, the small, frail woman who had entered her shop seemed to fill the chair, her personality making her seem bigger. 'I made my name in London when I was very young, quite by accident. I was working in a club and one night the cabaret didn't show so I volunteered to sing. It went down a treat.'

'Sounds wonderful.' Glancing at the takeaway cups on the counter, Stella felt like a terrible host. She cleared them away and turned to Vivien who was plumping one of the awful crocheted cushions and placing it behind her back. She was clearly here for a while. 'Would you like a cup of tea, Vivien?'

'Oh, that would be lovely. Yes, please.'

'I'm Stella by the way. Stella Harris.' She held out her hand for Vivien to shake and the old lady gently held the tips of her fingers.

'Vivien Griffen. Very pleased to meet you.'

Stella nipped out to the kitchen and put the kettle on. She searched for a nice cup and saucer but all she could find were builders' mugs ringed with tea stains. They were fine for her, but not suitable for a lady like Vivien. In the shop there was a range of pretty floral hand-painted cups that Stella had marked down. She ran back to grab one. When she re-entered the shop saying, 'I won't be a tick,' Lexi gave her a knowing look. 'Do you take sugar, Vivien?' Stella called on her way back to the kitchen.

Vivien must have been a little deaf, as it was Lexi who answered for her. Stella made the tea and returned with the cup and saucer.

'How lovely. So pretty. Thank you so much, my dear.'

'Have you got your shopping list prepared?' Lexi asked Vivien, finishing with Frank and standing up.

She took a sip of her tea, slurping a little. 'It's in my bag. And there's the cash too.' Vivien picked up her bag and took out her wallet. She removed the list and some notes and passed them to

Lexi. 'Make sure you get yourself a little something as well, won't you, Lexi.'

'No, I won't and you know it.'

'But you do this every week for me. I'd like you to get yourself a little treat. You work too hard as it is.'

'It's no bother,' said Lexi. 'I've got my own shopping to do anyway. I'll drop your stuff in later.'

Stella marvelled at Lexi. She was a mum, working in the café virtually full-time, and helping out this lovely old lady too. She was very kind. 'Where are your cute kids today?' asked Stella, realising they were missing.

'They're with their dad. We're divorced and he has them every other weekend. I don't get them back till tomorrow afternoon.'

'Oh, right.' Stella blushed. 'Sorry, I hope I haven't upset you.'

But Lexi gave a bright cheerful smile. 'Upset? Why should I be upset? Honestly, honey, I'm happy to have a break from them for a bit. I love them more than anything, but there are only so many arguments you can referee before you go a bit bonkers.'

Relieved, and feeling a kinship with Lexi, Stella ventured, 'I'm divorced too. But we never had any kids.'

'I was nearly married so many times,' said Vivien, sitting primly with her cup and saucer in front of her. 'I must have been asked … oh, at least five times in my prime. And once or twice when I was past it.'

'You've never been past your prime, Vivien,' Lexi replied. 'You just get better and better with age.'

Vivien guffawed. 'You have to play it cool, you see. Like you wouldn't even notice if they were around, that's the key. That's what I did and nearly every man I sang with fell madly in love with me.'

Stella repressed a smile and a hint of one passed over Lexi's lips. 'I'm sure they did,' Lexi replied. 'I'm sure you were the sexiest thing they'd ever seen.'

A group entered the shop and began cooing over the artwork.

Sensing a potential sale, Stella got up and went to greet them. She had researched the artists on her laptop and was giving a good pitch, even talking about where the painting had been done. If she could sell just one piece it would make her day. At three hundred pounds it would be a very good day's work, but not wanting to push she left her customers to it.

'Right, I should be going,' said Lexi. 'Or I'll get in your way. It's great to see you busy.'

'It's been lovely. Thank you so much for stopping by.'

'Yes, I should be off too,' said Vivien. 'Miles is coming to see me later.'

Stella's ears pricked up at the mention of his name. Whatever did snooty boots Parker want with lovely old Vivien? Not that she could ask.

'Tell him,' said Lexi, 'not to eat all the biscuits again.'

Again? So he was a regular visitor? Stella could feel how much she was scrunching her brow in confusion and made an effort to relax her face.

Lexi was just about to leave when she hesitated slightly. 'Hey listen, I've got a great idea. Why don't we have lunch together tomorrow, Stella? My kids don't get dropped off till late afternoon. We could have a nice Sunday roast at the Admiral Drummond?'

Stella paused. She'd had a few work friends back in Oxford but she only saw them on the odd staff night out. There was her sister, but she hardly went out now she had the kids as she hated leaving them with babysitters. Stella's heart pulsed a feeling of warmth around her whole body. She never dreamed she would make friends so quickly.

'If you're busy then that's fine,' Lexi said, a slight blush forming on her cheeks.

Stella realised that having taken a while to reply, it must have seemed like she was thinking of an excuse. 'No, no. I'd love to. That would be lovely. What time?'

The blush faded and Lexi brightened. 'One o'clock?'

'Sounds great.'

A petite woman from the group came over to the counter. 'Excuse me. I'd love to take that painting, please, if it's still available.'

Stella beamed. 'Of course.'

As Vivien and Lexi left, Stella made her way to the ladder tucked in the corner, ready to take down the painting. Eyeing the price tag once more, Stella decided she might need to do another happy dance. It was a good sale and maybe tomorrow she could go and buy a bed. All the worries and doubts created by the first few days' troubles and the hours and hours of hard work faded a little more. Things were definitely looking up.

Chapter 5

Lexi awoke on Sunday morning and her stomach squirmed, but it wasn't due to the half-bottle of wine she'd consumed the night before. She was nervous about having lunch with Stella. Rubbing her eyes, she tried to calm the silly fizzing in her tummy. The sun was shining in through the window of her bedroom, and she stretched out her arms and legs. Nothing beat a good lie-in.

Yesterday, after doing Vivien's shopping, she'd come home and had a long hot bath with candles and her favourite music playing, before curling up on the sofa with a face mask plastered on and giving herself a mani-pedi. Matthew Macfadyen in the film version of *Pride and Prejudice* had been her date for the evening. She loved the original TV series but who had something like eight hours free to get through it?

Climbing slowly out of bed, Lexi dressed in some capri trousers and a cute twinset. She loved a vintage look and felt that it suited her curvy figure. Her tummy wasn't exactly flat after two kids. Without clothes the stretch marks made her skin look more like an Ordnance Survey map, but she didn't care. Her body had delivered two amazing, if somewhat monstrous, children who she loved more than anything else in the world. She combed her hair and applied some make-up. She didn't wear too much on Sundays preferring to let her skin breathe, so it was a quick brush-over with some powder, a flick of eyeliner and a coat of mascara. Before long she was ready to go.

The Admiral Drummond did, without doubt, the best Sunday roasts in town. No fiddly little portions or elegant displays, just a mountain of food on a large plate covered in gravy. Lexi's stomach rumbled just thinking about it and by the time she had walked into town, she'd have earned it. She couldn't afford lunch *and* petrol so walking was her only option but at least it was another gorgeous day. After the weird cold snap they'd had a few weeks before, spring had finally started and the bare trees were showing real signs of growth, the world bursting into colour again. Lexi lived at the opposite end of town to the café, amongst the little terraces and cul-de-sacs.

Walking along, she passed the park where her children played at weekends in the summer, and she inhaled some of the fresh, clean air. Along the verges, clumps of daffodils planted by the local council were opening up, the gorgeous yellow heads bright and cheery. The brisk walk brought a chill to her cheeks as she took the road along the seafront. Every few yards a bench tempted her to take a moment to rest. Each had a small memorial plaque on them and Lexi enjoyed reading them as she passed. She liked walking on her own; it was far less stressful than walking with the kids. Ralph always tried to climb everything and Taylor spent most of the time trailing behind, twirling and singing as she went. Stretching out her fingers, Lexi suddenly missed their little hands in hers and her heart soared at the thought of seeing them again in a few hours.

The heavy wooden door of the pub required a good heft of the shoulder and Lexi pushed hard to get it open. It was a little darker inside and her eyes took a moment to adjust to the dimmer light. In the corner, Stella looked up and gave a smile. Thankfully, a bottle of white wine was already open and chilling in a wine cooler on the table. Lexi waved back. Stella was definitely turning into her type of girl. The pub was busy and loud with chatter and the scrape of chairs. The smell of roast beef floated on the air, making her mouth water.

'Hi,' Lexi said as she approached the table. A sudden surge of nerves flared up but she pushed it down and faked confidence. Slinging her bag down onto the floor, she kissed Stella's cheek.

'Lovely to see you,' said Stella. 'Thanks so much for inviting me.' A blush crept over Stella's cheeks, which made Lexi feel better; she was clearly a bit anxious too. Lexi sat down and poured them both a glass of wine.

'Thanks for ordering some wine. You have to have a glass with a big Sunday roast, don't you? How was business yesterday afternoon? Did you sell much more?'

Stella nodded as she sipped. 'Yep, I sold loads of Herbert's old crap and now I can source some new stuff. Nearly all the rugs went and most of the crocheted cushions though I'm still stuck with that horrible statue of the woman snogging a fish. I don't think any normal person's ever going to buy that.'

'It is hideous,' Lexi replied. 'I can't imagine what possessed Herbert to buy a lot of that stuff.'

'Weirdly, I think he was on track with some of the paintings and the ceramics. I just think his tastes were a little bit ...'

'Rancid?' Lexi offered and Stella laughed.

'Yeah. But then, he's a man so I suppose we can't blame him.'

'And from the paisley generation,' added Lexi. 'And even I don't wear paisley.' Her nerves disappeared as they decided to forgo starters to make sure they had room for pudding. They each ordered a full roast beef dinner and as the waiter moved away to see to another table Lexi asked, 'So, come on then, Stella. I want to know everything. What brought you down here away from your friends and family?'

'There's not much to say really.' Stella studied her wine. 'I was twenty-five when I married Isaac and we were together for ten years but then last year we split and he moved someone else in. Our divorce was finalised about a month ago.'

'That's rough, honey. This new relationship probably won't last. He'll soon realise everything he's lost.' Lexi thought about giving her a hug but not knowing her very well yet, decided not to. A look of pain flashed across Stella's face. It was a feeling Lexi knew well.

'I've got a sister still in Oxford, Abby, but she's got her own family. When we split, she wondered why I was so surprised and quite helpfully pointed out that it had been on the cards for ages.'

'That's nice of her.'

'Yeah. She's no-nonsense but she means well. And my parents live just down the road from them. After selling the house and splitting things fifty-fifty, I invested everything in the Admiral's Corner. There was nothing to keep me in Oxford. And as much as I love my family, a bit of distance is a good thing as far as they're concerned. So, here I am.'

Though she ended the sentence on an upbeat note, there was an undercurrent of sadness to the way Stella spoke. She must be a bit lonely, or at least, had been. And she hadn't talked of any friends. Lexi knew exactly how Stella felt. When the kids had started school she'd hoped she'd make some friends but it hadn't happened, and with always missing the other mums at drop-off and sometimes even pick-up time because of work, she never really got the chance to speak to anyone. She didn't have any brothers and sisters – only a mad mother who lived in Spain, and called every day to let her know she was still alive and hadn't yet drowned in sangria.

'Divorce is shit, isn't it? Was it amicable in the end?' asked Lexi.

'No,' Stella conceded with a small, sad smile. Lexi had seen that same expression in the mirror. It was a smile of miserable acceptance and pain pushed down. 'I threw things at him and left. Then we barely spoke. As we didn't have kids we didn't have to talk to each other and pretty much everything was done through angry emails or text messages from me, and sad, conciliatory ones from him. What about you?'

Lexi shuffled uncomfortably. She wasn't quite ready to go into all the details yet, fearing judgement, so she settled on a more non-committal reply. 'Similar.' She stared down into her wine. 'Except because the kids were so young we had to pretend to be civil to each other when we were both hurting like hell. It does make it quite difficult. There ended up being lots of late nights sobbing into pillows.'

Lexi looked back up at Stella. She was pretty, with lovely almond-shaped eyes. A little powder to take the shine off her nose and she'd look effortlessly amazing. In Lexi's view, those who didn't wear make-up had either tons of confidence and therefore felt comfortable enough not to, or didn't have any confidence at all and therefore didn't think they were worth it. She hadn't decided yet which camp Stella fell into but the idea that she didn't have much confidence made her incredibly sad and was something she wanted to change.

As the conversation lulled Stella asked, 'So what did you get up to last night? Did you have a nice relax?'

'Ah, it was blissful. After I got back from Vivien's I chilled out a bit. The house was wonderfully quiet and I sat with a glass of wine and watched *Pride and Prejudice*. And then I made a skirt from the last of a pale pink material I bought in the January sale. With a full net underneath, it'll look fabulous.'

'I can't believe you make your own clothes,' said Stella. 'That's an incredible talent. But the big question is who do you prefer, Colin Firth or Matthew Macfadyen?'

'Matthew Macfadyen of course.'

'Good choice.' Lexi grinned back just as the waiter brought over their food. 'This looks amazing,' said Stella, turning the plate slightly and studying the vast array there.

'Now I have a very important question for you,' said Lexi, popping her napkin on her lap. 'Do you eat all your vegetables first to get them out of the way, or all the meat, or do you eat a little of everything as you go? I've found that dinner tactics are a very important indicator as to whether you'll get on with someone.'

Stella paused, her face frozen.

'I'm joking,' reassured Lexi. 'It doesn't matter how you eat your dinner.'

Stella laughed. 'Well, I love cheesy veg so I tend to eat that first. Then stuffing, if I've got some, because that's my next favourite and then, once they've gone, I tackle the rest of my dinner in a little-bit-of-everything approach.'

'I approve,' said Lexi, taking another drink.

The two ladies consumed their dinner as if it was a military operation requiring concentration and stealth.

'I'm glad my trousers have an elasticated waist,' said Lexi, leaning back in her chair. 'I feel like I've ballooned.'

'Me too,' Stella replied. 'That was the nicest roast dinner I've ever had.'

Lexi patted her tummy like a pregnant lady. 'I think I'm having a food baby.'

'It doesn't show. You have such an amazing figure.'

'Really?' Lexi couldn't believe that anyone would say that of her. While she was perfectly happy and confident in her appearance, inside she gave a little fist pump. 'But I don't care how tight my trousers feel, I'm still having pudding.' She watched the waiter bring out a treacle sponge and deposit it in front of another customer. 'And I've already decided what I'm having.'

'That does look good,' replied Stella, following her gaze then perusing the menu. 'But I think I'll have trifle.'

They placed their orders and Stella topped up their wine. 'Thank you for coming to see me yesterday and for lunch today. It's made me feel really welcome here already.'

'It's been lovely,' said Lexi. 'And you're very welcome.' She spied a couple at a corner table flirting and chatting. 'How long do you think they've been going out?'

'Not long judging by how much they still like each other. Six months maybe? They're very touchy-feely and flirty.'

'Flirting? What's that?' Lexi asked with a smile.

'I think you spy someone across the room then throw your knickers at them, like at a Tom Jones concert.'

'Ah, yes. Thanks.' Both women giggled.

'I can't remember the last time I went on a date,' offered Stella, swilling her wine in her glass. 'I don't think I'd know what to do anymore.'

'Me neither. It'd be terrifying.'

'I know at some point I'm going to have to get back out there but I'm not sure I'm ready for it yet. Still, I don't want to end up a lonely old dog lady.'

'I thought it was cats?' Lexi replied.

'It is but I can't stand cats. It'll be me and Frank when I'm old and grey.'

'You have the dogs; I'll have the cats,' Lexi said. The waiter presented dessert and they ate in a comfortable silence. Afterwards, checking her watch, Lexi slugged back the last of her wine. 'Sorry to run but I have to get home before my horrible children arrive back.'

'Have you missed them?' asked Stella.

'Terribly,' Lexi replied, and a huge grin spread over her face. Even when she was calling them completely inappropriate names and moaning about the strange things they'd done, she did love them. 'Shall we split the bill?'

'Sounds good to me. I need to get back to Frank anyway.'

They parted ways at the door. Lexi started the walk back home, happy that she'd spent the money on lunch rather than petrol. The kids would moan about walking to school but the new blossoming friendship with Stella was worth every single penny if it helped to drive some of the loneliness out of her life. She never had time to think about it when the kids were around, but in the evenings, when they were in bed, there was no denying that it surrounded her till she felt like the last human being on the planet.

Chapter 6

Miles rolled over and draped an arm over Kiera. She was sound asleep next to him and hadn't stirred at all when he'd arrived back late last night. Even asleep she was beautiful and he wondered again how he'd ever managed to find someone like her. Her skin, bronzed from weekly tanning sessions, glimmered in the bright sunlight pushing through the gaps in the curtains, and her long blonde hair flared out covering the pillow. It was funny that she insisted she couldn't fall asleep if there was any light in the room and yet here she was sleeping soundly.

He rolled back the other way and looked at the alarm clock. It was just gone eight. And Monday again. How had another week gone by already? Another week where he'd been away rather than at home in his favourite place on earth. More meetings were being lined up for the weeks to come but at least for today he could relax. It was unusual to have had a meeting on a Sunday, but with clients over from the USA he couldn't really say no. It was unusual for him to sleep so late too, but the drive home had been a nightmare. Something was always going wrong at the moment, it seemed.

Miles lay on his back and pushed his arms and legs away from each other, stretching out the muscles. He rubbed his eyes with the heel of his hands then raked them through his hair. He needed a shower. Leaving Kiera to sleep some more – she loved to get at least eight hours – he snuck out of bed and headed to the bathroom. By the time he was back, she had begun to stir and smiled sleepily at him from under long thick eyelashes. 'Good morning, darling. What time did you get back?'

Miles rolled down the top of the towel circling his waist and took the one from his shoulders to dry his hair. Once he'd finished, he sat on the edge of the bed and gave her a long, lingering kiss. 'Almost four o'clock. The journey was a nightmare.'

Underneath the covers Miles could feel Kiera's legs against him. The best thing about them both working from home was that she was often there when he got back and they could spend time together when they wanted. Unless, of course, she had clients to meet – being a personal shopper, she preferred to travel to the designer shops in London. If she didn't work from home he wasn't sure they'd ever actually see each other.

'That was late.' Kiera combed her fingers through her hair then examined her nails. They were a shiny pink. The last time Miles had seen them they'd been blue. She must have had them done again. 'Do you like this colour? I can't decide if I do or not.'

He'd hoped she'd want to know why he'd got back so late and how the meeting had gone. It was a big one for him. One that would have made the difference between a bonus or not, which made the result all the more galling. 'I like the blue more. Shall I tell you what happened?'

'Hmm?' She stopped her examination and looked up, doe-eyed. 'Tell me about what?'

'The meeting yesterday. Shall I tell you how it went?'

'Oh, yes, go on.' She climbed out of the opposite side of the bed in her expensive silk pyjamas and Miles began to get dressed.

'So, first of all, the clients had planned to see a West End show so they wanted the meeting wrapped up quickly. Then after the show – which was awful, some musical about a dancing policeman

– they decided that despite assuring me they were interested in our new drug they didn't really need it after all. Then—' Kiera opened the curtains a little and stared down into the street. Miles frowned, unsure if she was listening. 'Then there was a massive pile-up on the M20 and it took me about five hours to get home.'

'I think we should go and see the lady who bought your shop this morning, don't you? She's opening up now.' Kiera stood on tiptoes to get a better look. 'She looks awful. I don't know what she's wearing. She looks like a mum. And not like Victoria Beckham mumsy – she looks like all those mums you see trudging to school, absolutely exhausted and pulling snotty-nosed children along. They all wear exactly the same outfit of jeans and jumpers; the jeans and jumper brigade!' She laughed at her own joke. 'The only mum who doesn't look like them is that Lexi from the coffee shop and I think she tries too hard.'

Miles liked Lexi a lot and hoped it was just some early morning grumpiness creeping out from Kiera. 'You're not even listening to me,' he said, giving his hair one last dry then throwing the towel into the washing basket. He'd meant for his comment to be slightly teasing but it came out rather sharply. Lately, she always seemed to be thinking about something else when he was talking.

Kiera turned, startled at his tone. 'I only got distracted for a minute.'

'I'm sorry,' said Miles, moving over and kissing her. 'I'm being grumpy. And we can nip in and see the shop if you want to.'

'If it's too painful we don't have to go. I just wanted to get a good look at our new neighbour. We can't ignore her forever.'

'You're right,' he conceded, going to find some clothes in his side of the wardrobe. He didn't particularly want to see the shop after that horrible dog had bitten him. Okay, he hadn't quite taken a chunk out of his hand, but Miles was still right. If it had been a child it could have been much more serious. He did, however, need to get over this feeling of injustice that Herbert had sold the shop to her just because he'd liked her more than him. *He* was perfectly likeable, Miles thought. Lots of people liked him. He just needed to wait and find a new place. 'Get dressed then,' Miles said cheerfully. 'We can go out for breakfast and call in on our way.'

Kiera went off to the wardrobe. 'Can we not go to that horrid café where that mad old woman keeps accosting you?'

'Vivien?' he said with a chuckle.

'Yes. She's awful and just prattles on about the good old days. I don't think I can cope with her this morning.'

Miles had a huge soft spot for Vivien. They'd been neighbours when he was young, before his parents moved. All the while he was growing up his mum had popped in to help her out when she needed it. Then as a grown man, when his parents had moved away, he'd carried on. Vivien had been there for him when he'd really needed it, when he hadn't felt able to talk to anyone else. Kiera had never had the patience for Vivien's stories so it was probably a good thing their paths didn't cross that often.

'We can go to the nice place in the centre of town with the big sofas and industrial tables,' Kiera said, pulling out different clothes from the wardrobe and examining them.

'But they make terrible coffee,' Miles replied, buttoning up his shirt. He spied some shopping bags in front of the wardrobe door. Lately, whenever she went to London to work she came home with more bags than her clients.

'I like their coffee. And they do a fabulous smashed avocado on rye.'

Inwardly, Miles groaned. He'd been travelling a lot lately and hadn't eaten last night when he got in. All he'd wanted was to get home as fast as possible and crawl into bed. What he really fancied this morning was a massive sausage baguette smothered in brown sauce and a large coffee the way Raina or Lexi made it. Raina didn't use fancy named beans just really good-quality ones – and she always got the temperature exactly right so you got the full flavour of the coffee and none of the bitterness.

Smashed avocado was fine if you weren't six foot two and absolutely starving. He'd be hungry again by eleven o'clock. Maybe they could call in and get one of Raina's cakes on the way back. Tucking in his shirt, he said, 'Shall we go then?'

Deciding between two different shirts, Kiera said, 'Go? Darling, I haven't even put my primer on yet, or chosen my outfit. Give me an hour and I'll be with you.'

Miles rolled his eyes and went downstairs to the kitchen. At least he had time to read the paper before they went out, but he'd need a snack to see him through till breakfast.

***

It was just gone ten o'clock when Kiera joined Miles downstairs. As usual she looked gorgeous. Her tall frame had been slipped into a pair of tight skinny jeans and her three-inch heels made her almost as tall as him. Her face was perfectly made up, hiding any blemishes, though he liked seeing the real her with the freckles, the imperfections; he had no idea why she hated them so much. As she passed, she pouted her lips, ever ready for a kiss. Kiera grabbed her Chanel bag from the kitchen side and gave Miles a peck on the cheek. 'All ready?'

'Yep. I'm gasping for a coffee.' Miles refolded his newspaper. 'And I'm starving.'

Kiera took Miles's arm and they walked through the back streets into town. Strolling along the tiny cobblestone roads amongst the old-fashioned houses, he took a deep breath and smelt the sea air. The beach was only a few streets away and you could hear the sea and its gentle, calming murmur. He loved Swallowtail Bay. When he was younger and first got the job, being away from home so often had been exciting. Now though, it felt more and more of a wrench each time he had to leave, and Swallowtail Bay pulled at his heart, whispering for him to come home. He couldn't really understand why, when they'd first met,

51

Kiera had wanted to leave so badly. She'd tried everything to convince her rich father to buy her a flat in London, but, ever business-minded, he'd been adamant she had to have a job before he shelled out on exorbitant London prices.

Miles could see it made perfect sense from his almost-father-in-law's perspective but Kiera had never really found a career she could stick at. Having a trust fund she could live off made it hard for her to focus too. Personal shopping was the closest she'd come, even if she was a bit picky as to who she took on. But since she'd begun travelling to London for her clients, she hadn't cared about moving there, happy to stay in Swallowtail Bay with him.

They passed the local butcher's and Miles nodded at the owner who raised a hand in greeting. Then there was the chocolate shop selling beautiful hand-crafted chocolates. How could anyone want to be anywhere else? Everything you ever needed and all the luxuries you didn't need but fancied were right here. This was perfect, idyllic. On the uneven cobbles Kiera swayed and tipped towards Miles. He wrapped an arm around her waist. Flat shoes were much more practical on roads like this, but Kiera wouldn't be seen dead in them. The only ones she owned were top-of-the-range branded trainers for her personal training sessions.

They entered the swanky new café and Miles ducked to avoid a low-hanging bare light bulb. The walls were painted a dark slate-grey and the lighting had a strange orange luminescent quality. With steel pipes fastened all around the walls he felt like he'd entered a spaceship. He looked at the chalkboard behind the cheery barista and ordered a large filter coffee and a cheese and ham croissant. Of course, it wasn't written as a cheese and ham croissant, it was written as a freshly baked artisan croissant made with Italian yeast, stuffed with Parma ham and organic Kentish goat's cheese, but it was basically the same thing. Kiera led them to a table in the window and sank into one of the old worn leather sofas. Miles sat opposite her and felt decidedly uncomfortable. How was he supposed to eat his food when it was about a foot higher than him?

'You're very quiet,' said Kiera, checking her reflection in a strange patch of stainless steel that had been pinned to the wall beside her.

'Am I? Sorry.'

'What are you thinking about?'

'I was just thinking about the shop,' he lied. Admitting he hated this place would be more than his life was worth. It was the type of place Kiera loved because it was more like somewhere you'd find in the city but it had never been Miles's scene. He liked places that were cosy and comfortable, where he could take his kids when he had some.

'Herbert's old shop? The one that woman stole from you?'

Miles had been so angry when he'd found out Herbert was going to sell to a stranger from Oxford rather than a local boy like him. The estate agent had said the main reason was because she was a cash buyer, but Miles had a large deposit and a business loan agreed in principle. There was no reason his offer should have been rejected. Deep down he knew it was because he'd pursued it too aggressively and this woman had taken the opposite approach and been super charming. He hated that he'd chosen the wrong tactic and had been ungracious in defeat. Something that still weighed on his mind. He'd even thought about getting Herbert's forwarding address and apologising, but hadn't yet been brave enough to ask.

'It's totally unfair,' Kiera continued. 'Herbert was just a dirty old pervert who preferred a woman.'

At the time, Miles had let his emotions get the better of him, ranting and raging in front of Kiera, but he was sure he'd never used words like that. Her loyalty was a wonderful quality but sometimes she was incredibly harsh and often spoke without thinking, saying whatever was on her mind. Whatever had happened, he shouldn't have been rude about Herbert who had been a kind and generous old man and a good neighbour. It was something he deeply regretted now. 'You shouldn't say that, honey,' he said gently. 'Anyway, it's all over and done with. Time to move on.'

'Poor darling,' Kiera replied, reaching out and running her hand over his cheek. 'You're really suffering, aren't you?'

'Let's just enjoy our breakfast,' Miles replied in a conciliatory tone. As their food was delivered, he leaned forwards and lifted himself from the depths of the sofa, hoping if he perched on the edge he'd be able to get to at least eye level with his croissant. 'Hmmm, this smells good.' He gave a small smile and took a bite. It was rather nice, but nothing could ever beat an enormous sausage baguette.

Kiera reached over, grabbed one of the celeb magazines from the rack on the wall and flipped the pages backwards and forwards. As she gossiped away her voice faded in his ears and he found himself thinking again about the town he'd grown up in and the idea of settling down. He and Kiera had been engaged for two years now and had never got around to setting a date for the wedding.

Miles recalled the day they'd met at the tiny Swallowtail Bay train station nearly four years ago. She'd just returned from a weekend in London and he'd been in Leeds at a conference. It was fate, he'd decided, because he'd been forced onto the train as his car was in the garage. He'd thought he knew everyone in town but as they went for a drink, she explained that though her parents lived there, she'd been sent to boarding schools her whole life and often stayed in London with friends. Miles's heartstrings had tugged so hard they almost shot out of his chest trying to wrap around Kiera. They'd been together ever since but, with his job and always being sent here or there, they'd never got around to organising the wedding. If he'd learned anything from losing out on the shop, it was that you never knew what would or wouldn't happen in life, and you couldn't keep putting stuff on hold. It was time to set that date, something he should have done a long time ago.

'Kiera,' he began a little nervously. 'What do you think about actually setting a date for the wedding?'

Kiera stopped reading and slowly turned her head. 'Really?'

Miles nodded. 'We've been engaged for two years and our parents keep asking if we've set the date yet. I think we should actually do it. Don't you?'

She slowly closed the magazine, considering what he'd said. 'Why now? You've not been bothered before.'

He'd hoped for a resounding yes and excitement so her reticence was a little worrying, even though it was a valid question. 'I just think we've let life pass us by long enough. Don't you want to?' he asked, as nerves bubbled inside him. 'It's about time we got another ring to go with that engagement one, isn't it?'

The gentle lines of her forehead eased as her grin grew wider. 'Of course I want to, darling.' She jumped up from the seat opposite him and onto his lap. Relief washed over him. 'Yes. Let's do it. But I get to pick the venue.'

'You can have whatever you want,' he said with a laugh. 'Just tell me the date and I'll turn up.' He kissed her and for the first time in a long while felt like his life was finally moving forwards. When the old man sat behind them loudly cleared his throat Miles pulled away. Kiera giggled and wiped the lip gloss from Miles's lips before returning to her seat.

'I was thinking we'd have a church wedding at the tiny church down the other end of town. The one with the cute gate over that little stream – we'll get amazing pictures there. I already know what sort of a dress I want. Then a big reception at the new hotel on the seafront. How about a spring wedding next year? We could get married a year from today? Or maybe April? March is still quite chilly. April has more sunshine. Oh my gosh, everyone is going to be so jealous.'

Miles sipped his coffee, glad that she was so happy at the prospect of finally becoming Mrs Parker.

'I've got to ring Claire and tell her. And we have to go shopping ASAP. There's so much to sort out. And I'll have to book Flavia to come down from London to do my hair, and Ronaldo to come and colour it. No one around here will be good enough. I need to look perfect. Actually, I might have to go up and see Ronaldo. He's so busy.' Miles nodded along, trying to keep up as the words tumbled from her mouth. 'Come on,' said Kiera, grabbing her bag. 'Let's head back. And we can stop by the newsagent's on the way. I want to buy some wedding mags. I haven't bought any for ages and all the fashions will have changed by now.'

Though Kiera's coffee and pain au raisin were barely touched, Miles quickly ate his croissant and did as he was told. Out on the flat surface of the road it was surprisingly hard to keep up with Kiera even in her insanely high heels. 'Do you still want to call in at Herbert's shop?' he asked, taking long strides.

'Oh yes, I think we should. If we're going to be neighbours we should introduce ourselves. And I want to see how much of an old perv Herbert really was.'

Miles bit his lip, wishing there was something he could do about Kiera's lack of filter.

The shop bell tinkled as he held open the door for Kiera and his eyes scanned the room. He couldn't believe the difference already. It was all so bright and spacious. Behind the corner of the counter Miles could see the dog asleep in his basket, thankfully on a lead. He wasn't as large as Miles remembered and the snores coming from that side of the room were decidedly unthreatening. Feeling foolish, he pretended nothing had happened.

'Good morning,' the woman behind the counter said in a genuinely cheerful voice. She'd been reading and the book rested on the countertop in front of her. 'Let me know if I can help with anything.'

Miles gave a quick smile and followed Kiera who was walking around touching things and checking prices. The woman behind the counter had resumed her reading. She was pretty and seemed placid and relaxed. Had he misjudged her? She must have been exhausted with all the work in the shop and scared for her dog. He had to admit he'd over-reacted too, embarrassed at being shocked by such a small, cute creature.

Kiera caught his eye and looked disdainfully around the shop. From the way the woman's gaze had frozen on Miles he knew that she'd recognised him, and as if to make matters worse, the dog woke up and stretched. Kiera watched on, appalled that the dog was there as the woman reached down to pet him. Watching her fuss over the small hairy thing made Miles feel even more silly for being scared, and further abashed about how he'd behaved.

When she'd finished browsing, Kiera went over and offered her hand. 'Hi, I'm Kiera. We're neighbours actually. I live at the Old Post House with my fiancé, Miles.' She turned to point him out even though they were the only ones in the shop. Miles gave a tight smile and nodded.

'Lovely to meet you. I'm Stella and this is Frank.'

Frank was sitting up nicely like a good, well-trained dog, waiting for another fuss. Stella must think him a complete idiot but that dog had actually frightened him when he'd snarled and snapped. Not that anyone would believe him when they saw the floppy ears and chubby body wobbling from excitement.

Stella, to her credit, didn't mention anything about their previous meeting, but politely smiled and said, 'Please let me know if you'd like any help with anything.'

'Oh, we're not buying anything from here,' said Kiera, and Miles wondered if she was this tactless with her clients.

'Oh. Right.' Stella's eyebrows lifted a fraction.

'We don't need anything at the moment,' said Miles quickly, trying to cover. 'But we did want to come and introduce ourselves.'

'Well, thank you. That's really nice. I hope I'll see more of you.'

'You probably won't,' Kiera continued, completely oblivious to how rude she sounded. Miles inwardly cursed and desperately searched his mind for something to say but Kiera was in full swing and he didn't want to talk over her. He'd just have to wait for a tiny gap and dive in. 'Herbert always sold so much crap and the shops around here are awful. I do all my shopping in London.' She flicked her hair back over her shoulder and gave Miles a half glance. 'Although you'll probably get an invite to the wedding.'

'Wedding?'

'Yes. I dare say we'll have to invite the neighbours – to the evening at least. We've just decided to set the date.'

'Congratulations,' Stella replied, and despite not knowing them she looked genuinely pleased at their news.

Now was his chance. Miles stepped forwards, desperate to change the subject before Kiera insulted the town or its inhabitants even more. The trouble was, he hadn't prepared a question and feverishly racked his brains for something interesting to say. He should have asked something personal and friendly, but all he could think to ask was, 'Are you planning on keeping the same stuff as Herbert? I know he sold the shop with a lot of stock left in it.'

'Umm, no.' Stella paused, clearly surprised at such a direct question and Miles scrunched his hands in his pockets, frustrated with himself. 'Not all of it. He did leave quite a lot but some of it was truly awful – no offence to Herbert. I'll keep selling the paintings and find some new artists, I think. Some of these are really good.'

Miles turned to where she pointed and saw that the paintings Herbert had kept piled up were now hung on the wall. They were all of the sea and something in the largest one caught his eye. It was an oil painting and the paint had been built up layer by layer. The colours of the shingle mixed and overlapped and the blue-green sea clashed with the lilacs, pinks and yellows of the sky.

He'd seen that sort of sunset before here, as if some great, powerful creator had knocked a paint palette over and every colour had fallen onto a canvas.

'It's beautiful isn't it?' a soft voice said from behind him. 'It's one of my favourites.' Without realising it, he'd wandered over to it and Stella had come up behind him.

'I don't think I've ever seen this one before.'

'It was under all the others at the bottom of the pile. I couldn't believe it when I saw it. The colours are outstanding.'

Miles found he couldn't turn away. 'They are. I wonder why Herbert didn't put it out.'

'I thought at first maybe he didn't like it but when I saw some of the truly awful stuff he was trying to sell I figured he must have just forgotten about it.'

At this he smiled and glanced at Stella. 'He did have some odd tastes.'

'He definitely did.' She laughed. 'I found a rug with a giant tiger's face on it in this weird shiny material. It was awful. I nearly kept it for the flat because I couldn't believe how bad it was. I think my mum had a painting like it over the fireplace when I was little. It must have been an Eighties thing.'

'Mine too,' Miles said, turning to face her, remembering the shiny tiger's face that had pride of place in their living room. Stella's eyes were a stunning brown, the colour of conkers with flashes of red like autumn leaves. Seeing Kiera approaching in his peripheral vision he pulled his gaze away. 'Definitely an Eighties thing.'

'Urgh, that's ghastly isn't it?' Kiera said, as she came to a stop next to Miles, pointing to the beautiful painting.

'Do you think?' he asked. Something in the painting had called to his soul and he could picture it hanging in the house.

'Hell yes. It's like a child's painted it and tried to use as many colours as possible. How much are you asking for that?'

A blush appeared on Stella's cheeks. 'Three hundred pounds.'

'Three hundred? I wouldn't give you ten pounds for that.' Kiera crossed her arms over her chest and went back to examining the shop. Miles thought it was worth even more.

'That's the wonderful thing about art, isn't it?' said Stella, moving back to the counter, her voice calm and cheery. 'Everyone likes different things. And what speaks to one person doesn't necessarily speak to another.'

Miles nodded his agreement, surprised that her opinion matched his own. 'Well, we should be going, Kiera.' It was probably best to move her along before she said something even ruder.

'Oh, I meant to ask,' said Kiera, surprising Miles. 'What are you doing about a website?'

'A website?' Stella echoed, her chocolate brown eyes open wide.

'Yes. You know, online. For the holiday lets and, I suppose, for the shop. Everyone books holidays online these days.' Kiera's heels tapped on the floor as she went to the counter.

'I hadn't actually thought about it yet. It's still early days.'

'You can't get started too early on something like that.' Her eyes ran up and down Stella and Miles felt his shoulders stiffen on her behalf. 'Did you know I'm a personal shopper? Even I've got a website.'

'Shall we get going then, darling?' he asked quickly, surprised at Kiera. She wasn't normally this tactless.

'I didn't but it sounds an amazing job. A website is the next thing on my to-do list, though,' Stella replied. 'Once I've sourced a few new bits for the shop.'

Kiera fished in her bag and pulled out her wallet, then extracted a business card. 'Well, when you do, I know this guy. His name's Jay and he did mine.'

Miles's shoulders tensed. Jay Adams was the local heartthrob. He looked like that bloke from *Outlander* – the tall Scottish one – and had been handsome since he was fifteen. Though they'd gone to different schools they'd played for the same football club as kids and Jay had teased Miles mercilessly about his teenage acne. Miles had been less than impressed when Kiera had hired him to do her website, but frustratingly, he was very good at his job.

Stella took the card. 'Thanks.'

'He's very, very good,' Kiera said and Miles swallowed down the tension Jay's name always provoked.

'That's really kind of you,' Stella replied. An easy grin came to her face brightening her expression. 'Thank you so much. Everyone's been really friendly. This is such a lovely town.'

'Well, I don't know about that,' said Kiera and with that she headed to the door, taking Miles's arm as she went. 'Bye.'

'Bye,' Miles repeated, surprised at how friendly Stella had been.

When they were out of earshot and nearly back at the house, Kiera said, 'Well, she wasn't what I was expecting. And having a dog in the shop is so … tacky.'

'What did you expect?' As Miles opened the small wooden gate leading to their house he didn't like to admit that Stella hadn't been what he was expecting either. On balance, he didn't really know what he'd expected. Someone he didn't like, he supposed, especially after their first meeting. But Stella Harris was proving very different to how he'd thought she was. As was Kiera. She'd been ruder than he'd ever heard her be before. Her sense of humour could sometimes be a little close to the bone but this had been something different. Perhaps her thoughts had been focused on the wedding and she hadn't realised how she'd come across. Yes, that must be it.

Kiera scrunched up her nose. 'I don't know. I just can't imagine her charming old Herbert at all. She seems too dull. A bit Plain Jane don't you think? Are you sure she wasn't a relation of his or something?'

It was possible. 'No one said she was.'

'Well they wouldn't, would they? They'd just want the quickest sale at the best price.'

Miles said nothing. Kiera's judgement might be a little harsh but she was right. If Stella hadn't even thought about the holiday let side of things or built a website she clearly didn't have a defined business plan. Miles felt the same frustration begin to rise up in him as he thought of all the hours he'd spent working out a sales plan and figuring out how much per square metre the shop was worth and therefore how much per customer he needed to make. He'd decided furniture was the way to go and found some very nice stuff locally. He'd even researched similar holiday lets up and down the coast to compare rates, facilities and how much he needed to spend to get them up to scratch. His jaw tightened at all the wasted hours, the late nights both home and away after long tiring days.

'Let's get the calendar out when we get home, darling,' said Kiera. 'We can fix a date for next year and I'll get calling the hotel and the vicar. How do you call a vicar? Do churches even have phones?'

Miles chuckled and slipped his hand into Kiera's. Life was still moving forward, he reminded himself. With the estate agents looking out for another property it surely wouldn't be long until he could stop travelling up and down the country. His dream of settling in Swallowtail Bay and one day starting a family would soon become a reality.

Chapter 7

After Miles and Kiera left, Stella fidgeted and fussed. So far all her energy had been put into the shop to ensure some money was coming in, but it would soon be holiday season and she had to be prepared. Kiera was right: she needed some online promotion for the holiday lets. She hadn't warmed to the woman who had an air of superiority, but then, she didn't much like Miles either. They were both snooty and suited each other in that respect. She should have known his girlfriend, or fiancée, would be just like him. But she had to admit, Miles's opinion on the painting had surprised her. She'd never imagined he'd have appreciated it. He seemed the nothing was ever good enough type, and she hadn't expected him to have such emotional depth.

The keys for the holiday lets had been sitting in a glass bowl on the Seventies dresser since she moved in last week. She hadn't let herself take a proper look yet, worried that if she went in she'd either panic even more that this new venture had been a bad idea, or stress herself out with the work involved. Either one would mean losing focus on the shop and she couldn't let that happen. The shop had to take priority as it was the easiest source of immediate income. But now that it was mostly under control, Stella could definitely take a look and move on to phase two of her plan: preparing the holiday lets for what she hoped would be a busy summer season. As she tapped her feet, feeling the need to keep moving, it seemed the hours ticked by slowly. When closing time rolled around, Stella unhooked Frank's lead from the chair and led him into the living room. Excitement tightened Stella's throat as she scooped the keys from the bowl and raced to have a good look.

Next door to the shop, an old Georgian townhouse had been converted into two apartments. The beautiful arched doorway with its panelled black front door stood out against the white-painted facade of the first flat. Above it, where the upper-floor apartment was, the exposed brickwork with its rich, earthy tones added a touch of period class. A large sash window stood next to the door, and though they were both beautiful they were covered in dust. *More things to add to the cleaning list*, Stella thought, but she could already picture the door, polished and shiny with two neatly trimmed bay trees in sky-blue pots either side. By the time she was finished, the outside would have regained its elegance and be enticing and welcoming to her visitors.

The front door opened onto a large black-and-white tiled hallway. To the left, a staircase led the way up to the second apartment while next to it, another panelled period door opened onto the one-bedroom flat. Stella let herself into the lower-floor apartment and all her excitement vanished. Though it hadn't been quite as bad as her own flat, it wasn't exactly ready to go either. When she'd first viewed it, it had seemed like a thorough clean and some new bedding was all that was required, but it had gone downhill since then. The wonderful period features that had taken her breath away the first time she saw them, including cornicing on the walls and around the ceiling lights, were cobwebbed and dusty. Everywhere there was a general smell of mildew, and the carpeted floor tiles were, for some unknown reason, sticky.

As she entered the kitchen, she could see it hadn't been cleaned after the last guests had left. Cups lay strewn over the side with blue fuzzy mould growing in them, and the beautiful white porcelain butler's sink was tea-stained and remnants of food clung on for dear life.

Stella continued her exploration fearing the worst but thankfully, the only bedroom was a pleasant surprise. It needed a dust and a good hoover but apart from the large antique French bed being left in disarray, it was passable. The white bathroom had a romantic, free-standing roll-top bath, though the smell from the drain and the long hairs left in it would kill any romantic notions stone dead. Getting closer, Stella scrunched up her nose at the funny smell coming from the plughole. Suspecting it was blocked and needed a good unclogging with something industrial-strength she'd have to apply wearing a hazmat suit, Stella mentally moved that to top of the list.

The good thing was, everything was white – all the furniture, all the bed linen, all the towels. Well, not quite white. They'd probably been white once, but right now everything had a hint of grey in varying shades. Stella made another mental note to purchase a tub of fabric whitener and empty the entire thing into the bath then chuck as many sheets in as possible. She might have to use her own bath until she cleaned the roll-top one, and leave them to soak for a good day or so, but with any luck, they'd get their colour back. She wasn't particularly hopeful as, closing the door, she climbed the stairs to the second flat.

The upper-floor apartment had three bedrooms and was more of a family affair with one double bedroom and two bedrooms with twin beds. The furniture was mismatched but seemed to be antiques Herbert had collected over the years. It was less elegant and more homely. Which was a nice way of saying it was an absolute mess. There were old grubby toys scattered all over the floor that looked like they'd been eaten and spat out again. The walls were scuffed and scribbled on and the double bedroom that Stella could imagine tired parents collapsing in after a busy day with the kids was the least relaxing space she'd ever seen. A large lumpy bed squeaked whenever you sat on it, the mattress so old it still had actual wire springs that poked through and tried to kill you in your sleep.

In the other bedrooms the walls were a weird pink colour that boys must hate, and the air was heavy and still. Here and there the same carpet tiles from downstairs were thin and threadbare with floorboards visible beneath. This one was going to need a lot of work, but at least with the high Georgian ceilings and large windows, there was a good amount of light in each room.

As she surveyed her new domain, plans were already forming in Stella's mind. She'd decided then and there that the following Sunday, when the shop was closed, she was going to come up here with a stack of cleaning materials and scrub everything from top to bottom. The awful, thin carpet tiles were going to be ripped out and the lovely floorboards underneath revealed. Then she'd sand them and either varnish or paint them white. She could use some of the rugs from the shop to cover any stains and maybe even reuse some of the cushions and furnishings. In the kids' bedrooms the last few ugly crocheted animal cushions might look fun and playful.

Stella closed the door on the holiday lets and her heart pinched at the fact she was doing this on her own. Not long after she and Isaac were married, she'd shared this dream with him and they'd spent an evening making plans of where they'd buy and what sort of property they wanted. On her own, Stella felt the smile of excitement fall from her face as she trudged back to Frank and another night trying to sleep on the living room sofa. As she re-entered the shop, *her* shop, she gave herself a good stern shake. She was just beginning to live her dream life. And that was something to be eternally grateful for even if she was having to do it on her own.

***

As the sun rose on Wednesday morning, the bright rays poking through the curtains, Stella woke up feeling that mid-week slump. The hard physical work of cleaning the shop and sometimes the stock, and the long hours of the last few days were taking their toll. There'd been a steady stream of customers and she'd managed to sell a few more things, but a lot of her working day was still punctuated by long periods of quiet – just her, Frank and the radio. Luckily, Lexi had said that Wednesdays in Swallowtail Bay were half-day opening. Stella hadn't thought that happened since the 1950s but apparently Swallowtail Bay was a law unto itself. It could work out well though, she thought, as she could use the afternoon to do all the admin tasks she didn't have time for in the evenings. Sat at the counter with only an hour till lunch and closing time, a sleepy Frank napping at her feet, Stella studied the screen of her laptop.

'Look at this one, Frank. It's very swanky and is just down the road.' Researching similar holiday let websites was proving fun, seeing what she liked and what might work for her. Frank snored loudly in reply. 'That's not very helpful, Franky boy.' He snored again.

The truth was the shop wasn't turning out to be as profitable as she'd hoped, even though it was early days. The sooner she got the holiday lets sorted out the better. It wouldn't be long till she really needed that income. Having bought the place outright she didn't have a mortgage to worry about, but she still needed to make money to pay the bills and, you know, eat.

'This one's gorgeous,' Stella said to herself as Frank still hadn't stirred. 'And it's much more family-friendly. Look, they've turned the kids' bedroom into a bit of a playroom as well. That's clever.' Just as Stella clicked to check out another property, the postman came in, bringing her attention back to the present. She trilled a cheery good morning.

'Here you are,' he said, handing over a stack of letters then bending down to give Frank a fuss. Frank finally awoke and lifted his head, grateful for the attention.

'Thanks. How are you today?'

'Oh, I'm fine, thanks. Just fine.' Frank rolled onto his back with his paws in the air inviting a tummy rub.

'You're such a tart, Frank,' Stella said, and the postman gave a chuckle as he left.

Stella picked through the pile of letters. Most were bills but one of the envelopes caught her eye. It was much smaller than the others, handwritten, but not in a hand she recognised. Placing the rest of the post on the counter, next to her mug of tea, she slipped a finger underneath the flap and pushed it up. The paper was thick and heavy and slightly scented. As her brain began to catch up with what her eyes were seeing it was like someone had pressed pause on her heart. It stopped then restarted with a double beat that made her breath come and go in uneven bursts. It was an invitation. And not a party invitation. There were no balloons or stars, or little silhouetted champagne bottles. There was only one person who would send her an invitation like this. Stella's throat tightened.

Together with their families,
Isaac and Ellie request the pleasure of
Stella and guest
at their marriage on
Saturday, 12th May at 1.30 p.m.
St Margaret's Church, St Margaret's Road, Oxford
followed by a reception at Henley Court Farmhouse
RSVP to Isaac and Ellie at isaacandelliearegettinghitched@
gmail.com

Stella felt her mouth fall slowly open and dry out. She took a deep breath in as tears stung her eyes. So they had made it last after all. Ellie had been the one Isaac had got with straight after their split a year ago. How could they be getting married when they'd been together for less than a year? All the hurt and anguish Stella had endured came flooding back in a great wave that made her recoil.

Isaac was the type of man who didn't do anything unless he was absolutely sure of it. Deep down she should have known he and Ellie would make it. A small, admittedly spiteful, part of her had hoped the relationship would fail. He always said he'd been decent and not acted on his feelings until they had officially split up, but no one liked to be passed over for someone else. Admitting that their marriage was over had left Stella feeling unlovable, ugly and low for months afterwards. It was often how she felt now, when she was alone in the night, feeling like the only person in the world still awake.

With trembling hands, she stacked the invitation, RSVP card and 'guest information' and pushed them back into the envelope. Screw admin and website stuff, her half-day closing would be spent in the café talking to Lexi. She had to tell someone how her life had just been tipped upside down.

Again.

***

After keeping it together until closing time, at exactly one o'clock, Stella flipped the sign and took Frank and his basket into the living room. Feeling a little guilty at leaving him, she took a biscuit from the packet on the side and gave it to him, before closing the door so he couldn't get out. 'I'll be back soon, Franky boy. Then I'll take you for a super long walk along the beach.'

As she left she picked up the invitation and marched next door to the café. It never closed when all the other shops did because people congregated there drinking coffee and eating cakes when there was nowhere else to go. It was one of the best day's trading of the week for them. Maybe next week Stella would try opening and see if any of the café customers came next door to her, but for now, she needed some space to clear her head and after being alone all morning, she desperately wanted someone to talk to.

Stella closed the shop door behind her, her eyes already moist with tears. She opened them wide, hoping they'd dry out. She didn't want to be a blubbery mess when she was talking to Lexi. Gazing at the trees lining the front of the church opposite, she saw tiny spots of pink blossom were beginning to form on the bare branches. In the sun, the gentle breeze lost all its coolness and though it felt more like summer than spring, Stella shivered. As Lexi had foretold, the café was busy with some of the regular old ladies huddled together with their china cups, and scones and jam, and some early tourists were tucking into tasty baguettes, sandwiches and paninis. She approached the counter and Lexi looked up with a smile that quickly faded. 'Stella, what's wrong?'

Certain that if she opened her mouth nothing but a sob would emerge, Stella held out the envelope then wiped away an escaping tear. Telling herself firmly to get a grip, she took a deep breath in.

'What is it, pet?' asked Vivien, craning her neck from her seat by the window, at the other end of the shop.

Great, thought Stella. *An audience.* This was just what she didn't need. She wasn't used to sharing personal information with people anyway and was taking a big leap in talking to Lexi. If she'd been sensible she'd have texted asking Lexi to come by later but it was too late now. Lexi put down the knife she was using to butter bread and took off her health and safety regulation latex gloves. She opened the letter, glancing back up at Stella as she did so, her eyes widening as she read the contents.

'Holy shit balls,' Lexi blurted, quietening at the swear words. She began to whisper, leaning over the counter towards Stella. 'What a twat. You don't mind me calling your ex a twat, do you?

But, I mean, what a twat. Did you have any idea this was coming?' Stella shook her head. 'Bloody hell. Right. You go and sit down; I'll bring you a coffee. And some tissues.' She turned to Raina who had come into the doorway. 'Read this.'

Stella didn't see Raina's expression as she was walking away but did hear her say, 'You look after her. I'll deal with the customers. Poor lamb.'

Stella made her way to a table by the window, hoping that watching the world go by would help her gain some perspective and get a grip on the emotions crashing around inside her. Vivien shuffled over and sat down too, her cup and saucer tinkling as her old hands shook. Stella couldn't think of a nice way to ask her to leave, and the kind, caring look on her face made it impossible to say anything at all. She'd just have to put up with another person knowing all about her private life and hope Vivien could be discreet. 'You look like you've had a real shock, dear. Is everything all right?'

Stella sniffed again, trying to control her emotions. 'I've just had some bad news, that's all.' The words *bad news* seemed too mild somehow considering her heart felt like it had been ripped out when it had only just begun to fit back in its rightful place.

Lexi joined her a few moments later with a tray bearing coffees for her and Stella, a fresh pot of tea for Vivien, carrot cake for each of them, tissues, and the invitation. Lexi picked it up again and reread it. She took a deep breath then blew it out, puffing out her cheeks. 'Stella's just had an invitation to her ex-husband's wedding.'

'Goodness gracious me, you poor thing.' Vivien reached out a wrinkled hand and Stella noticed her nails were painted a vibrant, saucy red, which made her smile despite everything else.

'Thank you,' she replied, taking the handle of her coffee cup and turning it towards her.

'That's so rough, honey,' Lexi said, shaking her head. 'Really rough. How are you feeling or is that a stupid question?' Stella

71

sniffed. 'Of course it's a stupid question. You feel hurt, angry, a bit rejected and maybe even a tiny bit jealous?'

Stella took a tissue from the packet and wiped her eyes and nose. Lexi was wonderfully astute, making this whole sharing thing a lot easier. 'All of the above. Plus I want to punch him in the face. Is that silly?'

'No. No, of course it's not. It's perfectly normal. I think I'd feel the same way if I suddenly got a wedding invitation from Will. I'd probably start throwing things too.'

Vivien began to pour herself another cup of tea. 'When I was young, I was very nearly married to another very famous opera singer. I can't say his name because though I say nearly married he already had a wife. He promised me he'd leave her – which he never did – and marry me. When he eventually told me he had no intention of leaving his wife I was utterly heartbroken.'

Stella blinked. She wasn't quite clear how the two situations were similar, but it was the thought that counted. There might have been a nugget of wisdom in there somewhere and Stella had simply failed to see it. She picked up her cup and cradled it in her cold fingers. 'I think a part of me hoped his first relationship since me wouldn't work out. That it wasn't that serious.' She shook her head. 'I know that sounds mean but it feels like more of a betrayal that he's gone straight from one love to another. If he'd had a few flings that hadn't worked out I don't think I'd have felt as much of a failure because he clearly wasn't that good at relationships either. But this ...' She picked up the invitation. 'It proves that he's really good at being part of a couple and I was the problem in ours.'

'It doesn't prove anything of the sort,' said Lexi, slightly cross. Stella looked up in surprise. 'Sorry, that's the voice I use on the kids when they're being naughty. Sometimes it just slips out. All it proves is that he's been lucky.'

'I agree, pet,' said Vivien. 'There's nothing wrong in being hurt. Some people are luckier in love than others. That's life, I'm afraid.'

Stella couldn't help the smile that tugged at her lips. She was beginning to feel luckier than ever sat here with these lovely people.

'I'd better help Raina,' said Lexi. 'I can see a whole line of our regulars coming down the street.' As the crowd outside drew nearer Lexi leaned towards Vivien and said, 'It's your competition.'

'My competition? Those old dears with the blue rinses and papery skin? Don't be silly, dear. They can't hold a candle to me. Some of them have never moisturised a day in their lives.'

Without reason, tears were suddenly threatening again and Stella found herself wishing Lexi was back with her. 'Sorry,' she muttered to Vivien. 'I'm sure it's just the shock. It'll wear off soon I should think. Sorry if I'm over-reacting.'

'I don't think you're over-reacting at all. I'd probably be even worse if I were you.'

The queue of old ladies came in and took up the rest of the available tables and chairs, rearranging them as needed. They plonked their shopping bags on the floor and some waved hello to Vivien who wiggled her fingers in return then turned her back with her head held high. She leaned in to Stella. 'I'm older than them but you wouldn't know it, would you?'

Stella suppressed a giggle and glanced out of the window as the high street emptied of people and the world of Swallowtail Bay went quiet once more. It was such a funny, friendly, odd little town, strangely untouched by time in so many ways. However upsetting this news had been, Stella was glad she was here. In just over a week, Swallowtail Bay and its residents had absorbed her into the community, and now she was turning to people for support like she never had before. She needed to get a grip though. Her future was here now not back in Oxford with Isaac.

She took a forkful of the huge wedge of carrot cake. The sweetness calmed her and she felt her shoulders relaxing down.

'Are you okay?' Lexi asked popping back over for a second.

'You seem very calm. I'd be destroying things or making voodoo dolls of them both.'

'I feel better having seen you and Vivien. When I was in the shop on my own I felt like everything was falling apart but I feel a little better having talked about it.'

'Getting news like that on your own always feels bad. It's like when you have insomnia and things start going round and round your head in the middle of night. You feel like you're the only person on the planet and everything is so terrible and tragic when really, it's just your brain magnifying everything.'

Vivien suddenly began again. 'When Giuseppe – I mean – when this gentleman I mentioned earlier told me he wasn't going to leave his wife I cried for two days straight. My best friend had to place cucumber slices over my eyes to try and take the puffiness down before I performed. I was in such a state it took every ounce of my being just to get up in the morning. I was utterly heartbroken.' Stella stared back and Vivien gave her a warm smile. 'Excuse me though, dears. I must just go and speak to Florence.'

Lexi shook her head as Vivien shuffled off then turned to Stella. 'I do love that crazy old bat. What will you do now?'

Stella pulled her shoulders back. 'I'm going to eat my cake, drink my coffee then go back to my shop and ring a website designer. My life has moved on, and I've got other things to worry about.'

'That's very grown up of you. You should be very proud of yourself.'

For a throwaway comment, Lexi had no idea how much that meant to Stella who had never before had friends to turn to in times like this and she was determined to solidify their friendship further. 'Are you busy this Saturday night? I wondered if you wanted to come round for dinner? You can help me make my mind up as to whether I actually go to this wedding or not.'

'Will there be wine?' asked Lexi, picking her cake up and enjoying a big bite.

'Definitely.'

'Then I'd love to. Will won't mind an extra night with the kids.'

'I might have to buy us a bottle of wine each,' said Stella. 'I think I'm going to need a whole one to myself.' With a small sigh and a horrible tension in her chest, she stood and headed back next door to the comfort of her shop.

Chapter 8

Miles followed Kiera and the manager around the posh hotel at the furthest end of Swallowtail Bay's seafront. Set far back from the promenade and within a couple of acres of lush green gardens, it had opened last year after a huge renovation. Miles had enjoyed watching the historic manor house returning to life. It was part of what had inspired him to look for a business here. Every time he had come home from a sales trip away, a new part of the stately home had been restored to its former glory, and now the eighteenth-century mansion welcomed visitors at an extortionate amount per night.

On their approach, Miles had eyed the three-storey building and imagined the views from the top rooms. Through the large sash windows you'd be able to see not only the extensive grounds, but also out towards the sea and the curve of the bay. It was a view he loved: a sweeping arc of coastline with nearby towns outlined on the horizon.

The plush deep-red carpet cushioned his heavy boots while Kiera, marching ahead with the shiny blue-suited manager, seemed oblivious to his pain. While she was correct that they needed to visit the hotel to make sure it would be large enough for the forthcoming celebrations (especially as Kiera had drawn up a provisional list of guests that amounted to over two hundred and fifty people – something he was yet to do), he was supposed to be spending this Friday scoping out some potential new clients for meetings next week. That meant a lot of work. Visiting this place in a couple of weeks would have been fine, he could have scheduled it in, but he didn't really have time for this today. If it made Kiera happy though, he was glad to do it.

The Langdon Mansion Hotel had made quite an impression on Kiera when they'd entered through the large automatic doors at the front. A receptionist had immediately walked over and greeted them in the enormous lobby. It was all very grandiose and expensive and Kiera had been swept away even though they hadn't yet got down to details. When the receptionist had fussed over her, complimenting her figure and dress, and then forced a glass of champagne into her hands, Miles knew he would be hard pressed to convince her it was too big and expensive for them. A few moments on a large purple velvet sofa and the manager had arrived. Miles had peered at him, sure he was wearing eyeliner and possibly mascara, and then they'd been whisked away on a grand tour.

Although she'd initially seemed a little reticent at the idea of actually setting the date, once Kiera had begun looking at dresses and table decorations, she'd become almost obsessed, turning down clients in order to do wedding research at home. Miles had tried to get her to slow down and not jeopardise her work, but there was no stopping her. Still, she deserved the wedding of her dreams and he assumed that she was just taking a holiday like everyone else did from time to time.

'So,' the manager began as he walked ahead with Kiera. 'You were thinking of having just the wedding reception here, is that right?'

'Yes, that's right.'

'Because we can offer civil ceremonies as well. A lot of people prefer to have the whole thing in one place to save transporting guests between different venues. It can get very stressful.'

'I understand,' she replied. 'But I'm happy to sort out any transportation. Anyway, I want a church wedding. We're not particularly religious but the church near us is so pretty; it'll be an amazing setting.'

The manager nodded and smiled, revealing a set of teeth he was clearly looking after for a horse. They hadn't just been whitened, they'd had at least three coats of Dulux Brilliant White, plus varnish. He ostentatiously opened a door. 'This is the ball-room,' he announced with a grand sweeping gesture that was more suited to *Strictly Come Dancing*. 'Our largest room, which can hold up to three hundred and seventy people, seated. We do have a smaller room called The Parlour that—'

'No, this will be lovely,' Kiera replied turning to Miles. 'Isn't it gorgeous? We can have the head table over there in front of the stage and circular tables with bright white cloths. The chairs can be covered as well with big gold bows on the backs. This will be just perfect.' The manager stood back as she surveyed the room.

Peering in through the doorway, Miles had to admit the grand ballroom was beautiful. Large windows lined one side with big draping curtains in a rich, dark red velvet that matched the carpet under his feet. The polished wood floor of the ballroom shone under the light from several ornate chandeliers hanging imposingly from the ceiling. 'It's lovely,' he replied, but he had the feeling it was also incredibly expensive.

Taking his subdued response as enraptured silence, Kiera held a hand to her chest and said, 'Oh, Miles, you love it too, don't you?'

The manager grinned and cocked his head. 'Wonderful. So when is the happy day?'

'We're flexible, actually,' said Kiera. 'But I definitely want a spring wedding.'

He sucked some air in through his enormous gleaming teeth.

'I should warn you we're pretty booked up for next year with weddings and other events.'

'And is everything confirmed, or are some bookings provisional?' Kiera asked.

Miles watched as the manager gave her a warm smile. 'Some are provisional, I have to admit.'

'Well, surely if we're willing to pay the deposit now we should get the booking over someone provisional who may later change their mind?'

Miles felt a rush of panic. They had no idea how much the place even was yet. He loved how she was throwing herself into the wedding preparations but it was important to be sensible. 'Kiera, hang on, we need to find out the price first.'

Her expression suddenly hardened and she walked over to him to whisper, 'Don't make a scene, Miles.'

'I'm not,' he mumbled back. 'But this place is undoubtedly horrendously expensive. It might not be worth the money. We haven't even looked anywhere else yet.'

'Of course it's worth the money.' Her eyes narrowed on him. 'And Daddy can pay the deposit if *you* don't want to—'

'No, Kiera.' He tried hard to keep his hand gestures calm so the manager wouldn't know they were arguing. 'We'll pay, this is our wedding. I'm just saying that—'

'We can talk about this at home, darling,' she said through a tense jaw though her voice was light. Pound signs must have been flashing before the manager's eyes going by the look he gave Kiera, and Miles was sure he'd overheard her saying her father would pay.

'Shall we have a coffee in the bar?' the manager asked. 'And take a look at the calendar? I'm sure we can find you a suitable date.' Kiera nodded and her dark blonde curls bounced in agreement. Torn somewhere between resignation and dread, Miles shoved his hands in his pockets and trudged after them. He hadn't expected them to be making any firm decisions yet. He'd joked that Kiera could take care of everything and he'd just turn up, but he hadn't actually meant it. He wanted to be involved and make joint decisions.

Soon they were sat in one of the lounges, which had an old boys' club feel to it. A long wooden bar ran the length of the room and the seating was a mixture of leather and velvet. The clever lighting of large glass balls and old elegant chandeliers gave the place a modern twist without being at odds with the period features. Some of the furniture was similar to what Miles had hoped to sell himself in the shop, but he refused to think about that anymore. It was time to force his life forwards, rather than looking back. The manager delivered a coffee for Miles and another glass of champagne for Kiera before disappearing off to get the calendar and the wedding pack, or as he liked to describe it, the best-day-of-your-life guide. As soon as he had gone, Kiera took Miles's hand.

'Oh, darling, isn't it just brilliant? It has everything we need and it is so elegant.' She sat back and stared around her. 'Beautiful isn't the word. Even the best hotels in London couldn't compare to this.'

'I'm glad you like it,' he replied, calmly. 'But we do need to think about the cost. I know you don't want to and I don't want to be miserable, but we have to be realistic.'

'Oh, don't be a spoilsport,' she said, frowning. 'Daddy will stump up a load. He's ecstatic we've set the date. He's been waiting for ages. If we ask him now he'll be too happy to say no.'

'That's not quite what I meant.' Miles frowned. He had always worked hard for everything he had and the thought of relying on Kiera's father was abhorrent to him. A contribution towards the wedding was a tradition he was willing to accept, or them buying Kiera's wedding dress he could understand, but he had no expectation of more and hoped Kiera didn't either. 'I meant that—'

'I'm teasing, Miles.' Kiera leaned forwards across the coffee table and stroked his knee. 'I'm not an idiot, but I really want this. I think this place is perfect and I can't imagine I'll find anywhere I like as much.'

The manager returned with his iPad and sat down next to Kiera. 'So, as you can see, The Ballroom is already fully booked for March and April, but I've got some space in May.' He showed Kiera the screen.

'Oh, but I really would like an April wedding though I'm flexible on the exact date. Is there nothing you can do to help me?' Her eyes scanned his name badge. 'Kevin?'

'I understand, Miss Delany, but—'

'Please, call me Kiera.'

The manager cocked his head, all sympathy. 'The thing is I want you to have the day you deserve. If we look at May you can see there are a few more available dates.'

Kiera turned to Miles, inviting him into the conversation, but he couldn't see what else could be done. 'There's not much we can do if it's already booked,' he replied.

Her eyes sharpened on him then went back down to the screen. 'Why is this day in a different colour to the others?'

'This one?' The manager pointed to the screen. 'This is a provisional booking.'

'And have the people got back to you yet?' Miles could see instantly where Kiera was going with this and a chill ran down his spine. He had no idea where this side of Kiera was coming from. The manager shuffled uncomfortably in his chair, clearly feeling backed into a corner.

'Well, no, but they still have a few days left before I can release the date.'

'I have an idea,' said Kiera, taking a sip of her champagne. 'Why don't I give you my credit card now to secure the booking, and you can give them a quick call and tell them that you've had to release the date as they haven't got back to you.'

A redness began to creep up his neck, turning his skin a ruddy colour. 'I really can't do that without giving them some notice, Miss ... Kiera.'

'Okay, well you could give them to the end of the day, couldn't you?' she replied, taking her credit card from her wallet and casually waving it back and forth. Miles felt like he was watching a different woman. Kiera had never acted like this before as far as he could remember. Something in his brain told him that since they'd got together he'd been away a lot but he pushed the thought away.

'Well, I suppose I could. Let me see when the provisional booking was made.' He turned the iPad away from Kiera and tapped the screen. 'Ahh, yes, the booking was made some time ago. Let me give them a call now.'

'Wonderful,' Kiera replied, grinning.

'Hang on,' interrupted Miles, who had watched with mounting alarm. They hadn't asked any pertinent questions yet. 'First off, can you confirm how much this will all be? And how much is the deposit?'

'Well, with maximum seating, a three-course meal, welcome drinks, table wine based on maximum seating, evening buffet – which is divine by the way – and the honeymoon suite we're looking at approximately ...' He shifted away as he typed on his iPad. 'I'd say about a hundred thousand pounds. And the deposit is twenty per cent.'

Miles swallowed in an attempt to stop himself shouting. 'A hun—'

'That's fine,' Kiera replied, giving Miles a warning look. 'My father is happy to pay. I thought you were going to say more, actually.'

Hearing that number had made him a bit hot and sweaty and Miles ran his fingers over his forehead, tracing the deep frown lines that were appearing as he aged. He hoped he'd get a good bonus this year – a *really* good bonus. No matter what Kiera said there was no way Miles would let her father pay and he took out his wallet to offer his own card. At the same time his phone beeped as a new email popped up from his boss asking him about the new clients he should have been researching. Damn it. He'd better send a quick reply now. He had no idea that weddings were so expensive. It was going to cost him a fortune. First though, he had to wrestle that mysteriously refilled glass of champagne from Kiera's hand before she spent any more money.

Chapter 9

Stella flipped the door sign to *closed*. It had been a good, busy Friday and the till was full of cash. She had just started counting it up when there was a knock at the door. A man in a black leather jacket with a mop of curly reddish hair and designer stubble gave her a cheeky grin. He flashed his eyes as she walked back towards the door and opened it a little. 'Can I help you?'

'Hi, I'm Jay, the website guy. You left a message on my phone.'

'Oh, right. Yes. Hi.' Stella opened the door wider and motioned for him to come in. He strode into the shop, looking appreciatively around him. A tight dark blue T-shirt covered a chiselled torso and his black jeans gave a hint of football player thigh. When Stella had imagined a techy computer guy she'd envisaged an overweight, beardy person with scrunched-up eyes unused to seeing daylight – either that or some nerdy, bespectacled, spotty youth. Judgemental, perhaps, but she couldn't help it. To be faced with this square-jawed hunk of man made her stomach squirm and her palms go clammy. As he held out his hand for her to shake, Stella was painfully aware that hers were damp. She tried to rub them on her backside without him noticing. 'Nice to meet you.'

His grin was worryingly disarming. 'I'm sorry I didn't call first, but as I was down this end of town I thought I'd pop by. How are you finding things?'

'I love it here. If I'm honest it's even better than I expected. Everyone's been so friendly and kind. I feel at home already.'

'Well, that's great to hear.' Frank wandered over and sniffed Jay's trainers. 'Who's this little guy?'

Stella was always grateful for Frank and never more so than moments like this. He was a good way of filling in gaps in conversation. 'This is Frank and he's a sucker for a fuss. He gets quite jealous if I'm getting all the attention.' When Jay smiled, Stella was sure she'd never seen anything like it before. His eyes were a light greyish-blue, almost iridescent. Her heart started to spin in her chest as he went back to fussing Frank behind the ears. Was there anything more attractive than a drop-dead gorgeous man with a dog? Possibly only a drop-dead gorgeous man with a baby and she wasn't in the market for one of those just yet. 'Did you want a tea or coffee or something?'

'Well, I was thinking …' He put his hands in his pockets and hunched slightly forward, rocking onto his toes then back onto his heels. 'I thought maybe I could take you for a drink and we can chat about your website over dinner? Kiera mentioned you being new to the area. I thought maybe I could show you around a little?'

Stella wanted to scream yes, but Frank reminded her that he needed a walk by rolling over with his paws in the air, waiting for his tummy to be tickled. He'd finally grown used to the postman through some treat-led bribery but he didn't always take to men. That he was behaving like this around Jay reassured Stella he was a nice guy. 'I'd really love to, but I'm afraid I need to take Frank out first. He's been cooped up in here all day.' She wasn't normally so forward but seeing his gorgeous eyes fall at the corners she said, 'Could we make it later?'

'I've got a better idea,' Jay replied with that dazzling smile again. 'Why don't we walk along to the Wild Goose and have a drink there? They let dogs in and I know that Don, the landlord, will love Frank. He's got a soft spot for King Charles spaniels.'

Stella tried to control the almighty grin spreading over her face. 'That would be great. I'll just put the takings in the safe and be with you in a tick.'

Jay wandered around the shop while Stella hurriedly stowed her money away and fetched her jacket and Frank's lead. When she walked into the living room to find it she grabbed her make-up bag and checked her appearance. Apart from desperately needing a haircut, she looked okay and the greys weren't showing through too badly. She applied a quick swipe of powder and another coat of mascara before grabbing her lip balm. There was no time to get changed so her plain T-shirt and jeans would have to do. At least she wouldn't look like she was trying too hard to impress him. Anyway, it's not like this was a date, which was good because she didn't know what to do on dates. She hadn't been on one in about fifteen years. Oh no, now she'd thought about the word *date* she felt completely terrified and jittery from the adrenalin running through her veins. Stella took a deep breath and went back into the shop to meet Jay.

Outside, the cool air helped to calm Stella's nerves and the conversation flowed more easily as they walked along the side of the shop and up towards the seafront. She kept the conversation about work where she felt more sure-footed. Anything personal and her heart started to beat rapidly and she stuttered.

'So how are you settling in?' Jay asked.

'Good. I love the shop and I think I've got my head around how the holiday lets are going to work. I just need to do a little bit of decorating and then I can start taking bookings for the larger flat. The single bedroom is almost ready to go. It just needs a good scrub and some new furnishings.'

'Sounds like you've got it all sorted out.'

The road grew smaller as they entered one of the tiny alleyways nestled between the fisherman's cottages. From the corner of her eye she saw him glance over.

'I think I do,' she replied trying to sound confident but as the road narrowed the gap between them became smaller and she was almost touching his leather-jacketed arm.

The wind grew stronger as they rounded to the seafront and stepped off the promenade onto the pebble beach, heading towards the shore. Jay pushed a hand through his hair and the curls twisted around his fingers, flying back the moment he released them. Frank, who would usually have stayed next to Stella or the sea, kept walking over and sniffing him. Stella searched for something to say to stop herself from imagining her hands in his hair. 'So have you always lived in Swallowtail Bay?'

'Yeah, born and bred here. I've moved away for jobs over the years but always end up coming back. Where did you move down from?'

'Oxford,' Stella replied with a pang, but as she looked out at the sea – a little rough today from the strong breeze – and watched the waves crash down disappearing to foam, the pain lessened. She dropped her eyes and studied the myriad colours of the pebbles, checking for shells.

'Wow. I worked there for a while after uni. It's a beautiful city.'

'It is.'

'Sounds like you miss it,' Jay said, as he glanced at her again.

Stella felt herself blush. 'I miss the place but—'

'But not what you had there?'

He'd hit the nail on the head. 'Exactly.'

Overhead, seagulls chased for food, and as the waves lost their ferocity on the shore they nudged the pebbles back and forth. Her eyes found a beautiful red stone and she stopped to pick it up. As she straightened, she saw Miles walking towards them. He gave her a polite smile but his face stiffened when he saw Jay. With a curt nod, he greeted them both. 'Stella. Jay.'

'Miles,' Jay replied cheerfully. 'How are you, mate?'

'Fine. Thank you.' And with that he marched off towards his house.

Stella wasn't sure what had happened between them but his face definitely changed when he saw Jay. Miles wasn't exactly an effusive man, but his stern expression had become even harsher as he'd cast his eyes on him. Perhaps he was as snooty with Jay as he was with her.

Jay broke the silence that had descended after their encounter with Miles. 'I don't get that man,' he said, still relaxed and cheerful. Stella raised her eyebrows enquiringly. 'He's just such a miserable git. I have no idea why he has to go through life being such a grump. I mean when you live somewhere like this ...' He gestured around him at the beauty of Swallowtail Bay. 'How can you be so miserable all the time? He still thinks he's too good for us all if you ask me.'

'Have you known him long?' It seemed she was right: Miles was snooty with everyone, not just her.

'Since we were kids. We went to different schools but we played for the same football team. He wasn't very good but I admired that he gave it his best shot.' It was such a nice thing to say that Stella smiled. 'But he always acted like he was better than the rest of us.'

She could well believe that. From their very first meeting he'd thought he was better at running a business than her, or would be, if he had half a chance. He'd just have to get over it and accept the shop was hers.

They carried on in an easy silence for a few minutes then Jay led them towards the Wild Goose pub that had just come into sight. Potted olive trees stood either side of a door complete with an old-fashioned bell pull, and the front was lined with old Tudor beams. Swallowtail Bay was proving to be as amazing as Stella had hoped it would be. It was full of buildings from every era and of every type you could imagine.

Like a gentleman, Jay opened the door for her and stood aside while she led Frank through. The barman smiled at them both. 'All right, mate. What can I get ya?'

The pub was tiny and Stella felt awkward standing there with Frank taking up most of the room until the customers at the other tables began turning around and cooing at him, which he loved.

'What would you like, Stella?' Jay asked. 'We can share a bottle of wine if you like?'

'That would be great. I don't mind red or white.'

'Shall we go for white as it's a lovely evening?' Stella nodded, and tightened Frank's lead so he'd sit down. 'A bottle of Sauvignon Blanc, please, Don.'

The barman turned to Stella. 'There's a water bowl out in the garden if he needs a drink but he's welcome in here too. I like dogs. King Charles in particular. Beautiful.'

'Jay said you did. Do you have any of your own?'

'Nah. Not anymore. It's hard to find the time to walk them with running the pub. We're open as much as possible, for breakfast right through till eleven at night.' The barman took a wine cooler and filled it with ice before taking a bottle from the fridge and supplying two wine glasses. 'There's not really enough time to walk them.'

'I can imagine,' Stella replied. 'You must work hard.'

'I do, but I love it. Wouldn't have it any other way. You've bought old Herbert's shop, haven't you?'

Frank stood and sniffed a passing stranger's leg and Stella gently tightened his lead again so he'd sit back down. 'Yes, I have.'

'Good. It's nice to see it being kept as a shop and not turned into another café. If you ask me we've got enough of those at the moment.' Don leaned on the counter, his great big hands the size of shovels splayed out. 'You can't walk two shops down the high street before you come to one and then two shops down from that there'll be another. And they all serve weird coffee with milk

89

that isn't actually milk. Stuff that comes from nuts or some such thing. Very odd.'

Stella giggled. 'It can be.'

'Thanks, mate,' said Jay, taking the wine cooler and the two glasses from the counter. When he turned to Stella he rolled his eyes and motioned towards the back of the pub. 'The garden's this way.' She moved aside to let him through and followed enjoying the 'oohs' and 'ahhs' Frank always received. Finally they were sat at a picnic table in the back of the pub. It was only a small courtyard garden, but the potted plants dotted here and there were beginning to flower, and it was quite a suntrap.

As they chatted, Stella began to wish she was on a date with Jay rather than it being a business meeting. He was charming and friendly, not to mention mind-blowingly handsome. Nerves wriggled in her stomach, once more reminding her to stick to business. Frank sniffed around the pot plants as Jay poured the wine.

'Did you meet Herbert before he left?' Jay asked.

She nodded. 'Yes, I did. He was a really nice guy. I'm happy that he's enjoying his retirement. I've only had the shop a couple of weeks but it's hard work. I can imagine after a lifetime I'll want to retire to Málaga as well.'

'I can't imagine him in Málaga in his budgie smugglers. Actually I can. Yuck.' He gave a shudder but then smiled and Stella's heart struggled under its loveliness. 'I'm happy the shop has gone to someone who clearly cares about it as much as he did.'

Her eyes flicked to Jay's left hand, holding the stem of his wine glass. No wedding ring, but that didn't mean he didn't have a girlfriend or a fiancée. He was about the same age as her so there must be someone – he was too handsome to be single. Not that it mattered as this was a business meeting, she reminded herself again. It was nothing to do with her.

'So I know a few things that I'd like on the website,' Stella said, trying to focus her mind. 'It needs to be for the shop and the holiday lets and I wanted a little bit of the history of the building in there too. Something to show how special we are. Did you know the whole lot used to be known as Admiral's Corner because an admiral actually used to live there?'

'I didn't know that. It sounds great.' He looked impressed then thoughtful. 'You'll need an online checkout facility and did you want a booking facility too? Or do you want people to enquire first?'

Stella thought for a moment. 'I think they should enquire. Until I've got used to all the changeover days I should probably keep things simple. Once I'm more experienced we can add that later, can't we?'

'We certainly can,' he said, tapping his index finger as he spoke. She liked him saying 'we'. 'Are you keeping the shop name as it is?'

'The Potter's Wheel? I don't think so. I don't think it represents all the different things I plan to sell. And from researching the history of the place I think it would be nice to have the apartments called something else too.'

'So what are you thinking of?' Jay sipped his wine.

She'd never seen a man drink in such a sexy way. He didn't swig with his mouth open or gulp it down. It was gentlemanly and made his mouth look nice. *Stop it*, she told herself. *Business meeting. Nothing else. Business meeting.* 'I've thought about it but I couldn't think of anything suitable. And some of the things I came up with were downright silly so I'm not going to tell you those.'

'Come on,' said Jay leaning forwards, a teasing glint in his eye. 'Tell me one.'

'No. Definitely not. Not till I've had more wine at least.' Was this flirting? Why was she doing that? Frank came back over and Stella leaned down and gave his head a stroke. He curled into a

91

ball in the sunshine and went to sleep at her feet. 'I still haven't come up with anything perfect.'

'It's funny, I didn't really know it was called The Potter's Wheel. I mean, I know it's written over the door but we've only ever known it as old Herbert's shop.'

Stella paused and played his words over again in her head. Why hadn't she thought of it before? It was obvious what the shop should be called.

'What is it?' asked Jay.

'I think that's it. I think we just figured out the name.' He looked confused. 'I'm going to call it Old Herbert's Shop in his honour. As the building was named after an admiral it kind of fits that the shop should be named after him, don't you think?' Excitement bubbled out as she spoke. Something about the name felt right.

'I do,' he replied, topping up their glasses. 'We definitely need a toast to that.'

Stella grinned and raised her glass. As the light changed from the brightness of day to a mellow evening glow, it dappled through the gaps in the buildings catching Jay's face and highlighting his stubble. She'd expected it to be red like his hair but it was more a mixture of browns and blonds. She dipped her eyes, not wanting to be caught staring. 'I thought I'd go back to the original building name for the apartments and keep it simple and classy. Just Admiral's Corner.'

'I think that deserves another toast. Cheers.'

'Cheers,' Stella replied. She had to stop smiling or her cheeks were going to hurt. She must look ridiculously silly, grinning like a lunatic with this man who was, quite frankly, out of her league.

'The website won't take long to build and I'll only charge mate's rates. We'll need some pictures of the stock and the apartments, and some nice descriptions as well. Once I've got everything up and running, I'll sit down with you and show you how to update everything.'

'Okay,' she replied tentatively.

'Don't look so nervous.' He laughed and reached out a hand across the table, resting his fingers lightly on hers. 'It's really easy, I promise, and I'm only down the road or on the end of the phone if you get stuck.'

'Thank you. I can't believe how friendly everyone is here.'

Jay moved his hand away and a prickle of disappointment passed over her. 'We try our best.'

Stella studied her wine happily. Here she was sat in a pub garden with a truly gorgeous man. If she turned up to Isaac's wedding with Jay on her arm she wouldn't be cast as the sad old spinster she so feared. In fact, people would be jealous as hell. Isaac's mother in particular, who'd never really taken to Stella. Stella chastised herself for being so petty. She shouldn't want to get one over on Isaac – she was a grown-up – but it was hard not to under the circumstances.

'Would you still like to have some dinner?' Jay asked. 'They do great food here. And with company to match, I can't think of anywhere else I'd rather be.'

Stella's breath caught in her throat. He couldn't have a girlfriend if he was saying something like that. As excitement mounted she tried to stop her voice coming out like a helium-filled squeak. 'Yeah, that would be great.'

'I'll grab us a couple of menus.'

As Jay left, Stella caught the eyes of a group of young women at another table following Jay as he went back inside. They turned to each other and giggled and Stella sat taller, pulling her shoulders back. She pretended that this was a normal meeting for her and not something so amazingly, brilliantly out of the ordinary. Jay arrived with the menus and another bottle of wine and they carried on talking about this and that as the sun set slowly.

When they were finished, they walked back towards the shop, and Stella congratulated herself on an evening in which she didn't embarrass herself horribly. Jay had been so easy to talk to and so friendly. There was no bravado, no false modesty and he didn't pretend to be something he wasn't. He wasn't stuck-up and snooty like Miles Parker. If things carried on going this well, she thought, there was every possibility she could ask Jay to Isaac's wedding, and even more possibility he might just say yes.

Chapter 10

On Saturday evening, Stella waited impatiently for a knock on the door from Lexi. She'd tidied the flat from top to bottom, cleaned everything including the Seventies kitchen units and pushed the windows fully open to finally get rid of the horrible smell of stale tobacco. As takings had been okay and sleeping on the sofa was giving her a terribly bad back, Stella had shelled out a little bit of money and replaced Herbert's skanky old bed with something simple and cheap from IKEA. As far as the flat went, she was actually beginning to settle in and it was feeling more and more like home. After locking up the shop, she'd quickly made a lasagne and side salad. Knowing that a lot of wine would be consumed tonight by herself if not by Lexi, a good carby dinner was definitely called for.

The back door to the flat, accessed through a small garden, was blocked thanks to the piles of rubbish in front of it, so Stella sat on her stool by the counter waiting for Lexi to arrive. Spying her approach she opened the door. 'Hi, thanks for coming.'

'It's my pleasure,' said Lexi, proffering a bottle of wine in one hand and wrapping the other around Stella's shoulders, pulling her in for a hug. 'And the kids have been absolute arseholes today so I was quite happy to hand them over to Will.'

Stella laughed. 'I'm sure they weren't that bad.' Lexi's ability to speak so honestly about her children was refreshing and not at all like Stella's sister who was sometimes blind to the faults of her offspring. 'I've made dinner and the wine is already open.'

They went through the shop and into the flat where Frank sat in the hallway, wagging his tail. He received a pat on the head as they walked past then followed them into the living room, charging forward to claim his place on the sofa but getting diverted by his food bowl.

'You take a seat and I'll grab the wine,' said Stella. She nipped into the kitchen and quickly poured it into two polished-up glasses she'd laid out in preparation. When she returned she sat in the armchair opposite Lexi who was snuggled on the large scruffy brown leather sofa.

'How do you like the flat?' asked Lexi.

'It needs a lot of work,' Stella replied, curling her legs under her. 'But I love the layout, and where I've added a couple of the paintings from the shop it's hidden some of the terrible wallpaper.' Two of the paintings had been so beautiful Stella had decided to keep them for herself and forgo, at least for now, the possible profit. One was of a dark and stormy sky over a raging sea. There was something so gothic about it that it put Stella in mind of *Wuthering Heights* and she knew then and there she couldn't possibly part with it. The other was a more abstract piece: swipes and slashes of colour in oranges and yellows on a plain canvas. The chaos of colour had sparked a strange feeling within – a sure sign it was meant for her. Both were placed either side of the large living room window under which Lexi was now sat.

'I'll just have to do bits as and when I can. I need to concentrate on the holiday lets first and get them ready to go. I've got a load of work planned for tomorrow. Which reminds me, Jay said I need some photos taken once they're cleaned.'

'Jay the website guy?' Stella nodded and swallowed her mouthful of wine. Frank managed to scrabble onto the sofa with an ungainly thump and plonked down next to Lexi. 'Jay the handsome website guy?'

'Umm hmm. Kiera, Miles's fiancée, recommended him and we met yesterday. I thought he'd be perfect for the job.'

'And is this just for the job of website guy or did you have something more romantic in mind?'

Stella kept her eyes down on her wine glass. 'We did have dinner last night but it was just a business meeting.'

'Ooooh!'

'I'm a bit out of practice when it comes to men,' said Stella, unsure why yet again she was sharing so much. Yet, each time it was coming more and more naturally. 'It was a really lovely evening.'

'Good, I'm glad. I definitely believe that love finds us when it's ready. I'm happy to wait and just concentrate on the kids at the moment.'

Stella smiled. Lexi really was a cool woman, content to be herself and live her life, knowing she would deal with whatever came her way. She also looked fabulous tonight, as usual, encased in a Fifties-style dress with a buttoned-up cardigan. Her hair was scraped back into a bun and she wore a headscarf, like housewives used to wear, but somehow, with just her flicky eyeliner and some mascara she looked incredibly chic. The vintage style really suited her.

'So when will your website be up and running?' Lexi asked, draining the last of her wine.

'By the end of this week I hope. Jay texted me earlier to say that he's already got a basic website sorted and it just needs the images and text. I've got a lot of it already written. I've been working on it in the shop during the slower times and if I can get the images up soon then we're sorted. I've already got a booking for the one-bedroom from someone who's stayed here before. They arrive on Friday.'

'That's so exciting.'

'I am quite excited,' Stella replied. 'I've left the one-bedroom up with the listings Herbert had already organised because once I've ripped up the floor tiles and sanded, apart from a good clean and replacing the bed linen, it's good to go. I've taken the three-bedroom one down until I've got it in a better state.'

'Is it that bad?' asked Lexi.

Stella sighed. 'There's nothing structural but it's tired and old—'

'Like me.'

'Hardly. I want to get the carpet tiles up there too and either sand or paint the floorboards, and move stuff around. That's my job for tomorrow. I've set my alarm for five so I can get Frank walked and then start as early as possible. I need to get as much done tomorrow as I can and then I'll work in the evenings too so I can get it back on the listings from next Monday. That's my deadline.'

'Wow. You're really self-disciplined.' Lexi twizzled her glass in her fingers. 'I can't believe you've moved here and taken over a business like it's nothing. You've made it look so easy.'

'You haven't seen me running around freaking out about stock levels, sales margins, and mark-ups. Or waking up in the middle of the night, worrying this is all going to go wrong and leave me homeless and bankrupt. I'm sure Miles Parker is thoroughly enjoying watching me all stressed out and manic.'

'Why do you say that?'

'Because every time he walks by he's always slyly peering in and sneering, judging every item I have in the shop. I'm sure he'd be over the moon if everything went wrong for me. The other day I nipped out the back to grab a cup of tea and when I came back he basically had his nose pressed against the window. I'm surprised Frank didn't bark at him. Then when he saw me he didn't even smile or say hello, he just shuffled off with his head down.'

'Poor Miles,' Lexi said, and Stella raised her eyebrows, unconvinced. 'He really isn't that bad, you know. He was probably just curious to see what you're doing with the place. Honestly, he is a nice guy really.'

'Well, I'm yet to see that side of him.'

'Anyway,' Lexi said brightly, 'I'm sure you'll make this place successful. The shop's doing okay, isn't it?'

'Yes, it is.' Stella tucked her hair back behind her ear. 'I just want to find some new stock that will sell nice and quick. I'll need a quick turnover to keep the money coming in. Stock can't just sit around. It's got to be in and out. And I can't sell it for less than I paid. I don't mind doing that with Herbert's old tat but going forward it's not sustainable.'

'It sounds like you've got it all sorted out.' After adjusting her hairband, Lexi said, 'I'd love to run my own business.'

'Really? Would you sell the clothes you make?' Stella could happily offer Lexi some space in the shop if she did.

Lexi nodded. 'And all things vintage. But I don't think it's on the cards for me. By the way, that lasagne smells great.'

'It should be done actually,' Stella replied, getting up to check. 'Do you want to sit at the table and I'll bring it in?'

Stella brought in a huge dish of steaming lasagne then went back to fetch the side salad and wine as Lexi moved to the small circular table at the far end of the room. At the moment it was nestled next to some more boxes of stock, but Stella was slowly selling all the old stuff and it wouldn't be long till the room was clear. After topping up their drinks, they ate with glee. 'How are the kids?' she asked Lexi.

'Oh, they're fine.' Lexi rested her elbows on the table and took up her glass. 'Will loves having them and they love seeing their daddy. It's better now the kids have got used to things. We had some bad times when Will and I had only just split. Ralph's behaviour went haywire and Taylor just shut down on me, but now we have a routine they're a lot happier.'

'Do you mind if I ask what happened with you two?'

Lexi took another sip and Stella noticed a slight tension in her expression. 'It's complicated really but suffice it to say things were tough after the kids were born. They're really close in age and it was exhausting having a newborn and a toddler. I didn't feel like me anymore, I just felt like … oh, I don't know … a housekeeper, a mother, a cleaner … Not a person.' She took a deep breath. 'Plus Will was out a lot working. Or in the pub.'

From the way Lexi looked at her, Stella knew it was time to change the subject. They both wanted this evening to be full of laughter and fun. 'Why were the kids arseholes today?'

Lexi gave an amused smile. 'Taylor decided to be a grown-up and got into my make-up bag and Ralph wanted to do some splatter painting and ended up completely covering my walls rather than the paper. My landlord will go nuts.'

'I take it Taylor's make-up didn't go well?'

'She came down looking like The Joker. Honestly, it was absolutely terrifying. And when she asked me if she looked nice, I kind of mumbled a yes and she could tell I was lying. She then had a complete hissy fit and told me I was the worst mum in the world and ran upstairs.'

'Oh no,' said Stella, imagining Taylor's confidence had been forever dented. Not to mention how heartbreaking that must have been for Lexi to hear something like that.

'It's not as bad as it sounds,' Lexi replied. 'She's told me the same thing three times this week already. I was more worried about getting the make-up out of my bedding because she face-planted my duvet wearing my favourite red lipstick. Makes you happy you haven't got kids, doesn't it?'

'Sometimes,' Stella replied. 'But I bet the cuddles are nice. I miss cuddles with someone.'

Lexi rested her knife and fork for a moment. 'Cuddles mostly mean snot or toothpaste-covered shoulders. But yeah, I do like cuddle time.'

'Oh, by the way,' said Stella, suddenly remembering. 'Did you want that roll of fabric? I saved it for you as no one else bought it. I thought it should go to a good home.'

'I'd love to,' Lexi replied, a slight blush coming to her cheeks. 'But I still can't afford it. Ralph needs some new school shoes. His are falling apart so I won't be able to buy it for a while.'

Stella suddenly felt very awkward and stupid for asking. She should have waited for Lexi to mention it and now she'd embarrassed her. Stella wanted to just give it to her, but she worried that Lexi might think it was out of pity and be even more offended. Stella quickly moved the conversation along. 'Oh, I bought cake for pudding.'

'Yay!'

'I got us a big, gooey chocolate cake from that bakery down the other end of the high street.'

'Our rivals?' asked Lexi scornfully.

'Yes. Sorry. But it wouldn't have been a surprise if I got it from you.'

'Traitor.'

Stella enjoying the teasing. 'And I bought some posh champagne cream too.'

'In that case,' said Lexi, 'I forgive you.'

'I'll clear this lot,' said Stella, thankful that the awkwardness she'd created had been forgotten. 'And fetch some bowls. I thought you could take what's left for the kids. There's far too much for me to finish on my own.'

'Aww, that's really kind. I'll help,' Lexi said, standing up and picking up the lasagne dish. 'That was so delicious. You're a really good cook.'

'I'm really not. There isn't much I can cook, but I can manage a decent lasagne.' Stella served out pudding, and they went back to the living room and curled up on the sofas with bowls of cake and lashings of cream.

'What are you going to do about your ex's wedding?' asked Lexi who was scraping out her bowl so as not to miss anything.

Stella sighed. She'd been trying not to think about it and had hidden the invitation in a drawer in the kitchen. 'I've got to go, haven't I? If I don't, I'm going to look like such a cow.'

'Do you think he's invited you out of spite or to show off?'

'No. He was always a really decent, honest bloke. He probably thinks it's a nice thing to do to show that he still thinks of me as a friend and that there are no hard feelings. It wouldn't even occur to him that if I turn up on my own I'm going to look like a lonely, sad loser.'

'No, you won't. You'll look like a strong independent woman who just hasn't found the right guy yet. Or who has concentrated on building up her new business before looking for love again.'

Stella smiled and placed her bowl on the floor beside her. She'd wanted friends like this her whole life. Like the ones you see in TV programmes like *Sex and the City* but she'd never had them before. Having Lexi around made her feel empowered and happy. She loved her new life and had never needed a man to make her happy before. Deep down she knew that the renewed feelings of rejection the invitation had inspired were making her focus on completely the wrong things but it was hard not to think about how she'd be judged by others. 'I really don't want to go,' she said with a childish whine. 'It'll completely suck but I know I have to. If I don't go, he'll think I'm still angry with him, which I am, but he doesn't need to actually know that.'

'You could always find a hot date to go with,' said Lexi, licking her spoon. 'Maybe someone like Jay? He is incredibly good-looking.'

'Is he? I hadn't noticed.'

Lexi gave her a knowing look then laughed. Could Stella really pluck up the courage to invite him to the wedding? It had seemed a good idea at the pub the other night but as soon as she was home she'd worried it would be too forward. They'd need to get to know each other better first, but there was plenty of time for that, wasn't there? She could start by calling him tomorrow to discuss the website again. With Lexi's encouragement, a smile started to pull at her cheeks. She was definitely going to do it. She was going to invite Jay to Isaac's wedding.

Chapter 11

From the window of his home office, situated at the top of the house in the converted attic, Miles had spent the week watching seemingly relentless activity at the shop. From his high view-point he could see into the courtyard garden at the back of Admiral's Corner, and since the previous Sunday he'd watched Stella, dusty and dirty, with her hair scraped back into a pony-tail, throwing carpet tiles down into the garden from the flats. She'd stop every once in a while and come down to load them into her car, presumably to take them to the tip. Either that or she was fly-tipping but he doubted it. He was beginning to think that she was like him: conscientious and thorough. Then once the tiles had gone, there was washing – tons and tons of washing. Every time she took a load in she'd smell the sheets and a sweet smile lifted the corners of her mouth, bringing joy to her face.

In between the washing and the tip runs there were car jour-neys out, coming back with a myriad of paint cans. At one point he actually found himself standing up and peering over his desk to see exactly what was happening. What Miles couldn't figure out was why he was interested in the first place. Over the week he'd even made excuses to Kiera that he had jobs to do so he could come up and see Stella working through the lighter evenings, going to and fro with mops and buckets and dusters. By the end of the week she looked exhausted but not unhappy or daunted. In fact, when he'd passed the shop to get his lunch one day, he'd noticed her eyes were bright and shining with happiness.

Miles stretched his arms up, determined to focus, and turned his attention to his laptop but the memory of seeing Stella that morning with an enormous wicker basket wrapped in cellophane and bursting with treats popped into his brain. A big box of chocolates sat at a jaunty angle between a bottle of wine and a candle. She had obviously prepared a welcome basket for her first guests. The light from the opposite window reflected off his screen and he went to pull the blinds a little. Before he did, he took a moment to admire the view. From this side of the house he could see between the roofs out towards the sea. It was a bright sunny day with just a slight chill to the light breeze and for a second he studied the waves cresting and crashing together. He wished he could be here all the time, but he'd be away again soon. At least it was Friday, even if he had some work to finish before the weekend.

Moving back to his desk, he began to answer an email from his boss and yet again couldn't stop himself from checking the window to see if there had been any further activity at old Herbert's place.

As he was alone, without Kiera popping in and out, he should definitely be concentrating on the task in hand. She was in London searching for wedding dresses with her friend, but as he thought of her an unsettling feeling began to ripple through him. She'd turned down yet another job to be able to go shopping, and most worrying of all was the way she'd talked about the potential client. She'd actually laughed about them, said that they were wasting their money, that they were beyond help. Kiera had been polite in her email response, but as she'd written it

105

she'd said such unkind things Miles had been too shocked to reply. He was sure she'd never done that before. He'd have remembered.

Now that Stella was working on the holiday apartments, Miles began to wonder what they looked like. When he'd seen them he'd imagined they needed extensive work: new furniture and lighting; changing fittings and fixtures; and adding fancy modern conveniences like a top-notch coffee machine and sound system. Something to really set the mood of a classy retreat but with a funky, modern edge. Stella mustn't have thought it necessary, and that made him even more curious. He really needed to concentrate. He had another sales meeting in a few days and had figures to prepare. Miles picked up his phone to double-check the meeting was still going ahead as voices below caught his attention.

Down in the street, a young couple pulled up at the side of the shop, giggling at one another. Just as they were making their way around to the front Stella came out to meet them. She had a great big, welcoming smile on her face and her cheeks were flushed. He thought of Kiera and the smiles she gave him. It was only since they'd set the date for the wedding that she smiled at him like that again. At the beginning of their relationship all her smiles had been like Stella's. Prior to the wedding announcement he couldn't remember seeing it for a long time. Miles shook the thought away and looked again out of the window. Stella shook hands with the guests and they chatted for a few moments though he couldn't make out what they said. They must have been talking about the building as the man looked up and Stella followed his gaze, pointing at something on the side wall. Then she led them away out of sight.

A sharp pain stabbed in his chest. He told himself it was indigestion but deep down he knew it was jealousy. He had imagined himself in that role, meeting and greeting guests, making their stays special, and it had filled him with a passion he hadn't felt before. Stella was being incredibly professional. It was a shame their first meeting hadn't gone how he'd planned. Miles knew he'd over-reacted and come across as a complete idiot. The second with Kiera hadn't gone much better. And then the other day, Stella had caught him having a sneaky look in and in his embarrassment he hadn't known quite what to do, so he just shuffled off into the café. All he'd wanted was to see if she had any new stock in yet. She'd been doing so well in clearing all Herbert's old junk he'd hoped to see some new items and wondered what they might be. In the interests of neighbourliness, Miles decided, he should probably try again.

He sat for a moment and jiggled his legs up and down in anticipation then grabbing his phone he headed downstairs.

The little bell tinkled as Miles walked into the shop and Stella looked up from behind the counter. The dog was, as usual, asleep at her feet. Miles cursed himself as Stella smiled down at the really quite sweet King Charles spaniel. Miles remembered now he quite liked dogs. Kiera had never wanted a pet but he'd always secretly loved the idea of having a little dog like that to take for spring walks along the beach, wrapped up in coats and hats, cheeks pink from the cold.

'Hello, Miles,' Stella said cheerfully. The light shone through the large shop windows onto her light brown hair and her lips were a pale pink. Under her gaze he stumbled for something to say. He should have thought ahead and prepared something. Normally, Miles was good at networking. No, he was *great* at networking – you kind of had to be in a sales role – so why did he struggle so much around Stella? Unable to think of a good opening line, he plastered on what he hoped was a confident grin and said, 'Hi. How's it going?' If he'd said that at a work event he'd be made to leave. It was the most unoriginal start to a conversation in the history of the world. Ever. Inside, he cursed. He wasn't going to begin changing her opinion of him that way, was he?

'Good. Thanks,' Stella replied but she seemed a little guarded as she glanced at him.

Miles gave a half nod and Stella stared for a moment then looked away to her paper and pen. He wondered what she was writing. He awkwardly rocked on his heels and then wandered around pausing at some of the new stock she had brought in, pleased to see that things were going well. He checked the price on the bottom of a gorgeous glass paperweight. It was made of clear glass except for a bright green streak that ran through the middle. Miles raised his eyebrows. The price was really quite reasonable.

'Can I help you with anything?' Stella asked. There was an edge to her voice and he wondered what he'd done now to offend her. All he was doing was seeing how much it cost. He'd imagined it being a lot more expensive.

'No, thanks. I was just browsing.' He opened his mouth to say something about the price but then closed it again as she watched him. He didn't want it to come out the wrong way. She gave him another almost wary glance.

The dog came out from behind the counter, his lead at full stretch as he sat down near Miles, expecting a fuss. Miles slowly reached out a hand but the dog pulled back and, embarrassed, he did the same.

'Don't worry about Frank,' Stella said, gently retracting his lead and moving Frank away. Her tone was a little more conciliatory than it had been earlier. 'He can get quite nervous around men sometimes.'

'At least he didn't try to bite me this time.' He'd meant it as a joke but as soon as he saw Stella's reaction he knew he shouldn't have said it. Whenever he was here, every time he opened his mouth both feet went flying in. She dropped her head and a flush came to her cheeks.

'I'm sure if he wanted to bite you he would have. He just wanted to warn you off trying to grab his collar.' Her tone grew sharp and it caught him off guard. He didn't want to go over old territory but for some reason, he needed her to understand that at the time he'd been trying to help.

'I really was only trying to stop him running into the road and killing himself.'

This time, Stella didn't say anything in reply and Miles turned his attention to another glass *objet d'art*. It didn't seem to have any practical purpose, being a sort of oblong shape with weird corners, but was pretty and had a matching green streak to the paperweight. He checked the price at the bottom and felt his eyebrows lift. Considering how unique it was, and that it was probably hand-made, the price was amazing. He was considering buying one for his office when Stella, who had misjudged his expression of surprise spoke.

'I think you'll find they're very reasonably priced. They're made by a local artist and each one is unique.'

'I'm sure,' he replied, putting it back. This time he made sure his eyebrows stayed still.

'They're actually very popular.' Again, her tone was cold and Miles had no idea why. He hadn't criticised them. He'd even made sure his eyebrows hadn't implied anything, so why she was being so defensive? It's not like he'd said something rude. He began to feel the pressure of the heavy, loaded atmosphere but again didn't know what to ask. Worried that if he asked a personal question she'd think he was prying, he pointed to a painting and said, 'Have you thought about selling some more of those?'

Stella dropped her pen onto her notepad and her eyes flashed. 'I will be getting some more artwork, but it won't be the same. I want to have some variety.'

'But if it sells well, why wouldn't you?'

'I'm likely to have the same customers coming back week after week so I need to have more variety in the art. People aren't going to keep buying the same type of painting. And I like exploring other artists.'

'So you're not going to stock any of the same artists as last time?' It was a genuine question but her lips tightened into a line. She seemed to be taking offence to everything he said.

Stella stood up and came to join him looking at the paintings on the wall. 'I didn't say that. I might keep one or two if I feel they really have something special but no one wants to buy exactly the same painting as someone else. I'm asking a lot of money so each piece needs to be unique.'

'I disagree,' Miles said, stuffing his hands into his pockets, glad that they were beginning to have an actual conversation. 'People buy prints of famous artists all the time.'

She pushed her hair back from her face and crossed her arms over her chest. 'But that's famous artists. It's not the same when it's local artists and I'm asking anywhere from one hundred pounds up. People want something of their very own that no one else in the town has. They don't want to visit their neighbour's house and see the same picture that they've got on the wall. And I can't base all my purchasing decisions on tourists because they make up such a small percentage of my customer base and don't generally buy big objects like paintings.'

'So you're trading on the whole "keeping up with the Joneses" mentality?' Wow, Stella really had done her homework, thought Miles. He'd come to the same conclusion when he was preparing his business plan and was impressed, but she was looking at him like she wanted to slap him. Colour flooded her cheeks and her pale skin tinged with pink.

'You have to understand your customers and local people are mine. While tourists will make up a huge part of my trade in the summer, I can't rely on the sales made in those few months. I need stock that will speak to my customers through the rest of the year. The ones who come in week in, week out for presents or homeware.'

'Speak to your customers?' He wasn't taking the piss, it was just a strange turn of phrase he hadn't heard before but again she seemed to be getting huffy with him.

'Yes,' she replied, indignantly.

'Sorry,' he said. 'It's just a funny phrase.'

She took another deep breath and as her chest rose and fell something happened to his insides. 'No it's not. It's true.'

'It is a bit funny,' he said trying to lighten the mood, but Stella was having none of it.

Marching back to the counter she said, 'Look, if you're not going to actually buy anything, perhaps you should leave.'

'Come on,' said Miles, shocked at her reply and trying again to bring it back to how well it had been going earlier. 'You have to admit that was a bit of a funny thing to say?'

'Funny?' Her voice echoed around the empty shop and Miles felt a mild panic rise within him. *Oh no*, he really shouldn't have said that. Why did he keep doing this to himself? It was a wonder he could speak at all with his massive boot lodged so firmly in his throat. Her features immediately changed, becoming hard and cold. 'How bloody dare you!'

Miles tried to remain calm but panic was surging through him. 'I'm sorry if I offended you. I was only trying to have a bit of a joke.'

'You come in to my shop smirking at the stock or making faces at the prices and then you criticise my choice of artwork and my reason for stocking it. You don't actually own this place, Miles. Technically this is none of your business.'

'I thought we were having a conversation. I was just offering my opinion—'

'I don't need your opinion.'

A horrible sinking feeling swamped Miles. He'd gone in trying to be neighbourly and smooth over their previous meeting and it had all gone wrong. For some reason Stella seemed to deliberately misunderstand everything he said or the words came out all wrong. 'Look, all I was saying was—'

111

'Perhaps you should leave.'

Seeing her normally plump lips in a tight, angry line, Miles sighed to himself. This really hadn't gone according to plan and he just couldn't figure out why or why he cared so much. 'Yes, I think I probably should,' he replied and with a strangely heavy heart marched away, unable to look back.

Chapter 12

Lexi grabbed her forehead with both hands in an effort to keep her head from exploding and tried to remain calm. Pressing firmly and attempting to keep her voice steady, she said, 'Ralph, I've asked you a million times, will you please put your shoes on?' Ralph's eyes, trained on the TV, didn't move. 'Ralph?' His head spun and he looked at his mother as if this were the first time he'd noticed her existence.

'Pardon?'

'Oh, for the love of—' Reining in her annoyance because he had at least said *pardon* rather than *what*, she took a deep breath and let go of her skull. 'Ralph, will you please put your shoes on?' He ran to the hall and found his trainers then back into the living room and put them on the wrong feet. Lexi rolled her eyes. How was this boy ever going to make it in the real world? How did he even manage to get through school? She squeezed her eyes shut and counted to ten. At least it was a Saturday and she didn't have the pressure of his teacher tut-tutting at her if she was late. 'You need to swap them over, darling.'

'Why?'

'Because you've got them on the wrong feet.'

'But I don't mind them like that.' His eyes went back to the television.

At this she smiled. 'I know you don't mind but it'll hurt your feet.'

'It won't. I wore them like this to school yesterday.'

'No you didn't, Ralph. You wore your proper school shoes and I made sure you'd put them on right.'

'But I wore them like this after PE and they were fine.' He was speaking to her over his shoulder.

'Ralph, please.'

'Oh, all right.' With his eyes still on the TV screen, he begrudgingly swapped them over.

At least that was one battle won. Now to chase Taylor. 'Taylor? Taylor? Come on, sweetheart. We really need to go now.' Taylor came down the stairs wearing a skirt she had folded over at the waistband to make even shorter, a crop top and Lexi's favourite pair of red high heels. Taylor paused in her favourite model pose – one hand on a jutted-out hip. *My daughter wants to be a hooker*, thought Lexi, desperately. *That'll be a fun conversation at parents' evening.* Lexi played it out in her head. *'How is my daughter getting on with her reading, Mrs Berry?'*

'Oh, fine.'

'Excellent, she'll be able to read her criminal record then. And maths?'

'Yes, she's very good at maths.'

'Fantastic. She'll have no problem counting out fivers in dark alleys.'

Lexi reminded herself, as she did every morning, that today she wasn't going to be a shouty mum. 'Taylor, you can't go out like that, sweetie. Can you please go back upstairs and get changed?'

'But I look cool!' Her eight-year-old tried to stamp her foot but in the high-heeled shoes nearly fell down the stairs. After Lexi had instinctively jumped forwards, and Taylor had regained her balance, her heartrate returned to normal.

114

'Taylor, get changed now. Please. You need something warmer – it's still cold outside. And you're not wearing my shoes.'

'But Mum, I can walk in them.'

'No, you can't.'

'Yes, I can. Look—'

Lexi's temper flared. Why did they have to argue with literally everything she said? 'Taylor Elizabeth Stockton, go and get changed.'

'But Muuuum.'

'No buts. I want to go into town and I want to go now. I need to ask Stella something.' She paused from delivering the blow they were going to hate most. 'And we're walking.'

'Oh why?' moaned Ralph, finally turning around. The little toad paid attention when he wanted to.

Lexi didn't want to admit that she was nearly out of petrol and didn't have enough money to fill up the car. What little she had she needed to keep for school runs this week. 'Because it'll be good for you.'

Taylor stomped off upstairs to get changed.

'Why can't we get the bus?' asked Ralph. 'I like the bus.'

Lexi grabbed her wallet from her bag and double-checked its contents, just in case a fairy had appeared overnight and added some spare change. Apart from the five-pound note she needed to keep it was empty. She fixed a smile and replied as cheerfully as possible, 'No, darling, we're going to walk.'

'Oh. But it's raining.'

'It's not raining.' She eyed the fine drizzle and threatening sky outside. 'It's just a bit grey. I'm sure we'll be fine. And we can take umbrellas just in case.' The sad look on her son's face yanked at her heartstrings. As always, she felt like a terrible mother. If only their family hadn't broken apart. If she and Will were still together they might be able to afford the bus. As it was, she was being forced to use some of the emergency money she kept in her knicker drawer to pay for dinner, and even that was going to have to be from the discounted aisle. She really was a failure. Feeling tears well up, she sniffed. 'I tell you what though, we can go by the duck pond and feed the ducks if you like.' There were a couple of slightly mouldy crusts in the bottom of the bread bin they could use.

'Yay!' Ralph smiled and seeing his bright blue eyes, Lexi smiled too.

Taylor descended the stairs in a pair of leggings and full-length top. Pausing on the final step she flung her arms in the air. 'I look like a farmer.'

A giggle erupted from Lexi, releasing a wave of love for her stroppy daughter. 'A what?'

'A farmer.' Taylor pouted.

Lexi went to her daughter, cupped her cheeks in her hands and placed a kiss on the end of her nose. 'Come on, Farmer Taylor. We're going to feed the ducks on the walk into town.'

After Taylor had flounced around and flung herself dramatically into her coat and shoes, they made their way to town, via the duck pond. Just around the corner from their house there was a little green and a small pond. Though Lexi's kids moaned about the drizzle when they were walking, they were still content to feed the fat, well-supplied ducks and splash in the puddles. Taylor, being a big girl now, had her own umbrella that she used as a prop as she sang and danced along, while Ralph was content to hold his mum's hand and together they sploshed their way along the cobbles of the high street, past the rainy windows of the boutique shops and posh cafés singing, 'Rain, rain, go away, come again another day'. It wasn't that long a walk, but with any luck, they'd be tired out by the time they got home.

Before long they were at old Herbert's shop and Lexi opened the door for the kids who charged in at full speed. 'Slow down, you two, there's precious stuff in here. Hi, Stella.'

'Hi, Lexi how—'

'Look at that doggy,' cried Ralph, running towards Frank who had woken up at the sound of the shop bell. At the thought of getting a fuss he sat up in his basket, wagging his tail so fast he could have taken off if he wasn't so fat.

'He's so cute,' replied Taylor, following her brother.

'This is Frank,' Stella said. 'And he really loves kids. You can stroke him if you like; he's very friendly. He won't bite, but he might lick you. He's quite a licky dog.'

Ralph and Taylor smiled and sat on the floor petting Frank while Lexi approached Stella. Her nerves had been mounting all the way into town but she'd managed to keep them at bay with the help of the children distracting her. Now there was no getting away from it. She had to ask. 'Stella?' said Lexi, moving to the furthest end of the counter, away from her children. Stella followed, her brows knitted together.

'Is everything okay?'

'Yes, fine. I just … I just need to ask you something.'

'Ask away,' she replied.

Lexi chewed the inside of her cheek. God, she hated being in this position. 'I was wondering if you were planning on getting a cleaner for the holiday lets?'

'A cleaner?' echoed Stella, her eyes wide in surprise. Lexi shifted nervously, hoping Stella would lower her voice. She must have flicked her eyes over to the kids because Stella's gaze followed hers and her voice quietened. 'I hadn't really thought about it yet but I suppose I'll have to eventually for the busy summer months. Especially if people come mid-week. Why do you ask?'

Lexi looked over to see Ralph trying to bat Taylor's hand away so she couldn't stroke the dog. They were occupied by their argument and not listening. It was about the only time she'd ever been grateful for one of their arguments. Feeling shame burn away at her cheeks she said, 'I wondered if you might take me on when you get to that point. I can make it fit around the café job. I've already checked with Raina. I really need the money at the moment.' If Stella wasn't taking anyone on yet she had no idea what she'd do. There wasn't much else that could fit in with school and the café.

Stella leaned in closer. 'Isn't Will paying his child support or something?'

'No, it's nothing like that. It's just that …' Lexi shook her head. 'With Will being a self-employed roofer he hasn't had much work lately. I know he'll pay me as much as he can and make up for this when he's getting the work in, but things are really hard for him right now, which means they're hard for me too.' She wondered if he still had enough money to go to the pub, like he had when the children were babies, leaving her tired and alone, but she hadn't asked him. There was no point in starting a row over the past when other things would most certainly get brought up.

'I see.' Stella nodded. 'Okay, I need to do the sums, but I should be able to give you a few hours starting now.' She was clearly thinking aloud and Lexi hated putting her on the spot like this. 'It'll have to come out of the holiday let profits but on the plus side it'll mean I don't have to keep shutting the shop to nip off and clean. I don't want people getting the idea the shop isn't open when they want it to be.' Lexi was relieved to see a big smile come to Stella's face. 'I don't know why I didn't think of it before actually. It could work out really well. My first people are due to go on Monday. Could you start then?'

Lexi nodded as relief eased the tension in her neck.

'Are you okay otherwise though? I mean, can you manage?'

'I think so. Things are tight, so I won't be buying that fabric any time soon, but I've got just about enough to pay the rent and I've already phoned the gas and electric companies and explained the situation. We've agreed that I'll pay a little each month and top it up when I can. They were really nice actually. I hadn't expected them to be.'

'I suppose it's in their interests to keep your business and have some money coming in even if it's not always as much as they'd like. They must know you'll pay.'

'I will. I've never missed payments before. This is the first time things have been that bad for Will. I feel really sorry for him. He's so stressed out.'

'And you?' Stella's kind smile and genuine affection nearly made her cry.

'I'm super stressed,' she admitted. 'I'm having to feed us on a really tight budget and that means lots of vegetables to bulk up meals, which the kids hate. I try and hide them but I haven't got time to mess about. They just have to force it down.'

'What will you do with the kids if you have to work after school?'

'I'm not sure yet.' Lexi shrugged. 'Raina said I could do earlies and Carol, who also works at the café, has agreed to do the afternoons, but there are some days we're not quite sure about yet. That way, I could work there in the morning and split the shift to do the holiday lets. After-school club costs money – money I don't have.' She rubbed her tired eyes. Since Will had come around a few days ago to explain that he couldn't make all of this month's payment she'd hardly slept.

'They could stay here with me, if you like?' Stella said, watching them happily playing with Frank.

'Really?' asked Lexi.

'Yeah, of course. They seem like little angels. They could do their homework or watch TV in the flat and you'll either be next door or upstairs if anything goes wrong. Frank should keep them occupied.'

Lexi didn't know what to say. She was desperately trying to hold back the tears forming in her eyes. She hated crying in front of the kids but this was more than she could ever have hoped for. 'Thank you so much.'

'Mummy?' asked Ralph. 'Are you crying?'

'No, darling,' she said laughing and wiping away a tear. 'I just had something in my eye.'

119

'Mummy?' asked Taylor. 'Can we get a puppy?'

'After what happened to Graham the goldfish? Not a chance.' Stella looked up with a quizzical expression. 'Don't ask,' Lexi replied. 'Just don't ask.' A strange banging sound came from next door. 'What's that? You never said you were having work done.'

'I'm not.' A redness flooded Stella's cheeks and she glanced at Taylor and Ralph, then back to Lexi and mumbled, 'It's the couple I've got staying. They haven't stopped bonking since the moment they arrived and the bedroom is right next to that wall there.' She pointed to the wall that separated the shop and the holiday lets.

Lexi's mouth fell open in surprise but she kept her voice low. 'Is that the bed bashing the wall?' Stella nodded. 'Oh my God! She'll get cystitis going at it like that.'

'Not to mention she's ruining my headboard. And my wall.'

Lexi, feeling like she could breathe for the first time in a week, began to giggle.

'What's that noise, Mummy?' asked Ralph.

'Just some hammering next door,' she replied, and she and Stella exchanged glances before bursting out laughing.

Chapter 13

That evening, Stella reflected on her conversation with Lexi with a heavy heart. She wasn't exactly rolling in money but so far she hadn't got into debt and while not making a profit as such, she wasn't spending more than she made and still had a very small amount of savings behind her. Life must be so hard for Lexi, even though she didn't always let you know it.

From the large living room window the sun lowered in the sky, flooding the room with light, and hungry seagulls could be heard overhead. Her laptop was open on the small table at the end of the living room as Jay was coming over to show her how the website worked, and to upload the images she'd taken after a big week of cleaning. There were fewer boxes than there had been last time and Stella smiled to herself. She was making slow but steady progress; she just wished she could do something more to ease Lexi's burden.

Rather than slipping into her unflattering but warm fleece pyjamas and big fluffy dressing gown, as she normally did after work, she'd not only remained dressed, but had even changed her top to something a little more flattering. Any agonies she'd had over dinner had been resolved when she'd discovered a meal deal in the supermarket. They could enjoy a nice three-course meal and a bottle of wine, and she'd even splashed out on a bag of salad to go with it. The plates were laid on the other side of the table and everything else was in the kitchen, ready to go.

Stella's phone rang and she answered it immediately when she saw Jay's name flash up. Her body fizzed with panic that he was cancelling on her. 'Hi, Jay.'

'Hi,' he said in the cheerful tone she had come to recognise. 'I'm outside.'

'Okay. I'll come and let you in.' Stella hurried out and opened the door. He was wearing the same leather jacket but this time he wore a navy sweater underneath. He ran his hand through his hair and her heart beat like it was about to have a full-on seizure. Seeing his face, she echoed his warm smile.

'I've got everything sorted out for your website. I can't wait to show you.'

Stella pulled herself together. 'I can't wait to see it. I didn't know if you wanted to eat before we looked at it or after?' He had lovely even teeth and a thin covering of stubble on his chin.

'Shall we eat after? It won't take long for me to upload the images and show you where everything is.' Stella led the way into the flat and Jay followed. 'It's such a nice place.' He didn't seem nervous at all as they entered the living room, which helped Stella relax.

'I know it's a mess and ridiculously Seventies, but I'll get round to sorting it once I've got the business up and running. I'm going to have to do a little bit at a time.'

'Good idea.' Jay stood surveying the living room with his hands in his jeans pockets. It emphasised how flat his stomach was and Stella had to draw her eyes away. 'I see you've got your laptop all ready. Do you mind if I drive?'

'Drive?'

'Control the mouse,' he replied and there was something disarming about the slightly mischievous glint in his eyes.

'Oh, sure.' Stella giggled then hated herself. She never giggled.

She laughed or chuckled, and occasionally snorted when something was really funny, but she wasn't normally a giggler. She had to get a grip. 'Did you want red or white wine?'

Jay shook his jacket from his shoulders and hung it on the back of the dining chair. 'White would be great, thanks.'

Stella made her way to the kitchen. She'd never seen a navy jumper look so sexy on anyone before. She'd always associated navy jumpers with accountants or civil servants, but then Jay seemed to break the mould as far as his profession was concerned. She turned down the oven so the Brie and mushroom pie would stay warm while they worked, and poured two large glasses of wine before going back to the living room, already feeling a little hot and flustered. After handing a glass to Jay, Stella then pulled out a chair and sat down next to him. 'I'm really excited to see the website.'

'It's a big thing. I know everyone seems to have websites these days but a good one that's easily navigable is essential, especially for the holiday lets. Speaking of which, have you got the photos?'

'Yep.' She pulled a memory stick from her jeans pocket and handed it over. Hopefully he wouldn't notice it had gone a little warm. He took it and plugged it in and the photos she'd taken flashed up on the screen.

'There's some great shots here,' he said, his eyes fixed forwards and his fingers whizzing about.

'Thanks. Some little touches like a few cushions here and there made a huge difference.'

Jay looked up and smiled, then took a sip of his wine. Stella really couldn't fathom why he wasn't taken already. He was so handsome and easy to be around. From their previous dinner together and the telephone and text conversations they'd had, she knew he had a fun side but was still a gentleman. 'So …' And he began taking her through the details of the website and uploaded the pictures they chose together. The second flat was now ready for bookings and he showed her where everything on the website was and how to update it. He even suggested a blog. 'You might not get millions of people reading it, but you're a sweet, interesting person and I bet they'd love Frank. You could look at other social media too.'

'Do you really think so?' It was all alien to Stella, being such a private person, but if it helped the business she couldn't really ignore it.

'Yeah, definitely. I can then link them to the website once they're up and running. They're easy to do. Just follow the instructions on the sites, or let me know and I'll do it for you.' Stella's head was whirling. Jay had said she was sweet and interesting. If that was really what he thought of her then that was pretty amazing. She hadn't felt that way in a long time. He leaned his strong jaw on his hand as he clicked some buttons and his sweet grey-blue eyes were bright with enthusiasm. It was endearing and very, very sexy. After a moment he said, 'It's exciting stuff, isn't it?'

'It is,' she agreed, taking a sip of her drink.

He suddenly sat back, taking his wine glass and looking down into it. 'Sorry.'

'Sorry? For what?'

'For getting all excited about the website. I don't mean to. I just really enjoy my job.' He kept his eyes down and Stella swore he blushed.

'It's okay. I do it about the shop too. It's pretty amazing actually, loving what you do.'

'It is.' Jay stared into her eyes as they connected over this shared experience. The space between them felt small and she had a sudden urge to lean forward and kiss him, but when her wine splashed onto her finger where her glass was tipping, she sat back and thought about the matter at hand.

'I know I need a picture of the front of the shop. I'll get that done this week. As soon as we get a good day and I've repainted the sign.'

124

'You're repainting it yourself?'

Surprised at his question, Stella felt flustered. 'Yeah. I can't afford a sign writer and anyway, I think it'll look nice if it's a little higgledy-piggledy. I'll draw it out first, of course, but how hard can it be?' Did he think she was mad or not capable of doing it? A sudden bolt of insecurity shot through her and she felt slightly foolish, but his eyes stayed on her.

'I think you're absolutely amazing.'

A firework went off in Stella's heart and she felt its light and warmth fill her body. 'I wouldn't go that far. I'm just skint.' Jay's expressive laugh echoed around the room. 'I'd better check on dinner. Are you hungry?'

'Ravenous and it smells delicious.'

Stella hurried off while Jay shut down her laptop. When she came back he was waiting at the table. They ate a small starter of baked Camembert with crusty bread, chatting happily about his work and her plans for the future. Then he helped serve out the pie while Stella prepared the salad. Conversation moved on to their respective pasts. Her curiosity was piqued when he mentioned Miles. 'I saw him the other day,' said Jay, 'moaning on about losing the shop to you.'

'Was he?' Stella asked, her fork ready with food but she was unable to put it in her mouth.

'Well, I think he was. I mean, he could have been talking about something else and I've got the wrong end of the stick.' That was very sweet of Jay, but she was sure he hadn't. After their last exchange Stella wasn't at all surprised Miles was going around slagging her or her shop off. A prickle straightened her spine.

'If he was saying anything about a shop selling stupid, over-priced stock then he probably was talking about me. He came in the other day and basically said as much.' She sighed, exhaling the tension from her shoulders. 'He wanted the shop you see, and he thinks he could do all this a lot better than me.'

'Well, he's wrong there, isn't he?' Jay gently laid his hand on hers. 'Try not to worry about Miles. Like I said before, he's always thought he was better than everybody else in this town.' He glanced at her before continuing as if confirming to himself that he should say more. His vulnerable expression made Stella's heart thump. 'When we were kids,' he began slowly, 'he used to take the mickey out of me for my accent – for being common. Not pronouncing my t's properly.'

'What?' Who the blimmin' hell did he think he was? 'That's so mean.'

Jay gave a self-conscious laugh and scratched the back of his head. 'It wasn't great fun, but it was a long time ago. I'm sure he's sorry for it now.'

'How can you be so nice about it?' asked Stella. The moment she'd met Miles she'd known he was a snooty prick and the other day had only proved it.

'Sometimes you have to let bygones be bygones, don't you? We were both kids. I'm sure he knows he was an idiot back then. But like I said, I might have misheard or got the wrong end of the stick with what he was saying the other day, so best not to go accusing him of anything.'

'I won't,' Stella confirmed, admiring Jay's sensitive nature. 'I'll be happy if our paths never cross again. I certainly won't seek out opportunities to talk to him.'

Jay's sweet smile got the evening back on track and eventually Stella took out their dessert bowls, cleared now of the delectable profiteroles she'd got in the meal deal, and came back to find him sitting on the sofa having topped up their wine glasses and placed them on the coffee table.

It was gone eight o'clock, and the sun had finally set. The noise of the gulls had quietened and now only a few birds could be heard singing themselves to sleep. Stella's nerves threatened to get the better of her and take her to the armchair, but she pushed them down and sat next to Jay. If she was going to invite him to Isaac's wedding she was going to have to sit next to him at some point. In her mind, the time spent at the dinner table didn't count as it was for business, but sitting on the sofa felt decidedly more personal. He turned his body and his knee rested against hers. She'd expected a bolt of electricity to shoot through her but instead the nerves in her stomach grew fierce. Jay rested his arm on the back of the sofa and said, 'Now that all the business stuff's out of the way, I really have to tell you something.'

'Oh?' Her mouth was dry and she suddenly craved a large drink of water.

'I think you're the most beautiful woman I've ever seen.'

Stella wanted to reply but couldn't think of anything to say and then, before she could open her mouth, his left arm reached forwards and he cupped her face, drawing her towards him. For a second, Stella allowed him to lead, though something inside her brain warned her that she wasn't ready for this. His lips touched hers and his kiss was soft and gentle. He pulled away for a second, studying her face. Jay was without doubt the most handsome man she'd ever seen so what was happening? Why wasn't her body burning with anticipation? Why didn't she want this? He kissed her again, more passionately this time but Stella's brain simply paused. She'd imagined kissing him and how wonderful it would be, but for some reason it wasn't making her feel how she thought it would.

She put a hand to his chest to gently ease him away but he misread her signal and instead grabbed her fingers and pulled her closer, his kisses becoming more passionate and eager. He finally paused, whispering, 'Where's your bedroom?' and nuzzling her neck.

She pushed her hand more firmly into his chest. 'My—? No, wait.'

'Why? What's wrong?'

'I'm sorry. I'm just … I'm not ready.' Unable to read the emotion that passed over his face, she said again, 'I'm really sorry.'

127

'Right. I—' He shook his head. 'I'm sorry, I thought … I thought you wanted to—'

Stella felt her face flame. 'I thought I did too. I just … I haven't been with anyone else since my divorce. It's been a while and I thought I was ready, but I guess I'm not.' She stared down at her hands in her lap.

'Right.' Jay also kept his eyes down. 'I umm, I should probably go then.' Stella knew she should say no and ask him to stay but the fact was she wanted him to leave. Damn it, she was useless at relationships. Jay leapt off the sofa as if she'd just told him she had bubonic plague and grabbed his jacket from the back of the chair. Stella stood up to show him out. 'No, don't worry. I can see myself out.'

'I'm so sorry,' said Stella. 'I didn't mean to lead you on or anything.'

'Honestly, it's fine,' said Jay, but she could tell by his tone of voice that she'd hurt and embarrassed him. At the doorway to the living room he stopped and turned. 'I still think you're the most beautiful woman I've ever seen. I'm sorry if I came on too strong. I'll, umm, I'll see you around.'

Stella waited until she heard the shop door slam then flopped back down onto the sofa. She hated herself for being so ridiculous, so prim and proper. She didn't have to be in love to sleep with someone. She could just do it because she wanted to. She was an adult! But then her indignation subsided. Who was she kidding? She'd never been like that. She only ever found someone truly attractive after she knew their personality.

Anger rose up inside her at her own stupidity and ridiculously Victorian attitude, and she punched a cushion. Before long, tears threatened her eyes. As she picked up her book in an attempt to think of something else, a tear fell onto the page, soaking into the paper. Then another. She quickly wiped them away, cursing her own stupid heart, and went to bed.

Chapter 14

When Monday morning came, Stella didn't have time to think about Jay anymore or the debacle that was Saturday night. She just really hoped there weren't any website problems, because she couldn't face seeing or speaking to him right now. Over the weekend, she'd played that evening's events out again and again in her head, wondering whether to text and apologise. But what could she say that didn't make her sound crazy? And to make matters worse, the sex-mad couple in the first apartment had been at it all weekend reminding her constantly what she was missing out on. At least they were leaving today, hopefully on time, and her new arrival would be in this afternoon.

Mr Nicholas had booked for one person so she'd made his welcome basket less romantic and included Earl Grey tea, coffee, biscuits, and a nice bottle of red wine – the one she hadn't used on Saturday night. She shuddered again at the memory and pulled the cellophane tight, fastening the bow at the top. As check-out time was at ten o'clock and check-in wasn't until three that afternoon, Lexi was going to split the cleaning and do an hour from 11 a.m. to 12 p.m. and then again from 2 p.m. to 3 p.m. This meant Raina still had help in the café over lunchtime, Stella didn't have to shut the shop, and Lexi could nip out to grab the kids from school. Stella could also pop up during her lunch break and make sure everything was fine, which is where she was off to now. Frank was happily settled into his routine of sleeping in his bed at the end of the counter and didn't bark every time she left him, so she put up her closed sign, just for a moment, and nipped to the lower-floor flat, taking the welcome basket with her.

A beautiful bright sun shone down on her as she opened the front door to Admiral's Corner Apartments. Stella had already installed two bay trees either side of the front door and inside the entrance hall she'd placed a welcome mat. When she entered the lower-floor apartment, Lexi was mopping the wooden floor-boards, including the skirting boards. Stella marvelled at her thoroughness. 'I'm almost finished,' Lexi said, ringing out the mop once more.

'It looks amazing.' Stella's eyes scanned the room. The small side table in the entrance hall shone and there wasn't a cobweb or mark on the walls. Though she'd removed as much of them as she could there were still one or two stubborn stains she'd thought needed painting over. Somehow Lexi had got rid of them. Stella walked on and popped her head inside the bedroom. It had been beautifully made up with a set of new bedding, and the cushions propped up invitingly. In the living room the cream leather sofa had been waxed and one of the uglier blankets from the shop placed artistically over one end so it looked inviting and comfy. Amongst the pale creams and whites of the flat the blanket looked chic and elegant. And the whole place smelt of something warm and spicy. 'It smells amazing too.'

'It's a tip my mum gave me.' Lexi ceased her mopping for a moment. 'You sprinkle essential oil on the hoover filter, and I had some sandalwood left so I thought I'd use it in here.'

'That's genius.'

Lexi smiled. 'I know, right.'

A variety of books, purchased at the second-hand bookstore

down the road, had been laid out on the coffee table and everything was spotless. Stella placed the welcome basket down on the counter top. The only unsightly thing was the used bedding that sat in a pile on the kitchen floor but Stella would soon be taking that with her. 'I can't believe what an amazing job you've done, Lexi.' She laughed. 'I really don't know how you managed to do it in the time available. It would have taken me ages.' Lexi poured away the water from the bucket and rinsed out the sink.

'You did most of the work and the couple who just left were lovely even though they were sex-mad. They left you a tip. Here.' Lexi pushed a small plate towards her. 'It was in the bedroom.'

Stella eyed the note sitting in the tray. She'd never considered that there'd be tips. 'Gosh, Lexi, they left us a tenner.'

'I know and a really nice comment in your visitors' book. That's a brilliant idea by the way.'

'Thanks,' Stella replied. 'I read it on a website somewhere. Here.' She gave the ten-pound note to Lexi who shook her head.

'No way. I can't take that.'

'Yes, you can,' Stella insisted, seeing the small beads of sweat forming on her forehead just below her 1950s head scarf. She waved the note again. 'Here. You've cleaned the place. You should have it.'

'No thanks, really. Especially as it's from your first guests, I'd feel terrible. You should definitely have it.'

Stella looked at the note in her hands. She really wished Lexi would take it, knowing how hard things were at the moment, but if she was adamant it seemed there was no changing her mind and there's was no way Stella wanted her to feel like a charity case. 'Here's an idea then, why don't we put this towards a couple of coffees and huge slices of cake for you, me, Ralph and Taylor? I'm betting you haven't had any lunch yet.'

Lexi nodded. 'Now that's a good idea.'

Stella grabbed the dirty washing and Lexi placed the mop and bucket in its cupboard before they headed downstairs. 'I think this is going to work out perfectly,' Stella said.

'Me too,' agreed Lexi and for the first time in a couple of weeks Stella saw a smile that reached Lexi's eyes.

At about four o'clock, a strange-looking man entered the shop. Pale and pasty, with dark shadows under his eyes his long, floppy hair kept falling down and he pushed it back with a strange flick of his hand. Even though the day was quite bright and sunny he wore a long leather duster coat that swamped his thin frame, and he carried two old, battered leather holdalls. 'Good afternoon,' said Stella. 'Please let me know if I can help you with anything.'

'I'm looking for Stella Harris,' he said in a very posh Etonian voice that was completely at odds with his appearance. 'I was told to acquaint her at this wonderful place of business.'

'I'm Stella,' she replied, edging around Frank, holding out her hand for the gentleman to shake. 'Pleased to meet you.'

'I, my dear madam, am Carter Nicholas.' His long pale fingers wrapped around hers. 'It is a privilege bestowed upon me, by myself, that I have booked one of the Admiral's Corner Apartments for this forthcoming week.'

'Oh, yes.' Once Stella had translated what he'd said into normal English, she knew exactly who he was. 'Mr Nicholas, how lovely to meet you. Let me just grab the key and I'll take you round. Everything's ready for you.'

A thin smile came to the man's face giving it some life but he still looked like he needed a good meal and some iron tablets. 'Wunderbar. Wonderful. Absolutely smashing.'

Stella eyed his two holdalls. 'Would you like me to take your bags for you?'

'No, no. I couldn't possibly ask you to do such a thing. It's fine, thank you. Not only would it be the height of un-gentlemanly behaviour, but this one's full of books. It's quite heavy.' He lifted it a fraction to show its weightiness.

Stella led the way, locking the shop door behind her. She'd only be a few minutes and there was no other way around it. Mr Nicholas followed behind with big loping steps, his shoulders rounding forwards as if life was dragging him down. 'Do you like reading?' asked Stella, trying to make him feel welcome. 'Or are you researching something?' A whole holdall full of books was a lot even for the most voracious of readers.

'Both actually,' he replied. 'I'm a poet so I read a lot and I find inspiration in the words of the great Romantics. Byron, Shelley, Keats. Geniuses all.'

'Oh, I see.' Stella had hated poetry at school – all those metaphors and fluty language. She kept her opinion to herself though. It was a golden rule that you didn't go about insulting your paying guests. Not if you wanted them to stay. 'Well, here we go.' Stella opened the black front door, glad to see it shining in the sunlight. The new welcome mat with 'home from home' written on it was pristine as she stepped through to the flat. When she opened the door, she enjoyed the impressed look on Mr Nicholas's face as he walked in.

'This is lovely,' he said heading down the hall and examining each room. 'Wunderbar.' At the end of the hall he spun on the spot so his long leather duster fanned out like Batman's cape. 'This'll be perfect for my writing. I can feel the inspiration already.'

'You plan to write while you're here? Isn't that a bit of a busman's holiday?'

He gave a slight chuckle as he dropped the luggage at his feet. 'My work is my life,' he replied sincerely, his eyes becoming doe-like. Then he relaxed. 'That sounded very dramatic, didn't it? I apologise. Sometimes I can't help but write when the mood takes me. The words dance around my head like music and I just have to write them down no matter what time of the day or night it is.'

Stella smiled, trying to figure out how old he was. He must have been younger than her but not by much. He had faint lines around his mouth but there was a youthfulness caused by his soft-looking skin. Clearly keeping out of the sun was good beauty advice after all. 'There's a welcome basket in the kitchen and I can swap the red wine for white if you'd prefer it.'

'A bottle of red will be lovely, Stella, thank you. Perhaps you'd join me for a glass this evening?'

Stella's mouth formed a circle of surprise. Had the world suddenly gone mad? She'd spent the whole of her life as a wall-flower except for a handful of dates before she met her ex-husband and none since they'd separated. It seemed for all Carter Nicholas's appearance of self-conscious quiet he was fairly forward when it came to asking someone out. 'That's really very kind of you, but I've actually got plans this evening,' she lied. The only plans she had were with Frank and her own bottle of red wine, and right now that's all she wanted.

'Of course, you have. My apologies.' He gave a slight bow as he pressed his hand to his chest and Stella shuffled uncomfortably under his gaze.

'Well, I'll leave the keys with you, Mr Nicholas—'

'Please call me Carter.'

'Carter, then.' She handed over the keys explaining which one was for the flat and which one was for the front door then made her goodbyes.

When he responded with, 'Goodbye, beautiful lady. I can already feel the salt sea air pulsing through my veins. Did you know Shelley drowned at sea? I wonder if his soul lives in the waters still.'

Unsure what sort of response was required here, Stella said, 'Well, I hope you have a wonderful time.' And left trying to repress a giggle.

What a strange man, she thought as she turned the shop sign back to open. Frank was awake and barking when she walked in and she leaned down to give him a big fuss. Thinking of Carter's face again there was something quite attractive in that

Byronic love-lost persona. Perhaps it was the tired puppy-dog eyes. She decided to have a look on the internet for Carter Nicholas. It would at least make the last couple of hours go quickly.

On Saturday morning, Stella was up early and in the shop, changing a display after a sudden flash of inspiration the night before. After changing some of the teacups around she decided to head to Raina's and get her coffee before Carter had the chance. Since arriving on Monday, Carter had delivered a morning coffee to her at precisely 9 a.m. when she opened the shop, along with a phrase of poetry from one or other of the great Romantics on a torn sheet of lined A5 paper. Each time he renewed his offer of a drink that evening, which Stella politely declined. She had no intention of mixing business with pleasure after how well it had gone with Jay. She was a business-only girl from now on. The pile of love notes Carter had delivered so far sat under the shop counter weighed down by the hole punch.

'Hey, what are you doing here?' Stella said to Lexi, as she snuck into the café checking behind her in case Carter was up and about. The man kept such strange hours Stella wondered if he ever slept. Lexi smiled, somehow still looking amazing, even at this time of the morning.

'Carol called in sick. She's got a terrible cold so I said I'd cover. Will's having the kids for me this morning and I'm only here till lunchtime. Morning, Vivien.' Stella turned and Vivien arrived looking resplendent in a long red coat, wide-leg trousers that dwarfed her tiny frame and a bow-tie blouse. Her hair was, as usual, perfect. She waved, shuffled to a seat using her stick for support and sat down. 'You're early today, Vivien. Everything all right?' Her voice carried a note of concern that Stella immediately picked up on.

The old lady huffed. 'Oh, I couldn't sleep so I decided to treat myself to breakfast out and then I'll have a nap later if I need it.'

'Good idea,' Lexi replied, relaxing a little. 'Do you want your usual?' she asked Stella.

'Yes, please.'

'Usual for me too,' called Vivien and Lexi smiled.

'I knew that already, m'lady.'

'How are you, Vivien?' asked Stella, joining her at the table. 'Do you mind if I join you for a minute?'

'Not at all, dear. And I'm very well, thank you. I'm going to get some shopping and I thought I might stop in at that nice little deli and get myself something posh for lunch.' Her small hands were laid delicately in her lap.

Stella was growing fonder and fonder of the old lady. 'Why not – you should definitely enjoy your retirement. I'm sure all those years in the opera had you working very long hours.'

'Oh, they certainly did. And we played hard as well as worked hard.' She sat back and patted her hair. 'They were very good times. Anyway, who have you got staying this week?' Lexi came over and deposited their drinks on the table then pulled out a seat and joined them for a moment.

'I've got a poet called Carter Nicholas.'

'Never heard of him,' Vivien replied.

'No, I hadn't either. So I searched for him on the internet and it turns out he's quite well-known. There were a few newspaper articles about him and he's won some posh prizes too. I didn't get a chance to actually read any of his poetry though.' Stella had been quite surprised at the findings and at having a prestigious poet staying in her humble holiday let. She just wished he'd stop with the poetry lessons every morning.

'Is he young?' asked Lexi.

'He's about my age I'd say. Maybe a bit younger.'

'I knew a poet once,' Vivien added with a dreamy, faraway look in her eye. 'His name was Gus and he wrote the most beautiful things. He was a little too obsessed with death though, for my liking. But most poets are, aren't they?'

'Was he one of the ones who proposed?' asked Lexi, sipping her coffee.

'Oh, yes, dear. Poor thing fell madly in love with me and was utterly heartbroken when I broke it off.' Stella suppressed a smile. It was difficult to tell how much of what Vivien said was actually true and how much of it was made up, or to be kinder, embellishments of the truth, but regardless, Stella loved listening to her stories. 'There's something rather wonderful about a poet's soul,' she continued. 'They're so romantic and turbulent. My affair was rather exciting for a while, then it all got quite tedious and I told him that he couldn't keep behaving like a hormonal teenager and had to grow up.'

'What happened next?' asked Stella, the strong flavour of her coffee waking up her taste buds.

A rather smug expression came to Vivien's face. 'He called me a cow and told me I didn't understand him. So I threw a vase at his head.'

Stella laughed. 'Sounds like you were quite tempestuous yourself.'

'I was. I was.' Vivien picked up her cup and saucer and sipped her tea.

'Let me get your toast,' said Lexi.

'And I'd better get back to work,' Stella replied. 'Here's hoping for a busy day.'

Just then there was a knock at the window and Stella looked up to see Carter peering through the glass, waving at her. He opened the door and came in.

'Good morning, beautiful creature. Good morning.'

'Good morning, young man,' replied Vivien. Stella didn't have the heart to say he'd been referring to her. He'd taken to calling her that and no matter how many times she asked him to stop, he didn't.

'May I join you?' Carter asked Vivien, flicking his hair back out of his eyes.

'Of course. You must be Stella's poet.'

'He's not *my* poet,' she said, quickly. Then felt herself blushing.

'I am indeed.' Carter glanced over his shoulder at Stella and she had to admit his eyes were rather sparkly. 'Would that I were more than her merest poet but alas …' He let the sentence trail away with a sad look in his eye. 'And you are?' he asked Vivien.

'My name's Vivien Griffen. You may remember me. I was an opera singer you know.'

'The name does ring a bell.' He was clearly lying to make her feel better, which was quite sweet. Stella decided to rescue him.

'Do you need anything, Mr Nicholas?' she asked.

'Carter, please. My dearest lady, I have asked – nay pleaded – that you call me Carter. Mr Nicholas sounds so old-fashioned.' At this Stella had to bite her lip. It was truly ironic given that he spoke like something out of a Shakespeare play. 'And no, not really. As you've beaten me in purchasing a finely made beverage for yourself this morning, I thought I'd drop this in to you.' He handed her the latest love note. Stella gave it a cursory glance as her cheeks began to flame in embarrassment. 'And I thought I'd see if I could tempt you to join me in a glass of wine this evening?'

Oh, for goodness' sake, thought Stella. Why wouldn't he just stop? 'That's really, very kind of you, Mr Nicholas—'

'Carter.'

'Carter. But I'm afraid I already have plans for tonight.' This time she wasn't lying. She was going to Lexi's and had no intention of cancelling.

'Oh, dear, that is a shame. Well, I shall try again tomorrow. "Faint heart never won fair maid,"' he proclaimed, raising a finger in the air. 'Perhaps next time.'

'Yes. Sorry.'

Carter sighed dramatically. 'Well, then I shall continue on with my walk. I can feel the souls of Byron and Shelley calling me towards the sea. It's doing wonders for my creative juices.' He flashed his eyes as he spoke and Stella heard Lexi hide her laugh behind a spluttery cough. Men didn't normally mention their juices to her. He waved goodbye to them all with a theatrical flourish and after the door had closed behind him and he'd walked off down the street, she turned to Lexi and rolled her eyes.

'That man never gives up. He's asked me every day if I'll have a drink with him and every single day I say no and he acts like I've never rejected him at all. He's either got the hide of a rhinoceros or he's deaf.'

'He must like you very much,' said Vivien.

'He can't do, he doesn't even know me. And anyway, I'm just not interested.'

'He was very handsome though.' Vivien leaned forwards trying to catch a glimpse of him as he went off down the street.

'Was he?'

'Yes, he was,' said Lexi. 'Definitely.'

'Oh.' Stella had never thought to look at him like that but he was a very nice, gentle man, even if he did speak like Ian McKellen. The love notes he gave her daily caused her acute embarrassment but were well-chosen romantic lines. Thinking now, his face had got some colour since coming to stay. The fresh air and brisk walks had brought a pinkness to his cheeks so his skin wasn't so sallow, and the dark circles had lessened his look of illness.

'I would,' said Lexi, with a mischievous grin.

Stella was agog. Not only was it too early in the day for this conversation but she'd never really considered how attractive Carter might actually be. 'Would you?'

'I would too,' replied Vivien. 'If I was twenty years younger.'

Stella's wide-eyed gaze shot to the older woman and Lexi giggled as she replied. 'If you were twenty years younger, Vivien, you'd still be forty years too old.'

'Cheeky girl,' Vivien harrumphed.

'Right, back to work for me,' said Stella, grabbing her coffee cup and taking it to the counter. 'I might have a top-up before I go though, Lexi. I think with Carter around I'm going to need it.'

The day was bright and sunny and though the air was still slightly cool, life felt exciting and full of colour. Spring was bursting into life all around her and the breeze carried a faint tang of salt from the sea. Across from her, the blossoms on the trees in the churchyard were growing from tiny pink spots to sweet little flowers. Even better, the shop was busy and time passed quickly.

Stella had made some good sales and moving around the stock had resulted in a few more of the older pieces Herbert had left finally leaving the building. By the time the evening came, Stella couldn't wait to kick back with Lexi and have a good chinwag over a bottle of wine. They were meeting at Lexi's at seven, after the kids were in bed. Stella had a sneaking suspicion the kids wouldn't be sound asleep when she arrived, but having seen them a few times in the café and a couple of times in the shop she didn't mind. In fact, she liked them very much. As much as she liked her own niece and nephew, if not more. Ralph and Taylor hadn't developed the sense of entitlement her niece and nephew sometimes had, according to her sister. The product of having money, Stella presumed.

Lexi had kindly said that Stella could bring Frank and so, at just gone half past six, Stella zipped up her coat, popped Frank's lead on, and they headed off for Lexi's house. Just as she was leaving the shop, Carter came out of the apartment clutching some papers.

'Hello, dearest, most beautiful creature. I was hoping to catch you.' His dark eyes had a slight twinkle to them, Stella noticed, as he flicked his hair back from his face with that odd, yet endearing movement.

'I'm just going out I'm afraid, Carter.' Stella pulled Frank back from sniffing Carter's long leather coat. She was a little worried he might start chewing on it.

'Oh. Oh, I see.' His eyes dropped to the floor and this time he seemed genuinely crestfallen. 'That's a shame. I've just written something amazing and I did so dearly want you to read it.'

'Me?' Why Carter would want her to read his poetry was beyond her. She hadn't claimed to know anything about poetry or even to particularly enjoy it. 'That's very kind of you but I'm sorry, Carter, I'd be a terrible critic. I know absolutely nothing about poetry.'

'But you don't need to be a critic, you just need to tell me if you like it.' He rolled the papers in his hand. Stella noticed how his smile was slightly lopsided. Perhaps Lexi wasn't so crazy after all, but she had to get on.

'Sorry.' Stella smiled apologetically. 'But I really have to get going or I'm going to be late. I'll see you later.' She pulled Frank's lead and guided him forwards. 'Walk on, boy.' She didn't turn around, afraid that Carter might be stood there dramatically clutching his scribblings to his chest. Stella pressed her lips together trying to stop the smile but once they were a good few paces ahead she let it engulf her. She couldn't wait to tell Lexi what she'd found on the internet about Carter Nicholas after a little more searching today.

The walk to Lexi's house gave Stella the chance to see other parts of Swallowtail Bay she hadn't explored before. As she walked the length of the cobbled high street and came out the other side towards roads filled with houses, the sun had almost set. An inky darkness flooded the sky with heavy stripes as she left the larger, more exclusive homes behind. Further on, it was clear she had left the posh part of town as the grand Victorian terraces were replaced with bungalows and quiet cul-de-sacs. Swallowtail Bay had been a small fishing village but as it had grown, the outer edges had housed a mining community thanks to the coal mine a couple of miles away.

Lexi's house wasn't quite on the edge of town, but it was a good mile from Stella's. Lexi had told her that all these houses were built for the coal miners and their families and had been little communities of their own. Stella could imagine it well: everyone knowing everyone else, neighbour looking out for neighbour. Even now, it seemed friendlier than the poshest part of town where Miles and Stella lived, where the houses, like their owners, seemed to look down on each other. The small patch of lawn in front of Lexi's house, enclosed by a tatty fence, was scrubby and littered with an assortment of footballs, some flat, some still round. Stella knocked on the door and Lexi opened it looking a little flustered.

'Hi.' She stood to one side. 'The kids should be in bed but they're not going quietly.'

Knowing how excited they got when they saw the fat little dog, Stella said, 'I'd better hide Frank then.'

'Yes, might be best. Come this way.' Lexi led Stella through the house to the back door and opened it to reveal a tidy back garden, half decked and half lawned. Two kids' bikes were leaning against the high fence that went all the way around. 'He can't get out,' she said. 'You'll be fine to let him off the lead.' Lexi started walking back into the house and Stella noticed how at ease she felt already. She unclipped the lead and Frank tore off to the bottom of the garden to chase a bird that had swooped in and immediately thought better of it. She left him happily sniffing his way around and went back inside just as Lexi shouted up the stairs. 'And if I have to come up there again you'll both lose your TV time tomorrow. Do you hear me?' A muffled grumble came back in reply. 'Hey babes,' she said, as she turned to Stella, all traces of the annoyed mum voice gone. 'I might have to murder my children but you don't mind, do you?'

Stella laughed. 'Not at all. How are they?'

'They're both being absolute dicks. It's like a tag team. As soon as one starts settling the other plays up. I've told them if they come down again I'm going to make them live in the attic with the spiders.'

'Mum?' called Ralph from the top of the stairs.

Lexi took a deep breath. 'Yes?'

'Can I have something to eat?'

'No!' Her hands shot to her hips. 'I've already told you twice, you've had dinner, pudding, two oaty biscuits, a yoghurt, a banana and a glass of milk. You're not having anything else. You'll only moan and tell me you've got tummy ache. Now go to bed, please.' She turned to Stella. 'I might as well have his ears surgically removed for all the good they are.'

'Can you tuck me in again?' called Ralph in a small, sweet voice.

'I'll be up in a minute,' Lexi replied, turning to Stella with a grin. 'Do you mind opening the wine?'

Stella went into the kitchen and let Frank back in from the garden. Though they weren't as close as some and never had been, she missed her sister and seeing her niece and nephew. Sometimes she felt so removed from them that she may as well have been on Mars. She really wanted to be Aunty Stella to Ralph and Taylor one day. Being called an aunty to your friend's children seemed even more special in a way.

'Busy day?' asked Lexi returning a moment later.

'Pretty good actually. I got some more of the old stuff shifted but I could really do with selling another painting or two.'

Lexi leaned back against the kitchen counter. 'Perhaps you need to organise an exhibition?'

Stella felt her eyebrows knit together as she thought. 'Like an art exhibition?'

'Yeah. We don't have many art galleries here. There's one down the other end of the high street but it does really weird super expensive stuff.'

'That's a great idea, Lexi,' cried Stella. 'I could do a whole meet the artists thing in the shop. Lexi, it's genius! I could clear out everything else and make it an exhibition space for a weekend. If I got everything on Sale or Return, or even took commission I wouldn't have to buy stock. Lexi, you are so clever!'

'I try my best,' she said handing Stella a very large wine glass full to the brim, then picked up her own and they clinked glasses. Lexi went into the living room and they flopped onto the comfortable sofas. 'So, tell me more about this amazing poet you've got staying. He's handsome in a Kiefer Sutherland in *The Lost Boys* kind of way but without the rugged sexiness. He's more a die-of-a-broken-heart type.'

'He is quite soppy,' said Stella, 'and his poetry's a bit intense.'

'Is it?' said Lexi. 'I can't imagine that.'

Stella nodded, grinning widely. 'With him going on about the Romantic poets I was expecting his stuff to be all old-fashioned and lovelorn, but I read one of his earlier that was all about decaying carcasses and lizard men from another planet wiping out the human race.'

Lexi's eyes widened in surprise. 'Really? Yuck, I don't fancy that much.'

'Me neither.' Stella took a sip of her wine. 'He asked me to read some just as I was leaving. Hopefully it won't be anything like that. He wanted me to tell him if I liked it and I'm not sure I'm a good enough liar to give a convincing reply. I know I'm still learning about the hospitality business but I do know it doesn't do to go around insulting your guests.'

'Best get your reply ready then. You don't want to have to make something up on the spot if he's written about lizard aliens taking over the world. Vivien was quite smitten with him. She's terrible. You'd think at her age she wouldn't even be thinking about sex.'

Stella had often wondered about Vivien and her stories and who better than Lexi to tell her the truth about the old girl. 'Are all the things she says true?'

'What? All the stuff about these legions of men falling madly in love with her? Yes, I think so. She certainly has a lot of photos of famous people in her house.'

'Have you been to her house much?' asked Stella.

'Yeah. You know I do some shopping for her each week now she's getting a bit older and there are quite a few photos of handsome young men on her mantelpiece. I'm not sure she knew all these great opera singers though or if she was a bit more middle of the road than she makes out. I had a little look on the internet when I first met her and she did sing in Vienna.'

'She's quite a character. I do like her.'

'That she is,' Lexi replied, smiling fondly. 'There's a few pictures of Miles too. He's maybe in his twenties in them. Maybe younger.'

'Miles?' Stella couldn't believe what she was hearing. Though she knew they were friendly she was very surprised to hear that there were pictures of him as a young man in Vivien's house. She hadn't realised their friendship extended so far back.

'Yeah. He's known her for years – since he was little.'

'Oh.' This revelation was showing a loyal, kind side to Miles that seemed completely at odds with Jay's description of him and what she'd experienced herself. As if reading her mind, Lexi mentioned the man she'd been trying to forget.

'How was Jay the other night?'

Stella paused, her skin prickling as she recalled the events. She hadn't told Lexi about Jay yet, having decided it was something she wanted to put behind her. Embarrassment caused her walls to build back up. But taking a sip of her wine and letting the warmth slide down into her tummy, she decided to tell the truth. 'Funny you should ask.' And she shared with Lexi the details of and told her of her stupid reaction to such a handsome man. 'I'm so embarrassed,' Stella said when she'd finished. 'I haven't seen him since. Or texted. I wouldn't even know what to say.'

'He's always seemed such a nice guy,' said Lexi. 'I'm sure he'll send you a text or something soon just to put your mind at rest that everything's cool.'

'I hope so. With being so busy it feels like it was ages ago but I suppose it really wasn't.' Frank came and curled up on her lap and she mindlessly stroked his long, soft coat. 'Do you ever miss sex, Lexi?'

'Not at all,' she replied. 'That's how I'll know when I've met someone worthwhile. I'll start to care about it again. At the moment, I get into bed and I can just about keep my eyes open to take my make-up off. Plus, after the kids were born I didn't feel like a woman anymore. I felt like a worn-out dishcloth most of the time. Still do now. Sex was the last thing on my mind.' Her tone changed slightly, tinged with disappointment and resignation. 'And when Will used to come home from the pub, having left me with the kids all evening, stinking of beer, it didn't exactly turn me on. I was just so tired from dealing with everything on my own all I wanted was to sleep. He couldn't quite understand that him rocking up and giving me a sloppy booze-ridden kiss and a quick squeeze wasn't enough to get me in the mood. I mean, don't get me wrong, I love my kids more than anything else in the world and I'd never be without them, but it is pretty non-stop. What about you?'

Lexi's honesty surprised Stella, given that she'd never said so much about her marriage before. She'd obviously felt incredibly low at times and had to struggle on without the emotional support she needed. Stella shrugged in answer to Lexi's question. 'Sometimes. Not as often as I used to. I've never been one to leap into bed straight away. It takes me a while to feel comfortable enough to do that. When everyone else at uni was having one-night stands I could never bring myself to do it. Even when I really tried. I think, like you, I need to feel loved and have a deeper connection.'

'I'm sure you'll meet someone soon who ticks all the boxes,' said Lexi.

'I'd better,' Stella replied, swilling her wine in the glass. 'I still need to find someone to invite to this wedding. And that definitely won't be Jay now.'

Chapter 15

Miles sat opposite Kiera in the nice seafood restaurant just down the road from their house. It was small, local and friendly, completely unlike the fancy restaurant at the Langdon Mansion Hotel. That was where Kiera had wanted to go for dinner tonight but Miles had left it too late to get a reservation. He'd been away all week on jobs up north and had completely forgotten to call them. By the time he'd remembered, no amount of pleading with the snooty maître d' had conjured up a table on a busy Saturday night and Kiera had sulked ever since he'd broken the news.

The cheerful notes of Van Morrison sounded from the speakers and Miles noticed other couples chatting or bobbing their heads to the music. Everyone else seemed relaxed and happy, but he was feeling distinctly on edge. Through the week, when he'd called and spoken with Kiera, there'd been a tension that travelled over the distance, seeping into his body. For some reason, they didn't seem to be getting on as well lately.

Tonight, the gentle light from the long tapered candle stuffed into a wine bottle lit Kiera's face, but she eyed it disdainfully and picked up her wine glass. Miles tried to ignore the sinking feeling settling in his stomach.

This had been their favourite restaurant once upon a time. At the moment that time felt like eons ago. He still loved it here. Loved the way the walls were covered in nautical paintings. None of them were famous, at least, he didn't think they were. Some were landscapes, some of ships or docks from all different eras. He especially liked the way the handrail along the bar was made of thick mariner's rope. He'd asked for a seat by the window and the friendly staff had been only too happy to oblige – service he couldn't imagine getting at the Langdon Mansion that seemed more of a do-what-you're-told kind of place. They were opposite the beach and from their table he could see a bright white moon glittering off the calm water below.

'Are you okay?' asked Miles.

Kiera huffed. 'I'm just bored of this place.'

'Don't you like it in here anymore?' Miles ran his fingers over the thick wooden table top feeling the nicks and crevices.

'It's all right,' she said with a shrug. 'I was hoping for something more classy.' She leaned forwards. 'My friends are texting me all the time to find out where things I'm wearing or looking at for the wedding are from, and what I'm doing for invitations and stuff. They're beyond jealous.' She started scrolling through her phone. 'I really wanted to go to our wedding venue tonight to post some pictures of the ballroom, but you didn't get a reservation.'

Stress stiffened his shoulders, but Miles was determined not to have a row. They'd been bickering a lot lately and he'd wanted tonight to be like old times. 'Isn't there something here you could use?'

'No,' she scoffed. 'I mean candles in wine bottles? It's so mid-Nineties.' Miles thought about saying that this place had been fine before but chose not to. There was no point.

At first, Kiera's enthusiasm for the wedding had been infectious and reassured Miles it was the right thing for them both, but lately it had turned from excitement to a spitefulness about her friends and the local area that had surprised and unnerved him. While he'd been away this week, sat alone in his room at the Travelodge, he'd realised that if he added up the time they'd spent together in the same space it didn't actually amount to much, even though they'd been a couple for almost four years.

A faint warning bell began to sound that he wanted to pretend was tinnitus. The truth was, he was seeing a different side to Kiera at the moment, or, he thought with a creeping dread, he was seeing a side that had always been there but he hadn't realised it. Kiera was getting more and more obsessed with making her friends jealous and it sent a shiver down his spine. He'd really wanted to reconnect with her this evening, to talk about some of the things they used to – movies, TV shows, music – the stuff other couples talked about all the time. In the past, their conversations had flowed so easily but lately they were becoming stilted and strained. Perhaps though, he was being grumpy. He was feeling very tired tonight.

The waitress came over to take their order and Kiera looked up from her menu, scrunching up her nose. 'Do you know when the menu will be changing? It's been the same for ages and I'd so love something different. To be honest, I'm bored of this now.' She closed the menu and waved it at the waitress.

Slightly thrown, the waitress said, 'Oh, umm, I'm afraid I don't know. I'd have to ask the manager, but I can certainly pass on your comments.'

'Yes, please do that,' Kiera replied. 'Otherwise people will stop coming. I know I won't be coming back until there's something different to have. There's the Langdon Mansion just up the road now, so you've got some big competition. The food there is much, much better.'

Miles opened his mouth to speak because not only had Kiera been unspeakably rude but also they'd never actually eaten there so Kiera had no idea if the food really was better or not. It was certainly more expensive and more fancy-sounding, but that didn't mean it tasted better. Miles glanced at the waitress apologetically. 'What are you having for a starter, sweetheart?'

Kiera sighed and read her menu once more. 'I suppose I'll have the scallops *again* and then the Dover sole.'

Miles gave his order and said, 'Thank you,' as Kiera clearly wasn't going to. He took the menus and handed them back.

How could Kiera not like this place anymore? The staff were so friendly and helpful, the food gorgeous, and the roaring log fire was perfect on a chilly spring night like tonight. Miles took a moment to watch the beautiful colours of the flames and listen to the comforting crackling sounds. Kiera took out her mobile phone and started tapping away on the screen. 'What are you doing?' he asked, nicely. He was careful to keep his tone light so as not to provoke her.

'I'm just tweeting about how awful this place is.'

'You can't do that,' Miles said quickly, leaning over the table. He hated this side of social media. Everyone felt free to tell everyone else how wrong they were. Sometimes he really thought that no matter how good Twitter and these things were, life was better without them.

Kiera looked up and her features were arranged in a horrible sneer. 'Why not?'

'Because this is our local restaurant. We won't ever be able to come back here if you do that and they find out.'

'Who cares if they do? It is awful.'

Miles ran his fingers over the table top again. 'No it's not, it's fine. It's completely fine. You're just being—'

'What? What am I being?'

Her voice was rising and Miles searched his mind like it was a thesaurus, trying to find the right words. *Unreasonable?* No, he'd get the silent treatment all evening. *Rude?* Definitely not. That would put him on the sofa tonight. *Snobby?* Not a chance. He'd get a firm slap before he reached the second syllable. 'I think you're just being a bit … sensitive to things at the moment.'

'Oh, am I?' She flicked her hair over her shoulder in annoyance and sat back, watching him. Before he had chance to answer she continued. 'Anyway, I've sent it now.'

Miles felt a wave of panic. Was he making too much of this? Being too sensitive himself because he loved this town and felt protective towards it? 'You really shouldn't have done that, Kiera. You can't go slagging people off.'

'I really don't see why not,' she replied, sarcastically. 'I'm allowed an opinion.'

'Of course you are, but we live here. They'll find out. And don't you see that the things you do affect me as well?'

Kiera's disdainful expression cut straight to Miles's heart. 'It doesn't affect you at all.'

'Of course it does.' He ran a hand through his hair in frustration. It was growing longer and beginning to curl again. 'I live here too. And I like it here. Now I can't eat at my favourite restaurant anymore.'

'*This* is your favourite restaurant?' she mocked.

'It used to be yours.' He took another sip of wine, trying to relax.

Kiera shrugged, her anger seeming to abate. 'Well, now I know better. Besides, I was thinking that once we were married we could look at moving to London.'

The pit of Miles's stomach dropped to the floor. Kiera knew how much he loved it here, that he wanted to settle and raise a family here by the seaside. Somewhere green with wide open spaces. And Kiera, he'd thought, was on board with the idea too. Although she'd mentioned moving to London when they first got together, she hadn't spoken of it for a long time and he'd assumed that as with some of the jobs she'd tried, she'd simply lost interest. He'd thought she was happy with the way their life was going. Had he been wrong?

'London is the kind of lifestyle we *should* be having, Miles,' she continued. 'Not being stuck in this place with only three different restaurants.'

'I thought you were happy here,' he said, concern threading through his voice though he kept it low.

A tap at the window drew his attention and Miles looked up to see Jay and he felt his insides tumble. He was clearly waving at Kiera who responded with a wide smile. Jay then nodded in Miles's direction and walked on into the night. Kiera watched him go until he was out of sight but then kept gazing out of the window. He wondered what was going through her brain. When she turned to look at him again, she'd softened.

'Let's talk about something else.'

Miles felt his shoulders relax a little, thankful for the change of topic. Hopefully now they could get back to reconnecting. 'Have you had any new clients lately?'

'A few enquiries,' Kiera replied, sipping her drink. 'But no one who's worth my time.'

'Oh. I thought personal shoppers helped everyone.'

'I'm not going to spend hours on tedious mums who are only going to bore me to death talking about their children, and go back to being part of the jeans and jumper brigade two days afterwards. It's a complete waste of my time and beyond boring.'

He was unable to hide his shocked reaction and Kiera glared at him challengingly then dropped her eyes to her glass. From the corner of his eye he saw the waitress pause behind the pillar, plaster on a smile and bring their food. They must be the worst customers in the world and he felt humiliation burn his skin.

'Is there anything else I can get you?' she asked in a cheery voice after putting the plates on the table.

'No, that's fine, thank you,' said Miles.

Again forgetting to say thank you, Kiera sighed, pulled out her napkin and made out that there was a plate of sprouts in front of her rather than a delicious meal that she hadn't had to prepare herself. Miles tried to save the evening and bring the conversation back to more neutral territory.

'I'm away again next week from Tuesday. I'm back up north.

A couple of the companies loved my pitches. I think I'm quite close to sealing the deal.'

'Okay,' said Kiera with absolutely no enthusiasm whatsoever and silence descended.

Miles spread his smoked mackerel pâté onto a piece of warm, freshly made bread, savouring the enticing aromas, and popped it into his mouth. However good the Langdon Mansion Hotel was, he couldn't imagine it making anything better than this. The smoky taste tingled his taste buds and the warm, soft bread was deliciously chewy. But as soon as he swallowed, his mind kept wandering to the woman before him. The woman he felt he'd never known before.

How could someone have changed so much in such a short amount of time? Or had she always been like this and he'd never noticed? Hopefully it was just wedding stress and once they were married he'd have back the woman he fell in love with. When they'd first got together she was a strange mixture of confidence and vulnerability. Those flashes of insecurity had spoken to his protective side but, somewhere along the line, they'd diminished and now there were times when her self-confidence bordered on arrogance.

Miles shook his head, admonishing himself for thinking such things about the woman he loved, the woman he was about to marry. But it had left him with another disconcerting question floating around his already crowded and confused mind. One that he suspected he already knew the answer to: had he changed that way too?

Chapter 16

After a wonderful evening spent at Lexi's, Stella approached the door to the shop, fumbling in her pocket for her keys. She suddenly realised how tired and squiffy she was and told herself off for not having more control. And she wasn't just physically tired, she was tired of being on her own. More than anything she wanted to be held by someone who cared about her.

A sudden surge in her heart made her glimpse at Miles's window. A light was on, but she didn't see anyone. Not that she wanted to be held by *him*. She had no idea why her head had turned his way. But thinking back to what Lexi had said about him and Vivien, could it be there was a loyalty somewhere within him under that harsh exterior? Most teenage boys wouldn't be seen dead with an old lady and that he was still friends with her now showed an unusual level of devotion. She still couldn't figure him out though and all that Jay had told her weighed heavily on her mind. Maybe it was the idea of loyalty or faithfulness she craved right now. Though Jay had many positives, perhaps that had been lacking and that was why she hadn't connected with him enough to sleep with him. Frank pulled at his lead and Stella shivered in the cold, clear night.

As she drew her eyes down from gazing at the stars, she noticed there was a single red rose taped to the door along with a note. It was a poem. A terrible poem left by Carter. Thankfully, not his usual fare of post-apocalyptic lizard men and the end of the human race, but a love poem full of emotion and romantic notions. Stella giggled as she read it. He really should stick to writing about miserable things, but she appreciated the sentiment. And there were one or two phrases that caught her eye. The poem was about a hard-working woman whom he referred to as the 'beautiful creature', or 'Aphrodite' and amongst the drivel – phrases like, 'My heart is overflowing with love, you fit me like a hand in a glove,' – the way he described the woman's heart and soul was quite touching.

Stella's hand flew to her heart as she read it in the lamplight, realising it was about her. The coffee-coloured hair and brown eyes told her so. But in amongst the terrible rhymes he described her as having a gentle soul, a heart begging to be given to others and a spirit that called to the wounded. Stella held the single, perfect red rose. You had to admire the effort.

This was the poem he had tried to show her earlier, Stella realised with a stab of guilt, then a warm, fuzzy feeling grew inside at the idea of someone being so in love with her they wrote her poetry. No one had ever done that for her before. A strange longing for strong arms around her began to build. For someone to kiss her and make her feel like a woman again. Sometimes she felt so much like a robot it was scary. And Carter wasn't unattractive. Lexi and Vivien had said he was handsome, and now she pictured his face she could see it too. Stella hesitated for a moment. She didn't want things to end up the way they had with Jay. But would they?

The problem with Jay was that he was so good-looking it was intimidating. She'd felt at such a disadvantage to him, like she wasn't on a level playing field. He'd been in charge and that had made her feel weak and vulnerable. But did she feel like that now? No, she didn't. It wasn't that she felt Carter was beneath her or anything so pompous. It was more that she felt equal to him and picturing his face in her mind she realised how harshly she'd judged him.

A light was still on in the apartment and Stella hoped for a glimpse of him. She spotted him at the window and he looked back at her warmly. If she knocked on that door she knew what would happen, but the thought of it didn't fill her with fear as it had with Jay. Something stirred. Something she hadn't felt in a long time: a yearning, and a readiness to let feelings back in she'd kept at bay. Taking Frank through to the flat, she popped him into her bed before heading back outside.

Somehow she knew that Carter would be a gentle and caring lover, which was what she wanted right now. It had been a very, very long time since she'd spent the night with anyone, and he would hold her close and encircle her with his arms, chasing the loneliness away. Stella closed the shop door behind her and carried on without looking back. With each step her heart raced faster and her stomach knotted with anticipation. Her hand hesitated at the door to the apartment, and she took a deep breath before knocking.

Carter opened, wearing a plain white T-shirt and grey jogging bottoms. His hair was ruffled and messy and he stood back, his smile one of surprise but still gentle and welcoming. Stella stumbled over her words still clutching his poem and the rose. 'Umm, thanks for the poem. It's umm … it's very nice of you.'

'Did you like it?' he asked softly.

'Very much. No one's ever written me a poem before.'

He opened the door a little wider. 'Did you want to come in? I just opened the Baileys hoping you'd knock.'

Baileys? The idea of him running to the fridge and opening a bottle of Irish cream liqueur made her want to giggle. It wasn't exactly champagne on ice, but luckily, she quite liked Baileys. She thought about it for a moment, making doubly sure she was ready. His meaning was clear – her meaning was clear. What else would she be doing knocking on his door in the middle of the night? And he was leaving on Monday. Stella knew that unlike with Jay, she really wanted this and after swallowing down her nerves amid rising anticipation, she answered, 'Yes, please.'

And the door closed behind her.

A bright light shone in Stella's eyes and she opened them slowly. She was still in Carter's bed and he was fast asleep next to her. Rose petals covered the floor where he'd sprinkled them over the bed and she spotted one out of the corner of her eye, dangling from her hair. She hoped there weren't any stuck to her bum. A bubble of excitement then fear churned in her stomach. A part of her wanted to stay there. The night had been wonderful, if a little over-the-top romantic with lit candles and piano music playing. She'd forgotten how enjoyable sex could be and she'd missed feeling that physically close to someone. She wondered if he might accompany her to Isaac's wedding, but she didn't have time to ponder the thought any further; she had to go and walk Frank. The poor thing would be wondering where she was. In fact, she could hear him barking.

Stella grabbed her underwear from the floor next to the bed, shaking out even more rose petals from her bra, and tried putting it on without getting out from under the covers or waking Carter. She hadn't missed the awkward morning-after moments. Finding her jeans and T-shirt she pulled them on and carried her shoes to the door. Carter never stirred as she slipped outside, but there seemed to be an unspoken understanding of each other's expectations. A beautiful day had dawned, she noticed as she walked out into the street. The sun blinded her and she shielded her eyes against it.

'Oh, there you are,' said a male voice. She turned to see Miles. His eyes were narrowed and Stella was unsure if it was caused by the bright morning sun or if he was being his normal judgemental self. 'Did you know your dog's been barking for the last half an hour?'

'Really? I didn't realise it was that long.' Poor Frank. Another petal fell from the back of her head and floated on the gentle breeze down to the ground. Stella watched it, as did Miles with wide surprised eyes. Clearing her throat, she edged around him and unlocked the shop.

The door connecting the shop and the entrance hall of the flat was closed but Stella could hear Frank on the other side barking and scratching to get out. 'Hello, darling,' Stella said, opening the door. Frank waddled towards her, his tail wagging so much he did a strange sideways shuffle. He jumped up and began licking her outstretched hand. 'Hello, my boy. Here I am.' Miles was still watching her from the shop door. 'Did you want something?' Stella asked. If he was going to start moaning at her about the noise Frank had made she'd have to try very hard to keep her temper. Her mouth felt like someone had thrown sawdust in it and her head was thumping. She'd enjoyed the sex last night but a part of her felt like some sleep would have been a better choice. And she'd definitely drunk too much Baileys.

'I was just seeing if everything was okay. I didn't know if something had happened to you or Frank – you don't normally leave him on his own.'

Stella paused. 'Really?'

A faint smile spread over his mouth and he put his hands in his pockets. 'Yes. Is that so hard to believe?'

All the emotions of last night had left her exhausted and tetchy and the answer was yes, she did find it hard to believe. 'You don't even like my dog,' she replied cautiously. She didn't bother to add, 'Or me'. At her tone his eyes shot to the floor and then back up to meet hers. Her embarrassment at being caught scampering out of Carter's flat made his unexpected concern even more off-putting. 'Well, good morning,' she said, and walked to the shop door. She had no idea why she'd said good morning like a

Victorian maiden aunt. It made her sound like an idiot but she couldn't think of anything else without a bucket load of coffee.

Miles peered at her through the glass for a second, then walked off back towards his house.

Stella had no idea what to make of that strange exchange and as Frank pawed at her leg she turned her attention to him instead, thankful that dogs were much easier to read than men.

Chapter 17

Just under a week later, Miles stood at the bar on the busy Saturday night waiting to be served. He'd been coming to The Chain and Anchor ever since he was old enough to drink. Younger actually. There might have been a few sneaky underage pints when he was at grammar school. It was a wonder he ever got served with all the acne he'd had. A cold shiver ran down his spine at the memory. The few friends he'd had didn't tease him, but Jay Adams – captain of the local football team – had, and it had affected his self-confidence. In fact, it had destroyed it. Miles raised his hand and rubbed his chin. Most of the scars had faded but there were one or two he never failed to notice when he was shaving. The emotional scars had lasted far longer.

Jay had always made sure Miles felt small, colluding with his mates so Miles was the last one picked at football. He had never felt good enough. All he'd wanted back then was to be liked by the cool kids. Cool kids like Jay. A memory he'd kept pushed down made its way to the surface: a recollection of Jay asking him to join him and his mates on a night out. Miles, with his unworldly misplaced trust, had thought things were finally looking up, that they were seeing past all the things he couldn't do and getting to know the real him. But of course he was wrong.

When he'd met them that night they'd belittled him, called him repellent, told him he should wear a bag over his head, then wedgied him. He hadn't gone back to football after that.

When years later he'd met Kiera and she'd been interested in him, he couldn't have felt further from the teenage loser he'd been back then. Glancing at her now, he noticed her long soft hair was gently curling about her shoulders and she looked cute pouting as she redid her lipstick, but he couldn't stop the niggling feeling that something wasn't right anymore.

A rising doubt kept popping up even though he repeatedly pushed it down and did his best to ignore it. His brain wasn't helping because if it wasn't thinking about Kiera, it was thinking about Stella and when he did, an emotion he couldn't quite identify niggled at the back of his mind. For some reason, an image of Stella kept appearing when he least expected it. And now, thanks to Jay, memories he didn't want to think or feel again were resurfacing too.

'What can I get ya, mate?' asked the young barman.

Miles was taken by surprise by his bright blue hair and decided he was getting old. This guy didn't look old enough to have left school let alone have a job. 'I'll have a pint of Shin Splints and a large Chardonnay, please.' The barman nodded and began preparing their drinks. Miles reached in his back pocket for his wallet and as he turned, caught sight of Jay in the corner. Suddenly it was like he was fifteen again and he felt exactly the same way he had that night. Miles tried to shrug it off, reminding himself he was a grown, successful man now, and no longer a loser. But he still didn't trust Jay even after all these years.

Kiera denied it, but Miles was sure Jay had made a play for her when they'd been working together on her website. The thought had flashed up again the other night at the restaurant when Jay had tapped on the window. He'd always enjoyed stealing Miles's girlfriends on the very odd occasion he'd got one while his face was covered in spots. And there was still something sly

161

about him Miles didn't like. Jay's voice, fuelled by the empty pint glasses in front of him, rose above the din.

'So there we were, me doing my thing, sorting out her website and, well you know what happened next.' He gave a self-satisfied laugh. His friends guffawed along with him. 'I know a gentleman should never kiss and tell but, mate, let me tell you, she might have been out of practice, but she was more than willing to learn.'

Miles wrinkled his nose in disgust as the other men at the table jeered and laughed. The man was a pig, and so were his idiotic friends. All of them still like a bunch of horny teenagers. He felt sorry for whoever they were laughing at. Jay had always been too smooth and Miles had no idea how the women of Swallowtail Bay hadn't figured him out by now. One of Jay's friends, a guy Miles had known from football, stood and collected their pint glasses. 'But she's only been here a couple of months. That's fast work, innit?'

Miles felt a prickle of tension grab the back of his neck. Stella had only been here a couple of months and Kiera had given her Jay's card. Jay raised his annoyingly chiselled jaw and shrugged. 'Honestly, mate, she was well up for it.'

'All part of the service, hey?' The man walked over and waited beside Miles at the bar. 'All right, Miles? How ya doing?'

Not for the life of him could Miles remember the guy's name. He'd have to bluff it out. 'I'm all right, mate, cheers. You?' The guy put down the glasses and shook Miles's hand.

Another surge of laughter came from the corner and the man looked over and back to Miles. 'You know Jay, don't ya? He did your website, didn't he?'

'Not mine, but my fiancée's.'

'D'ya know, that man gets more sex than any other bloke I know. Who'd have thought being a website designer got you laid, hey?' Miles gave a small nod, wishing the man would stop talking. 'He's just done the website for that bird who bought old Herbert's shop and she jumped into bed with him the first chance she got! Women, hey?'

So he had been talking about Stella. Miles could feel his features tighten as he struggled to understand why he was so bothered by it. The guy must have seen something in the unspoken response as he said, 'Oh, sorry, mate. You were after that shop, weren't ya?'

Anger began to rise up in Miles's body. Every fibre of muscle and sinew was on fire and the back of his neck grew hot. 'I was interested for a while but it didn't work out.'

The man grabbed his shoulder in a giant hand and squeezed. 'That's shit. Never mind though, mate. Plenty more fish in the sea and all that. Plenty more shops on the high street.' He laughed at his own joke.

Miles gave him a polite smile but couldn't get away quick enough. 'My fiancée's over there so I'd better get back to her. Nice to see you again.' He picked up the drinks and stalked off to Kiera and their quiet seat in the corner. The pub was busy and he had to wind his way through the crowd. The fire in his stomach bubbled away and rose into his chest to set his lungs alight.

'What's wrong with you?' asked Kiera in an amused voice. She took her drink from him and had a dainty sip. 'You look cross. What did that man say?'

Miles took a big mouthful of his drink and tried to figure out exactly what was going through his brain. He was normally a clear-headed, logical thinker, but a great mishmash of emotions surged through him, fogging his mind. Why was he so angry? It wasn't that he was attracted to Stella and jealous, but for some reason an image of her gathered in his mind's eye. It was her face the moment they'd connected over the beautiful painting. Her deep brownish-red eyes, her light brown hair and her perfect peaches-and-cream skin.

Vivien had told him Stella's story one day in the café and there'd been something about her bravery he approved of. The old girl had too. He took a sip of his drink. Jay Adams? He hadn't thought Stella the type of woman to be so easily flattered and easily tempted. Lexi had said she was lonely but she seemed too cheerful for that. And how did everyone think what Jay was doing was okay? Sitting there telling the pub about his private life like love was some sort of competition. It beggared belief.

'Miles,' said Kiera, sharply. 'For God's sake, what's the matter? You look like the whole world's ending.'

He took another sip of his drink before saying, 'Jay's telling everyone about him and Stella sleeping together.'

'So?' A horrid smirk passed over Kiera's face. A look he'd noticed more and more recently.

'So he's being really rude and crass about it. If they did sleep together he shouldn't be going around telling everyone. It's not very decent of him.' Kiera flung her hair back over her shoulder and smiled. Something about that smile put Miles on edge. It wasn't genuine; it was a weird, almost smug smile. 'Why are you smiling?' he asked. 'You wouldn't like it if he slept with you and then told the whole town. He shouldn't be doing it.'

'He didn't really sleep with her,' she replied, nonchalantly. 'She said no, actually.'

'What? How do you know that?'

'We're friends. He told me. He thought they were going to and just as he was making his move, she said no.'

Miles's glass paused at his mouth. He felt the ale touch his lips then lowered it down. This news was worrying on so many different levels. Not only had he not realised Kiera and Jay were still so close, but why would Jay do something like that? Was his ego so fragile that he had to lie? And this could ruin Stella's reputation. He hated gossip. 'So why is he telling everyone that they did?'

'Because I told him to.'

'You did what?' Miles hadn't meant to raise his voice and the people at the tables near them turned and stared. He turned his glass in his fingers and studied it for a moment trying to calm the anger and confusion rising inside him. He couldn't believe what he'd just heard.

Kiera sat back and toyed with her phone, saying it again slowly like it was all perfectly reasonable. 'I told him to.'

'Why would you do that?' he whispered.

She put her phone down and looked up. 'Don't look at me in that judgemental way of yours, Miles.'

'I think we should leave,' he said. He had to get out and understand what was happening and he couldn't do that with all the noise of the pub ringing in his ears.

'But I've only just got my drink.'

'I don't want to talk about this here.'

'Then change the subject.' She looked up from under her eyelashes almost flirtatiously. 'I'm not moving until I've had my drink.' Though he was frustrated, he couldn't pick her up and carry her outside. Miles gulped some of his pint, trying to figure out what to say next but changing the subject was impossible. 'You don't seem to realise, Miles,' she continued after drinking some of her wine, 'I'm trying to help you.'

'How is that helping me? How is slandering someone and ruining their reputation helping me?' How could Kiera think he'd want such a thing? She knew how much he hated gossip. More and more he felt like he didn't know her anymore. And what was worse, she was turning into the type of person he didn't want to know. Keeping his annoyance contained in just a whisper took a huge amount of control.

Kiera's face, however, remained placid. 'Because it hurt Jay's feelings and we wanted to get back at her. She was being a tease. Plus I thought it might make her leave so you can get the shop.' She sat back and sipped her wine like she was a saint who'd just performed their most benevolent miracle to date.

After Kiera's mention of moving to London the other night, something didn't sit right. Even when she was saying supportive things she always sounded somewhat reticent. Something was going on, but right now he couldn't figure out what. 'Make her leave?'

'Yes.'

'But it would ruin her life. What if people find out and think I put Jay up to it? Everyone knows how much I wanted the shop. My reputation will be ruined too.'

'Well, then we just start again somewhere else. There are millions of shops and holiday lets available all over the place. Or we move to London.' She adjusted the sleeve on her pretty top and suddenly the penny dropped.

This whole thing was a win-win for her. If the business failed and Stella sold up, Kiera knew he'd find it hard to take it over. He'd already told her that if the shop came up again he'd be too worried the town would think him a vulture. They'd been known to boycott stores for less. And if Stella didn't sell up and leave, Kiera and Jay could leak it that Miles had made up the lie to try and ruin both his and Stella's reputations. Kiera knew Miles's reputation meant everything to him. If the town hated him they'd never step foot in any shop he owned and he'd have no choice but to move away. Maybe move to London with Kiera. 'Is that why you did it?' he asked quietly. 'To get me to move to London?'

She tossed a curl over her shoulder and played innocent. 'I don't know what you mean. I told you, I did it for you. To help you get the shop you've always wanted. That's what you've always said to me.'

'I told you last week I was looking at new properties now. What you mean is you were going to pretend I was the one who let slip the gossip.'

'I really don't know what you're talking about, Miles.' Her brow wrinkled in fake confusion, her voice sweet and sickly with pretend innocence. He felt betrayed but when he looked at things from Stella's perspective things were even worse.

'What if Stella really is as lonely as Vivien said and she becomes depressed? How would you feel then? How would that sit with your conscience?' Miles's own conscience pricked as he recalled their interactions. He'd been offhand and rude when he first met her and her dog, still pained that he'd lost out on his dream. Kiera had then made things worse with her rudeness. A trait he realised now had always been there but he'd been blind to. Then when he'd tried to make amends he assumed he'd just stroll in and Stella would forget all about his ill manners. Even if some of his bad manners had been down to nerves, shame burned in his brain. He'd been such an arse. He'd been conceited and arrogant all because he felt Herbert had wronged him, when in fact Herbert could sell the shop to whomever he wanted and Miles had been ridiculous to think otherwise. Moreover the thought of Stella crying herself to sleep because her business was failing squeezed the life out of his heart.

'My conscience would be fine because I did this for you, Miles,' Kiera answered coolly but her words lacked conviction. 'I did it for the man I love. Not that you seem very grateful.'

Slowly, Miles realised something terrible and painful. The woman in front of him was unrecognisable. Worst of all, she didn't love him at all. Not really.

'I'm not grateful,' he replied, still struggling to keep his emotions contained within a whisper. His thighs tensed and he had to stop himself from rising out of his chair. 'I think it's a terrible thing you've done. You're going to have to tell Jay to stop lying.'

Kiera shrugged. 'Fine.'

'If he's lied about this, what else has he lied about? His qualifications? His work history?' He'd mumbled it more to himself than Kiera but she was on him instantly.

'What do you mean "what else has he lied about?"' She mimicked him in a bratty, childish voice.

They were on the verge of making a scene and this was a definitely a discussion to have behind closed doors. 'I really think we should go home. You've nearly finished your wine. Let's discuss it there.' He rose and grabbed his coat from the back of the chair. Kiera knocked back the last of her drink and stood too, slamming the glass down. They managed to make it outside but she paused in front of the large window onto the street, framed by the lights inside like an actress on a screen.

'What did you mean, Miles?' she spat, her features pinched as she played up to the crowd glancing at them from inside.

'What I said,' he protested. 'If he's lied about this he could have lied about other things.' His brain flew to the thought of Jay and Kiera working together and the pit of his stomach filled with dread. 'How could you two do this to Stella?'

'Oh, get a grip, Miles.'

'How can you so willingly ruin someone else's life just to get what you want?' From the corner of his eye he could see people in the pub watching, all pretence of not noticing gone. After taking a big breath he urged her once more to move. 'Please, Kiera, let's just go home. We're embarrassing ourselves in front of everyone.'

'Oh, so I embarrass you now, do I?'

'Kiera, please?'

She met his gaze, glanced in though the pub window, and suddenly her face changed from hard and angry to distraught. 'How can you treat me like this, Miles?' For the first time her eyes were glistening with tears. He wanted to believe they were real but he could see from the rest of her face they weren't. He'd seen her cry properly when a relative had died. Her face had scrunched up as big, fat tears ran down her face. She'd gone red and blotchy but he'd still thought she was beautiful and that he was the luckiest man in the world. He'd held her tightly through the night as she cried on his shoulder. What was happening now was completely different. It really was like watching a film. Only one or two tears escaped and she dabbed gently at the corner of her eyes with her fingertips.

Staring ahead, Miles realised that the niggling doubts that had been slowly mounting since he'd suggested they set the date for the wedding weren't superficial at all. A deep crevasse had opened up in their relationship. It had been growing from a tiny crack for months and months. The wedding had brought out a different, spiteful side to Kiera and if he was honest, he didn't even enjoy being with her anymore. There was something lacking in her soul. He wanted and needed something substantial in the women he was to spend the rest of his life with. Kiera had used and manipulated people to get what she wanted, not caring for the consequences or the impact on their lives. She wasn't the woman he'd thought, or rather convinced himself, she was.

In the hotel, he'd been right when he reassessed his life. They'd been together for four years but with having been away so much, the time they'd actually spent together was less than half that. Travelling for work had made every return home feel like a honeymoon period so he hadn't really got to know her at all. Not all the different sides to her character – the good and the bad. Being in love with someone meant loving all their negative traits as much as the positive ones, but that wasn't the case for him and Kiera, and he had a suspicion there was much about him she wouldn't like either.

Miles walked ahead, and as he neared the end of the street she began to follow, staying a few paces behind, her heels clacking on the ground. Anger radiated off her. At least this way they could retain some dignity. In the cold night air, without the noise of the bar surrounding them, he felt more clear-headed, and as he opened the front door to the house, and placed his keys in the glass bowl, he knew what he had to do. It was the best decision for both of them. The only one that would give them each a real chance at happiness.

Miles strode into the silent living room, lit only by the light from the hall and cleared his throat. 'I think we should have a bit of time apart, Kiera. I think we need some space from each other.'

'Are you breaking up with me?' she shouted, her voice carrying a high-pitched, almost hysterical edge. From the doorway she threw her coat onto the sofa or possibly at him, but it veered to the side.

'I need some time to deal with what you've done.'

'So you are breaking up with me. You're really not the man I thought you were.'

'No,' he conceded. 'I'm not the man I thought I was either.' He'd become a selfish, self-pitying dick and it was time to change. That wasn't who he was deep down.

From the hall doorway she glared at him, her arms crossed over her chest. 'By the way, just so you know, Stella might not have slept with Jay when he did her website, but I did when he did mine.'

Miles looked up into her eyes. He'd thought he loved those eyes once, but looking at her now, seeing her clearly for the first time, he realised he'd loved the outer shell of her soul not the very heart of it. And really, somewhere deep down, he'd known the truth about her and Jay. He just hadn't let himself believe it. For Jay it would have been the ultimate win. He'd always hated Miles for having money, teasing him for pronouncing his t's properly, calling him 'pizza face' and reminding him how ugly he looked with angry red spots plastered all over his cheeks. Miles bit his lip as remembered hurt almost drowned him.

Kiera's smile was spiteful and he saw now the hard edge of the spoilt rich kid she really was. They'd never really connected on a deeper level and he'd been swept away by her. He'd still felt like the teenage acne-ridden loser who'd hit the jackpot with such a gorgeous, clever woman. He'd been too proud to admit they weren't right for each other.

'Did you hear me?' she shouted. 'I slept with Jay Adams.'

'I know you did,' he replied. 'I think I've always known.'

'Then you're a complete idiot.'

'Yes,' he said, finally swallowing his pride. 'I am.'

***

The next morning, Miles woke from an uncomfortable night on the sofa, fully dressed and with an aching back, to find Kiera slamming about upstairs. Trying to be adult about everything he got up and went upstairs to find her in the bedroom, shoving things into her Louis Vuitton suitcases.

He stayed in the doorway and leaned against the frame. 'I'm sorry it's ended this way, Kiera. I really am. I guess we just weren't right for each other.' She straightened up without speaking, her face perfectly made up and without a hint of puffy eyes, and before he could react she'd thrown a bottle of perfume at him. It shattered against the wall near his kneecap, sending shards of glass over the floor and releasing a heady, sickeningly strong scent of vanilla that attacked his nostrils.

'Just fuck off, Miles, you pompous prick,' she spat, marching to the dresser and returning with a bundle of underwear.

Well, that certainly told him, didn't it? He backed away and went to the kitchen to have a coffee as there didn't seem anything else he could do right now.

Half an hour later, a loud thumping told him Kiera was descending the stairs. He went to help with her luggage but as he began to climb the first few steps with an outstretched hand the look she gave him made him flinch. Had she been holding a knife he was sure she wouldn't have hesitated in driving it deep into his chest. He swallowed hard and moved aside.

'I'll come and get the rest of my stuff when I bloody well want to and if you try and move any of it I'll remove your balls with a pencil sharpener and wear them as earrings.'

'Okay,' Miles replied, his voice wavering a little. He cleared his throat and told himself to man up. He should have expected this response from Kiera.

Unable to watch her struggle he opened the front door for her. She shoved into him with her shoulder as she passed and he produced a rather unmanly 'umph' sound. She pulled the suitcase behind her down the path towards her car. Knowing it was going to be too heavy to carry, Miles followed her. She wouldn't want him to help but there was no way she'd be able to lift it without hurting herself. She yanked open the boot, but when she turned to pick up her case she spotted their immediate neighbour looking through her net curtains.

'Come to get a good eyeful have you, Mrs Chapman?' she shouted, flailing her arms around. 'Nosy old cow! Yes, we've broken up because Miles—' she pointed at him just to make sure everyone knew who she was talking about '—is a complete dick who doesn't appreciate me. All right? So fuck off!'

Miles felt his face flame and couldn't bring himself to turn and look at the expression on Mrs Chapman's face, though he could well imagine how shocked the mild-mannered, grey-haired old lady would be. He turned his head the other way only to see Stella walking Frank back towards the shop. The dog's legs were wet and straggly from being in the sea and Miles suddenly imagined walking with them both along the beach. In his mind, they'd be laughing while Frank frolicked near the shore. Though Stella's pace slowed for a second she didn't stop and stare and Miles was incredibly grateful for that. It was very decent of her. He just hoped that Kiera didn't see Stella or she might start swearing at her too and that made him feel strangely protective.

Kiera marched back into the house and was soon making it down the stairs with the second suitcase. Miles worried she wouldn't fit it all into her sports car and glanced at the boot. If he was lucky it would just about fit or it would have to go on the back seat and he couldn't imagine how awkward prolonging this moment while he fidgeted about with suitcases would be. Whether Kiera shouted at him or not, he decided to move the other case so both would fit.

'Get your bastard hands off my stuff, Miles Parker, or so help me God I'll—'

'I'm only trying to help,' he said, cutting her off. Poor Mrs

Chapman had heard enough bad language for one day. 'I didn't think they'd both fit.'

Kiera stood next to him, her eyes fixed on his. 'Whether they fit or not is none of your business. You just wait until my father gets hold of you, you weak little runt. He'll have a field day. And don't try and find me. I'm moving to London. I've already talked to Daddy and he's going to buy me a flat so I can start my life again. Away from you. And good fucking riddance. I've always been far too good for you.'

Now with no idea of whether he should help her move the suitcase or not, Miles stood stock still. He was slightly worried she might have a weapon concealed somewhere and the look in her eye made him think of Hannibal Lecter when he had that mask thing on in *Silence of the Lambs*.

'Well, are you going to put my suitcase in or not?' Kiera demanded. 'Don't you think it's the least you could do?' Miles leapt to do it just to get rid of her before she had another go at him but had to duck out of the way as she almost slammed the boot on his head. With a final toss of her hair and a one-finger salute to poor Mrs Chapman who looked terribly shocked but hadn't yet moved away from the net curtain, she stomped to the driver's side and got in. As she pulled away she said, 'Goodbye, Miles, you utter f—' but the rest of her words were cancelled out by the screeching of tires as she drove down the road and out of Miles's life.

Miles felt his shoulders relax and the muscles of his stomach loosen. Yes, Kiera had made them both the subject of gossip with her really quite fantastic exit, but at least it was done. And for some reason, he didn't really care that the town would be talking about him for the next million years. He raised his eyes to the sky and took a breath in. The salt sea air filled his lungs, reminding him how much he loved being here in his hometown. And he felt oddly positive about what his life would be like now. As he lowered his head back down he saw Stella peering from her shop window, but as soon as she realised he was looking she ran away into the depths of the store. Closing the garden gate and turning to walk back down the path, he saw that Mrs Chapman was still watching.

'Morning, Mrs Chapman,' he called with a wave. 'Lovely day, isn't it?'

Chapter 18

Stella sat with Lexi early Monday morning having a quick cup of coffee before starting work, feeling tired and a bit down in the dumps. On Friday, Carter the poet had left, and while they had swapped numbers she wasn't sure that she wanted to stay in touch. He'd been lovesick and forlorn, only stopping short of reciting another poem in front of a shop full of people when one of the customers had told him to put a lid on it. Though sweet to begin with, Stella had found his constant compliments and ardent assurances a little dramatic, not to mention tiresome. But she was happy for their night together, and as mercenary as it sounded, she was still contemplating him as her date for Isaac's wedding, even though the idea of making conversation during the long drive to Oxford, then spending a whole day with him, was torturous. Possibly even more torturous than the wedding itself.

To make matters worse a drunk had checked in to the holiday let and Stella was worried that the flat was going to end up stinking of booze because the man was clearly sloshed from the moment he arrived. When he'd nipped out shortly after checking in, coming back with a carrier bag full of clinking bottles, it was clear he had every intention of spending the entirety of his stay that way.

The family that had been due to arrive on Friday for her first booking in the large flat were running late and didn't arrive until gone eleven o'clock that night, which meant Stella had to remain fully dressed and presentable rather than in her jimjams with no make-up on, to settle them in. She'd done it, of course, with a smile on her face and a cheerful, professional manner but there was no denying she was knackered when the alarm had gone off that morning and she'd had to drag herself out of bed to walk Frank before a full, hopefully busy day in the shop. *Her shop*, she reminded herself, shaking off the self-pity. Self-pity was fine for a few minutes but too much of it was just self-indulgent.

And she had to admit her lethargy today was partly her own fault. Rather than being sensible yesterday, on her only rest day, she'd taken advantage of the good weather and had been up a ladder painting the sign. She'd done the first coat before giving Frank his walk and then the second coat a couple of hours later. That was of course after she'd watched Kiera's amazing departure from Miles's house. She'd been surprised at how gentlemanly he'd been while Kiera had flounced around and shouted at him. He'd even tried to help her with her bags. Stella had felt a little sorry for him as he'd watched on in embarrassment.

In the afternoon she'd sketched out the new lettering and given that a first coat too. It still needed another, but that would have to wait until next weekend. She was just too dog-tired to do it in the evening and the nights were still quite damp.

'So Miles and Kiera have broken up then,' said Lexi. She giggled as she said, 'It sounded amazing.'

'It was quite a spectacle,' Stella replied. She'd forced herself to walk on to the shop even though she'd secretly wanted to stand and watch. She wondered who'd instigated the split and she did feel a little bit happy she wasn't going to be walking past the shop anymore, looking in with that smug smile of hers.

'Poor Miles. They were never really suited in my opinion. Or Vivien's either. She heartily disapproved of Kiera.'

176

'What exactly is the connection between Miles and Vivien?'

'For a woman who loves to talk she's almost cagey about it really, which tells me it means a lot to her. All I know is that Miles had a bit of a rough time as a teenager and she was a sort of substitute mum sometimes.'

Stella couldn't imagine Miles having had a rough time with his good looks and firm self-assurance. Plus, he seemed the type of guy who didn't care what other people thought. She sipped her latte as Lexi continued speaking.

'Anyway, are you sure you're still okay to watch the kids after school for a bit? It's not a problem if you can't.'

It *would* be a problem if she couldn't, Stella knew that, but it wasn't a problem in the slightest. She was really looking forward to it. 'Of course it's still okay. If you drop them in straight after school they can do their homework and watch some TV in the flat until you finish at the café.'

'Thanks, honey. I really need the extra hours and as Carol's cold has turned into pneumonia I can't leave Raina in the lurch. They don't have to do all their homework as it's not due in until Friday but if they could make a start that would be great. I try and get them to do a little bit each night. What's the new posh family like? You said when you spoke to them on the phone they were so snobby you could hardly understand them.'

Stella sighed. 'They are literally the worst. The kids are awful and have done nothing but moan—'

'Sounds like my kids.'

'They're nothing like your kids. Your kids are lovely and sweet and kind and have lovely manners. These are little monsters. Every time they walk past the shop I can hear them whinging about iPads and Xboxes. The father's always on his phone, yaying or neighing like a bloody horse about something that is apparently crucially important to his business, the mother leaves everything to the nanny so she doesn't break a nail or drop her martini, and the nanny is so far up her own arse I'm surprised she can see.'

Lexi giggled. 'Oh dear, how long are they here for?'

'Four weeks,' Stella replied, stressing the sentence. 'I've got a feeling this is going to be the longest four weeks of my life. The nanny's already been to see me three times since they arrived, moaning or treating me like a maid, asking me to fetch this and that. To be honest, I have no idea why they booked down here and not somewhere a bit posher like that big fancy hotel down the seafront.' Stella fiddled with her phone. 'And the bloke in the one-bed I swear had twelve bottles of red wine in his carrier bags the afternoon he arrived. I feel like I just got mixed up in an episode of *EastEnders*.'

'It does sound like it.' Lexi laughed and stood up from the table. 'Sorry, but I'm going to love you and leave you. It won't be long and the breakfast lot will be in.'

'Yeah, I'd better get going too,' Stella replied and hugged Lexi goodbye.

The day's trading was horribly slow and time dragged on for Stella. She would definitely have to explore this art exhibition idea a bit more because if she didn't make a few bigger sales things were going to get very hard indeed. And there had been a couple of weird things that day that had unsettled her.

A couple of young women came into the shop seemingly browsing but when Stella had gone up to say hi, they'd looked at her like she smelled of dog poo and had then proceeded to whisper about her. She could be being paranoid, and it was quite possible they were talking about something completely different, but Stella didn't think so. She just hoped they didn't know Miles and that he'd been at it again, slagging her off behind her back.

Then later, a couple had come in, pretending to look at the art, and when Stella introduced herself to them, they said, 'Oh, yes, we already know who you are.' Stella dearly wanted to believe the shop was beginning to gain a good reputation in the town but their raised eyebrows and smug smiles had set her teeth on edge. She'd shrugged it off though, knowing you couldn't please all of the people all of the time.

By late afternoon, after Lexi had dropped the kids in and Stella had settled them with some biscuits and juice to start their homework, the day had become overcast and grey, and a light drizzle was beginning to descend. Stella spent most of her time looking at the celebrity gossip websites on her laptop after answering all three of the holiday enquiries she'd received, plus completing a quiz to find out her skin type. Tiny droplets of rain slid down the big front windows when the bell over the door tinkled and Vivien walked in.

'Hello, Vivien, how—' Stella's foot immediately stopped tapping along to the radio. 'Gosh, you really don't look well, Vivien. Are you all right?' Stella jumped up from her stool and went to help the old lady who, rather than looking polished and elegant as usual, looked wobbly and frail. Vivien struggled to catch her breath but as she did a little colour returned to her cheeks. Stella guided her to the wingback chair near the counter. It had become her usual seat whenever she popped in, and Stella had left it there rather than move it backwards and forwards all the time.

'I'll be all right in a minute, dear,' she puffed. 'It's just getting old.' She rested her cane on her lap and closed her eyes.

'Can I get you a cup of tea?'

She shook her head gently. 'A glass of water would be lovely, thank you.'

Stella nipped out to the kitchen, checking on the kids as she went. They were both sat at the table working hard. Lexi was doing an amazing job; they were brilliant kids. When she came back she noticed Frank had moved from his basket and was sitting by Vivien's feet, guarding her. It was worrying. He did that whenever Stella was ill, like he could sense something was wrong. Stella noticed Vivien's hands shaking as she put the glass

179

of water to her mouth. 'Shall I call someone to help you back to your house? I know it's not far but you can't go on your own like this.'

'No, no, dear, that's fine. I'll be right as rain in a jiffy.' She sipped the water again but her skin seemed so much thinner today. It was like she'd suddenly aged by ten years.

The bell tinkled again and this time Miles walked in, brushing some rain from his hair. He hadn't worn a coat and his shirt was dotted from the drizzle. He gave a nod towards Stella and his face was, as usual, stern and forbidding. It wasn't until he saw Vivien that his expression softened, quickly turning to concern. Kneeling down in front of her he took her hand. 'Vivien, what's the matter?'

'You look like you're going to propose,' Vivien said with a chuckle but that one short sentence seemed to have taken all the air from her lungs. As she took some deep breaths, a smile gave her face more life, and Stella felt her worries subside a little. 'What should my answer be, Stella?' Luckily, Stella was saved the embarrassment of having to say that she'd rather marry a fish than pompous, grumpy Miles Parker, by Vivien answering her own question. 'I think I'd say yes.'

'Well, thank you very much,' Miles replied, and something about the softness of his voice and the gentle lines of his face made him look distinguished rather than hard. Even Frank gave him a sniff and Miles looked at him rather fondly before patting his head and standing up.

'Miles,' said Stella tentatively, 'I was wondering if you could take Vivien home? I don't think she should go on her own today. She still looks a bit peaky to me.' He turned to Stella and she was struck again by how handsome he was. Maybe it was the dark, cloudy sky outside and the soft lights of the shop but he really did look different. He'd be perfect to invite to the wedding if he wasn't such a miserable toad. 'If you're too busy, I'll close the shop and me and the kids can take her ourselves.'

'You will not,' Vivien replied. 'You're not losing business on my account. And those kids don't need to see me all tired and out of puff.'

'Business?' Stella echoed. 'Chance would be a fine thing.' The slight turn of Miles's head made Stella wish she'd kept her mouth shut and the note of regret out of her voice. Something flitted across Miles's eyes that she couldn't read. Glee?

'I'm happy to take you,' said Miles. 'As long as I get a cup of tea at the end of it.'

'I think I've got some Battenberg in the cake tin as well.'

'Then the deal is sealed. But you're not going anywhere just yet; you finish your water and when you're done I'll get the car.' Miles placed a hand affectionately on her shoulder.

'You can tell me all about you and that strumpet splitting up.' It wasn't a question, it was an order.

Stella started. 'How did you—'

She paused, expecting Miles's face to cloud but was surprised to see a smile forming. 'I should have known you'd know already. It's all around town now, isn't it?'

Stella stared dumbfounded. Who was this easy-going man in front of her?

'It is,' Vivien replied. 'And I want all the gory details. You were far too good for her anyway.'

Miles grinned. 'You would say that though, wouldn't you?' He bent down and gave her a kiss on the cheek.

Why would Vivien say that? Was she his nan or great-aunt or something? Lexi had never said they were related and neither had Vivien for that matter, but there were pictures of him as a young man in her house. It was all very odd.

'Umm, thanks, Miles,' Stella said. She'd expected more of a battle, or a rude 'I'm too busy' reply. What was currently happening was all completely unexpected. As if to confirm that Vivien was now able to leave, Frank removed himself from her feet and went back to his basket.

'No problem.' Miles bent down and gave Frank another fuss. 'He's a really lovely dog, isn't he?'

'He is,' Stella replied, ensuring her voice stayed level and didn't carry even a hint of I-told-you-so. 'He's a sucker for a fuss and thinks all humans are there to give him one. Or a treat.'

Miles's face broke into a disarmingly relaxed grin. 'So he should.'

Clattering voices rang from behind Stella as Ralph and Taylor came out into the shop.

'We've done our homework, Stella,' said Taylor, taking long confident strides. 'Vivien!' she said when she saw the old lady and ran over to give her a hug. The fondness in Vivien's eyes radiated through her smile as she encircled the young girl, followed quickly by Ralph. 'Why are you sitting in the shop?' asked Taylor, her youthful forehead crinkling in confusion.

'Oh, I often sit here for a bit,' Vivien replied and though it was true, Stella sensed a hint of a lie. 'Are you coming to see me on Saturday?'

Taylor shook her head and sensing his chance Ralph answered for both of them. 'We're going to Daddy's this weekend—'

'Ralph! I was going to say that!'

Ralph grinned triumphantly. Stella decided to step in as Vivien was still looking quite tired. 'So you've done all your homework for today?'

'Yep,' Taylor replied. 'We've done all our spellings and I've done half my maths. Ralph hasn't; he didn't want to.'

'Well,' said Stella, 'Mummy did say you didn't have to do it all, but I'm sure she'll be pleased you've both made such a good start.'

As if they'd only just noticed him, Taylor and Ralph both turned to Miles who smiled down at them. Stella was unsure if they'd ever met him before. It hadn't come up in conversation, and she was just going to introduce them when Vivien said, 'You two remember Miles, don't you?'

Taylor nodded while Ralph looked uncertain.

SHELVING
3/28/2025

Qty: 1

Location:
AA-AA-AAA-17-R

Customer PO #:

* 1 1 2 3 - 2 5 0 3 2 1 *

Title:
Who Put the Spell into Spelling?

Order Qty: 4

'Hi, kids,' Miles replied. 'How's school?'

'Boring,' Taylor replied and Ralph giggled.

'Yeah, really boring.'

'Do you know I can do this—?' announced Taylor, kicking her right leg high into the air. 'I want to do gymnastics but Mummy says I can't yet. I don't think we can afford it.'

Stella watched on with mounting worry. She didn't have enough experience with kids to handle this kind of thing. She wanted to defend Lexi but she had no idea what to say. To her surprise, Miles responded well. 'It looks to me like you don't need gymnastics. That was amazing.'

'Don't do it in here though, dear,' said Vivien. 'You might knock something over.'

The doorbell tinkled again and as the grown-ups looked to the new arrival, the kids went and played with Frank. Stella's smile quickly faded and she plastered it back on as the nanny walked in and spoke to her while staring down her slightly too long nose. 'Ah, there you are. I'm afraid I need to complain again. The DVD collection that you advertised really is completely inadequate. There are only DVDs for younger children. We need some for older children. Hector and Lucas are ten so they like things like *The Avengers*, *Thor* and *Deadpool*.'

Deadpool! There was more swearing in that film than you'd find in the navy. Stella bit her lip to keep her words from escaping. From the corner of her eye she could see Ralph looking both jealous and shocked. 'Of course. I'll nip out and get you something more suitable.'

'Okay,' the nanny replied, with a sigh indicating that Stella's response just wasn't quite good enough.

'I'll be closing soon, so I'll have them with you in an hour.'

As she turned, her long ponytail swished around and almost hit Stella in the face. The nanny was very tall and naturally slim with one of those athletic frames. The poor thing had no boobs to speak of but Stella was immensely jealous of her sharp cheekbones. She'd always felt her rounded cheeks made her look like a hamster hiding food. The nanny spotted Miles and, suddenly, a large smile spread over her face. 'Hi, I'm Josie. Do you work here too?'

Stella cringed, awaiting Miles's terse and grumpy response. She couldn't have been more surprised when he very calmly said, 'No, I live nearby though, just down the road.'

'Oh, so we'll be seeing a lot of each other then.' She dipped her head so she was looking at him from under her long eyelashes. Stella couldn't do that sort of thing. It just made her double chin stand out. Josie's voice became a bit huskier. 'That'll be nice.' Was she flirting? With Miles? She'd only just laid eyes on him. Fair enough he was attractive but still, that was fast work. Josie turned back to Stella. 'So we'll expect the DVDs shortly then? An hour is quite a long time to wait.'

'Okay,' Stella replied, remembering that no matter how hateful her customers might be they were her source of income and had to be looked after. She gave her best, happy grin and hoped she didn't look like a lunatic. 'Yes. I'll drop them in in a few minutes.'

'Are we going out?' asked Taylor from her seat on the floor at the end of the counter and Stella gave her a smile. It looked like they were. Josie left with a curt nod towards Stella and a lingering look at Miles. Poor Vivien was ignored completely.

'Well, she was awful,' said Vivien as Josie walked past the window back to the apartments. 'Thinks quite a lot of herself, doesn't she?' Taylor and Ralph giggled.

'You're funny when you're mean, Vivien,' said Taylor.

'They do require a lot of looking after,' Stella replied tactfully. 'But to be fair she's right. Most of the DVDs are quite old and for younger kids. I've been meaning to get some other ones but haven't got round to it yet.'

'I've got some you can have,' said Miles. 'I've got all *The Avengers* ones, but I'll leave out *Deadpool* if you want? I don't think it's appropriate for ten-year-olds. You can keep them, if you like.'

'Oh.' Stella was completely thrown. 'Umm, thanks. That'd be great.'

'I'm not allowed to watch *Deadpool*,' said Ralph looking very solemn indeed. 'Mummy says it's not appropriate.'

'Mummy's right, darling,' said Vivien, kindly. 'She always knows best.'

Miles nodded his agreement. 'Mummy's definitely right on that one, Ralph.' He turned to Stella. 'I'll run and get them now for you while Vivien finishes up. Bye, kids. See you soon.' He walked out of the shop and began a slow jog to his house. Stella watched him go, admiring his tall frame and muscular thighs, wondering how and when Miles had been taken over by aliens. Vivien placed her now empty glass of water on the counter. She had a lot more colour in her cheeks and her skin had lost the horrible grey, transparent tinge it had when she'd walked in.

Eyeing Stella, Vivien said, 'See he's a lovely man, really.'

Stella gave a quick smile and bent down to hide behind the counter, giving Frank a quick cuddle. Taylor and Ralph really were the loveliest of kids and she made a mental note to tell Lexi how good they'd been when she saw her. A moment later she stood up. 'Right, kids, can you go and put everything away in your school bags ready for Mummy – and make sure you've had a nice big drink.'

Vivien sat a little straighter. 'And I'd like a hug please.'

Both obliged and Stella watched a warm light fill Vivien's face. She hoped one day she'd get hugs like that off these two.

'Can we have another biscuit?' asked Ralph on his way back around the counter.

'I know where they are,' added Taylor, helpfully.

Stella grinned. 'Yes, of course you can. Go on then, quick sticks.' When they'd gone she checked Vivien over once more. 'You're looking much better now. Have you been to the doctor's?'

'Oh, I don't need that. What's he going to say? He'll tell me I'm ancient and it's to be expected at my age. And look, here's

185

my knight in shining armour bringing the car round. I used to have a chauffeur in my heyday you know. Handsome man. Very much in love with me. See you later, my dear.' Stella helped her out of her chair then assisted her to the door.

'You take care of yourself, Vivien.' Miles took over and steadied Vivien as she lowered herself into his car, then from the backseat grabbed a stack of DVDs, including all the ones Josie had asked for. 'Thanks, Miles. This has really saved my skin. I'll give you some money for them, of course.'

'No, I won't hear of it. It's my pleasure. Glad I could help.' He climbed into the car and drove off and Stella walked back into the shop.

Miles had never been that nice before, and yet, Vivien had always spoken so highly of him. Was it that Stella kept catching him on off days? She thought back to their previous encounters, replaying his rudeness, his attitude towards Frank and her stock. Had she misjudged him?

'I have no idea what's going on here, Franky boy, but I don't trust him. No one goes from being so mean to so nice without a reason.' She crossed her arms and looked out of the large shop windows into the street. She still didn't know what he'd come in for. 'I think he's up to something.'

Chapter 19

Early Friday morning, Miles loaded his suitcase into the back of his car. The consistent drizzle that dampened the start of the week had cleared, and spring was giving way to hints of summer, warming the gentle breeze. The sun was already climbing rapidly – a huge yellow ball in a clear blue sky. He had a long drive ahead of him for a sales meeting in Leeds and had booked a hotel for overnight. There was no way he could make it there and back in a day, and as he didn't have Kiera to worry about he could take his time and please himself.

It was weird how everything in his life seemed suddenly more relaxed. He wasn't as anxious about work and being away, and he wasn't even stressed that the properties the estate agent had shown him yesterday hadn't been what he was looking for. As nice as they were, they hadn't felt right, but he didn't mind waiting for something perfect. There was no rush anymore, with anything. For a while at least, Miles was quite happy to let life roll on of its own accord.

Over the road, Stella was just returning from a walk with Frank when the dog stopped to sniff something. She smiled down at him and gave his lead a gentle tug just as the nanny, whose name escaped him, approached her. From the look on Stella's face, it was clearly another complaint. Though her smile remained intact he could see a slight tension around Stella's mouth and eyes. Then the nanny turned, spotted him and waved. Miles waved back and continued his work under the bonnet, checking the car over, as he did before any long journey, trying not to get oil on his jumper. Dealing with customer complaints couldn't be much fun, but he still longed for that sort of problem rather than the same old stuff he dealt with now: sales targets, budget forecasts, driving up and down the country giving the sales patter. He still really wanted what Stella had, but contented himself with the thought that it would happen one day if he just kept plugging away.

'Are you going somewhere nice?' asked a soft voice from the side of the car. He looked up from under the open bonnet to see the nanny standing there, all fresh-faced and cheerful in tight Lycra leggings and a crop top. She must have been out for an early morning run.

He stood up and scratched the back of his head. 'Umm, no not really. Well, I'm going to Leeds, which is a nice place, but it's for work.'

'Oh, right.'

He heard his own reply and wished he was better at making small talk. He was okay in professional situations and networking events, turning a switch on and off, but in social situations he had to work hard as all those insecure feelings from his youth flooded back. Especially with Stella – for some reason she made him feel self-conscious. It suddenly occurred to him that when he found someone new he was going to have to get to know them, and that required a lot of conversation, most of it awkward and nerve-racking.

'It's Josie, by the way. We met in the shop the other day.' She jutted out a hand and Miles shook it.

'Yes, I remember.' He remembered meeting her, but couldn't admit to having completely forgotten her name. 'I'm Miles.'

Josie pushed her ponytail back past her shoulders. If she'd

been out running she didn't look it; her face wasn't at all sweaty or pink and the goosebumps on her skin told him the crop top might have been an aesthetic rather than practical choice. 'So what do you do?'

'I work for a pharmaceutical company.'

She raised her eyebrows, impressed. 'When do you get back?' Josie's gaze was so intense he walked to the back of the car and bent down into the boot, pushing his bags around and pretending to check something.

'Not till the end of the week. Which reminds me,' he said, thinking out loud, 'I really should ask someone to keep an eye on the place for me.'

'I can.' Josie bounced on her heels like a child and Miles realised she wasn't just fresh-faced, she was young. Really very young. Probably in her very early twenties. From her smooth, unlined skin she really couldn't be any older than twenty-three. He was thirty-seven, the last year of being able to say he was mid-thirties. Soon it would be late thirties and that meant midlife crisis territory.

Straightening up, he pushed his hair back from his face. 'That's kind of you, but I should probably ask someone who's here all the time.' He thought about Vivien but she hadn't been too well lately and was getting too old for that sort of thing. Kiera had left creating such a scene, he didn't really want to add to his embarrassment by asking the neighbour, Mrs Chapman. She'd been careful to ignore him as much as possible. He could ask Lexi, but she had enough on her plate as a working single mum.

It was then he thought of Stella. She was up at the crack of dawn, like him, and had been very caring and considerate when Vivien had been ill the other day. As she was just over the road she really would be the perfect choice, but was it too much to ask? Shamefully, he'd been such a dick the last few times they'd met. It would serve him right if she said no. He realised now how much of his attitude had been due to all the stress he was under, even though he hadn't realised it at the time.

'Well, if you change your mind, you know where I am.' Josie pulled her ankle up behind her to stretch out her leg, then the other. 'Have a safe trip.' She let go, pouted a little, then bounced off back to the flat.

After closing the boot he went around to the front of the car and pulled down the bonnet before heading over to Stella's shop. As he rounded the corner he saw the newly painted sign and a warm glow released inside. She'd called the shop Old Herbert's Shop, which was actually a fitting tribute to the old boy. He smiled to himself. It was a much better name than he'd come up with when he was writing his business plan.

Stella was already tidying and sorting stock when he knocked on the front door. He startled her and as she walked over, he mouthed the word 'Sorry,' but her smile was polite rather than friendly. Seeing her features up close he noted that she had an expressive, naturally pretty face. If her smile was genuine and reached all the way to her deep brown eyes they'd sparkle and he wished he hadn't been so arrogant and taken that sparkle away.

Opening the door she said, 'Hi, Miles, you're up early.' There was trepidation in her voice and he couldn't blame her for being on her guard. It was nothing more than he deserved.

'Yeah, actually, that's what I came to talk to you about. I, umm … I was wondering if I could ask a favour.' He suddenly felt very silly and scratched the back of his head.

'Sure, come in.'

'The shop looks great,' he said, trying to be more sociable. Stella had been working incredibly hard, he could see, and the other side of the shop had been cleared of even more stock. Most of the items were new and the place was almost unrecognisable. It was light, airy and full of beautiful pieces of art and an array of homeware from hand-painted dinner services to unique and unusual decorations.

'Oh, thanks.'

He paused, putting his hands in his pockets. 'And I love the name. What made you think of it?'

Stella's eyes widened in surprise. 'I don't know really. I was talking to Jay when we were discussing the website and it just sort of came to me. It seemed right to keep it but it needs another coat of paint, which is on my list for Sunday.'

Miles remembered his and Kiera's row and Jay's lies in the pub. He felt a cold shiver run down his back. Stella clearly didn't know what they'd been saying about her. Should he be the one to tell her? Could he do that? He couldn't just blurt it out right now, especially as they were beginning to have a proper conversation. Perhaps he could let Lexi know and ask her to warn Stella. He presumed she would prefer to hear it from a friend though something about that felt cowardly. No answer seemed right. He'd have to think about it more before he did anything; it was important he made the right decision. One thing he would do though, was try to put a stop to the rumours if anyone mentioned it to him.

'Are you okay?' asked Stella. He'd stood staring in silence like a creepy weirdo.

'Yeah, I'm fine, sorry, I was just admiring some of the new paintings.'

Again, the pale skin of her forehead wrinkled. 'Right. So, what did you want to ask me?'

Miles felt his neck muscles tighten with nerves. 'I know this might seem a little odd but I was wondering if you'd keep an eye on my place overnight. With Kiera gone there isn't anyone there and I have to go away for some meetings. I'll be back Sunday night but …' He shrugged, unwilling to mention that he was too embarrassed to ask Mrs Chapman.

'Oh. Umm—'

'You don't need to do anything, just … you know, keep an eye out.' Stella looked like he'd just asked her to go skinny-dipping with him. 'If I'm honest, I could ask the neighbours but since

191

Kiera left in such dramatic style I'm a bit embarrassed to.' Why had he just told her that? Her face softened and he saw a hint of a smile lift the corners of her mouth.

'Of course. Should I take your mobile number in case anything happens?'

'Yeah, that'd be great.' He pulled out a business card from his wallet and handed it to her. She had long slender fingers but a blister had formed by her thumb and her palms were red and sore-looking. She was working hard to make this place successful and Miles both admired her and felt guilty for having thought it was all coming so easily. In contrast, he'd recently discovered Kiera hadn't been working for months. All those supposed trips to London to meet clients were lies. She'd just gone shopping and was living off her trust fund. The fact that she'd always come home with so many bags should have told him so but he'd been blind to it all. 'Feel free to call or text if anything happens. And, if I can ever return the favour I'd be happy to.'

'Sure. No problem.' She nodded and her hair bounced around her face. A slight curl had developed at the front and Miles suddenly wondered what it would be like to wrap it around his fingers.

'I'd better get going.' Miles pulled his mind back to the task at hand. He edged towards the door and noticed the dog bed sitting empty. 'Is your dog not well or something?'

'Frank?' She looked confused then she glanced at the dog bed. 'Oh no, he's fine. He's just lazy. He likes a nap between his morning walk and me opening the shop. He's fast asleep on the sofa in the living room.'

'Oh, good. Well, thanks again and I'll see you tomorrow.'

'Sure.' She nodded. 'Safe journey.'

Closing the door behind him he looked up again at the newly painted sign. The wobbly writing only added to the charm. And this time it only hurt a tiny bit to admit that old Herbert had made the right choice after all.

Chapter 20

Lexi was running late. Again. After three arguments with the kids – one about shoes, one about coats and one about scooters – she had bundled them in the car, had another row about Taylor not yet being old enough to go without a car seat, and pulled up in front of the school. Thank God it was Friday.

Things were still not picking up for Will, which meant money was desperately short. She'd taken extra shifts at the café and was grateful for the work Stella had given her, even though she felt guilty for eating into her profits. Lexi comforted herself with the thought that she was able to feed her children for another week and was only a month in arrears with her streaming service so they'd let her keep it, which meant she could watch her favourite programs and stay relatively sane.

Will was picking the kids up from school because he was having them for the weekend and Fridays were turning out to be her busiest day. She split the morning shift in the café, then cleaned the holiday flats until three, when she'd get the kids, drop them at Stella's and go back to the café to work till five. They loved their time with Stella and it was proving an absolute godsend. Lexi was grateful to have found such a friend. Raina was as supportive as ever and even kept her supplied with cake including some to take home to the kids.

Lexi appreciated all the support she had, but wished her children didn't have to see all this, or be passed from pillar to post quite so much. Other kids in school didn't. And they didn't have to see their mum working her fingers to the bone and falling asleep during cuddles in the evening. So often her head would drop to the soothing sounds of CBeebies and sometimes she'd even wake herself up with a loud snore. What kind of a mum was she? She felt guilty ninety-nine per cent of the time and the other one per cent she was asleep.

After the morning café shift, Lexi took her bag from the worktop out the back of the café and rummaged for her keys. 'Right, I'm off next door, but ring me if we get a sudden rush and I'll pop back in.'

'Oh, I'm sure we'll be fine,' Raina replied, happily cutting some lettuce.

'You always say that,' said Lexi. 'But promise me?'

Raina looked up with a scowl. 'I promise. Now be off with you.'

As Lexi approached the door to the holiday lets she noticed the awful drunk bloke had left the front door open when he'd vacated, or the nanny had, and cursing, she went to the lower-floor apartment. Lexi fumbled for the right key. 'More haste less speed,' she told herself. She was always rushing these days.

The acrid smell of vomit hit her nostrils as soon as the door was open. She blanched and peeked inside. The place was an absolute mess. Empty wine bottles littered the hallway and she walked through to see a toilet bowl full of sick. The bed sheets were rucked up and the bedroom stank of stale alcohol with more bottles scattered over the floor. She held her breath and prepared for the living room. Food wrappers, magazines, and general dirt and debris were strewn everywhere. Lexi tried to take a quick breath in and raced round opening all the windows before she went to get Stella. She had to see this in case she wanted to keep some money from his deposit.

Lexi pushed the shop door with such force she had to catch it before it bounced off the wall and broke all the glass. Even Frank looked up as she marched in. Luckily there were no customers. 'Stella, you have to come and see the flat. I don't want to touch it until you've seen it.'

'What? Is it really that bad?' Stella stood up, her eyes wide in panic, but Lexi couldn't lie.

'Yes. It's awful. And it stinks of sick.'

'Oh no.' Stella ran a hand through her hair. 'I was worried this might happen. I saw him go to the shop and come back with another full carrier bag. I was hoping it was mostly food but it obviously wasn't. Oh God.' She rubbed her hand over her forehead. 'Let's go then.'

Stella shoved Frank into the flat then flicked the sign to closed and locked the door. When they reached the apartment Lexi let Stella go first and she stumbled in shock. 'Eww, it reeks in here. This is even worse than I thought.' She turned to Lexi as they wandered through, pausing at the living room door. 'I'll help you clean this. You can't do it on your own.'

'What about the shop?'

'It'll just have to stay closed. We've only got a couple of hours. How the hell are we going to get rid of that stink?'

Lexi, who after having two children, was well practised in getting rid of the smell of sick, said, 'If we can get rid of the source of it and open all the windows it should clear pretty quickly. I'll spray air fresheners everywhere too. If we're lucky the next people will be late arriving and we can give it a good airing. Have you done the gift basket?'

'Yeah. It's down in the flat. I'll bring that up later. Right.' Stella rolled her shoulders back and Lexi found her calm demeanour reassuring. 'Shall we separate or tackle each room together?'

'Let's work together,' Lexi replied. 'I think if we start in the

195

bathroom that'll make a big difference.' She went through to the kitchen and opened her cleaning cupboard, pulling out the tray of products. She grabbed her rubber gloves plus a pair for Stella, and all sorts of different spray cleaners and bleach, before leading the way.

Stella retched when she entered the bathroom. 'Oh, that is so gross.'

'You get used to it when you have kids, but yep, it is pretty gross.' Lexi flushed the toilet, pushed the already open window as wide as it would go, and poured half a bottle of bleach down the toilet and the sink. Stella opened a couple of bin bags, chucked the dirty towels into one and emptied the bin into another. From behind the cistern Lexi found an empty bottle of Merlot and another hidden behind the door. After a good scrub round, the smell, in that room at least, began to fade.

Next was the bedroom. Stella carried the bin bag of dirty washing and she and Lexi approached the bed with caution. As they pulled back the sheets a surge of queasiness overtook Lexi when she smelled, then saw, the pile of sick in the middle. The man had tried to cover it up by pulling the sheets over it, but once it had been revealed the whole room reeked. Luckily, they hadn't tugged the sheets and sent it flying over the walls like a disgusting Jackson Pollock. 'If this man ever comes back,' said Lexi. 'I'm going to rub his face in this like people used to do to dogs. That is so gross. Even my kids manage to get their sick in a bowl or down the toilet.'

Stella nodded, looking slightly shell-shocked. She clearly hadn't bargained for this sort of thing. 'I think I'll be emailing and letting him know I'll be keeping some of his deposit for new bedding.'

'Some? You're way too nice. I'd keep all of it.'

They worked in harmony together, clearing the rubbish, cleaning the surfaces with disinfectant, then sweeping and mopping the floor. How he thought they wouldn't discover the bottles under the bed Lexi had no idea. The man must have drunk nothing but wine for his entire stay. The living room was tackled with equal frenzy and finally the hall. By the time they finished at a quarter to three, only fifteen minutes before check-in time, the apartment smelt only vaguely of sick but very strongly of disinfectant.

'It smells like a public toilet,' moaned Stella. 'What can we do?'

'Don't panic,' Lexi replied. 'I've got a plan. I reckon if we keep the windows wide open, it'll be fine in an hour.'

'But it's already nearly three. They could turn up any minute.'

Lexi shrugged. 'You're going to have to convince them to go for a walk first if they arrive soon. With any luck they'll be super late. Or see if they're hungry and send them into me and Raina. We can do them a nice afternoon tea on the vintage cake stands. Make it an added extra.'

'Thank you,' said Stella, taking Lexi in a big hug. 'I don't know what I'd have done without you today.'

Lexi returned the embrace feeling the same. 'You're welcome, sweetie. I don't know about you, but I'll be ready for a big glass of wine tonight. I'd better get back to the café.' She hurried past Stella towards the door.

'I'll definitely be having a large glass of wine – white, not red though,' and she gave a theatrical shudder. Stella followed Lexi out of the apartment and locked the door behind them.

'Have you heard from the poet at all? I've been meaning to ask,' said Lexi.

'No. Nothing. I've texted him but he hasn't responded. I'm guessing his love for me was fleeting.'

'How do you feel about that?' she asked with a grin.

'To be honest I'm not the slightest bit bothered,' Stella replied evenly. 'The only thing I'm bothered about is that I'm not going to be able to ask him to Isaac's wedding so I'm back to square one.'

At the bottom of the stairs Lexi gave Stella a quick hug. 'Don't worry, honey, I'm sure things will work out in the end.'

Stella headed off into the shop and Lexi went into the café. Her feet, back and neck were already aching as she made her way past the busy tables. It was going to be a struggle to get through to the end of the day. She knew that this evening would end up like all the others – with her falling asleep on the sofa, only this time without the kids. Another pang of guilt hit her as she thought of them with their daddy. Sometimes she really missed them – all of them.

Saturday morning Lexi woke up on her own to the sounds of birds singing outside and the house silent. There was something completely delicious about waking up naturally and not being jumped on by small creatures even if they did hug you in the process. She'd already decided on a lazy breakfast of toast topped with poached eggs and the bit of ham left over from the kids' packed lunches. It was the sort of thing her children would turn their noses up at and moan about all the time she was eating it, which stopped her feeling like a grown-up. Sourdough would have been even better, but at an extortionate amount per loaf she couldn't afford it. Lexi stretched out her arms and legs and after another snooze decided to get up. She wasn't due at Vivien's until eleven so for once she was able to take time over her make-up and wear her very favourite dress.

The sun warmed Lexi's face and she enjoyed listening to the quiet around her as she walked into town, stopping off at the shop to stock up on some of Vivien's essentials. She knew her shopping list pretty well by now and it was always the same. If she got most of it now she could pop out later for any extra bits.

As she walked down the high street, taking the time to really look around, she smiled at the people having coffees outside in the sunshine. They had an amazing array of artisanal shops now: cheese makers, bakers who were amazing but thankfully didn't sell the same things as Raina, and a chocolatier. Swallowtail Bay had changed a lot since she was a kid. A gloriously blue sky with not even a hint of cloud formed a canopy over her head.

Vivien's house was about ten minutes further along from Stella and Miles's homes in the very poshest part of town and down a wide tree-lined road. Every garden was well tended with mature plants and bushes; some even had enormous trees in them that only helped to illustrate the age of the property. Lexi approached the gate to Vivien's beautiful old townhouse with its smaller, secluded front garden and walked up the path. Every time she entered through the little iron gate she felt like she was entering another world. The type of world that featured in Victorian novels about fairies. Maybe she and the kids could make a fairy house next weekend. With a grin, she knocked on the door. There was no answer and she waited a few seconds before knocking again, louder this time. Vivien didn't like to admit it but she was going a bit deaf.

Again Vivien didn't answer and Lexi hoped she hadn't forgotten and gone out. She didn't get much time to herself so when she did she liked to make the most of it and a wasted trip because Vivien had somehow forgotten would ruin half the day. But it wasn't normal for her to forget anything. She was still sharp as a tack. Lexi clenched her jaw and knocked again using the knocker this time, bashing it down as hard as she could. No sound came from inside and Lexi's frustration was suddenly replaced with fear. Her body hardened and with trembling fingers she took the spare set of keys from her bag and unlocked the door.

'Vivien?' Lexi called, walking down the large hall, her kitten heels tapping on the gorgeous blue geometric tiles. 'Vivien? It's Lexi.' A sudden gasp emerged from Lexi as she rounded the door to the living room and saw Vivien lying on the floor, fully dressed but unmoving. Throwing the shopping bag down she ran over to her. Vivien's face was grey and her skin cold. Her eyes were closed as if she was sleeping. Shaking all the way to the tips of her fingers Lexi felt on Vivien's neck for a pulse. There was nothing. Panic had stolen the strength from Lexi's hands and scared she'd done it wrong, she felt Vivien's wrist but there was still no pulse. A sudden queasiness rose up from the pit of her stomach, tightening her throat. Lexi's eyes filled with tears and though she knew it was of no use, she took out her mobile phone and dialled an ambulance.

A couple of hours later, after the appearance of both the ambulance and the police, and numerous questions, Lexi sat outside on the doorstep, with a tin foil blanket wrapped around her shoulders. She'd swept that step so many times and, remembering Vivien, traced her fingers over the grout.

'Can we call anyone to look after you?' asked the kind policewoman. She'd arrived a few minutes after the ambulance and seeing the state Lexi was in, had been calm and caring.

Lexi shook her head. 'No, thanks. I'll be fine.'

'We'd really prefer for you not to be on your own at the moment, Miss Durham. You've had a bad shock.'

Lexi wiped the tears from her cheeks. She couldn't seem to stop them no matter how hard she tried or how much she told herself Vivien was old and wouldn't have lived forever. 'I'm just going to walk around the corner to my friend's shop. It's not far. She'll look after me.'

'All right then. You can go whenever you like – there's nothing more we need from you. I just wanted to make sure you'd be okay.'

'That's kind,' Lexi replied, but inside she felt like a robot. The emotions of the last few hours had been so extreme she felt like a washed-out version of herself; grey and bereft of colour, turning invisible. She scrunched up the tissue in her hand and stood on shaking legs. Another wave of nausea washed over her and swirled in her stomach. Lexi gave the policewoman a faint smile and stumbled away.

The air felt colder than it had earlier that morning and she pulled her jacket tighter around her. The birdsong that had sounded so sweet now stung her ears as their sharp calls pierced the cocoon of grief. Though she tried to fight back tears they wouldn't stop coming. As it was such a nice day, Stella had wedged the shop door open and was busy arranging stock when Lexi walked in.

'Hey you— Oh, honey, what's wrong?' Stella immediately placed her arms around Lexi, her brow furrowed.

'It's Vivien,' she snivelled. 'She's dead.' She collapsed onto Stella's shoulder and sobbed.

'What?'

Lexi struggled for breath against the anguish pushing up from her lungs. 'She's dead. I went round there this morning with her shopping but she didn't answer. When I opened the door she was lying on the floor—'

Stella wiped a tear from her own eye. 'I can't believe it. I just can't believe it. I mean, she looked a bit peaky the other day, but …'

Lexi felt Stella's arms tighten around her and they both cried. 'I'm going to miss her so much.' They both looked up as a customer walked in then immediately turned around and walked back out again.

Stella started patting her back. 'She was really lovely.'

'Oh crikey.' Lexi shot backwards. 'What will I tell the kids?'

'I can tell them if you want, Lexi. I don't mind.' Stella wiped her eyes and Lexi saw the mascara run down her cheeks.

'No, it's okay.' She tried to pull herself together but her nerves were completely shredded. 'I'd better tell them. As their mum I should be the one to do it.'

Stella found a tissue in her pocket and blew her nose. 'Did you want me to stay over tonight so you're not on your own?'

Lexi thought about it but decided she would probably be better off alone. She didn't need anyone seeing her all snotty and puffy, but one day she'd tell Stella how much that gesture meant. How much having her as a friend meant. 'No, thanks, Stella. I think I'd prefer to be on my own with a bottle of wine.'

Coming back again and again, the question was rolling around her head: how the hell was she going to tell her children? How could she comfort them after something like this? They loved Vivien almost as much as she did.

Chapter 21

Just over a week later, Stella and Lexi were clad in black at the sweet little church across the road from the shop and around the corner from Vivien's house, saying goodbye to her. Lexi, having been closest to Vivien, had taken her loss hard. The kids too required a few days off school because they'd grown so fond of the old lady that they'd been heartbroken by her sudden death.

Stella watched Vivien's sombre-looking solicitor, Mr Beck, clad in a black suit with black tie, looking suitably mournful. Lexi had said that as Vivien didn't have any family he had followed the instructions set out in her will and arranged everything as Vivien had requested.

'At least it's a sunny day,' Lexi said, wiping at her eyes before the coffin had even arrived. 'Vivien would have been happy it was sunny.'

In the churchyard, stood in the shade of the pink blossom trees, Stella rested her head on her shoulder. 'You're doing really well, honey.'

'I'm trying not to cry too much in front of the kids.' She looked over and Stella followed her gaze to see Will, Lexi's ex-husband, a giant of a man, holding tightly onto his kids' tiny hands. They were crying too and Will hugged them close to him and stroked their heads. He looked uncomfortable in his suit but smiled sweetly at Lexi when he saw her looking over. Given her vintage style, Stella had always imagined someone equally as stylish, but Will's sandy-blond hair, weather-beaten face and thin layer of stubble were anything but. Lexi wiped again at her red nose. For once she hadn't bothered with her usual eyeliner, and her blood-shot eyes stood out against pale white skin. 'I wasn't sure about bringing them, but Will and I talked it through and he thought it would be good for them to say goodbye too. He said he'll take them home if it gets too much and they're not staying for the wake. He's been absolutely brilliant.'

'He seems a lovely man.'

'I'm nothing but trouble to him,' Lexi replied, suddenly collapsing into tears again.

'No you're not.' Stella patted her arm. 'You're wonderful and amazing, and brilliant.'

Lexi took a deep breath trying to control her erratic breathing. 'Suck it up, Lexi,' she told herself out loud. 'Suck it up. Oh, great, now Mr Beck's coming over.'

Mr Beck approached, his combover flipping the wrong way in the breeze. 'Miss Durham, the hearse will be here soon.'

'It can't. There aren't nearly enough people yet.' Lexi gaped around in panic. A fairly decent number of the townsfolk were in attendance, all clad in black and grey. The old ladies who Vivien teasingly referred to as her competition were wiping at their noses with delicate handkerchiefs but Lexi had hoped to see more. 'Didn't you say there was a guest list already prepared?'

'Yes, but—'

'Is everything all right?' asked Miles.

Stella glanced up to see him looking completely, mouth-water-ingly gorgeous in a well-tailored black suit. He must have heard Lexi's voice climbing and come over to help. He gave Stella a polite smile. She kept her mouth closed for fear her tongue would roll out like in old cartoons. She knew she shouldn't be thinking anything of the sort at a funeral, but Miles had suddenly shot up to the premier league looks-wise. His light brown hair had grown a little longer and she noticed now how it curled at the front. His suit fitted well over his broad shoulders and his peacock-blue eyes scanned her in her smart black dress. In her heels she was almost as tall as him and being on eye level she could see that his were a bit puffy and rimmed with red. Again, she wondered what the connection was between him and Vivien because he'd clearly shed a tear for her too.

'Are you okay, Lexi?' he asked again.

Lexi's voice carried a hint of panic as she spoke to Mr Beck. 'Did you invite them all? Did anyone RSVP?'

'I don't think you RSVP to funerals,' said Stella, softly.

'What's going on?' Miles asked again, gently. 'Is there anything I can help with?'

'I did, Miss Durham,' Mr Beck confirmed. 'But the list was rather long and … how can I say this kindly … fanciful.'

'Fanciful?' Lexi and Stella replied in unison. 'What do you mean fanciful?' Lexi asked.

Stella turned to Miles and his sad, solemn expression softened her heart. 'We're discussing the guest list Vivien prepared. Lexi's concerned Vivien wouldn't be happy with the turnout.'

Miles nodded.

'The trouble is,' said Mr Beck in his dulcet tones, 'the list included quite a lot of famous actors and singers and arty sort of people. I'm not sure any of them will come. I think we will have to proceed as we are when the hearse arrives.'

Miles turned to Lexi. 'I know this is hard, Lexi, but the church is quite full inside and there's still people arriving now. All her friends are here, which is the only thing that matters. I'm sure what would mean the most to her is that you're here.'

Lexi sucked in a deep breath and looked up to heaven. 'Okay.'

The hearse arrived and upon seeing it, a flood of tears escaped from Lexi. She pulled out another tissue and Stella found her own. But just as the coffin was removed and they made their way towards the church doors, a large black car parked just outside the church. Then another. Stella's mouth dropped open as the doors opened and elegant aged singers and some actors she recognised from old Hammer Horror films exited car after car and made their way into the church. One old lady, who walked with a stick and looked as if Lexi's daughter had done her make-up, greeted Lexi at the door. 'I can't believe our dear Vivien has left us,' she said, carefully wiping at her eyes. 'I always thought I would go first. She had such vim and vigour. And no one screamed quite like her.'

'She did,' replied Lexi, too shocked to cry.

From the doorway, Lexi and Stella looked on as more and more cars arrived and old stars of stage and screen filled the pews in the church. Whispers from the crowd met Stella's ears and she couldn't help but smile. Vivien would have been overjoyed at such an exit.

Lexi, Will and their children made their way to the front pews, followed by Miles and Stella. The solicitor sat at the back. During the service Ralph and Taylor looked around slightly dumb-founded, their eyes welling with tears, but holding tight to Will's hands. Lexi tried to smile at them but couldn't stop weeping and when Ralph flung himself into her arms, Stella was also unable to hold back any longer. She saw Will take hold of Lexi's hand and give it a squeeze. It was a wonderful gesture and seemed to calm Lexi a little as she stroked Ralph's head. Taylor cuddled closely into her arm.

Then the vicar asked Miles to give a reading and Stella's heart jumped. She looked to Lexi who shrugged; she couldn't have known he was doing it either. Miles stood up, pulled a piece of paper from his inside jacket pocket and made his way to the front. Where he stood, the great big stained-glass windows lit him from behind. The sun streamed in sending beams of light to the ground and it felt like Vivien was giving one last farewell.

Stella had expected a cold speech, but as Miles began, his voice shaking, she was surprised to see tears form in his eyes.

'Vivien and I have – had – been friends since I was young and a bit of a lonely teenager. She was an incredible woman – an incredible friend.' He stopped, his Adam's apple bobbing as he swallowed down a great lump of emotion. 'I know this poem was one of her favourites so I'll try and do it justice.'

Stella felt her eyes widen in shock. She couldn't imagine Miles as a lonely teenager. Surely he'd had millions of friends? One of the popular kids according to Jay, always teasing him about not pronouncing his t's properly. Confusion flooded her brain and she watched him with interest. Miles paused at the end of his first sentence, swallowed again, then took a deep breath as a few tears escaped down his handsome face. Stella could see how hard it was for him. He read beautifully and with a depth of emotion she wouldn't have credited him with. At the end, as her own tears escaped, Miles took his seat next to her. She heard a deep exhalation of relief and watched the fumbling of his fingers as he refolded the piece of paper and tucked it back into his pocket.

The service ended and they all made their way outside to the graveside. Lexi said goodbye to her children, cuddling them and assuring them she was okay, and Will too gave her a strong hug. Stella wished their marriage hadn't ended. They seemed so right for each other and from the tender glances between them, they clearly still cared about each other very deeply. It was such a shame. But then, life didn't always turn out how you wanted it to.

When Lexi rejoined them, Vivien's coffin was being slowly lowered into the ground. Her bottom lip wavered and without her children watching, she let the emotion overtake her. Stella wrapped her in a hug and looked up through blurry, watery eyes to see Miles wiping at his own cheeks.

After the burial was finished, the guests walked back towards the front of the church. They left Lexi behind to have a few minutes by herself at the graveside while Miles and Stella walked on, chatting to different people as they went. One of the old ladies Vivien had never really liked said, 'I meant to ask Lexi what actually killed her,' and began walking towards her.

Stella opened her mouth to speak when Miles said, 'Let's leave Lexi alone for a while, shall we? She was very fond of Vivien. Besides, I believe it was a heart attack.' Stella silently thanked him for steering them away. Lexi wouldn't be able to cope with some of their more direct questions right now. As the more famous guests climbed into their waiting cars and departed, everyone stared open-mouthed, probably thinking, as Stella did, that Vivien was still a surprising old lady. Lexi came back to join them and Miles turned to her. 'Lexi, I know Vivien was fondest of you, but did you want me to go over to the hotel and greet people for the wake? I – I didn't know if you'd like a few minutes before heading over?'

'That'd be great, Miles. Thank you.'

He gave her a nod and headed off.

'What's got into him?' asked Stella. 'It's like he's a completely different person lately.'

'He's been really sweet. He even sent me some flowers the other day.'

Stella looked up. She couldn't understand this change in Miles's behaviour. His relationship with Kiera couldn't have been to blame for all of it but he had been nicer since they'd split. 'Shall I wait in the car for you?'

'Yes, please. I won't be long.'

From the car window, Stella watched Lexi walk back towards the grave. Suddenly she realised that Jay wasn't there. There was no reason that he should be really – he'd never mentioned knowing Vivien that well – but when so many of the town had attended, she'd have thought he would too. He was still looking like the only man she could ask to Isaac's wedding, if she could summon up the courage to speak to him again. Either that or go on her own. Then she saw Miles's car departing and had a crazy idea. She really wanted to show everyone that she wasn't a lunatic running off to a new part of the country to follow a silly dream. That was what Isaac's parents had thought. If Miles came with her, it would show them she'd made friends and was building a new life for herself. And Miles owed her a favour after all, even if it was a pretty big one to ask.

'Are you okay, sweetie?' Stella asked, as Lexi opened the door and climbed in.

Confusion flooded her face. 'Mr Beck has asked me to drop by his office as soon as possible to discuss Vivien's will.'

'Really? Why?'

'I don't know.' Poor Lexi looked completely shell-shocked.

'You could be mentioned in it,' said Stella. 'Perhaps she left you a bequest.'

'As long as she didn't leave me her debts.' Lexi's shoulders slumped down in exhaustion. 'I've got enough of my own.'

Stella's heart lurched. If only there was something she could do for her friend. Her best friend, she realised with a sudden grateful rush, but she knew there was nothing. Grief had to take its own course and all she could do was be there for her. Which she would be. Every step of the way.

Chapter 22

Despite the kids' protests that they needed just one more day to get over Vivien's death, Lexi deposited them at the school and beat a hasty retreat. They had both cried and it had wrenched her heart out when the teachers cajoled them into class while they told them how sad they were. But Lexi knew that what they needed was calm, normality and routine. It was hard for her too, but the more they stayed off school, the harder it would be to go back. The headteacher had kindly rung her an hour later to confirm that the kids had calmed down and were enjoying a normal school day, so she didn't have to worry. It had been a huge weight off her mind.

Now all she had to stress about was what the solicitor could possibly want with her. She and Vivien had been close but she'd never mentioned leaving her anything in her will. Perhaps she had left her the pretty full-length mirror from her bedroom, knowing how much Lexi liked it. But what if it was something awful? Lexi had no idea what that could be, but she really couldn't cope with anything else right now. Being with Will at the funeral had brought back a whole heap of memories and feelings, and her heart felt fit to bursting with the weight of it all.

Mr Beck was seeing her at eleven o'clock and Raina had said

she could take as much time as she needed. Everyone was being so sweet and kind. Lexi felt her eyes well up again but she looked to the sky to dry them and took a deep breath. She was bored of crying now and there was no point in destroying her eyeliner. The day was warm as the last month of spring had begun and they were edging towards summer. The sky was a bright clear blue, almost shiny, and clouds were few and far between. She'd only worn a cardigan over her dress today and took a moment to enjoy the sun on her skin.

The solicitor's wasn't based in a new shiny office building because, thankfully, there weren't many of those in Swallowtail Bay. It was actually nothing more than a renovated Victorian house. Mr Beck's office even had an old Victorian fireplace in it, filled with wood stacked in an arty fashion. He sat behind a large old-fashioned dark wood desk, and looked even older in the dim light that struggled to come through the small window behind him, shaded as it was by a large hydrangea bush.

'Thank you for coming, Miss Durham. Normally we would simply write to anyone mentioned in a will, but Miss Griffen gave us very specific instructions regarding you.'

'Oh, okay,' Lexi replied, shifting in her seat opposite him. Her insides felt as knotted as Ralph's shoelaces when he tried to tie them.

'Would you like a cup of tea or coffee before we begin?'

'No thank you.' Lexi pushed down the uncomfortable feeling in her stomach and felt her shoulders tense up. She couldn't eat or drink anything right now. Mr Beck picked up a folder, opened it and then peered over the top at Lexi. Patience wasn't a virtue Lexi had been blessed with and she had to hold herself back from shouting at him to hurry up. Eventually, he spoke.

'Miss Durham, apart from a bequest of some vinyl records and some books to Miles Parker, Miss Griffen has left all her property and monies to you. The mortgage on the house has been paid for some time and Miss Griffen had a substantial amount in savings. After inheritance tax, over three hundred thousand pounds has been bequeathed to you.'

Lexi's mouth fell open and she leaned in close, fearing she had misheard. 'I – I'm sorry, what?'

Mr Beck smiled and his face became softer and more kindly. 'I understand it may be a shock, but Miss Griffen has left everything she owned to you. We'll begin the process of transferring everything to your ownership within the next few days. You're welcome to enter the house as soon as you wish and I understand you have a set of keys already?'

'Yes. Yes, I do. So – wait – hang on a minute.' She was now resting on the edge of his desk for support. Her brain was foggy and it was like she was in a dream, or drunk. 'Do you mean to say she left the house to me?'

He nodded. 'And everything in it, and all her money too. Apart from the items left to Mr Parker.'

Unable to speak as her mind whirled around, Lexi paused. 'So what do I do with the house?' If her brain was a cartoon character it would have its fingers in its ears and be running around in circles shouting 'aaarrrggghhh!' Instead of relaxing at such incredible news, the knot in her stomach had tightened so hard it felt like it had pulled in all her other internal organs. Her heart refused to beat and her ribs felt like they were collapsing inwards.

'Are you sure you wouldn't like a cup of tea or coffee, Miss Durham?'

'No. Honestly, thank you. I just – I just don't understand.'

Mr Beck was being very patient. 'The house is yours,' he said with a smile. 'You may do with what you wish. You can move into it or sell it.'

'I couldn't sell it.' The reaction was pure instinct – a way to preserve Vivien's memory – but could she live there? In the house her friend had died in?

'You have some time to think about it. You can't sell until

we've transferred the deeds but that won't take long. Take your time to make a decision.'

'No. No. I mean I just couldn't. It was Vivien's home and it's such a lovely house.'

'That's for you to decide. But we'll be happy to offer advice or provide any assistance you require. All our fees are on our website.'

'Yes, of course.' She nodded. 'Thank you.'

'If you've no further questions there's nothing else I need to tell you at this stage, but please feel free to call me if you think of anything. We'll send you a letter shortly with full details.'

Mr Beck stood up and Lexi knew that was her cue to leave. Her legs wobbled and her head spun, leaving her light-headed. Then as she left, a huge grin spread across her face. Her stomach unknotted and her heart felt about to explode. How could this have happened to her? She shook her head in pure disbelief as she walked to Stella's shop.

'Are you okay?' asked Stella from behind the counter.

Lexi paused in the doorway, still unsure if she was in a dream. 'Vivien left me her stuff.' The words still didn't quite register with her brain.

'What stuff?'

'Everything.' Suddenly she wanted to laugh. 'Her house, her possessions … everything.'

Stella stared at her. 'I can't believe it. That's amazing.' She leapt up from behind the counter and took her in a hug. Lexi was too shocked to even close her arms around Stella and they hung loosely at her sides.

Lexi laughed disbelievingly. 'I'm not broke anymore and we can move in as soon as we want to. We just have to wait for the deeds to be transferred.'

'She really was very fond of you, wasn't she?' Stella said.

'I had no idea she'd do this though.' It was all utterly unbelievable.

'Well, that's clear from the look on your face.' Stella laughed.

'I'm so shocked. I don't know what to do. I'd better tell Will and I'll have to tell the kids tonight.'

'I can't think of anyone who deserves it more,' Stella said. 'Shall I go and get us celebratory coffee and cake from next door?'

'I'll go,' said Lexi. 'I need to tell Raina.'

'You're not going to quit your job, are you?' Stella asked, concerned, but the idea hadn't even entered Lexi's head.

'No! Gosh no. I just want her to be one of the first to know, that's all.' Just because her luck seemed to be changing a little didn't mean she could turn her whole life upside down and no one had supported her more than Raina.

'I'm sure she'll be happy for you.'

'She will. I know she will. Can I have another hug first though, please? I'm all shaky and weird.'

Stella obliged. Lexi hadn't felt this way since they had handed over her newborn children. It was a moment of pure pleasure – of peace and tranquillity, and of everything being right with the world. In fact, this was even better than the days the nurses had plonked her wriggly babies on her chest because the house wasn't going to learn to talk back, she thought with a smile. She'd always known Vivien was a kind and caring soul but Lexi had never expected anything like this. Closing her eyes, she gave thanks to the wonderful old lady for changing her life.

Chapter 23

Miles heard the good news about Lexi from Raina a few days later when he stopped in for a late lunch. His nostrils filled with the smell of cooked bacon and sausages, but in front of him, beneath the glass, was such an array of ingredients he just couldn't decide what to have. Bright lettuce and tomatoes glistened; a bowl of fresh flaky tuna looked inviting next to a plate of sliced good quality ham and next to that was juicy and tender rare roast beef. Then there were all the cheeses: Stilton, Brie, feta, good old cheddar. Maybe he could get two baguettes and have one for supper. 'I can't believe it,' he said, smiling. 'So Vivien left her everything?'

'Oh, yes,' Raina replied in her soft Irish accent from the other side of the counter. 'You're not cross, are you?' She eyed him suspiciously. 'She's a good girl and she deserves it.'

'No. Not at all.' Confusion pulled at his features. 'Why would I be cross?'

'I think Lexi was worried you might resent her as you and Vivien were close too, you being friends with her since you were young and all that.'

'Of course I don't resent her. Vivien and I were friends, but I didn't do anything near what Lexi does – I mean did – for her.'

215

A lump formed in his throat, temporarily halting his mounting appetite. He still hadn't quite got used to speaking about Vivien in the past tense. 'I used to pop in when I could, but Lexi saw her every week, did her shopping, cleans for her too, sometimes.' He'd done it again, he should have said cleaned. Miles swallowed down how much he was going to miss her. 'Lexi deserves it. No one works harder than her.'

'It'll certainly make life easier for her. She's a good girl. It's nice to see things working out for the nice people for a change, isn't it?'

'It certainly is,' he replied, finally picking out what he was going to have for lunch.

Raina placed her hands on the top of the counter. 'Now have you decided yet, young man, I can't wait here forever. I've got a business to run.'

Miles smiled. 'It really is your own fault, you know, making everything look so great. But, I have decided and I'd like a roast beef and Stilton, please.'

'I could have told you that's what you'd order when you walked in here. You should just let me decide next time.'

'Maybe I will,' he teased. 'In fact, I'd like another one for my supper later. Why don't you choose that one for me?'

'Right you are.'

Raina set about making his two baguettes and a few minutes later he took his carrier bag with him as he left. 'Thanks, Raina. This smells delicious.'

'Enjoy it. And be good.'

Miles left the shop, closing the door behind him. How could Lexi worry he'd be upset or angry that Vivien hadn't left him her house or money? She'd left him her vinyl records and some of her books, including her poetry books, the one that contained her favourite he'd read at the funeral. That was more than enough for him. Lexi, kind as always, had offered to get them for him when she began sorting the house and Miles was happy to wait.

216

He didn't want to add any more pressure on her at the moment. He knew he'd get them eventually, and he'd treasure them. But Raina's words worried him. Had he really come across as that sort of person who begrudged another's happiness and good fortune? He was more relaxed now and, though he felt bad to admit it, happier since Kiera had left, but the thought that people thought of him as such a … such a … dick was shaming.

As he walked past Old Herbert's Shop, the name making him smile once more, he realised he had a good excuse to pop in and speak to Stella. If he really had been coming across so horribly he needed to fix it. He walked through the already open door and smiled at Frank.

'Hello, boy.' Frank wandered over to him, stretching as he went, then sat at his feet, waiting for a fuss. The lead was only just long enough to reach him and as he bent down he saw more new stock, blankets and cushions this time piled high on the old wingback chair Vivien used to sit in. They were in muted golds and mustardy browns and very good quality. The price Stella was asking made them a bargain and he wondered again where she was getting her stock from. If he did open a business he'd have to ask her for some tips. After scratching Frank behind the ears, Miles turned to Stella. 'He's got used to me now, I think.'

'I think he has.'

'I just popped in to say Raina told me about Lexi. I'm really pleased for her.'

Stella's eyes, warm and friendly, were sparkling at her friend's good fortune and Miles felt the force of her kindness. 'It's such amazing news, isn't it? I'm glad something good has come out of such a horrible thing.'

'Yes. Vivien really was incredible.'

'She was. I didn't know whether to use her chair at first but I didn't really want to move it either, so I kept it where it was and put it to good use. I couldn't keep looking at it all empty; it was like I was still waiting for her to pop in.'

'I think she'd be really pleased she's still centre of attention,' he joked, lifting the mood. 'I bet they're selling well. They look great.'

'They are actually,' Stella replied proudly. 'I think the colours are a good choice. They'll go in anyone's homes and on nearly any colour sofa.'

Conversation was going well for once and Miles found he wanted it to continue. 'It wasn't until the day of her funeral I realised all Vivien's stories were true. I'd always thought she made them up, or at the very least over-exaggerated.'

'Me too.' Stella's eyes opened wide in agreement. 'I felt so bad when all those old opera singers turned up—'

'Giving it all, "Darling," this and "Darling", that,' he said, waving his hand around like the Queen.

'Yes, exactly!' Stella laughed and her face illuminated with the warmth of her smile.

Miles searched for something to say, refusing to lose momentum. 'How are the holiday lets going? Is that awful family still here?'

'Yes, for another two weeks. They're not that bad now they've settled in actually. The other flat is free this week and, to be honest, I'm quite relieved. With the funeral and everything it would have been hard to manage without Lexi's help.'

'It must be difficult doing it all on your own.' Miles was careful to keep his voice and expression neutral and not sound at all judgy like he had done in the past. He was doing everything he could to control his manner and not let his nerves get the better of him, as he'd previously come across so badly.

After studying him for a moment she answered. 'It is sometimes but I've got Lexi for moral support. That smells delicious,' she said pointing to his carrier bag. 'Late lunch?'

'Yeah. Well, one is a late lunch; the other a late dinner, probably. I'm a bit lazy when it comes to cooking.'

'It can be hard when you're on your own.' A fleeting look of sadness passed over her eyes and was then engulfed by a fierce pink blush that galloped over her cheeks. 'Wait – sorry, I – I didn't mean to remind you that—'

Miles laughed and held up his hand. 'It's okay. I know what you mean.' To think that she was being nice and trying not to remind him of his break-up after how pompous and obnoxious he'd been to her – she must have the temperament of a saint. 'Anyway I need to have something now because I've got to go away for a networking event this evening and the catering can be quite hit and miss. Those little canapés don't fill you up and there's never enough to go round.'

Stella's face relaxed. 'Do you need me to keep an eye on the place again?'

'No that's okay, I'll be back in the early hours. Just not sure what time. Thanks for the offer though.'

'Sure.' Stella hesitated as if she was unsure about her next sentence. Her cheeks reddened even more and she picked up a pen, fiddling with it. After another glance in his direction, she seemed to make her mind up. 'Miles, I wondered if I could ask a favour in return?'

'Of course.' Internally he could have fist-pumped the air; he was so pleased she felt she could ask him something. It meant things were moving on from the dreadful start they'd had.

'It's a bit of an odd one, but I'm really, really stuck.'

Miles smiled. 'Go on, try me.'

Still tapping the pen she spoke quickly. 'I was wondering if you fancied coming to a wedding with me? Not like my date but – it's next weekend in Oxford and I haven't got anyone else I can ask.' The blush had spread over her neck and she kept her eyes down on Frank, still absent-mindedly tapping. 'I still don't know that many people here.'

He had to be honest, it wasn't what he'd been expecting and he was taken aback. He'd thought she might ask him to walk Frank or help with a delivery; she had a lot more paintings coming in at the moment, he noticed. But Stella was nice and he really did admire her spirit in moving somewhere new and starting a business. And, despite being ridiculously awful to her, when he'd asked her a favour she hadn't even flinched in saying yes. If he wanted a chance to prove to her, and the town, that he wasn't a stuck-up idiot, this was it. 'Okay, then. Yeah. I'd be happy to.'

The relief on Stella's face was palpable. 'Oh, good, thanks. You won't have to drive. I'll do all the driving so you can have a drink and relax. And I won't introduce you as my boyfriend, or anything, just a friend.'

She was babbling a little and Miles felt his heart wriggle in his chest. 'Okay, well, whatever you want. So you'll text me when we need to leave and stuff, yeah?'

She nodded. 'I will.' Miles gave Frank one last pat and turned to walk away. 'Miles?'

He spun back at the sweetness of her tone and saw again the genuine smile on her pale pink lips. 'Thank you.'

As soon as he stepped outside he was accosted by the horrible family loading themselves into an enormous people carrier, parked on the double yellow lines out front. Josie sidled over and he felt his good humour begin to fade.

'Hi, Miles. What are you up to today?'

Inside he groaned but made an effort to smile back. 'Hi, Josie. I'm just off to work in a bit.'

'Anywhere exciting?'

'No, not really. You?' He nodded to the car.

'Oh. We're off to the theatre this evening. We're having an afternoon in that town, oh – what's it called? The one with the theatre and museum?'

'Halebury?'

'Yes, that's the one. We're staying at a hotel there overnight.' She leaned in and whispered, 'I don't see why when Roger could easily drive but he says he wants to drink and Hermione won't drive at night.'

'Couldn't you drive?' he asked. 'If you really don't want to stay overnight.'

She cocked her head like he'd just said something ridiculously stupid. 'But then *I* couldn't have a drink, and believe me these kids drive you to it.'

He wasn't sure she should be talking about her employers, or their children, like that to a complete stranger. She must have thought they were on better terms than they actually were.

'Come on, Josie. We're ready to go,' called the man he presumed was Roger.

'Listen, Miles, I was wondering if you fancied having a drink together sometime?' She placed her hands in the pockets of her jeans and was jutting her chest out.

Miles knew from the tension around his eyes his expression was that of a rabbit caught in headlights. Some men – men like Jay – might have been flattered, but she was so young the offer made him feel very uncomfortable. 'Umm, Josie, listen, I'm quite a lot older than you—'

'So? I don't mind.' She fluttered her eyelashes at him but all it did was cause another wave of panic and he answered bluntly without thinking.

'I do though. Sorry.' Her face changed in an instant and her eyes narrowed on him. It reminded him strangely of Kiera.

'Fine,' she replied, just as Roger called her again to get into the car.

Miles turned and began to walk away hearing her huff in reply to them both. With a sigh he knew he'd had a lucky escape, but the kids didn't seem as fortunate as she chastised them. He felt a little sorry for the two boys who were clearly going to be on short shrift that afternoon until one of them called Josie a name ten-year-old boys shouldn't know and he marched on before his ears turned blue.

Chapter 24

Stella rolled over and glanced at the clock. It was two in the morning! She pulled the pillow down over her ears to shut out the noise. The horrible family must have decided to come home rather than stay in Halebury. That awful Roger had enjoyed telling her of their plan to spend even more money and stay overnight in the nearby town. Maybe the hotel hadn't been up to their exacting standards. Urgh, they didn't have to make quite so much of a racket though. They really were the worst. Luckily, Stella was bone-tired and her heavy eyelids closed again almost instantly. The next thing she knew the alarm was going off and the sun shone in through the bedroom window. It was time to start the day.

At eleven, Stella took a quick break from what had been a fantastically busy morning to let Frank out the back for a wee. Just as she returned to the shop she saw the horrible family pull up on the double yellow lines out front. Weird, she thought they'd come home last night. Maybe they'd gone out early. Stella tutted. They could have easily parked at the side of the shop where there weren't any lines, rather than breaking the law. Leaving the hazards on, they all climbed out and Josie and the children ran inside. A few minutes later Stella heard an ear-splitting scream and the kids and Josie came charging back down the stairs to where Roger was unloading the boot.

Stella ran to the shop door and stuck her head out. 'What's wrong?' she asked as Hermione, the mother, grabbed Josie by the shoulders and demanded to know the same.

'We've been robbed,' Josie shouted, tearfully.

At the same moment, just to make matters worse, Miles walked around the corner from his house and stopped abruptly, surveying the scene. Hermione let go of Josie and her hands closed around her face. Her voice was hysterical and punctuated by gasping breaths. 'What do you mean we've been robbed?'

'Someone broke in and they've taken everything. All our clothes are everywhere, the TV's gone and loads of other stuff.'

Stella's whole body went cold and her arms and legs felt like lead. The only thing she could hear was the hard pounding of her heart and blood thumping in her ears. Josie and Hermione turned to her, as did Miles. Stella glanced over their faces and ran as fast as she could next door and up the flight of stairs to the flat. The door was flung open and still on its hinges but the wood frame was splintered and cracked where a crow bar or something had forced the lock. She went in and saw that every room was ransacked. Josie had been right: clothes had been thrown everywhere, the contents of a chest of drawers had been removed and the wardrobe doors were left open, sticking out into the chaos. All the TVs were missing as were the stereo and the DVD player.

Miles had followed Stella in and stood beside her. She turned to him, unable to say anything, or figure out what to do next. Josie, Hermione and Roger were frantically searching the room. The two children stood on the landing, peering in the doorway. Roger pushed past Stella to the bedroom and they followed behind, watching him check the bedside cabinet. The drawer had been left open but he glanced in it, then searched around the

223

floor. 'They've stolen our money,' he said, before rounding on Stella. 'I had a thousand pounds in that drawer.'

'A thousand pounds?' echoed Stella, willing her brain to work faster. Before she knew what was happening he was in her face, clicking his fingers in front of her eyes.

'Hello! Anybody in there?'

'There's no need for that,' said Miles, taking Roger's hand and pushing it back towards him.

'I'm so sorry,' said Stella. Every muscle twitched as the fight or flight response took hold and she had to resist the urge to run away. 'I'd better call the police. I'll replace your money, of course.'

'Just wait,' said Miles. 'We'd better let the police deal with this first before you go promising anything, Stella.'

'Are you calling me a liar?' demanded Roger, squaring up to Miles.

Panic washed over Stella as she worried that on top of everything there might now be a fight. Miles didn't flinch but looked Roger in the eye and said calmly, 'I'm saying we need to report this to the police first, then Stella can talk to her insurers and find out what she needs to do.'

Roger backed away as Hermione dramatically flung herself into her husband's arms, weeping. He looked at Josie. 'Get the children and everything of ours you can find. We're leaving. Now.'

'Oh, Dad,' one of them moaned. 'Can't we stay? This holiday has only just got exciting.'

'I'll go and call the police,' said Stella and through her tears caught Miles's eye. His face was a mixture of concern and sympathy, which was sweet of him, but there was nothing he could do to help. As she looked around, the pounding in her chest returned. 'Oh no! I left the door open. Frank!' As she'd just come back from letting him out she hadn't had a chance to fasten his lead back onto his collar.

Stella charged back down the stairs and out into the street to see the shop door wide open. How could she have been so stupid?

Charging in, she ran around the counter shouting his name, but Frank wasn't there. He'd gone. Tears stung her eyes and she pressed her hand to her mouth to stop the sobs from escaping.

'He can't have gone far,' said Miles, appearing at the shop doorway, having followed her down. 'We'll find him.'

Stella ran into the street, her body moving on instinct rather than through controlled movements. She looked around, desperately trying to think. It was a bright sunny day and even though there was only a slight breeze she was shivering, her chest juddering with fear. 'He knows his way to the beach. I bet he's gone there.' She walked fast, glancing around, calling his name all the time, but each time she did it became a little more shaky – a little more desperate. Miles came too, also calling out, but Stella knew Frank wouldn't come for anyone but her. As panic took over she began running, Miles keeping pace. 'Frank? Frank? Here, boy, come on.' But he was still nowhere to be seen.

As she approached the road to the beach her lungs constricted, pushing all the air out. If he'd been hit by a car trying to cross and was lying in the road she'd never ever forgive herself, but thankfully he wasn't. They ran between oncoming cars, Stella calling again and again, frantically turning her head left and right in the hope that she'd spot him. At the top of the beach she paused and a bolt of relief soothed her as she saw him down at the water's edge chasing the seagulls who responded with flapping wings and angry caws. She let out a breath and cried. Without thinking she grabbed Miles's arm and pointed him out. 'There he is.'

Miles smiled and it helped her calm down and breathe. 'Frank!' Stella called as they headed down the stony beach. Frank looked up upon hearing his name, his tail wagging like it was all a great game, his long ears flapping in the breeze. A seagull landed behind him and he turned suddenly, heading into the water. At first Stella wasn't concerned; he'd need a bath when she got him back but that wasn't a problem. She'd close the shop and snuggle up with him on the sofa – once she'd sorted out the burglary that is. She called his name again to distract herself from the thought of that and bring him near. All she wanted was to have him back. But then he began going deeper into the water and panic gripped Stella once more.

The sound of the waves had brought her here to Swallowtail Bay and often at night she'd hear it in the background – a gentle white noise to help her sleep – but right now the waves weren't gentle and the sound didn't relax her. They were strong and crashing onto the shore, dragging the pebbles and engulfing them. Frank wasn't swimming anymore; he was struggling in the water as the strong spring tide pulled him further and further away. Her throat tightened like someone had punched it and tears fell again. A strange sound came from Frank, something between a yelp and a bark. He was panicking, thrashing about. 'He's going to drown,' she cried. 'Oh, please no. He's going to drown.'

Just as she was about to run into the water Miles came charging forward, running full pelt towards the sea. He threw his phone and wallet onto the ground and dived straight into the cold, white waves. From the way the water pushed him backwards she could see the strength of the current but still he pressed on. Frank was desperately scrabbling around and the look in his deep dark eyes was one of pure terror. Stella's heart broke apart but Miles was almost there. He was having to swim now, his strong arms cutting through the rough water until he gently caught hold of Frank who struggled mercilessly, making Miles's job twice as hard. Somehow Miles remained calm and in a flash he was back on the beach soaking wet and shivering. Stella ran towards them, taking Frank from his arms and cradling him like a baby. The poor soaking wet dog shivered and he pressed his cold wet nose to her face, whimpering. Miles stood next to her, his arms crossed over his chest, his whole body shaking.

'Thank you. Thank you so much.' A crowd had gathered at the terrifying spectacle and they began to clap. Miles nodded at them, embarrassed and freezing. 'You'd better get changed before you catch pneumonia,' Stella said, aware that he had saved her and that she'd been stupid running off leaving the door open. Speaking of which, she hoped her entire shop hadn't been robbed, but even if it had, Frank was more important than that. She couldn't believe that Miles had done that for her. Leapt into a freezing sea to save a dog he didn't even like. Underneath his blunt exterior there seemed to be more to him. No matter what Jay had said, she couldn't deny how heroic and selfless he'd been. It seemed there really was a depth to him she hadn't credited.

And now, she owed him big time.

The family left as soon as the police had taken their statements. They completely blanked Stella as they climbed into their car, and it wasn't until Roger was just about to get in that he interrupted her apologies to say, 'You'll be hearing from my solicitor.'

Once Miles had changed into clean, dry clothes he called a joiner friend to come and fix the door and stayed with Stella while she made her statement. 'They left mid-afternoon yesterday,' she told the policeman, sat in her living room, a blanket around her shoulders. 'I didn't see them go. I was serving customers.'

The policeman nodded. 'The front door onto the street wasn't damaged. Could it be that it was left open?'

'Maybe. But if it was it would have been them that left it open. Once the guests are in I don't bother them. I leave them to their holiday. They have keys.'

The policeman nodded and she shuddered; she was in shock from everything that had happened that day. She just couldn't get warm no matter how many cups of hot sweet tea she drank or how many blankets were wrapped around her shoulders.

'I'm sure it wasn't your fault,' said Miles. 'These things happen. *They* must have left it open when they left for Halebury.'

Stella sniffed twice and looked down at Frank who was still shivering in his basket even though she'd added extra blankets and wrapped him up like a sausage. Burying her face in her hands she collapsed into tears. 'What am I going to do now? They'll take everything I've got.'

'Your insurance will cover a lot of it as you've reported it to the police,' said Miles. 'You'll just need to get the incident number for when you contact them.'

'Thanks,' she replied, wiping her nose. She really was grateful to him, not just for saving Frank but he'd been so practical this afternoon, locking the shop for her and reminding her to get information for the insurance people. Though normally level-headed, it was the advice she needed while her brain was mushy with shock.

Miles placed a hand gently on her back. It sent a shot of heat up her spine, causing her to turn to him, but then he removed it looking embarrassed. 'I'll nip next door and see if Lexi can come over. You shouldn't be alone right now.'

'You're being very kind. Thank you.'

He gave a half smile. 'I'm not actually as bad as I seem. Did you want me to come back and wait till she arrives?'

'Yes, please. I'd appreciate the company.' And the thought of Miles's company was a pleasant one. Miles walked away while the policeman asked some more questions. When he returned the policeman had gone.

'So what's the official verdict?'

'They think that either I or one of the family left the front door open and someone just chanced their luck. I woke up in the night thinking I heard them come back but it must have been the burglars. That helps them with the timing. They're going to check CCTV and see what they can find.'

'Well, at least that's something.'

Stella leaned down and gave Frank another cuddle. The dog looked up with his large soppy eyes and the mass of blankets wiggled where he was trying to wag his tail.

'He knows you're upset,' said Miles, almost fondly.

Stella wiped her cheek. 'He does. Sometimes he comes and sits on me when I'm feeling unwell and barks at anyone who goes past like he's guarding me. He did that to Vivien that day she was poorly. Thank you for saving him. I don't know how I'd have coped if I'd lost him on top of everything else.' Saying it out loud brought a wobble to her voice again.

Miles cleared his throat. 'I'm glad I could help. Lexi said to pack a bag; you're staying at hers tonight. And you're to bring Frank.'

Good, thought Stella, sadly. She really didn't want to be here anymore. She'd tried so hard to make her dream a reality but it was all being torn away from her. If only she could turn the clock back and not even try at all. Maybe even go back to before she and Isaac split and save their marriage and stay in Oxford. It would stop all the heartache of ending up a failure.

Chapter 25

Miles knotted his tie and ran a hand over it to ensure it was straight. He'd chosen a light grey suit for this wedding. Somehow it didn't feel right to wear the same black one he'd worn to Vivien's funeral.

It had been less than a week since the burglary and Miles was sure Stella wouldn't be in the mood to go, but he'd promised he would and she hadn't told him otherwise. He was meeting her at the shop at eight-thirty to ensure they had plenty of time to get to Oxford for the ceremony at one o'clock. He shrugged his jacket up onto his shoulders, tucked his wallet and keys into his pockets and made his way out.

As he turned the corner he could see Stella through the large glass windows of the shop. She was wearing a fitted pale blue dress the same colour as the sea, with a lace edging that finished just above the knee. Nude high heels showed off her shapely legs – legs he'd never imagined she had in the jeans she usually wore – and her hourglass figure was shown off to perfection. Her hair was loosely piled on top of her head with tendrils framing her face and though her make-up was minimal, she looked amazing. She didn't need much to accentuate her pretty features and yet, she was entirely herself. Kiera had always worn make-up like a mask, hiding her true self. Stella looked up at him as he pushed open the door.

'Hey, Stella. Are you ready to go?'

'Yes, I think so.' Her eyes widened a fraction as they ran over him and he nervously flattened his tie again, hoping she approved. 'Frank is at Lexi's for the day. I've got a card with a gift voucher in – unoriginal I know, but I couldn't think what else to get them and I didn't want to take something from the shop in case it seemed a bit weird or boastful. So, I've got my bag with my money, keys and make-up. Yep, I think we're all set.' She gave him a half smile but her voice lacked its usual enthusiasm. Not surprising given everything she was going through. The fact that she was smiling at all was a miracle.

'I get the feeling you're not looking forward to this.'

'I'm not really. But it's too late to pull out now.'

'You could blame the burglary.' Worried he sounded like he was trying to get out of it, Miles added, 'I mean – I'm happy to go still, just, you know, if *you* didn't want to.'

'If I was going to use that as an excuse I should have done it days ago. Never mind. We've got our glad rags on now so we might as well go. And you can drink *all* the free beer. Knowing Isaac's parents it'll definitely be a free bar.' With a slick of pale pink lipgloss, Stella's smile was even more dazzling.

'So who's Isaac?' Miles asked and she froze, slowly turning back to face him.

'Sorry, didn't I tell you? It's umm, it's my ex-husband's wedding.'

'Your ex-husband?' Astounded she'd agreed to go at all, Miles rearranged his shocked features. Before, his surprise had often come across as judgemental and he didn't want to slip back into old habits. If Kiera suddenly invited him to something there's no way he'd go. It just showed Stella's kind nature and incredible strength of character. 'Wow.'

She hesitated, fiddling with her handbag. 'Are we still okay to go? I know it seems weird and I'm sorry I didn't mention it before, I just—'

'You just thought that being the pompous idiot I've made myself out to be I'd have a tantrum and refuse?' Miles watched a range of emotions pass over Stella's face from fear to amazement, to a wry and extremely pretty smile. He'd hit the nail on the head. 'I won't lie, I am surprised. I'd find it difficult attending my ex's anything, let alone her wedding. But then, if Kiera invited me to something it would only be out of spite.'

'Isaac's not like that,' she assured him, cocking her head slightly to one side. 'He'd never think to do such a thing. I'm sure he's invited me to show there are no hard feelings and that he wants us to be friends. He's a nice man, really.'

Miles wanted to ask what had happened between them but was afraid of pushing his luck and asking too personal a question. He popped his hands into his pockets. 'Well, you're a much nicer person than I am.'

'I don't think that's true,' Stella replied and a strangely loaded atmosphere descended.

As the blush rose up Stella's face and Miles warmed from the compliment, she dropped her eyes and led the way out, locking the door behind her. Miles followed to the car, unused to being the passenger. As they drove past the shop on their way out of town, he caught Stella glance at the door to the holiday lets and read the concern in her face.

'Have you heard anything more from the family?'

She sighed. 'Yes, I got a letter from their solicitors about two days after they left telling me I was being sued for five thousand pounds.'

He flinched. 'Five thousand pounds? How can they possibly claim so much?'

Stella's hands shifted on the wheel. 'A grand for the money he says he had in the bedside cabinet, another for the possessions that were damaged – kids' toys and stuff though they didn't bring

232

much with them – and the rest is emotional damage to him, his wife, the nanny and the children.'

'Emotional damage?' Miles's voice dripped with derision. 'Those kids were completely fine.'

'I don't know. I suppose shock can take some time to come out, can't it.' She shrugged. 'It is what it is. I'm going to have to stump it up and hope the insurance company pays me back. They're demanding the money pretty quickly.'

'But that's nonsense.'

'The insurance company said it's going to take a while to get sorted. There's the police investigation, and I can't prove who left the door unlocked. They said it's my decision if I settle or not.' She glanced out of the window again. 'I'll really miss Swallowtail Bay if I have to leave.'

Miles's face shot to Stella's. He didn't want her to leave either, especially under such circumstances. It just wasn't fair. A red flag began to wave in Miles's brain but he couldn't pin down exactly why. It must have been the reference to Stella leaving. He hadn't realised the burglary could cost her everything. As this was probably the last thing Stella wanted to discuss today, he changed the topic to something lighter.

They made great time to Oxford, listening to the radio, discussing music and films and discovering they actually had a fair amount in common. As they pulled up onto the gravel parking area in front of the church, Stella seemed to hesitate.

'It'll be okay,' Miles said. 'They don't know about the burglary, do they? And you don't have to tell them. Just pretend it hasn't happened and try and enjoy yourself.'

'Okay,' Stella said, taking a deep breath. 'Let's go then.'

The church was big and grand, much larger than the small sweet one they had buried Vivien in at Swallowtail Bay, and full of people. The familiar pull of home filled Miles. No matter how pretty somewhere was, it wasn't a patch on his and Stella's hometown. Miles saw an older couple in the front pew scowl and whisper to each other. He took them to be the ex-husband's parents. After fiddling with his cravat, the ex-husband made his way towards them.

'Isaac, you look fabulous. Congratulations,' Stella said, holding out her hand.

For a second Isaac stared at her, then he took her hand and pulled her in and kissed her cheek. 'Stella, you look lovely. I'm so glad you could make it.' Something about the way he spoke with such unbridled joy and enthusiasm made Miles think of a giant puppy. 'And who's this?'

'This is my friend Miles.'

'Congratulations,' said Miles, shaking Isaac's hand too. 'I hope your day is everything you want it to be.' From the corner of his eye he caught Stella's cheeky smile.

'Ellie should be here any minute. Unless she's jilted me – which I really hope she hasn't.'

There was something very warm about Isaac's easy, friendly manner and he could see that Stella was right. Isaac hadn't invited her to make a petty point about how his life had moved on – something Kiera would do – he was genuinely pleased she was there to share this moment with him.

'I'm sure she hasn't,' replied Stella. 'I see your parents have spotted me.' Miles followed her gaze, as did Isaac, to the two sneering faces he'd spotted before.

'Just ignore them, Stella,' Isaac said. 'You know what they're like.'

'Do they approve of Ellie?' There was no jealousy in her voice, only a slight teasing.

'They do,' he said reluctantly. 'Sorry.'

'That's okay. I wish you both every happiness.'

Isaac took her hands in his. 'Thank you, Stella. That means so much to me. We shared such a huge part of each other's lives, I'd hate for us to not to be friends.'

'Me too.'

Miles couldn't believe what he was seeing. Recalling Kiera's theatrical farewell, he couldn't imagine her ever being so gracious, but Stella seemed the type of person who brought out the best in people. It wasn't surprising her first husband had been a nice man. However it had ended, they were clearly both okay about it.

'I need to get back up front, but you guys take a seat. I'm so happy you could make it, Stella,' he said again, giving her another kiss on the cheek. 'And nice to meet you, Miles.' Isaac disappeared, almost breaking into a run he was so excited.

'He seems nice,' Miles said, as they edged their way along a pew to the end. Stella's hand brushed against his and the warmth and softness of her skin kindled a tingling that ran up to his chest. From the quick glance she gave him, he wondered if she'd felt it too.

'He is. He's a good man and I'm happy for him.'

Miles stared at her. 'You really are, aren't you?'

'I really am,' Stella replied as if she had only just realised it herself. 'When I think about it we did just grow apart. I want him to be happy. Don't you want Kiera to be happy wherever she is?'

Miles thought for a moment and realisation dawned. 'I do actually. But, weren't you hurt when it ended?'

'Very.' She admitted it so openly that Miles had to stop his mouth dropping open. 'And angry. And I felt rejected. But I've come to realise that sometimes things don't work out the way you think they should and I do like my life in Swallowtail Bay.' A sudden sadness washed over her features that Miles could tell had nothing to do with the wedding and everything to do with the shop, the burglary and the horrible family suing her for a ridiculous sum of money. Yet again there was a red flag flying somewhere in his brain, telling him he'd forgotten something or made a mistake, but he couldn't place why. 'Do you ever think about Kiera?'

'Sometimes. I've kind of trained myself that once something is done I don't think about it again.'

'Does it work?'

He thought of the shop and how hard he'd found it to let go. 'No. Not always.' The grin that spread over Stella's face was cheeky and Miles mirrored it.

Everyone stood up and the bride entered. She was a pretty girl though not as pretty as Stella, and she looked a bit meringue-like in the large poufy dress, but then every bride should wear what she wants on her wedding day. The service was long, very long, and he and Stella glanced at each other from time to time, repressing a smile. Neither of them sang the hymns and when Miles first noticed he leaned in and whispered, 'You're not singing.'

'Neither are you,' Stella teased.

'But you were singing in the car.'

'Car karaoke is one thing, but hymns are out of my vocal range. Too high. What's your excuse?'

'Tone deaf.' And Stella's eyes sparkled as she silently mouthed the words.

Before long they were making their way to the wedding reception being held at an enormous farmhouse on the outskirts of Oxford. A jazz quartet were playing as they arrived and waiters and waitresses were handing out glasses of orange juice or champagne. Fairy lights hung from the white walls giving everything a soft, pretty glow. White tablecloths covered the tables and everywhere were rather extravagant displays of pink flowers.

'Which table do you think we're on?' asked Miles, taking an orange juice for himself and handing one to Stella.

'Somewhere near the back I'm sure.' Again there was no bitterness in her voice. In fact, Stella sounded like she was actually enjoying herself. Miles looked around.

'Have you noticed there aren't any children?'

'Aren't there?'

'No. I think that's such a shame. I love seeing kids at weddings

236

all overexcited and dancing like idiots. It makes me feel better about my dance moves.'

Stella laughed and sipped her orange juice. 'I won't drag you up to the dance floor so you don't have to worry.'

'Good.' They moved to the side to let some other people through and again his body touched Stella's. Being close to her made him hyper-aware of everything he was doing but she didn't immediately move away. When she did he had a sudden urge to take her hand and pull it back. 'Do you mind if I have a beer or two with dinner? I'm happy not to drink if you prefer.'

'Of course I don't mind.' Where Stella's hair was piled onto her head, Miles could see the full beauty of her profile. He found himself thinking about kissing her long, graceful neck and hoped he wasn't blushing, turning his attention away to the monstrously huge flower display next to him. 'You're doing me such a big favour, please enjoy yourself.'

'I am enjoying myself actually. You're not bad company.'

'Neither are you,' she joked.

'Are you surprised?' He wasn't sure he was going to like the answer but he'd asked now, and trusted Stella would at least be honest with him.

She hesitated. 'A little.'

A prickle of shame stung the back of his neck and he reached a hand back to quell it. 'I was awful to you when you arrived and I'm embarrassed by how I behaved. I am sorry for being such an arse.' Stella's glass stilled in mid-air. She clearly hadn't expected such an apology from him. He wanted her to see what he was really like, not the self-indulgent man he'd been before. Feeling embarrassed, he motioned to the seating chart. 'We'd better take our seats. I think they're arriving soon.'

Along with the other guests they found their table and sat down. Miles was next to a large woman in an enormous fuchsia dress and matching feathery fascinator, the colour of which matched the blobs of blusher on her cheeks. Her name was Fiona and she had more lipstick on her teeth than on her lips but had a kind and happy face. Stella was next to an old man called Jack with receding, slick-backed grey hair.

'Are you with the bride or groom?' asked the woman, swatting away a bright pink feather that bounced back and tapped her on the nose.

'Groom,' Miles answered, glancing at Stella. She was chatting away to the old man, making him laugh as though they were old friends. She really did have a way with people, such an easy, unassuming manner.

'I'm with the bride,' Fiona said. 'She's my goddaughter. Don't you think she looks gorgeous?'

'She looks lovely,' Miles replied, politely. She was pretty but he wouldn't go so far as to say gorgeous.

The woman poured herself a large glass of white wine from the bottles in the middle of the table. 'This is Isaac's second marriage, you know. He's divorced. Don't know why it didn't work out but sometimes things just don't, do they?'

From the corner of his eye Miles saw Stella's back stiffen then relax as Fiona passed no judgement.

'I don't know about you young 'uns, but I'm absolutely starving,' said Jack, taking a bread roll from the basket in the centre of the table and cutting it open.

'I'm quite hungry too,' said Stella, smiling at everyone.

'And are you with the groom's side too?' asked Fiona.

Miles caught the mischievous twinkle in Stella's eyes as she replied. 'Yes, I'm Isaac's ex-wife.'

Fiona coughed as her wine went down the wrong way. She grabbed her napkin and wiped at her mouth. 'Oh, I'm so sorry. I didn't mean to embarrass you before.' Her cheeks blazed even redder under the pink blush. 'He's always spoken very highly of you.'

'We're still friends,' Stella admitted taking a bread roll herself and giving Fiona a disarming smile. 'He's a lovely man and I'm very happy for him and Ellie. Like you say, sometimes things don't work out but it's fine, really. He looks incredibly happy – and Ellie too.'

'Well that's lovely of you, dear. Not all marriages end so amicably.'

'When I left my first wife,' said Jack, 'I came home to find all my stuff in bin bags out in the street. Same with the second actually.'

Miles glanced at Stella and she flashed her eyes at him.

'I'm here on my own,' replied Fiona a note of sadness in her voice. 'I wasn't sure about coming. I don't much like going to things on my own, but since my Ken passed away, I have to or I'd never leave the house.'

'I'm sorry to hear that,' said Miles.

'Thank you. The worst thing is,' Fiona continued, 'you don't have anyone to dance with, do you? And there's nothing worse than sitting out all night.'

'Well, maybe you'll have a dance with me later?' asked Miles. Stella's head spun towards him. Even though he wasn't really much of a dancer, Fiona seemed a nice lady and he wanted her to enjoy herself.

The meal was served and, unusually, conversation flowed easily. Any time there was a lull Stella would ask a question and everyone would soon be talking again, sharing memories, experiences or jokes. She had a natural flair for putting people at their ease and seemed genuinely interested in whoever she was talking to, listening intently to what they had to say. At his networking events everyone was out to speak to the right people and say the right thing. Eyes would flit about the room and there would be a lot of polite nodding, but Stella's eyes never wavered from the person in front of her and she remembered everything they said. It was such a unique quality. Miles had the sneaking suspicion that Isaac had been a fool to let her go.

After the meal, the music started and the first dance began.

As 'I Believe in a Thing called Love,' by The Darkness started up, Isaac and Ellie went from refined, almost shy man and wife to two idiots rocking out on the dance floor, imploring their friends to come and join them. Guests flocked up, laughing and joking, and soon heads were bobbing up and down. Stella and Miles stood up but didn't move from their table. Near the end of the song she leaned in to Miles. 'I did not expect that!'

'Me neither.' The way her eyes sparkled when she smiled made them seem bigger, browner and deeper, and he had to draw his gaze away.

'They look so happy.'

Unable to read her tone, Miles turned to her. 'Are you okay?'

Stella's eyes met his but there were no tears, and no pity or disappointment in her face. 'I'm totally fine. I'm really, really happy for them.'

A round of applause started with whoops and whistles following. The music changed to something orchestral and Isaac danced with his mum while Ellie danced with her dad. Couples joined them, swaying to and fro.

'Oh, look at that,' said Fiona, putting a hand over her heart. 'Isn't that lovely?'

'Would you like to dance?' asked Miles and Fiona's puffy cheeks rounded as she grinned.

'I very much would, young man.' Seeing Stella approve of his actions made him feel ten feet tall.

'Well,' said Jack. 'If that young man is dancing with you, Fiona, then perhaps the lovely Stella would like to dance with me?'

'I'd be delighted,' she replied, pushing her chair back. 'But just so you know, I'm not interested in being wife number three.'

'Number three?' Jack look confused. 'I'm on the lookout for number five now, sweetheart.'

Stella and Miles laughed as everyone went to the dance floor. He might have been imagining it, but he was sure that as he and Fiona turned and twirled, Stella watched him from time to time.

The evening wore on and while Stella sipped her tonic water, giggling with the other guests at the table, Miles saw Isaac and his new wife making their way around the room. His stomach tightened a little as they approached. Stella's evening had been nice so far; he didn't want it to go south now.

'Stella,' said Isaac. 'I want to introduce you to Ellie.' Ellie gave a timid smile.

Stella stood up and kissed Isaac on the cheek then held out her hand to Ellie. 'I would give you a kiss on the cheek too but I wouldn't want to ruin your lovely make-up.'

Ellie instantly relaxed and the tight smile loosened to something more genuine. 'Most of it's sliding off my face from all the dancing anyway.'

Stella really did have a gift when it came to people. She gently pecked Ellie's cheek and stood back surveying them both. 'You look beautiful, Ellie, and your dress is stunning.'

'Doesn't she look amazing?' said Isaac, gazing lovingly at his new wife.

'I'm really very happy for you both,' said Stella. 'This is my friend Miles.'

'How do you do?' Miles replied, shaking Ellie's hand. 'Can I buy you both a drink?'

'Oh, no, I've had bucket loads already,' said Ellie.

'Me too,' added Isaac. 'I should probably drink some water or something before I fall asleep. I'd be in big trouble then and not just with Ellie.'

'No, your mum and dad would go bananas. I hope you've had a lovely time?' Ellie's eyes flitted between them.

Miles said, 'We have. It's been lovely. Your godmother has been wonderful company.'

'Aunty Fi? Really? Not everyone says that. And how was Great-Uncle Jack?'

'He's been lovely,' Stella replied. 'He's quite a character.'

'That's a nice way of describing him. Isaac's parents hate him with a passion. I had to put him as far away from them as I could.'

'They can be quite … firm in their views, can't they?' said Stella.

'God, yes. But for Isaac's sake I'll put up with it.'

Stella smiled as Ellie's cheeks coloured. She suddenly looked down at her empty glass, probably worrying she had said the wrong thing.

'That was a great choice for your first dance,' said Miles, steering the conversation to something more neutral. 'Really good fun.'

'Thanks,' said Isaac. 'It was Ellie's choice actually.'

'I wanted something I wouldn't cry to.'

'It was brilliant,' said Stella. She reached behind her and took the white envelope from the table. 'I've got you both a card and a gift voucher-thing. I know that's not very original, but I didn't know what you wanted.'

'That's really kind of you,' said Ellie, taking the card. 'We didn't expect you to get us anything. Isaac was so worried you wouldn't come.'

'Really?' She turned to Isaac.

He shuffled his feet. 'Well, you know.'

Stella gave his hand a squeeze. 'Idiot.'

'That's what I told him,' said Ellie. 'He's always said such lovely things about you. I'm really happy I got to meet you.'

'I'm really sorry,' said Stella, 'but we need to get going soon. We've got quite a long drive back.'

Isaac nodded. 'Of course. But perhaps you'd think about coming and staying one weekend? Have you visited Oxford before, Miles?'

'Once or twice for work, but I've never had the pleasure of relaxing and enjoying the sights.'

'Then you must come and visit. I know where all the best pubs are.'

'That sounds great,' Miles replied, glancing at Stella. He wasn't really sure what he should be saying as they weren't a couple but replying as if they were felt strangely right and Stella hadn't stopped him. Isaac and Ellie made their farewells and continued around the room talking to everyone. 'Do we really have to go or is that an excuse?' asked Miles.

'We really do actually. It's already ten o'clock.'

'Really?' Miles checked his own watch even though he knew Stella wasn't lying, then felt like an idiot for doing so. 'I never realised it was that late.'

'It's been a lovely evening, hasn't it?'

Before he could stop himself, he said, 'Time for one last dance?'

'Sure.'

Miles took Stella's hand and led her to the dance floor as a slow song came on. At first he was pleased because slow ones were easier to dance to, you just rocked a bit and shuffled around in a circle – even he could manage that. But as he took Stella into his arms and held her close his whole body filled with longing. His hand sat gently in the curve of her waist as if it had been designed to go there by some Cupid-like creator and after a moment her body moved closer to his, pulled by an invisible force. The gap between them disintegrated to nothing.

As she was nearly as tall as him their mouths were dangerously close together and he wanted more than anything to kiss her perfect pale pink lips. He could smell her perfume, and when she raised her eyes to his, their brilliance and clarity penetrated right through to his heart. With a gentle sway their lips brushed, sending a shockwave through his body, and in that instant he decided to kiss her. She didn't pull away and the kiss they shared was tender and sweet. Had they been alone he'd never have stopped, but as the music came back into his ears he remembered where they were and, unsure if Stella would want something like this to happen so publicly, he didn't try to kiss her again and just held her until the end of the song.

From the way her eyes dropped and she bit her lip, the pale

colour of her cheeks flooding with pink, he could tell she was embarrassed. He too felt like the shy teenage boy he'd once been and chose to keep quiet, seeing if she mentioned it first. When she didn't and they went back to the table, his insides squirmed around like someone had put them in a washing machine.

They said goodbye to Fiona and Jack, Stella being her normal cheerful self, and made their way to the car. Without the bright sunshine, the evening had turned chilly and Stella shivered a little in the cool breeze.

'Did you want my jacket?' asked Miles, thankful for a chance to speak and break the silence that was enveloping them now they were alone.

'No thanks. I'll be fine once we've got the heater on in the car.'

As he watched the streetlights fly by, remembering the kiss that now felt so monumental, as if it changed everything for him, he realised how much he'd misjudged Stella. He'd made assumptions about her that weren't true and he felt the weight of that guilt as from the corner of his eye he studied her beautiful face. He wanted to know what she thought of the kiss – the incredible kiss – and drew the subject back to the wedding in the hope that it would come up. 'How was all that for you? The wedding,' he added quickly, not wanting to be too obvious.

'It was fun. I had a ...' She hesitated and Miles's chest tightened with apprehension. '... A nice time.'

Was she talking about the kiss? he wondered. He hoped she was. 'What actually happened between you and Isaac, if you don't mind me asking?'

Stella glanced over and gave him a smile. 'We just grew apart over time. Luckily, he didn't do anything awful like cheat on me. He and Ellie didn't get together until after we split. He was decent and told me he had feelings for someone else before acting on them.'

'Not like Kiera then,' Miles commented, watching the rhythmic glow of the streetlights through the windscreen.

'She cheated on you?'

'Yes, with Jay.' He could feel Stella's eyes on him but he didn't turn. He didn't want her to pity him, and what's more, he knew the inescapable moment was coming when he'd have to tell her about Jay. It was going to be hard, it would ruin her evening, add stress on top of everything else she had going on, and it would hurt her, something he'd do anything to avoid. Even though he'd tried to quash the rumours someone might still say something and if she found out he'd known and not told her she'd never trust him again. He couldn't abide the thought of that. He wanted Stella to respect him as much as he respected her. A stone-like dread settled on his chest.

'Jay Adams?'

Miles nodded. 'It was when they were doing her website. I don't know if they slept together since, but ...' He paused gathering his courage. He had to do it but he'd worked so hard to put that smile on her face, he didn't want to wipe it off. 'Stella, I'm sorry. I found out that they were both lying, saying you slept with Jay, and that's when it all came out. That was when I ended it—'

'Wait, what?' Stella's head spun to look at him then shot back to the road. 'He was saying I'd slept with him?'

'Yes, I'm sorry.'

'You knew?' Her voice grew stronger with controlled anger, even though her eyes remained on the motorway. Miles knew he deserved it. 'Kiera and he concocted this plan to discredit me and I'm afraid you got caught up in it.'

'Me? Why?'

'Kiera wanted me to leave Swallowtail Bay. I think she and Jay were going to leak it that I started the rumours so I'd be embarrassed and leave town. It's a small place and people would boycott any shop I owned if they thought that I'd done something like that. I'm truly sorry, Stella. I've been doing everything I can to stop the rumours. Letting people know Jay isn't a reliable man. I didn't know how to tell you. I'm sure no one believes him.'

'So everyone thinks I'm a slapper?' Stella said angrily. 'Well, that explains my whispering customers the other day.'

Bloody gossipers. 'People who know you will know you're not. I don't think you are,' he added, hoping it would help a little. He wanted to tell her how much that kiss had meant to him, the feelings it had stirred. 'I'm so sorry you got caught up in this.'

'And I thought he was nice.' Stella shook her head, incredulously. 'I'm so stupid.'

'No, you're not,' Miles said firmly. 'People don't know what Jay's really like. They never have.'

'What do you mean?' Though she was still looking forward he could see her brow rucked up in confusion.

Miles ran a hand through his hair, resting his elbow on the windowsill of the car door and his forehead in his hand. 'Jay likes to show the world this image of a nice guy, but he's not. He's petty and small-minded. Ever since we were kids he used to love getting one over on people, especially me.' He paused again, summoning up his courage. As painful as it was to talk about he wanted Stella to know everything. At least then, if she never spoke to him again he'd have no regrets. 'I used to have bad acne as a teenager – he used to call me pizza face.'

'That's horrible.' The genuine disgust on Stella's face made him feel justified in disliking Jay.

'It gets worse. Once he and his mates made out they were finally going to stop teasing me and be my friends and … when I met them they wedgied me and told me I was repulsive and should wear a bag over my head.' The deep emotional scar smarted again and he swallowed down the pain. 'Luckily I had Vivien.'

She glanced over. 'At the funeral it seemed you were close.'

'My parents worked long hours and even though I was old enough to be left alone, sometimes I came home so demoralised from the teasing, I'd nip next door and sit chatting with her. She always listened.' She'd been an unlikely audience for him, but her sage advice and kooky outlook had taught him it was good to be different. 'Jay used to steal my girlfriends, if I was ever lucky enough to get one and he used to tease me for pronouncing my t's properly – calling me posh and Little Lord Fauntleroy.'

'I'm sorry, Miles. Jay had it the other way around when he talked to me.' From her expression she must have expected him to be cross but he just gave a resigned shake of the head.

'I'm not surprised.'

'He said you used to tease him for being common. Making fun because he *didn't* pronounce his t's properly.'

'I didn't. I promise.' He willed her to look at him and when she did those same clear, perceptive eyes were warm and understanding.

'I believe you. It looks like he's screwed us both over.'

'As we got older it seemed to die down, though we never really liked each other. I guess sleeping with Kiera was a final way of getting to me.'

Stella sighed with a devastating tiredness. 'This is all such a fuck-up, isn't it? Why is life always so complicated?'

Miles started at her swearing. He hadn't heard her swear before and with such vehemence either. He hoped against hope she wasn't referring to their kiss. A moment he found himself wanting to repeat again and again and again. 'Did you want me to speak to Jay for you? I didn't confront him directly when I first heard, I'll be honest. I didn't really know what to do. But I should have. I'm sorry.'

'No, it's fine. Thanks for the offer, but I'll be speaking to him myself and giving him a piece of my mind.' The anger died from her voice and she sighed again as her shoulders slumped down. 'I might as well just sell up anyway.'

'Why would you say that?' said Miles. 'The business is doing well, isn't it?'

'With Jay telling the town I'm an easy lay and people gossiping about me, and the horrid family suing me, I really don't see the point in going on. I can't afford to pay them five thousand pounds. Not unless they agree to me paying in instalments.'

'You shouldn't be paying anything at all. Not until they can prove you left the door open. It must have been them.' Miles thoughts shifted. Something about what he'd said was ricocheting around his head and suddenly he remembered.

Replaying that afternoon in his mind, he recalled the nanny chatting him up and his brusque rebuttal that had immediately changed her attitude. Though he'd walked away he'd assumed she'd closed the front door before charging into the car and telling off the two boys, but when he thought back, he hadn't actually heard it close. It always made a slight thump and a click when the lock connected – he remembered from all the times he'd viewed the property. What if it hadn't closed and been left ajar?

A sudden coldness washed over him but his palms and the back of his neck felt clammy. He swallowed hard as he realised what had happened. It was his fault. *Oh shit.* He glanced at Stella from the corner of his eye. Fuck, fuck, fuckety, fuck, fuck. Kiera had told Jay to lie because of him and now the family were suing her for the robbery when that was his fault too. How the hell was he ever going to put this right? If she found out she'd never speak to him again and the thought of that left an empty, hollow feeling in his soul.

Miles bit his fingernails. He hadn't bitten them in ages. Stella was special and had stirred something meaningful within him and he couldn't, or rather, wouldn't, let that go. He had to find a way of putting this right.

'Don't even think about selling up,' he said to Stella. 'We'll think of something.'

This time she pulled her eyes away from the road, and pain and disappointment were etched on her face. 'I wish I could believe you. But unless you know something I don't, the whole thing seems pretty pointless to me.'

Miles bit his nail once more, his jaw firmly set. This problem was of his making and he needed to solve it. There had to be a way out of this mess and it was up to him to find it.

Chapter 26

'He said what?' asked Lexi, as she and Stella gathered at the pub for Sunday lunch. While eating her Yorkshire pudding she'd told Lexi about Jay and his lies over Miles. Lexi, as Stella had suspected, was as dumbfounded as she'd been. 'I can't believe it. I just can't believe it. Why would Jay go along with Kiera and lie like that?'

'He obviously cares a lot about his reputation as the most handsome man in town,' said Stella, pushing some leftover cabbage around her plate. 'Maybe he'd told his friends he was going to get me into bed and couldn't deal with it when I said no. Miles said with Kiera wanting to manipulate him into leaving he thinks they were going to leak it that Miles started the rumours to make life difficult for him.' She forked the last bit of roast beef into her mouth, remembering everything that had happened yesterday, including the kiss.

The pub was busy and loud with chatter, but Stella found it comforting knowing life was still going on around her, even though hers felt like it was falling apart. From their seats she could see out of the window to the sea on the horizon and on this clear but cloudy day, a few small sailing boats sat happily bobbing about. The noisy calls of seagulls outside mixed with the soft background music inside and Stella felt happy to be back in Swallowtail Bay.

'What an absolute plank,' said Lexi.

'You're not with the kids now,' she replied, teasingly. 'You can swear.'

'Then Jay's a complete dickhead.' Lexi wiped her mouth and threw her napkin down.

'Better?'

'Yes. I can't believe he lied about Miles like that as well.'

'I know,' said Stella. 'I'm going to give him a piece of my mind when I see him next. I take it you hadn't heard anything?'

'No, of course not,' said Lexi. 'I'd have told you. And him.'

Stella relaxed. Of course she would have. 'Miles apologised to me for not confronting him straight away but he said that it was the night he broke up with Kiera, so I don't blame him. If he had done I'd probably have been annoyed at him for sticking his nose into my business. Sometimes I think he couldn't have won with me before. And it explains those gossipy visitors that day Vivien came in looking unwell. I thought they were gossiping about me because of Miles. Jay said he'd been slagging me and the shop off behind my back, but I don't believe that anymore. They must have heard what Jay was saying about me and come to have a butcher's at the town bike.'

'It must have been hard for him to know what to do for the best. You know, make an even bigger deal of it or see if anyone actually does pay attention.'

'Jay Adams is an arse,' Stella said with a sigh.

Lexi gave her hand a squeeze. 'He really is.'

'The worst thing is, Miles and I had actually had a nice time up until then. I saw a different side to him. He was really chatty and kind and he even danced with this lonely old woman we met at the wedding. He was completely different.' *And then there was the kiss*, she thought. The sweet, tender, gentle kiss that had made the hairs on the back of her neck stand on end.

'See,' said Lexi, 'I told you he wasn't as bad as he seemed at first. And actually, he's even better since he and Kiera split up. You sound like you'd see him again if he asked.'

Stella knew she was going to have to tell Lexi about the kiss at some point so just blurted it out. 'He kissed me.'

Lexi's eyes widened and a huge grin spread over her face. 'He kissed you? Miles kissed you? When? And why didn't you start with that instead of Jay Adams being a prick?'

'I didn't really know what to make of it,' Stella replied, feeling her body growing hot as she remembered the sensation of his lips on hers or the way she'd wanted the kiss to never stop. Totally unlike when Jay tried to kiss her. As soon as he'd tried she'd known it wasn't right but when Miles had kissed her, it was like everything else had faded away to nothing and there was only him and her. The real him, not the version she'd seen and, she knew now, misjudged.

'What was it like? Was it one of those low slow romantic ones or a passionate bodice-ripper behind the bike sheds?'

Stella giggled at Lexi's descriptions but remembering it made her lips tingle again. 'It was really sweet and gentle and … I don't know—'

'Special?'

Stella just shrugged. It had started feelings in her she'd thought were long dead but she hadn't had a chance to really analyse them and decide what they meant to her. The wedding itself had helped her realise how over Isaac she actually was and how much of the hurt their divorce caused had faded. 'Anyway, I never thought there'd be a fun side to him. He seemed so cold and austere to me. And when I met Kiera I thought he was only after someone as window dressing for his own perfect life, but after sitting in a car for a few hours with him—'

'And snogging his face off,' Lexi added in a whisper as she leaned in to her.

'—and kissing him once,' Stella corrected, 'and laughing and joking, I realised there's a caring side I hadn't seen before.'

'Wow.'

'Yep. I know just how to keep my life simple. The only good thing to come out of yesterday is that I do finally feel like I'm over Isaac, or more precisely, over our split. I think it was the feelings of rejection that took the most time to fade, but we had actually just grown apart.'

Lexi rested a hand on her shoulder. 'Good for you, honey. I'm proud of you. Have you heard any more from the horrible family?'

Stella picked up the dessert menu. 'Not since I got the letter telling me they're suing me.'

Lexi took another menu but paused before reading. 'I can't believe they want five thousand pounds. It's bloody outrageous. Are you going to do what your insurers said and settle?'

'I don't know.' Stella took a deep breath. 'I haven't got that sort of money so I'd have to get a loan from the bank and I'd have to put it against the property. The business isn't really viable enough to get a business loan so it'll have to be a personal one. I've got a meeting with the bank booked in but I'm worried they might refuse when they find out what's happened, and I can't lie and pretend it's for something else.'

Stella rubbed her head. She'd had a headache ever since she got back last night. After her conversation with Miles about Jay and the way he'd gone all silent about the horrible family, the journey had been one of quiet concentration. She'd focused on the road any time her thoughts began to wander to other subjects. She didn't want to cry in front of Miles and knew that if she thought about it too much that's exactly what would happen. Even sleep hadn't cleared the throbbing in her temples and her head felt sore as if her brain was bruised.

'I'd lend you the money,' said Lexi. 'But I don't know when all the legal stuff will be sorted out. It could be ages until that happens.'

'I know you would, sweetie.' Stella took her hand and squeezed it. 'And I really appreciate the thought but I need to get out of this mess myself. Anyway, what does Will say about this newfound wealth?'

'He's pleased for me.'

'He was really sweet at the funeral.'

'Yeah. He's a gentle giant.' Lexi looked up at her, blushing slightly. 'But don't go getting any ideas – we're not getting back together.'

'Shame.' It was Stella's turn to tease and she received a mock scowl from Lexi in response. 'Anyway, a little bird told me it's your birthday soon.'

Lexi's head fell into her hands. 'Oh, I wish Raina would keep her mouth shut.'

'What are you doing to celebrate?'

Her fingers opened a little and her eyes peeked out. 'Drowning my sorrows in wine and eating my body weight in chocolate?'

'What about a party?' asked Stella. She'd suddenly had a very good idea.

'A party? Where?'

'In the big apartment. We could use the three-bed apartment then you and the kids can stay over too. We've both had a rough time lately so why don't we have a party and celebrate the only good thing to come out of it – our friendship.'

'But won't you have a booking?' asked Lexi.

'I'll block it out. I'm probably ruined anyway so let's make use of the space while we can.'

'You're not ruined,' Lexi reassured her. 'But it's a great idea. If you don't mind?'

'I definitely don't,' Stella confirmed lifting her glass in a toast. 'To friends.'

'To friends,' Lexi replied, clinking glasses.

A party was a great idea and it didn't matter if she lost a booking. After all, right now, Stella had nothing else to lose. 'I don't bloody believe it,' said Stella, steadying her wine glass.

'What?' asked Lexi.

'Look what the cat dragged in.' Stella watched as Jay Adams closed the door behind him and strolled up to the bar, resting one leg on the metal beam that ran around the bottom. He had one hand in his jeans pocket and the other was gesturing to his mates. Something about his stance reminded Stella of a puffed-up peacock. He hadn't noticed she was there and an unsettling rage was growing inside her. Stella wasn't quick to anger but knowing what he'd been saying about her and the things he'd said to Miles when they were younger gave her a strong wish to smack him in his incredibly handsome face.

'What are you going to do?' asked Lexi as Stella rose from her chair.

Figuring she had nothing much to lose, a thought flitted across Stella's brain and before she had a chance to assess it as either good or bad, her legs were moving and she was edging out from behind the table. 'I'm going to tell that conceited idiot exactly what I think of him and his lies.'

As she marched towards him, a surge of fear threatened to turn her around, but for the sake of what little dignity she had left she pressed on. Jay had his back to her when she tapped on his shoulder. He turned and, seeing her face, something akin to fear settled on his.

'Stella, hi, how are you? Is everything okay with the website? Do you need any adjustments?' He gave her a grin designed to appease. She could imagine him practising it in the mirror.

Stella smiled. 'Yeah, actually. I could do with a new banner that says, "Despite what a pathetic scumbag says, I did not sleep with Jay Adams."' A titter from behind her right shoulder showed that his friends appreciated her mic-dropping line and inwardly she cheered. A glorious blush took the edge off his sharp cheekbones and intimidating good looks. His mouth opened but Stella wasn't ready to let him speak just yet. 'Who the bloody hell do you think you are? You might be handsome but there are some women who see the beauty in a soul, not just a face.' She suddenly thought of Miles and pushed it away so as not to derail her flow. The pub had grown silent, watching the spectacle. 'I can't believe that because I didn't jump straight into bed with you the moment you asked, you decided to lie! Is your ego really so fragile that you can't take a single rejection? It's despicable. It's sad, Jay. Really sad. I feel sorry for you—'

'Wait, Stella.' He glanced over her shoulder at his friends who were sniggering. 'I don't know what you've heard, or from who but—'

'I've heard the truth, Jay.' She thought about telling him exactly what she knew about his and Miles's past but she didn't think Miles would want his feelings broadcast in the pub and so she contented herself with an ominous, 'And I know what you did to Miles.'

It was strange that she'd never doubted what Miles had said. She just knew that he only said what he thought was right or knew to be true. It was a quality she liked. Lexi had come up behind her as moral support and Jay continued, his eyes wide like an animal in a trap. 'Stella, honestly, there's been a misunderstanding—'

'No, there hasn't. You're an absolute dick. A pathetic example of what a man should be.'

'You should be ashamed of yourself,' Lexi added, using the mum tone she normally reserved for her kids.

As the two ladies turned and walked away, Stella twisted for one last shot. 'Oh, and part of the reason why I didn't jump straight into bed with you was because you're a crap kisser.'

Lexi threaded her arm through Stella's as they made their way back to their seats. Passing a table, Stella heard a woman whisper Miles's name and tuned in to what they were saying. 'Miles said it wasn't true. He said that Jay couldn't be trusted. Toxic masculinity, he called it.'

Stella resisted the urge to turn her head and ask them more. So Miles had tried to stop the rumours and defend her. It seemed

256

she really had misjudged him. They took their seats as Jay left the pub, head down and red-faced.

'That was epic,' said Lexi, sipping her wine.

Adrenalin had caused Stella's hands to shake but as the pub chatter started again and one of the locals raised his glass to her, Stella knew she'd done the right thing. If only the rest of her problems could be sorted so easily.

Chapter 27

Miles said goodbye to the estate agent and made his way to the café after seeing another property. It was a gorgeous Victorian house on the seafront that had been converted into two flats. It lacked a shop, but would be a great holiday let and what's more it needed minimal work. Conveniently, it was also only a few minutes away from his house. *This really could be the one*, thought Miles with a grin. Since he'd stopped constantly looking backwards and started going with the flow a bit more, he felt so much more positive. Life was definitely looking up. He checked his phone and seeing no emails or phone calls stuffed it back into his pocket. Apprehension tensed his shoulder a little and he forced himself to relax. He left the wide road that ran parallel with the beach and carried on down a small side street, back towards home and the café.

The weather was changing, leaving the chill edge of spring and leaning further and further towards summer. The days felt longer and warmer as the sun shone just a little brighter. Clear, crisp May skies were beginning to carry a summer heat with fewer and fewer clouds and the sea was losing its ferocious edge, the waves calming to a gentle ebb. As he walked on, the smells of salt and seaweed disappeared, replaced by freshly baked bread, and the sounds of the tide gave way to the cars and chatter of the high street.

When he walked into the café, he glanced at where Vivien used to sit and a pang of grief hit him. He really did miss the old bird. She'd been fun and so full of life, and knew how to live and love. Lexi's cheerful voice cut through his thoughts before they turned maudlin. 'Hey, Miles. How's tricks?'

'Not bad, thanks. You?'

She flashed a brilliant smile but there was a sadness in her eyes as they darted to Vivien's spot. 'I'm okay thanks. Missing Vivien but, you know.'

'Yeah I know. I was just looking at her old seat.'

Raina popped her head out from the back of the shop. 'We've kept her special cup and saucer. It's on the shelf up there.' She pointed to where it sat. 'No one else gets to use it now.'

'That's sweet,' he replied. 'You guys are quiet today.' Unusually the shop was completely empty.

'Ah, well, the morning rush is over. You'll be having a late breakfast then, I take it? Or is it an early lunch?'

'Early lunch. How's Stella?' he asked Lexi.

'Urgh, not great. She doesn't think she'll have a business once this whole robbery thing is sorted out. Anyway, where've you been the last few days? We haven't seen you for ages.'

Miles kept his face placid. 'Oh, I had some things to sort out.' He couldn't resist checking his phone again. All he needed was an email or call to confirm it was done and he could relax. Knowing this was all his fault was driving him crazy, not to mention complicating his growing feelings for Stella.

'So what can we get you today?' asked Raina. 'Or am I guessing again?'

Miles grinned. 'Can I have a black coffee and …' He perused the board. 'One of your bacon and Brie baguettes sounds good.' Just then his phone rang. He'd never moved so quickly before and Lexi must have noticed his eagerness from the surprised

259

look she gave. He turned away as he answered. 'Miles Parker speaking.'

The voice on the other end hesitated and Miles's heart flew up into his throat. He worried it was bad news. 'Oh, hello, Mr Parker, it's Reginald Beck here.'

'Good morning. You have news for me?' Aware that Lexi and Raina were behind him, he edged a little further away. As long as he kept his responses general, they'd never guess what he was doing.

'I do. Good news. It's done. Their solicitors presented the offer to settle out of court and it has been accepted. With your permission I'll arrange for the transfer of funds immediately.'

A big smile took over his face. 'Yes. Yes. Please do. And thank you. Thank you very much.'

'No need to thank me, Miles, it was such a generous offer they'd have been fools not to accept. Are you positive that you want to offer so much? It's not too late to take the offer off the table or change the amount.'

'No, thank you, Mr Beck. I'm positive. Let's proceed as soon as possible. Goodbye.'

Mr Beck rang off and Miles turned back round to see Lexi and Raina eyeing each other suspiciously. Raina spoke first.

'Now, what are you doing talking to Mr Beck the local solicitor?'

Damn it, thought Miles. He should have been more careful and not said his name.

'And what are you proceeding with?' asked Lexi, who then gasped excitedly. 'Have you found a property to buy? That's great! I know you've wanted to get somewhere here for ages. How fab that—Oh, wait—' Lexi's phone began to ring. 'Sorry. It's Stella,' she said to Riana. 'Do you mind if I take this? She really needs a friend right now. The bacon's just finishing anyway.'

'No, of course not,' Raina replied, still watching Miles. Lexi made her way to an empty table and sat down.

His heart filled with joy knowing he'd done the right thing

not just for his conscience, but for Stella too. Lexi answered and as she spoke her face changed. Miles tried to keep his eyes on the sizzling bacon but couldn't stop glancing over as she spoke. Raina too watched on with concern.

'Hey honey, don't worry. There'll always be quiet days, we're quiet too … I know, but sales will pick up soon and as soon as this whole mess is sorted you'll feel better. Why don't you concentrate on the exhibition? It's only a week or so away isn't it? You need to stay positive … Don't talk like that, you can't. You need a coffee, that's all. I'll nip one over in a minute.' After a second she hung up and took over preparing Miles's order. 'I'm going to call in and see Stella as soon as we're done. She's really upset, talking about putting the place on the market. I really hope she doesn't.' Lexi looked up and grimaced. 'Oh, sorry, Miles, that was insensitive of me.'

'No, no,' Miles replied. He couldn't wait for Stella to receive the news that the case was dropped. She just had to hang on until then.

Raina patted Lexi on the shoulder. 'Why don't you head over now? I'll do Miles's lunch.'

'Are you sure?'

'Yes, go. You might as well as we're quiet.'

Lexi made two takeaway coffees and began to head out. Miles knew he had to get Lexi to convince Stella not to put the place on the market. 'Listen, Lexi, don't let her make any hasty decisions. Not yet.'

'I know. I'll try.' But it seemed she was only half listening as she removed her apron.

'Lexi, you really, really, need to make sure she doesn't do anything yet.' Raina, who was as wily as anyone could be, had narrowed her eyes on him. He was being as subtle as a brick in the face. 'Just, don't let her do anything hasty.'

Raina wrapped up his baguette and placed it on the counter. 'Miles?' Lexi said, pausing near the door.

He felt heat rise on the back of his neck. 'Look, I have to go,' said Miles, quickly, reaching out for his food but Raina pulled it back, holding it hostage.

'What's going on?'

'Nothing.' He gave a half laugh. 'I just remembered I've got some stuff to do. Can I please have my lunch?'

Lexi walked back to the other side of the counter so she could face him. 'No. You're acting weird. Now what's going on?' Her face clouded then suddenly cleared as she leaned across the counter. 'Oh my God. It's because of the kiss isn't it? You've really got the hots for Stella, haven't you? It wasn't just a one-off. Is that why you're being weird? You went a bit odd as soon as I mentioned her and started looking all shifty. And now you're going all red.' She pointed her free hand at his face. 'You do!'

Miles panicked. He did have the hots for Stella, quite a lot actually, and Lexi pointing it out like an excited teenager wasn't helping. But now wasn't a good time to try and do anything about it. Though he didn't know her inside and out, he knew that Stella would reject him just because everything else was so utterly rubbish right now. With so much hanging over her she wouldn't feel free to start a new relationship if she thought there was a chance of having to move away.

'Oh, leave the boy alone, Lexi,' said Raina, pushing his lunch towards him. She crossed her arms over her chest and Miles had the sneaking suspicion she'd figured out the truth about his conversation with Mr Beck. 'Let him go and have his lunch. Look what you've done to him – you've made him all red and splotchy. And you've got to get next door to Stella, so off with you.' Raina gave Lexi a gentle shove towards the door.

Without thinking Miles raised his hand to his face to see if it was as hot as he felt. It was.

'You know,' said Lexi as she walked to the door again. 'If you did have the hots for Stella you'd make a great couple.'

'Go away, Lexi,' he shouted back without turning around, but the thought had occurred to him too and he grinned. He heard the door to the shop close and looked up to see Raina with her arms folded across her chest.

'Now, young man, what have you done?'

'What?'

'You know full well what I mean. What have you gone and done? You can't fool me. I've been around the block a few times and back again. So, come on, tell me the truth or I'll charge you double for your baguette. It's not just that you fancy that young lady next door, is it? What was all that about not letting her sell up and Mr Beck proceeding?' Raina's head tilted as she began to understand what he'd said. 'You've paid them off, haven't you?'

Miles sighed and scrunched the curls at the back of his head. He should have known she'd guess. 'Yes. I made the decision to settle out of court on Stella's behalf.'

'Why ever did you do that? You can't buy a woman's affections you know. Especially not a self-sufficient woman like Stella.'

'I know,' he added. 'But it was my fault.'

'How could it have been your fault? They left the door unlocked not you. It's their fault.'

He shook his head. 'No, it was mine. Josie, the nanny, tried it on with me and when I didn't know what to say I ended up saying, quite bluntly, that I wasn't interested and she got annoyed. She couldn't have shut the door properly when she stomped off to the car. I didn't realise at the time; it was only later during the wedding. I had to sort it out, Raina. There's no way Stella should lose that place because of me.'

'So you've paid everything and they've agreed they'll drop it?'

'Yes. I made them a generous offer on the condition that they cease all proceedings. Stella will receive an email or letter from their solicitors over the next couple of days confirming it. But, Raina—' his tone grew stern '—I don't want her to know it was me, okay?'

'Why ever not?'

263

Miles took a step towards the counter and rested his hands on top. 'Because she's so nice she'll think she has to make it up to me all the time or pay me back and – and it'll embarrass her. She doesn't need to know.'

'But won't the solicitors tell her?'

'It's been made clear the details aren't to be included, just the fact the case has been dropped.'

Raina's smile said that she read him like a book. 'So you thought of everything then.'

'I hope so.' Before he'd have said yes, he had, but he wasn't that arrogant anymore. 'You have to keep this a secret Raina, okay? You can't tell her.'

With a sigh she said, 'Okay. If you insist.'

'I do,' he said 'Now, if the interrogation is over, I'm leaving with my lunch.' Raina simply harrumphed in response.

Chapter 28

It was Sunday, and Lexi and Stella were stood in the living room of Vivien's old house. It was the first time Lexi had been in there since Vivien had died and she was grateful for Stella's moral support. She shook her head in disbelief. 'I still can't believe that Vivien left everything to me. I mean, why me? I'm nobody special.'

'I think you're wrong there,' said Stella. 'And Vivien saw it too.'

'Hmm.' Lexi still wasn't convinced and kept worrying Mr Beck would call saying it was all a mistake. 'Anyway, how are you?' Lexi asked eagerly.

Stella perched on the edge of the old worn sofa and Lexi joined her. 'To be honest I'm still in shock. I can't believe they dropped the case just like that. I was sure Roger was the type to try and rinse me for every penny I had.'

'I wonder what made him change his mind.'

'I have no idea. I always thought I was a pretty decent judge of character but maybe I'm not.'

'Maybe they realised one of them had left the door open.'

Stella nodded. 'Maybe. But to get an email out of the blue from their solicitors? Crazy.'

'I wish I'd seen your face,' Lexi said with a grin.

'It was like this …' Stella widened her eyes and her mouth

265

dropped open in a caricature of shock. Lexi giggled. 'After that I was so elated I was all motivated again and got a few more artists lined up for the exhibition. Hopefully that'll generate some sales. This week I'll clear the shop so it can be an art gallery for next weekend. I've decided I won't move Vivien's chair – I'm going to put my favourite piece on there and use it like an easel.'

'That's a lovely idea,' Lexi said, smiling.

'Listen to me,' said Stella. 'I should be the one asking how you are.'

'I think I'm okay.' She looked around the living room, a familiar and yet unfamiliar sight. Everything seemed different. Every corner was crammed with beautiful dark wooden furniture. It sucked in the light, making the room darker, but Lexi had grown so used to it she couldn't imagine any other sort of furniture in there. The thought that one day soon she might be living in this very house, her children tearing up and down the stairs, was mindboggling. 'It still just feels really weird. Like this is all a dream, or at some point someone's going to jump out on me and tell me it's all been a huge prank. Apart from Vivien dying that is; I know that was real. But this house …' She didn't know how to finish the sentence and traced her finger over the sofa.

Stella placed a hand on her shoulder. 'I understand, honey. But this is what Vivien wanted and she'd want you to be happy. Not feeling guilty.'

'I can't help it, it's every woman's default mode.'

'That's true.' Stella stood and held out her hands to Lexi. 'Come on, this place won't clean itself.'

Lexi placed her cup down on the coffee table. 'Thanks for doing this. Right, my mum always said to start at the top and work down so, shall we?'

Stella nodded and picked up a black sack. Lexi grabbed a broom and they headed upstairs to start cleaning and sorting out Vivien's things. The bare dark wood floorboards of the stairs creaked under foot and Lexi's hand traced along the heavy wooden banister. She'd polished this for Vivien, and remembering her friend brought tears to her eyes.

'Are you okay?' Stella asked, seeing her face as they got to the landing.

'Yeah, I'll be fine.' Lexi took a breath and willed her eyes to stop because Stella was right: Vivien would want her to be happy. The walls of the landing were covered in photos and paintings. There were sepia pictures of Vivien's mother and father, and judging by the clothes, their parents too. She would keep all these for sure. She owed Vivien that much and wanted everyone who came into the house to know about her.

'The house is huge,' said Stella. 'How many bedrooms is it?'

'Four,' said Lexi. 'And a smaller attic room upstairs. And the bathroom is huge.' Though it felt strange saying it amongst her mixed emotions she couldn't wait to move in. She was beginning to feel that Vivien wanted her and her children here, bringing life to the lovely old house. Her rented house was tiny and she was constantly patching up torn wallpaper or scrubbing off scuffs from the walls. Her landlord wouldn't let her put up pictures and she desperately wanted some of the kids on display. Despite their constant gurning she did have a few nice ones of them and even some where they were hugging each other. She could just picture them framed nicely on the stairs snuggled between some of Vivien's.

'Just remember you deserve this,' said Stella, and Lexi nodded. Stella went off to clean the bathroom and Lexi entered Vivien's enormous bedroom.

It was located at the front of the house and had two large sash windows through which sunshine streamed in. A large tree outside shaded the room a little and Lexi threw open the windows to invite in the fresh air. When she saw the four-poster bed, complete with a deep pink bedspread and a gazillion cushions in different shapes and sizes, she smiled. Old Vivien knew how to live in style. There was also an old-fashioned dressing table and mirror, still strewn with trinkets. Somewhere were the things she'd bequeathed to Miles, and Lexi had promised to find them for him. He'd been very patient and hadn't even mentioned them, knowing how hard she was finding accepting this new situation. Sniffing, Lexi gave herself a mental shake; time to crack on. Against one wall were two large dark wood wardrobes and when Lexi opened them, her mouth dropped.

'Stella? Stella? Come here. Quick!'

Footsteps pounded into the room and a breathless Stella arrived. 'What is it? Are you okay?'

'Look at this.' Lexi pointed to inside the wardrobe. Stella joined her and her mouth dropped open too. The wardrobe was fit to bursting with exquisite vintage fashion. Lexi ran to the other one and opened it too. It was also stuffed full, the bottom lined with shoes and handbags, and in the corner of the room were a stack of hat boxes.

'Wow, this is amazing.' Stella pulled out a delicate grey silk evening gown that could have been haute couture it was so beautiful. 'What will you do with it all?'

Lexi shook her head. 'I don't know.' It was like being given one last present from Vivien, and Lexi closed her eyes and gave thanks. 'I mean … I really don't know.'

'You should sell it,' said Stella, running her fingers over a gorgeous but tiny sequined gown.

Lexi turned to her. 'Sell it?'

'Yeah.' Seeing Lexi's shocked expression, she added, 'Not in a horrible get rid of things way,' she reassured her. 'But you could start that online vintage clothing business you talked about.'

'What?' Lexi's brain had paused. It was all so overwhelming.

Stella continued and it was wonderful to see the same enthusiastic woman Lexi had met when she first arrived in Swallowtail Bay. The one who was never daunted by hard work or problems. 'All this combined with the clothes you make yourself – you could be a huge hit. You could sell online, have a rail in the shop, do fittings from home—'

'Me?' asked Lexi.

Stella nodded and placed a hand on her shoulder. 'Yes you. You probably couldn't give up the café just yet, but you never know, maybe one day. This could be the start of something wonderful.'

'Just like living here?' Lexi felt her breath leave her chest. 'Do you think I could really do it?'

'Of course you could.'

Overwhelmed by the sudden changes in her life, Lexi sat down on the edge of the bed and felt the tears fall down her face. Whenever she was with the kids she'd swallowed them back down, putting on a brave face, but now she was with Stella she could let them fall. 'I can't believe this is happening. For so long I've felt like I was being punished for everything I did.'

Stella joined her and placed a hand on her back. 'Punishment for what?'

Lexi wiped her tears away with her fingertips. She knew she should have used waterproof mascara today. 'Nothing. Never mind. I'm just tired.' But she couldn't stop the tears from coming now she'd started.

'Please tell me, Lexi.'

Lexi studied Stella's face through misted eyes. For so long she'd been alone without someone to talk to, someone to confide in. Could she take the final step and open up completely to Stella? She trusted her, and no one could blame her any more than she blamed herself. Sucking in a breath she said, 'It was my fault Will and I split up. I ruined my family.'

'No,' said Stella, now rubbing her back in gentle, soothing circles. 'Sometimes things just don't work out.'

Lexi shook her head. 'You don't understand. I cheated on Will. I—' The words fell away. Her friendship with Stella meant so much to her, she didn't want Stella to think less of her but she couldn't bear to lift her head and see her response.

'What happened?' Stella's voice was gentle and kind, carrying no judgement or reproach.

'It was after Ralph was born. There's only two years between the kids and I felt rubbish after having two kids so close together. My body felt gross and not my own – I'll save you the gory details. And I was so tired with a toddler and a newborn. I was exhausted all the time and I felt so low. My self-confidence was through the floor.' Lexi pulled a tissue from her pocket and twisted it in her fingers. 'Will was working all the time because we needed the money as I didn't have any coming in. But then, within weeks of Ralph being born, he started going to the pub after work. We hardly ever saw each other and when we did we were both either so exhausted we hardly spoke or all we talked about was the kids. I began to resent him going out to the pub instead of doing his share at home. I hardly left the house because I didn't have time for a shower or anything. I'd always think, "I'll have one when Will gets home," then he'd go the pub and I never got the chance. I just felt so low. Then Ralph got colic and was up all night. Taylor joined in too because Ralph would wake her and I was surviving on pretty much an hour of sleep a night if I was lucky. I didn't know what day it was and honestly felt at times like I was going mad. I asked him to stop going but he said he worked so hard he deserved to unwind.'

'But what about you?' asked Stella. 'You deserved to unwind too. Did he stop going?'

'No. After that we ended up arguing all the time. Then one day I met this guy in the park and it all snowballed so quickly. He was so nice to me and kept paying me compliments. When I was with him I felt like more than just a mum and a wife; I felt like a person again and one someone wanted to be with. I just got swept away in this made-up world and – and I slept with him. It was only once and as soon as I did it I regretted it. I knew I'd risked everything and that underneath it all Will was a good man. He was just tired and stressed like me. But the guilt was too much. After a month I came clean to Will and he said he could never forgive me.' She wiped another escaping tear away.

'I threw everything away including the love of my life because I'm stupid.'

'You're not stupid,' said Stella. 'And we all make mistakes.'

'Do we?'

'Of course. You should see some of the things I wore in the Nineties.' Lexi laughed and Stella continued. 'But seriously, you can't keep beating yourself up about something that happened in the past. I can't even imagine how you must lose yourself when you have kids. Isaac and I couldn't make our marriage work and it was only the two of us. Throw in kids and I can imagine it's even harder to remember that you're a couple. And it sounds like Will didn't exactly help matters, disappearing to the pub instead of being there for you. He has to take some blame for this too, Lexi.'

Lexi sniffed again. Unburdening all of this felt so good, but the guilt remained and she suspected it always would. 'Do you really think so?'

'Yes, I do.'

'I think I've had to keep this all bottled up for so long I just made it all my fault. In my mind, Will was blameless and I put it all on me.'

'Sometimes circumstances force us into making the wrong choice, but that doesn't make you a bad person.'

Resting her head on Stella's shoulder, Lexi said, 'Thank you, sweetie.'

'Things are changing for you now, Lexi. And I know it's scary, but you're not on your own anymore. I'm here for you and so is Raina. And maybe Will realises the mistakes he made in the past too. Time to start afresh.' They sat unspeaking for a moment while Stella rubbed Lexi's back, then in her usual cheerful voice she tried to chivvy her up. 'Right, come on. We've got a whole lot of work to do today so no more lazing about. Let's do the bathroom together. The shower screen's got more limescale than a scaly lime.'

271

Lexi stood, feeling like a load had lifted off her chest. For the first time she could see that she hadn't been completely to blame for the situation her family was now in. Both she and Will were equally responsible that things hadn't worked out. She'd always regret that night and feel a certain level of guilt for it, but Will wasn't the angel she had decided him to be. His disappearing off to the pub instead of being there for her had a huge impact on their situation too. Hearing someone else say it made all the difference. Maybe this new start was a chance to leave some of the past behind and start afresh. Though he'd never said anything, she knew Will felt sorry for neglecting her and not realising the depth of her isolation. They could both have a fresh start. It was what Vivien wanted for her.

Closing her eyes, she took a second to ground herself in this moment of freedom before starting the cleaning again, but as she left the bedroom she glanced again at the wardrobes full of gowns. *Thank you, Vivien*, she said to herself. *And thank you, Stella.*

Chapter 29

A week later and it was finally time for the gallery exhibition. In between recovering from her shock over the horrible family dropping their case and helping Lexi sort out some of Vivien's house, Stella had spent every spare minute preparing the shop to exhibit paintings rather than everything she normally sold. She cleared the dressers and moved them to the corners of the room to give as much wall space as possible. She'd slowly been clearing the stock away too to fit in more paintings. Stella yawned as a moment's tiredness weighed on her eyelids. She'd been up late hanging pictures, but the gallery, as she was calling it today, was nearly ready to go.

When she'd first had the idea, the family were still suing her for thousands of pounds and she'd felt like she was just going through the motions. All the while there'd been the possibility of losing the shop and having to sell up, she'd lost her normal energy. A draining lethargy had stolen the movement from her limbs and everything had seemed such hard work. Even her walks with Frank felt like a chore and she'd stopped enjoying the smell of the sea and the feel of the pebbles beneath her feet. That had changed now though and she was feeling more and more like her old self. Back to jumping out of bed in the mornings, Stella was once more savouring the feel of the cool breeze on her cheeks and breathing in the fresh sea air, enjoying its salty tang.

This morning, Stella had risen even earlier to take Frank for an extra-long walk; she didn't need him getting bored during the day and pestering her. Plus it was party night and her sister and niece and nephew were coming down. When she hadn't been sorting the shop, she'd been readying the holiday lets so her family could stay in one and Lexi the other. Though Lexi was as close as family now, even closer maybe.

Stella had taken a tennis ball with her and they'd walked up and down the beach with the sun slowly rising in front of her. It had grown from a pale and watery light shyly peering over the horizon to a fantastic blinding orb, promising a bright and sunny day. She threw the ball for Frank once last time and watched his big floppy ears flapping as he ran back to her with it in his mouth. More than ever lately her thoughts wandered to Miles, the wedding and the kiss. She hadn't seen him for the past few days and hoped he would call in today. She'd missed him and wanted desperately to share her news that the case was dropped. Hopefully she'd get a chance to tell him later. As he knew it was the art exhibition today, she couldn't imagine him not popping in. Calling Frank back to her, she clipped on his lead and headed home.

Just before opening time, Stella found the painting she loved most and placed it on Vivien's chair. It was the one that she and Miles had both admired all those months ago. She couldn't understand why it hadn't sold before now. To her it was the most beautiful piece she'd stocked. If it was still there at the end of the day, she decided, she would put it in the flat and buy it herself in instalments. Maybe here was where it was meant to stay. Surveying the shop once more, checking everything was perfect, she switched on the radio, went to the door and flipped the sign to *open*.

Some of the artists had agreed to stop by to talk to the customers about their work, and a few arrived shortly after nine, but no actual customers. Stella made the artists tea and chatted to them, telling them it was always a little slow first thing, but inside she prayed hard things would liven up soon. She took her seat behind the counter in a funk, making idle chitchat as her favourite jazz radio station played out. Stella had secretly hoped, as she had on her very first day of opening, for a line of people waiting to get in, but for fifteen minutes no one had so much as walked past. Gradually, a few people called in, and a few more, and a few more. And before long the shop was full. Soon it was packed and she had to move sideways to get through to greet everyone and let them know she was here to help. The artists too seemed happy chatting to customers, describing their inspiration and techniques for the paintings.

When one of the artists called her over, Stella was worried it was to complain about something, but when the customer stood beside them asked to purchase the painting, Stella couldn't stop a great big happy smile from taking over. All morning she was called here, there and everywhere to take down, wrap and sell paintings. The day was going better than she ever could have hoped for.

With so many people in, the shop grew hot and Stella wedged the door open, pausing a moment to feel the breeze on her face and take a big deep breath. Inside her was a mass of excitement and she felt almost shaky with it. With the sun out and the weather warm, the high street was busy and more and more customers were heading towards her. As she went back inside she looked out through the large side window and saw Miles coming down the street. He smiled when he saw her and Stella's heart wriggled.

'Wow,' he said, edging his way inside the doorway. 'This is going well.'

'It really is,' Stella replied, unable to hide her enthusiasm or relief. They made their way back towards the counter.

'And I see you've kept Vivien's chair out. That's wonderful.' He paused a moment, examining the piece and Stella wondered if he remembered it. 'I've always loved that painting,' he said slightly mournfully.

'Why don't you buy it?' she teased.

'I just might.' He gave another smile that made her legs melt beneath her. She replayed the kiss at the wedding and swallowed. 'This is amazing. You should be so proud of yourself, Stella. What an incredible thing to do. I can't imagine there's ever been this many people in here before and from the looks of it the paintings are selling fast.'

Stella savoured the compliment. 'I owe it all to Lexi really. This was her idea. One artist has gone to get some more paintings. I'm just worried that I'll sell so much to local people today no one will ever need another painting again.'

Miles gave a loud, easy laugh and it brightened his face. More than ever the hard edges she'd seen at first vanished. 'No, you'll turn them all into collectors and be made for life.'

'With any luck. Will we see you at the party tonight?' She tried to keep her voice level but her heart was ricocheting around her chest in the hope he'd say yes.

'Of course. I wouldn't miss it.'

'Stella!' Lexi's voice carried over the noise and she waved above the shop full of people.

'Excuse me,' Stella said to Miles and made her way over. She hoped he would stay but when she turned back he'd gone and from the corner of her eye she caught a glimpse of him walking back towards his house. She still hadn't got to tell him about the email and cursed herself for forgetting. 'Hey, Lexi.'

Lexi took her in a huge hug as did Ralph and Taylor who were right beside her. 'It's so busy!' Lexi said.

The same huge grin appeared on her face. 'I know. I'm so pleased.'

Ralph looked up with big round blue eyes. 'Do you have any kids' paintings?'

'Sorry, Ralph, I don't. But I could run some kids' art workshops during the winter, couldn't I?'

'That's a great idea,' Lexi replied.

'Can we come?' asked Taylor.

Before she could answer, an Irish voice drifted towards them. 'Now, I can see two little munchkins who look like they need some chocolate cake.'

'Raina!' they both called and Taylor jumped up and down on the spot, the idea of chocolate cake proving too much.

'Pop next door when you've finished,' Raina said to Lexi, 'and tell Carol to get them both some cake.' Lexi nodded in response and then eyed her kids as if to say, 'Only if you behave yourselves.'

'Can we go and stroke Frank?' Ralph asked Stella.

'Of course. You know where he is.' Small enough to make their way through underneath the mass of elbows and arms, they scurried over to the counter and Frank immediately perked up when he saw them.

Raina gently laid her hand on Stella's arm. 'This is going grand, isn't it?'

Stella nodded. 'If things carry on like this for the rest of the day I might have been able to pay that horrible family off after all. I know they've dropped the case but do you think I should send them something to apologise?'

'Absolutely not,' Raina said sternly and Stella felt herself stiffen in surprise. She'd never heard Raina's voice anything other than soft and lyrical, and from Lexi's face, she hadn't either. 'You don't need to go doing that; enough money's been spent already.'

'What do you mean?' asked Stella, a sudden pressure on her chest.

Lexi sharpened her gaze too. 'What's going on, Raina?'

'Nothing.' Raina started fiddling with the sleeve of her top and kept her eyes low, unable to meet their gaze.

'What did you mean enough money's been spent already?' asked Stella.

'It's just a turn of phrase.'

Lexi cocked her head. 'Umm, no it isn't. And why did you get so cross?'

'I've no idea what you're talking about,' Raina continued. 'My tone of voice was perfectly normal.'

'No it wasn't,' Lexi replied, her voice matching the noise in the room. 'And you've got that look about you.'

This time Raina looked up indignantly. 'What look?'

'That look that says you know something no one else does and we're all really thick for not working it out.'

'I do not,' Raina protested, her accent becoming fiercer as she defended herself.

'You bloody well do,' Lexi continued. 'Come on, what do you know?'

Stella watched on with a strange feeling in her chest. What did Raina mean enough money had been spent already? Okay, the email Stella had received had been a bit vague on details but how could Raina know more? 'Raina, if you know something, please tell me. I have a right to know.' Someone called Stella's name trying to get her attention, but she kept her gaze focused on Raina. 'Raina, please. I have to see to that customer. If you know something, tell me now.'

'You really should, Raina,' added Lexi.

'Oh, all right,' she conceded. 'You two are like the mafia. The family dropped the case because Miles paid them off.'

Stella's face froze. 'What? When? Why?'

Raina sighed and explained again to Stella. 'He paid them off because he realised it was his fault the door didn't shut. Josie, that hussy, was flirting with him and when he told her to go on with herself, she didn't shut it properly. Probably too busy flouncing around like she owned the place.'

'But why would Miles do that for me?' asked Stella. Now Raina really did look at her like she was stupid.

278

'He felt responsible so he made them a generous offer and they've taken the money.'

'How generous?' asked Lexi, reading the shock in Stella's face.

Raina shrugged. 'I don't know. Enough.' Stella stood stock still despite her name being called again. 'Come on now, girl, you should be pleased.'

'I am,' Stella replied but her head was buzzing. 'I just— How do I—How am I ever going to repay him?' she said, her voice barely more than a whisper. 'I was being sued for five thousand pounds and if he's made them a generous offer it must be more than that, plus what? Paying their costs? If he's shelled out all this money, how am I going to pay all that back? How do I even talk to him about it? Why would he do that for me?'

Raina's voice was back to being stern, making Stella and Lexi jump. 'Because he likes you, Stella. He wants to help. Is that so hard to imagine?' Stella looked up, her head filled with worry. Her name was called again and she knew that if she didn't put a professional smile back on her face she'd lose the sale. Her body didn't want to move but she forced herself to mumble a goodbye to Lexi and Raina before stumbling off to her customer. She served them on autopilot, her arms and legs working but her brain silent.

It wasn't until later that afternoon, when someone tried to purchase hers and Miles's favourite painting, that she had an idea of what she could do to say thank you. But would such a small token of gratitude ever be enough?

Finally, it was party night and Stella couldn't wait for Lexi to see the place. In the large flat, patched up and tidied after the burglary, she'd hung bunting in the shape of 1950s dresses around every room. Balloons were strung up in the corners and the kitchen was full of booze and food. She'd plugged in her iPod and put it on shuffle, smiling as Eighties hair-metal filled the silence. She'd promised Lexi music, but she hadn't promised good music. As excited as she was for Lexi's arrival, she was also nervous. It had been months since she'd seen her sister, Abby, and they'd be here soon too. On top of all of this, she was going to see Miles for the first time after learning what he'd done for her and her mind had been in a whirlwind ever since.

There weren't enough words to express how thankful she was to have the whole mess off her back but she couldn't let him pay out all that money. She just couldn't. When she'd added up the takings only an hour ago, she'd had to double, and then triple count just to make sure there hadn't been a mistake. She'd made so much money she was actually going to be able to pay some of it back to him. She'd been working on the assumption that, if they were suing for five thousand pounds and Miles had made a generous offer, he must have at least matched it, or gone over. And though she couldn't pay him it all in one go, she could pay him some now and the rest over the months to come. Stella was sure she would be in Swallowtail Bay forever now that she wouldn't have to leave. She didn't want to be anywhere else. Glancing at the corner of the kitchen and the large parcel wrapped in brown paper, she hoped that combined with some of the money, it would be enough to start with.

Stella heard a knock at the door and opened it, leaving it that way for the other guests to arrive. Lexi laughed as she walked in. 'Wow, it looks so pretty!'

'Do you like it?'

'I love it,' she said, taking Stella in a huge hug.

'Happy birthday, sweetie,' Stella said, and kissed Lexi's cheek. She looked incredible in another vintage dress. It wasn't one of Vivien's as she'd been a different size to Lexi, clearly petite from the get-go, but Lexi was wearing one of her pillbox hats in a deep red that matched the halter-neck wiggle dress encasing her. She looked sensational, like Marilyn Monroe. Stella smoothed down the little black dress Lexi had convinced her to wear. It was shorter than anything she would have chosen herself, but all that climbing up and down ladders and squatting down for things in the shop had done wonders for her thighs.

'Aunty Stella,' shouted Taylor, wrapping her bottom half in a hug. 'Do you like my dress?' She did a spin, holding out the bottom of the skirt and Stella laughed.

'Yes, I do. You look amazing. So pretty.'

Ralph hugged Stella too. 'Hi, Aunty Stella. Look I'm wearing a coatwaist.'

'Waistcoat, darling,' said Lexi, looking adoringly at her son.

Stella's heart filled with love; they'd called her aunty! 'You look very smart, Ralph. Have you guys been good today? Good enough to get your chocolate cake?' They nodded and Stella and Lexi smiled at one and other.

'They've actually been okay, but God knows what their dentist is going to say on their next visit. They've had enough sugar to kill an elephant. Anyway, go on you two. Go to the kitchen and get a drink.' They skipped off, the excitement radiating off them.

Stella and Lexi went to the living room. The music blared from the speakers. After getting a drink the kids joined them, dancing like lunatics. Lexi kept looking out of the window and Stella couldn't figure out why she was so nervous. 'Do you always get like this?' she asked.

Lexi nodded. 'I don't have parties. The last time I had a party I didn't have kids. I'm terrified people won't turn up.'

'Me too,' Stella said in a serious tone and Lexi spun around in panic. 'I'm kidding! Of course people will turn up. But before they do, I have something for you.' She went to the kitchen and came back with another brown paper parcel. This time it was a long tube shape and she'd tied a bright red ribbon around it in a fancy bow.

'What's this?' asked Lexi, her eyes widening in surprise. 'Gosh, it's very heavy.'

'Open it and see.'

'Can we open it?' asked Ralph bounding over with Taylor following.

'Please, Mummy?'

Lexi rolled her eyes and kneeled down so the kids could help. 'I suppose so. I haven't got to open any of my other birthday presents on my own yet, have I? Even the ones Daddy brought me.'

Stella raised her eyebrows. 'Oh?' But Lexi didn't get chance to answer as the kids tore away at the paper.

Lexi gasped when she finally realised what it was. 'Oh my gosh.' Stella smiled at her friend's reaction – her best friend's reaction. 'It's the fabric. The teapot design. I was going to buy this when Vivien's money came through.'

'Well, I wanted to get you something special. Something meaningful. And I know how much you've always liked it. I hid it away so no one else would buy it. Now you can start your business with a whole load of dresses made by you, in lots of different sizes, as well as the ones Vivien gave you.'

'I can't believe it. That's so thoughtful. Thank you.' She stood and took Stella in a huge hug, both of them tearful and grateful for each other.

Female voices rang out from the hall. 'Hello?' A bunch of women, followed by a throng of excited, screeching children rushed in. It was some of the mums from school and Stella smiled as Lexi went to greet them. Next to arrive was Will with some of his friends and the gentle kiss he gave Lexi, along with a besotted, admiring glance filled Stella with hope for them both. She'd definitely been right at the funeral; there was still love there and if they both realised their past mistakes, she could definitely see them making it this time.

Before long the place didn't seem half as empty and while everyone else was laughing, joking, dancing and having fun, she found herself checking her watch, disappointed that Miles hadn't yet arrived. The kiss had done things to her heart and body she hadn't experienced in such a long time; it was like being in love for the first time all over again. Yet, with the benefit of age it felt deeper, stronger and more real than fleeting first loves usually were.

Stella had spent a long time trying to figure out why he'd helped her. His guilt was an admirable reason though she hoped he felt the same things she was feeling. Since the kiss, Stella had come to realise that a deep affection had been growing so steadily and slowly she almost hadn't known it was happening. At the wedding she'd seen a different, caring side to Miles. Days were spent hoping he'd pop by, wondering if and when she'd see him again.

The music had been turned up and the bass pounded in the floorboards, but taking refuge in the hall she heard footsteps on the stairs and turned to see her sister, niece and nephew making their way up. They'd grown so much she hardly recognised them. 'Abby! Robert, Lucy! You've got so big!' Though they'd never been the closest of siblings, absence had made the heart grow fonder.

'This place is amazing,' Abby said with genuine enthusiasm. 'And we peeked into the shop – it's big, isn't it? Are you only doing paintings?'

'No. Not exactly,' Stella replied with a laugh. 'I turned it into an art gallery for the day. I'll tell you about it later.'

When they got to the top of the stairs, her niece and nephew gave her a hug but, as they hadn't seen her for a few months, were shy and timid around her. Stella vowed to change that. She'd block off the large flat for a few weeks every year and invite her sister down so they could spend some quality time together. Her mum and dad too, if Abby agreed, though living closer to them, Abby might want some peace from them too. Stella turned to her sister. 'Let's put your bags in the bedroom for now and I'll introduce you to everyone. You're going to love my friend Lexi and she has two kids about the same age as Robert and Lucy.'

Once her family were settled, and after a few more trips to the door, Lexi confirmed that almost everyone they'd invited was here and told Stella to go and enjoy the party. Seeing the smile of pure happiness on Lexi's face had made it all worthwhile. So many people had come to wish her happy birthday, and seeing her dancing with Will and her children filled Stella's heart with love. As she poured herself a large white wine in the kitchen, she could never have imagined she'd make such friends in just the few months she'd been here.

'Can I get one of those?' asked a deep voice from the doorway and Stella looked up to see Miles. She felt her knees go wobbly and nonchalantly rested her hand on the counter for support.

'Of course,' she replied and poured him one. As she handed him the glass their fingers touched, igniting her feelings once again. She wanted his fingers in her hair, pulling her towards him for a kiss. The thought of it made her lips tingle and Miles's deep blue eyes, as still as the sea on a summer's day, looked at her as if he could feel it too. 'I was worried you'd changed your mind,' said Stella, her voice quiet and wavering. She cleared her throat and tried to control it.

'I wouldn't miss Lexi's party,' he said. 'We've been friends for too long.'

'That's nice of you.'

Miles, looking disarmingly sexy leaning against the doorframe, fixed his eyes on her. Stella wasn't sure what was happening or how he felt. She still didn't know how to read him and, concerned he might assume she was wasting money on the party after all he'd shelled out, she said, 'Listen, Miles, I really want to talk to you about paying you back the money you spent. I'm so grateful but I just don't feel comfortable with it. The art exhibition went really well and I can pay you back a lump sum now and then a little a month maybe—'

Miles's face suddenly darkened and his eyebrows knitted together. His voice was harsh, like the old Miles, and it sent a chill through her. 'So, Raina told you, did she?'

'Please don't be angry with her. It wasn't her fault.' It completely was but Stella wasn't going to land her in it.

He raked a hand through his hair but smiled. 'She never could keep a bloody secret. I should have known better than to tell her. The trouble is you can't get much past her.'

Stella felt the colour rising to her cheeks as the heat built within. 'She said you thought it was your fault?'

'It was my fault. Josie was so busy trying to chat me up and I was so busy trying to escape that I didn't realise the door hadn't closed. If I had, you wouldn't have been robbed.'

Stella wanted to reach out and take his hand and tell him it was okay, but she still didn't know how he truly felt. He might think the kiss at the wedding was a mistake he wanted to forget all about. Instead she said, 'You shouldn't blame yourself, Miles. It was just bad luck. These things happen.'

Miles looked up at her from under his thick black eyelashes. His curls had grown even longer and were falling into his face. Stella felt her body tense.

'You're too nice,' he replied. 'Far too nice.'

'I'm not.' She felt the intensity of his gaze. 'We have to decide how I'm going to pay you back. I can't pay it back in one go. It'll have to be instalments but—'

Miles shook his head. 'No. I won't hear of it.'

'But, Miles—'

'No, definitely not. It was my fault and my job to put it right. Which I've done. The matter is closed.'

'Miles, you can't really expect me to—'

'Closed,' he said again sternly, but his expression was one of teasing.

'Miles?'

'Still closed.' He sipped his wine.

Stella felt a laugh rise up and explode from her mouth at how silly he was being. The mischievous twinkle in his eye softened his face. Feeling her heart stirring in a way it hadn't done in a long, long, time, Stella drew her eyes down to her watch, worried that if she kept staring at Miles he might think she'd gone mad. 'Well, I wanted to give you this as a thank you.' She hopped off the stool and handed him the painting.

Confusion drew fine lines over his forehead. He placed his wine glass down and unwrapped it carefully, then a smile pulled the corners of his mouth upwards. 'The painting. You shouldn't have. You should have sold it.'

Stella stood beside him admiring the colours once again. 'You said you liked it and I thought it might be a small way to show my appreciation.'

'You liked it too, I thought.'

'I do. But I'd rather it went to someone who truly deserves it.' Standing so close to him, Stella felt her skin prickle. His arm reached out and he rested his hand on the frame. She wondered how they'd feel wrapped around her waist and when he turned to her, Stella felt her heart thumping against her ribs.

'I didn't just do it because of guilt,' Miles replied, coolly.

'No?' Her voice sounded tiny in her ears. He was so close she could smell his aftershave, see the rise and fall of his chest, and the flecks of lighter blue in his navy eyes.

'I did it for you.'

'For me?' A giant lump formed in her throat.

'Yes.' She saw the flash of the shy teenager he'd described to her once before and spotted a tiny scar on his cheek. 'You must know how I feel about you ...'

Stella felt a strange tingling like pins and needles all over her back. 'I—'

'I've never felt this way about anyone before.' His hand reached up, his fingertips about to brush her cheek. 'There's something special about you, Stella. You're brave, kind, funny, patient.' Stella shook her head, unable to speak, and his hand dropped as he turned away. 'You don't feel the same way?'

'I do,' Stella said quickly, grabbing his arm and pulling him back to face her. She hadn't realised herself until lately the depth of her feelings for him. It had been so long since she'd felt anything so meaningful.

Miles pulled her into a tight embrace and focused his gaze. 'I was such an arse when we first met. I was rude and judgemental and—'

'Sssh,' she said, pressing a finger to his lips. They were soft and then she replaced her fingers with her lips and kissed him quiet.

When they separated, he said, 'I'm sorry it took me so long to realise how special you are.'

Maybe one day she'd tell him that the same thing applied to her too.

Epilogue

A few months later, Stella and Miles walked hand in hand along the beach at Swallowtail Bay enjoying the bright mid-morning sun. They were on their way for their usual Sunday lunch at the pub and enjoying some special time together.

It was now the height of summer and with Old Herbert's Shop being so wonderfully busy and the holiday lets fully booked, Stella was happily exhausted. Now the investigation was over and the police had checked the CCTV footage, the insurance company had paid out some money, conceding that the outer door to the apartments was open but the inner one had been locked. Between the money she got back from that and the art exhibition, she'd been able to pay Miles everything he'd shelled out. Not that he would have minded if she hadn't been able to pay him back for months, even years. He was kindness itself. Generous, funny, smart and caring. Everything she'd thought he wasn't.

Miles's holiday lets had just opened for bookings and he too spent most of his week manically charging around Swallowtail Bay. Gone were the days when he would have to drive off here and there for meetings. He'd made the decision with Stella, to quit his day job and focus on the holiday lets. There was even talk of her leaving the flat and moving in with him, giving her another property to add to her portfolio, but there was still a way to go before they were ready for that. The Seventies kitchen remained intact but at least it wasn't leaking. As much as Stella liked the idea, that was definitely in their future, not their present.

Up ahead, Lexi and Will walked together, her arm linked through his. In her dress she looked like something from an old black and white movie. Lexi and the kids had moved into Vivien's house and within a week of doing so, it was like they'd lived there all their lives. The children loved it and in the hallway now hung pictures of them next to those of Vivien at her most young and beautiful. Lexi and Will were taking it slowly but their relationship was going from strength to strength. Lexi spent most of her time worried about the kids, feeling guilty she was messing them up by going back to their dad. She'd even contemplated staying single and repressing her feelings, but Stella had convinced her to be brave and open her heart once more. Both she and Will had clearly learned from their mistakes and no matter what, they were raising their children to be wonderful human beings full of kindness and compassion.

Down on the beach, the tide rolled in and screams and yelps carried on the breeze from Ralph and Taylor who were running along with Frank, chasing the seagulls and arguing over who got to hold his lead. Lexi was still working in the café and doing some cleaning in the holiday lets while she tried to get her vintage clothing business off the ground. She, Stella and Miles had been working on a business plan and it wouldn't be long, Stella was sure, before *Vintage Designs* would be taking Swallowtail Bay by storm.

'Hang on, kids,' Lexi called, and Ralph and Taylor came back up to the promenade to where Lexi and Will had stopped. When Stella and Miles caught up with them, they all took a moment to admire the commemorative bench and the beautiful silver-plated inscription. As soon as Vivien's money had come through, Lexi had arranged for the bench to be installed and had worked with Miles on what the plaque should say. Every time Stella read it a smile came to her face. It summed up the old woman so wonderfully and contained all her joy and love of life. Below her name and the dates of her birth and death, it simply read:

'He was madly in love with me, you know.'

Will wrapped an arm around Lexi's shoulders and they carried on towards the pub. Ralph and Taylor sped back down towards the sea with Frank beside them and Stella took a huge breath in as she snuggled into Miles. Swallowtail Bay was well and truly her new home and as a great ray of light shone out from behind a passing cloud, it seemed Vivien was smiling down on them all yet again.

Acknowledgements

I'm so thrilled to be launching this wonderful series with HQ Digital who are, without doubt, the most insanely talented bunch of people you'll ever come across. I really can't thank them enough for all the hard work they put in on my behalf, helping me make my dreams come true. It's such a pleasure working with you all, especially the lovely Abi Fenton who always helps in figuring out the bits that aren't quite working and most importantly, gives me the courage to fix them! I'd also like to thank one of the sweetest people, ever, Vikki Moynes, who has now moved to another publisher but was instrumental in the first round of edits for this story.

It's also time for a huge shouty thank you to all the amazing readers and book bloggers who have been so kind as to read my books. There really is nothing better than reading a review and knowing that someone enjoyed your story. It makes all the self-doubt and days spent thinking I'm the worst writer in the world all worthwhile!

And finally, I really need to thank my family for constantly supporting me. My kids put up with me writing away in the corner during school holidays, and my husband, parents, and in-laws are always there with words of encouragement when it's not going well. I love you all millions!

Hi, lovely readers!

Can you believe we're here at the exciting launch of this new series: Swallowtail Bay? How did you find your first visit? I really hope you enjoyed it. The second book in this series, *Summer Strawberries at Swallowtail Bay*, is out in June, so I hope you'll come back and meet some new residents and see what they're up to.

In the meantime, it would be lovely to connect on social media if, like me, you prefer procrastinating instead of doing actual work. My website's: www.keginger.com; or I'm on Facebook at: www.Facebook.com/KatieGAuthor. And I'm still wasting far too much time on Twitter too where I'm @KatieGAuthor.

See you again soon and happy reading!

Best wishes,

Katie

xxx

9 780008 380540